P9-AQM-415

SEVEN TO

LOGO DESIGN BY **VINCENT KUKUA**
COLLECTION DESIGN BY **JEFF POWELL**

IMAGE COMICS, INC.   IMAGECOMICS.COM

ROBERT KIRKMAN—CHIEF OPERATING OFFICER
ERIK LARSEN—CHIEF FINANCIAL OFFICER
TODD MCFARLANE—PRESIDENT
MARC SILVESTRI—CHIEF EXECUTIVE OFFICER
JIM VALENTINO—VICE PRESIDENT

ERIC STEPHENSON—PUBLISHER/CHIEF CREATIVE OFFICER
COREY HART—DIRECTOR OF SALES
JEFF BOISON—DIRECTOR OF PUBLISHING PLANNING & BOOK TRADE SALES
CHRIS ROSS—DIRECTOR OF DIGITAL SALES
JEFF STANG—DIRECTOR OF SPECIALTY SALES
KAT SALAZAR—DIRECTOR OF PR & MARKETING
DREW GILL—ART DIRECTOR
HEATHER DOORNINK—PRODUCTION DIRECTOR
NICOLE LAPALME—CONTROLLER

GIANT
GENERATOR   *image*

ISBN 978-1-5343-0698-1

SEVEN TO ETERNITY VOLUME 3: RISE TO FALL. First Printing. March 2019. Published by Image Comics, Inc. Office of publication: 2701 NW Vaughn Street, Suite 708, Portland OR 97210. Copyright © 2019 Rick Remender and Jerome Opeña. All rights reserved. Originally published in single magazine form as Seven To Eternity #10-13. Seven To Eternity™ (including all prominent characters featured herein), its logo and all character likenesses are trademarks of Rick Remender and Jerome Opeña, unless otherwise noted. Image Comics® and its logos are registered trademarks of Image Comics, Inc. No part of this publication may be reproduced or transmitted, in any form or by any means (except for short excerpts for review purposes) without the express written permission of Image Comics, Inc. All names, characters, events and locales in this publication are entirely fictional. Any resemblance to actual persons (living or dead), events or places, without satiric intent, is coincidental. PRINTED IN THE U.S.A. For information regarding the CPSIA on this printed material call: 203-595-3636. For international rights inquiries, contact: foreignlicensing@imagecomics.com

ETERNITY

WRITTEN BY **RICK REMENDER** DRAWN BY **JEROME OPEÑA**

COLOR ART BY **MATT HOLLINGSWORTH** LETTERED BY **RUS WOOTON** EDITED BY **SEBASTIAN GIRNER**

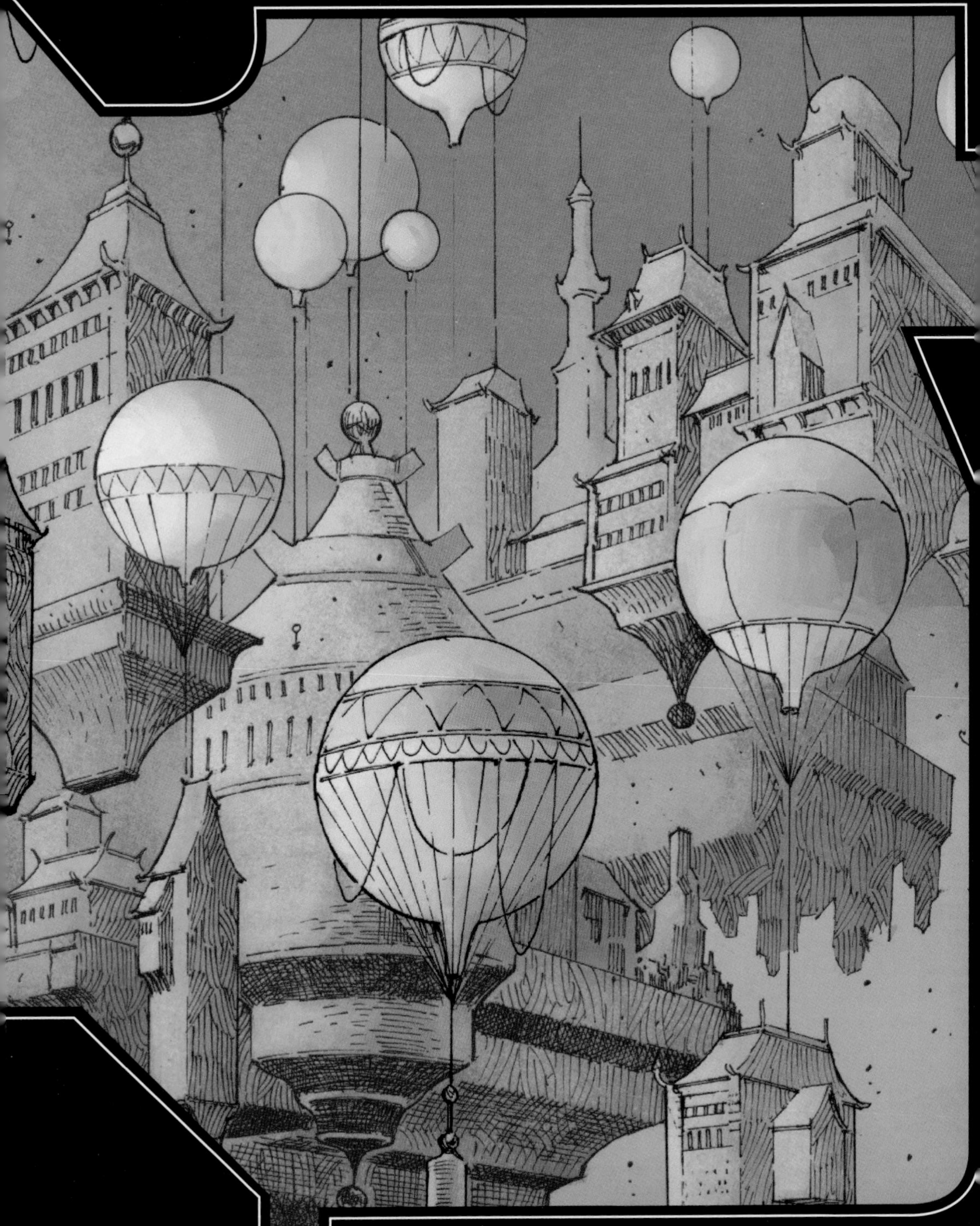

SEVEN TO ETERNITY CREATED BY **RICK REMENDER** AND **JEROME OPEÑA**

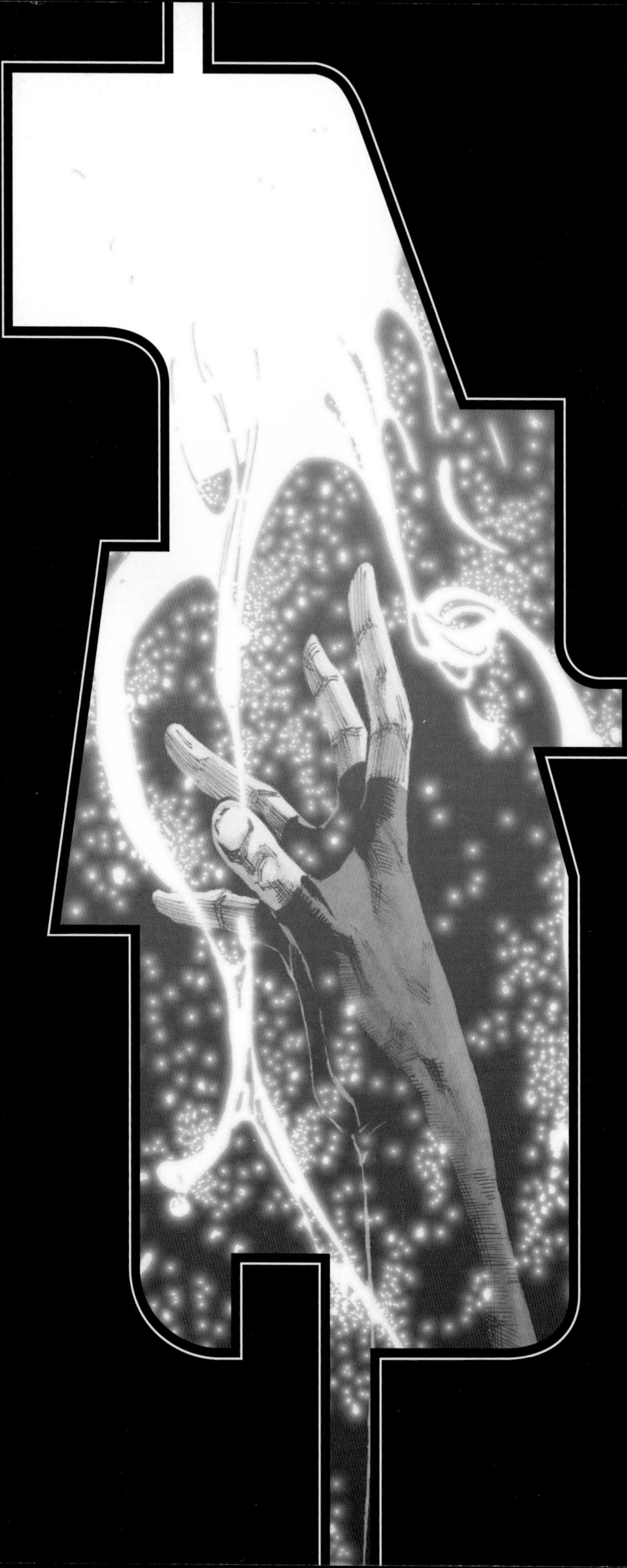

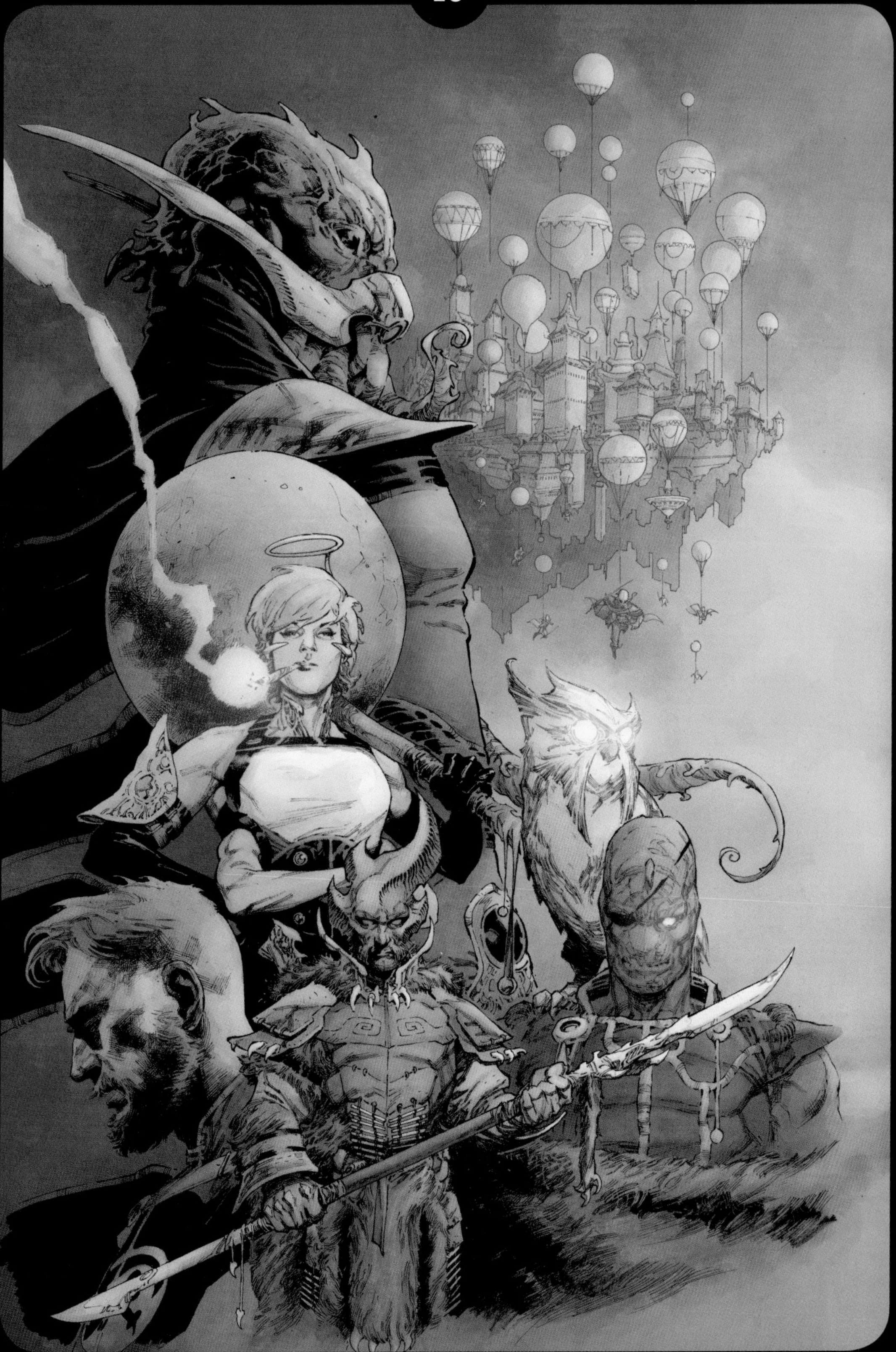

FROM THE JOURNAL OF ADAM OSIDIS

Did I ever tell you about The Great Hollow where the Moss Weavers dwell? Or maybe you've heard the rumors? Either way you know it's never a rational person's first choice to enter. We entered out of necessity, to avoid bounty hunters, acolytes, and vengeance seekers. None of the morbid rumors did the treacherous, subterranean labyrinth justice.

We were there for over a month. Time I didn't have to lose. What little I had left was quickly disappearing. It did offer a respite from the consumption eating through me; we had bigger troubles. No suns, no moons, nothing to gauge night and day—no landmarks to help find our bearings. It was then, when we were utterly lost, and time circled around us, that my trial became clear; I'd lost sight of more than just the days.

The Moss Weavers grew so high you'd climb for hours and never near the top. Every step they'd further their pull, the longer the connection, the closer the melding. The Moss Weavers are a mystery, but they are certainly kin to the Swamp. Only instead of expelling their poison onto any who visit, the Moss Weavers draw from the mind all evil, a cleansing that might sound pleasant but is, in fact, a vile madness.

As spiritual corruptions seeped from me I was forced to process each through dream. To relive each choice, each failure, each sinful motivation. Sleep was no safe harbor, but a conjured world where I was back home on the ranch, with Nival and the children, facing each challenge together, a unified front to hold back the current—a world where I never left.

Waking was no better. The darkness plays games on the eyes, hallucinations like migraines, flashes of the last look Pa gave me. Pa, who according to Garils, had turned down an offer to save Pete. Pa who isolated his family from the world.

That last time I saw him—the dull flat thing in his eyes...

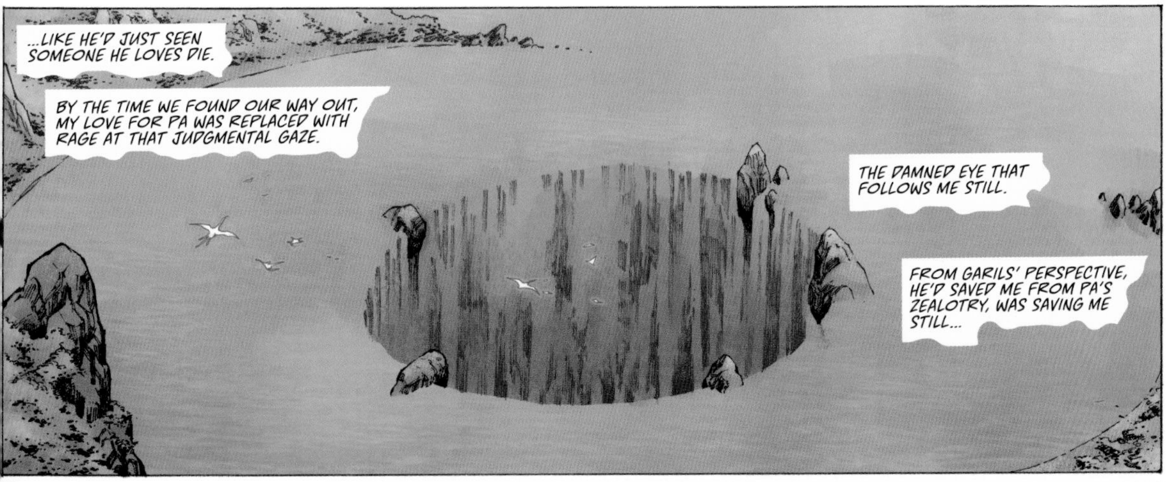
...LIKE HE'D JUST SEEN SOMEONE HE LOVES DIE.
BY THE TIME WE FOUND OUR WAY OUT, MY LOVE FOR PA WAS REPLACED WITH RAGE AT THAT JUDGMENTAL GAZE.
THE DAMNED EYE THAT FOLLOWS ME STILL.
FROM GARILS' PERSPECTIVE, HE'D SAVED ME FROM PA'S ZEALOTRY, WAS SAVING ME STILL...

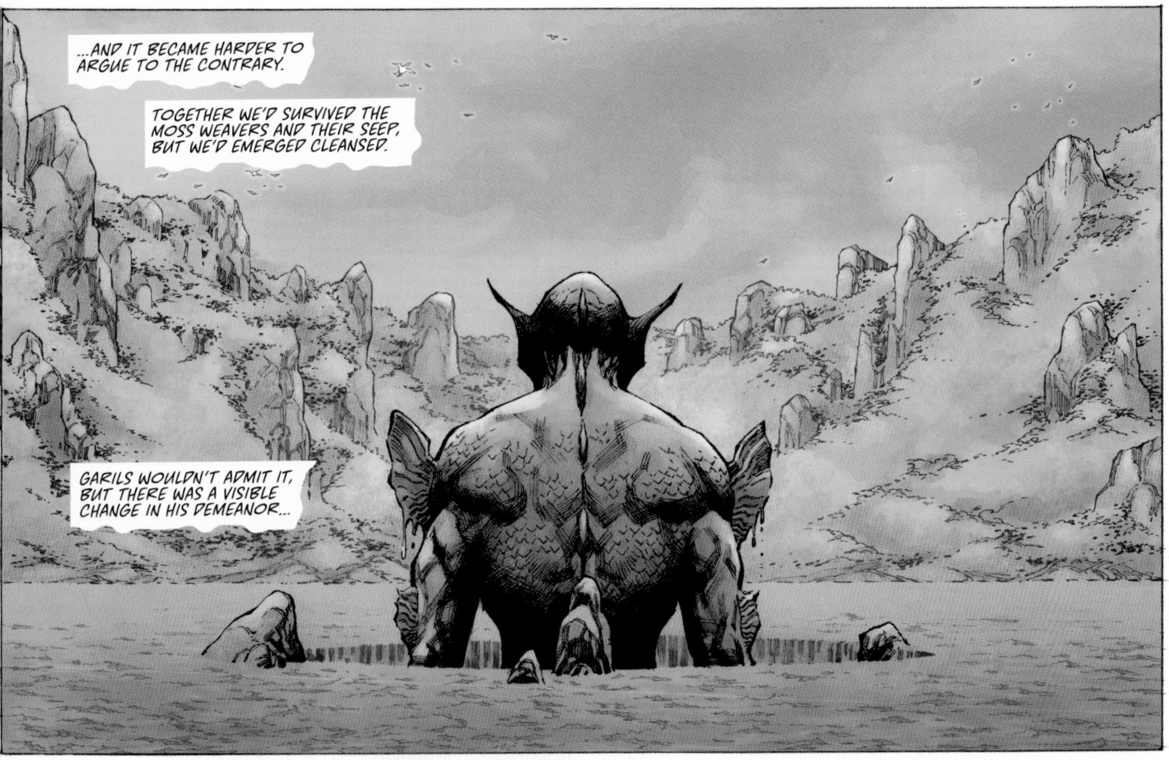
...AND IT BECAME HARDER TO ARGUE TO THE CONTRARY.
TOGETHER WE'D SURVIVED THE MOSS WEAVERS AND THEIR SEEP, BUT WE'D EMERGED CLEANSED.
GARILS WOULDN'T ADMIT IT, BUT THERE WAS A VISIBLE CHANGE IN HIS DEMEANOR...

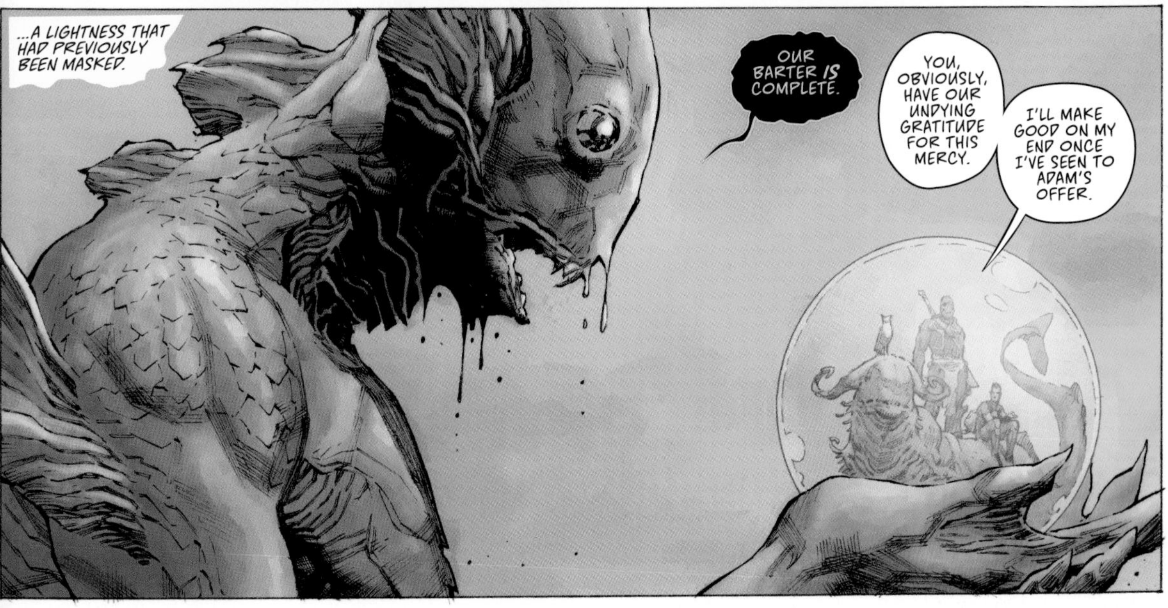
...A LIGHTNESS THAT HAD PREVIOUSLY BEEN MASKED.
OUR BARTER IS COMPLETE.
YOU, OBVIOUSLY, HAVE OUR UNDYING GRATITUDE FOR THIS MERCY.
I'LL MAKE GOOD ON MY END ONCE I'VE SEEN TO ADAM'S OFFER.

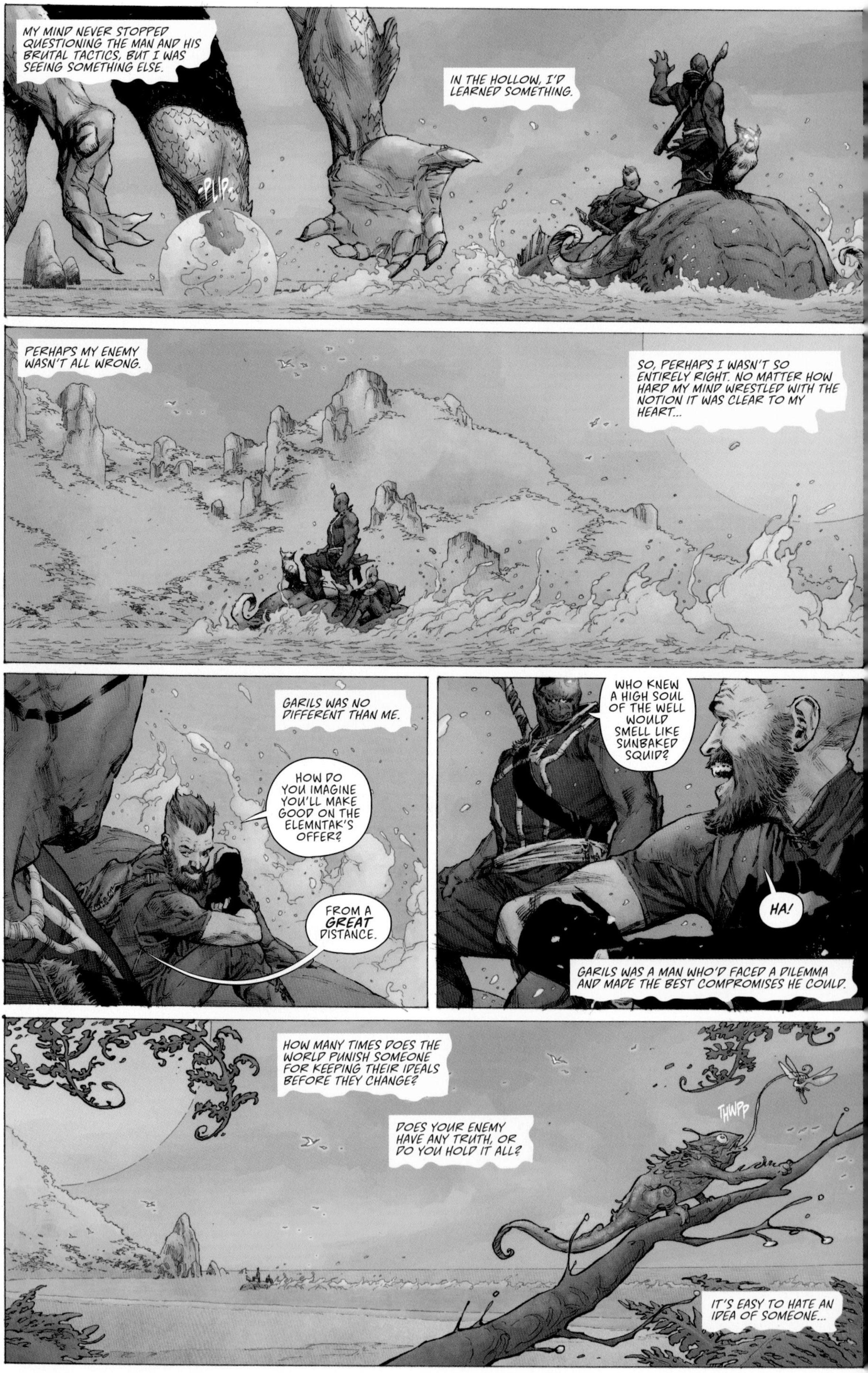
MY MIND NEVER STOPPED QUESTIONING THE MAN AND HIS BRUTAL TACTICS, BUT I WAS SEEING SOMETHING ELSE.
IN THE HOLLOW, I'D LEARNED SOMETHING.
-PLIP-
PERHAPS MY ENEMY WASN'T ALL WRONG.
SO, PERHAPS I WASN'T SO ENTIRELY RIGHT. NO MATTER HOW HARD MY MIND WRESTLED WITH THE NOTION IT WAS CLEAR TO MY HEART...
GARILS WAS NO DIFFERENT THAN ME.
HOW DO YOU IMAGINE YOU'LL MAKE GOOD ON THE ELEMNTAK'S OFFER?
FROM A **GREAT** DISTANCE.
WHO KNEW A HIGH SOUL OF THE WELL WOULD SMELL LIKE SUNBAKED SQUID?
HA!
GARILS WAS A MAN WHO'D FACED A DILEMMA AND MADE THE BEST COMPROMISES HE COULD.
HOW MANY TIMES DOES THE WORLD PUNISH SOMEONE FOR KEEPING THEIR IDEALS BEFORE THEY CHANGE?
DOES YOUR ENEMY HAVE ANY TRUTH, OR DO YOU HOLD IT ALL?
THWPP
IT'S EASY TO HATE AN IDEA OF SOMEONE...

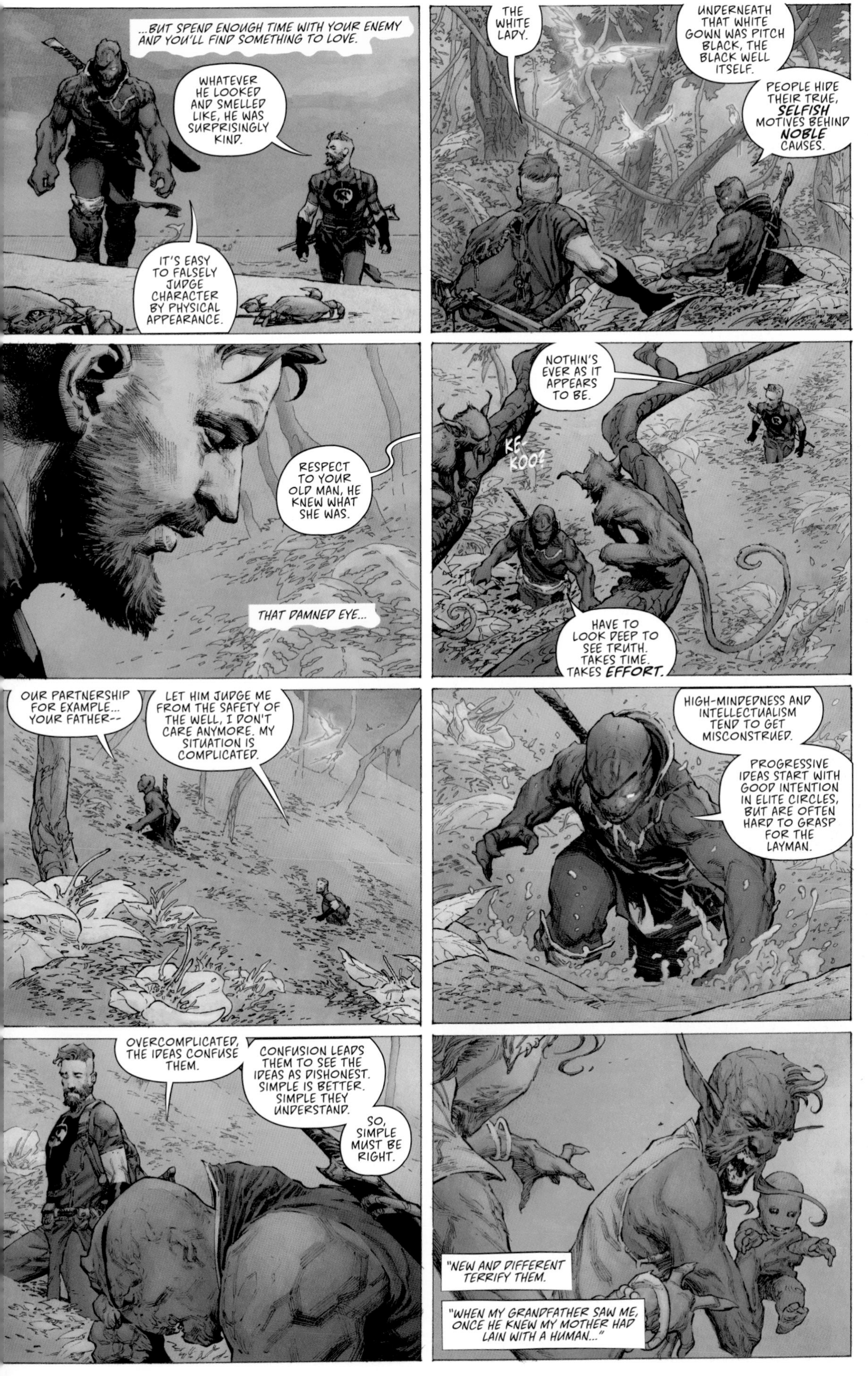
...BUT SPEND ENOUGH TIME WITH YOUR ENEMY AND YOU'LL FIND SOMETHING TO LOVE.
WHATEVER HE LOOKED AND SMELLED LIKE, HE WAS SURPRISINGLY KIND.
IT'S EASY TO FALSELY JUDGE CHARACTER BY PHYSICAL APPEARANCE.
THE WHITE LADY.
UNDERNEATH THAT WHITE GOWN WAS PITCH BLACK, THE BLACK WELL ITSELF.
PEOPLE HIDE THEIR TRUE, SELFISH MOTIVES BEHIND NOBLE CAUSES.
RESPECT TO YOUR OLD MAN, HE KNEW WHAT SHE WAS.
THAT DAMNED EYE...
NOTHIN'S EVER AS IT APPEARS TO BE.
KE-KOO?
HAVE TO LOOK DEEP TO SEE TRUTH. TAKES TIME. TAKES EFFORT.
OUR PARTNERSHIP FOR EXAMPLE... YOUR FATHER--
LET HIM JUDGE ME FROM THE SAFETY OF THE WELL, I DON'T CARE ANYMORE. MY SITUATION IS COMPLICATED.
HIGH-MINDEDNESS AND INTELLECTUALISM TEND TO GET MISCONSTRUED.
PROGRESSIVE IDEAS START WITH GOOD INTENTION IN ELITE CIRCLES, BUT ARE OFTEN HARD TO GRASP FOR THE LAYMAN.
OVERCOMPLICATED, THE IDEAS CONFUSE THEM.
CONFUSION LEADS THEM TO SEE THE IDEAS AS DISHONEST. SIMPLE IS BETTER. SIMPLE THEY UNDERSTAND.
SO, SIMPLE MUST BE RIGHT.
"NEW AND DIFFERENT TERRIFY THEM.
"WHEN MY GRANDFATHER SAW ME, ONCE HE KNEW MY MOTHER HAD LAIN WITH A HUMAN..."

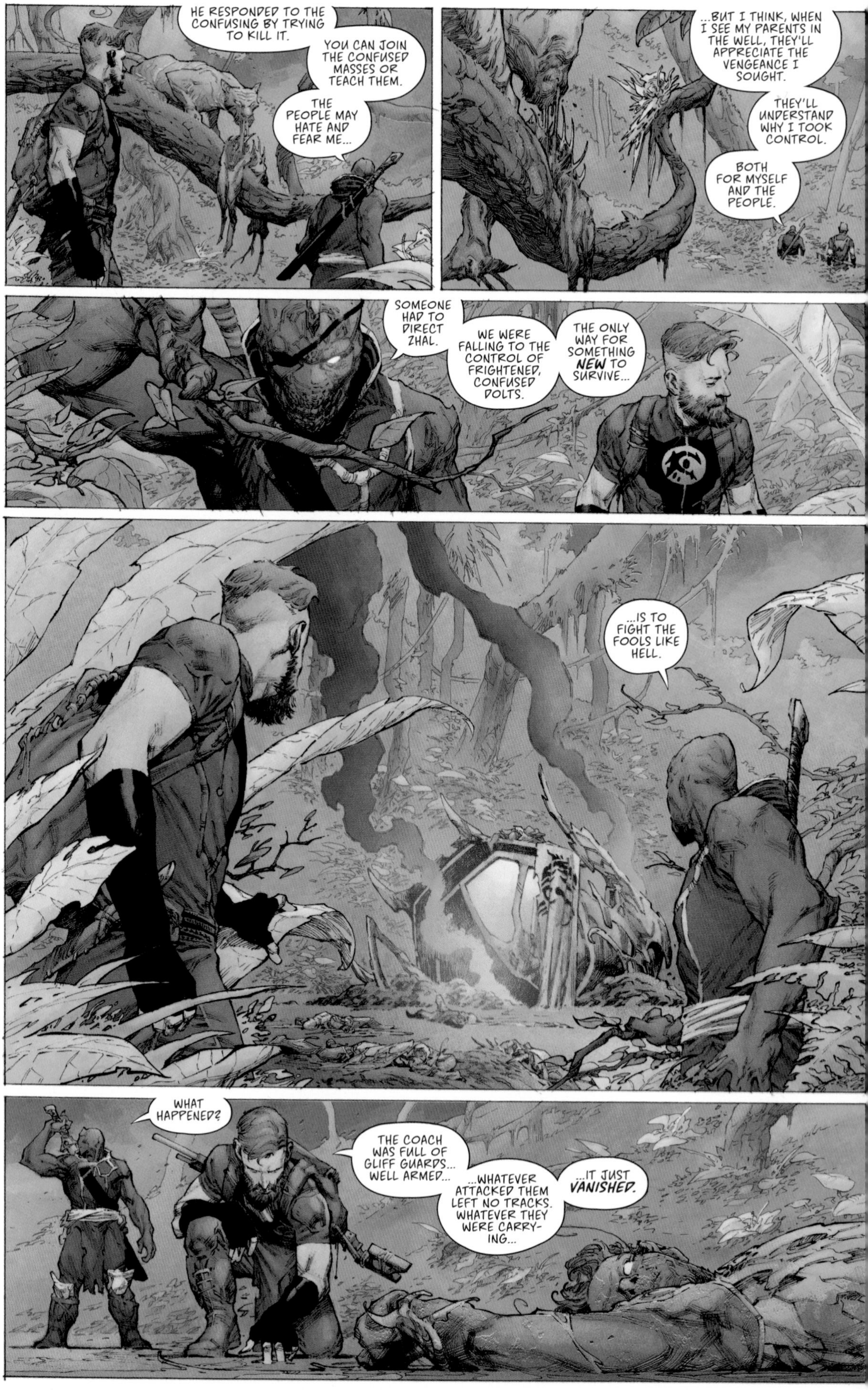
HE RESPONDED TO THE CONFUSING BY TRYING TO KILL IT.
YOU CAN JOIN THE CONFUSED MASSES OR TEACH THEM.
THE PEOPLE MAY HATE AND FEAR ME...
...BUT I THINK, WHEN I SEE MY PARENTS IN THE WELL, THEY'LL APPRECIATE THE VENGEANCE I SOUGHT.
THEY'LL UNDERSTAND WHY I TOOK CONTROL.
BOTH FOR MYSELF AND THE PEOPLE.
SOMEONE HAD TO DIRECT ZHAL.
WE WERE FALLING TO THE CONTROL OF FRIGHTENED, CONFUSED DOLTS.
THE ONLY WAY FOR SOMETHING ***NEW*** TO SURVIVE...
...IS TO FIGHT THE FOOLS LIKE HELL.
WHAT HAPPENED?
THE COACH WAS FULL OF GLIFF GUARDS... WELL ARMED...
...WHATEVER ATTACKED THEM LEFT NO TRACKS. WHATEVER THEY WERE CARRY-ING...
...IT JUST ***VANISHED.***

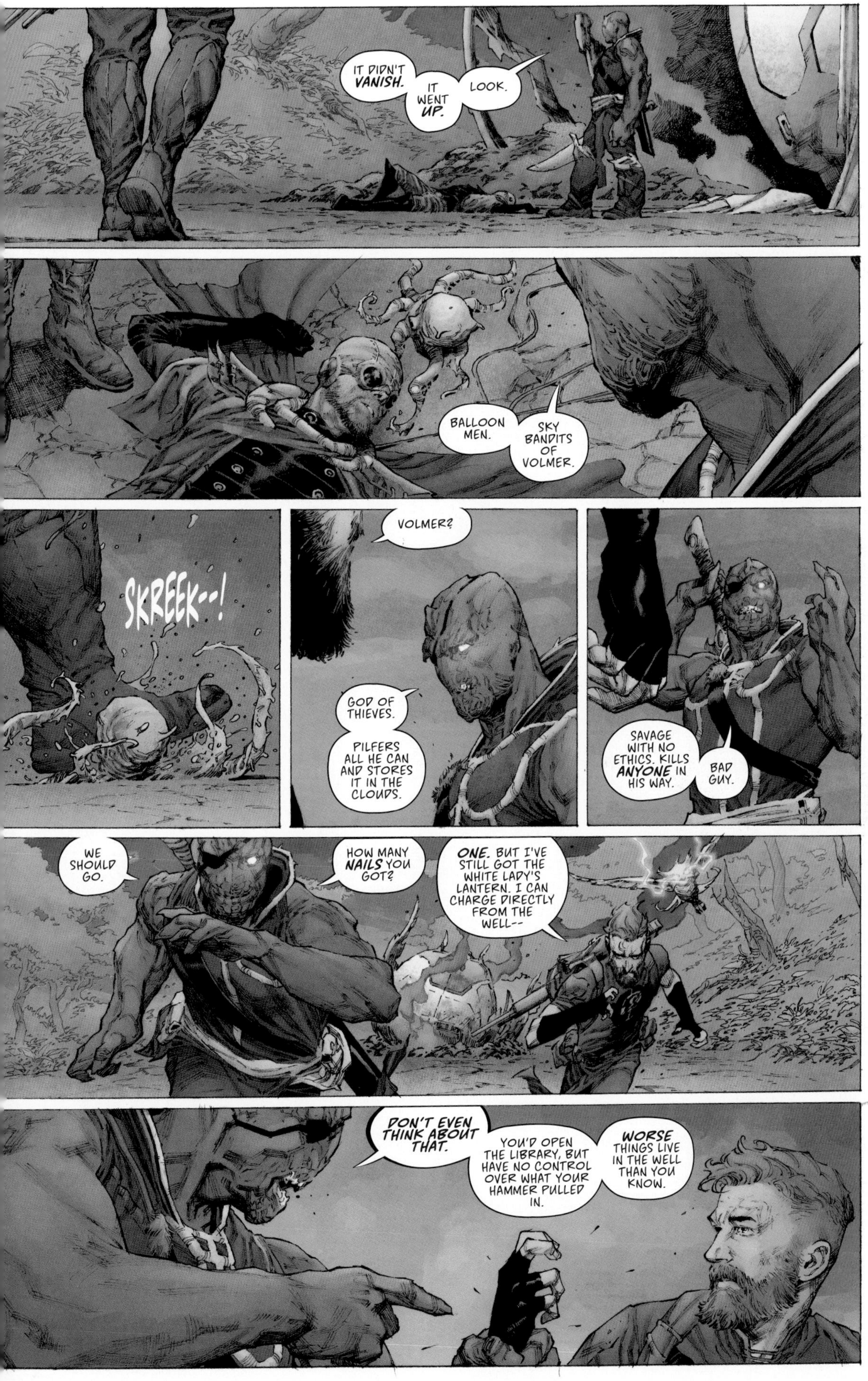
IT DIDN'T VANISH.
IT WENT UP.
LOOK.
BALLOON MEN.
SKY BANDITS OF VOLMER.
SKREEK--!
VOLMER?
GOD OF THIEVES.
PILFERS ALL HE CAN AND STORES IT IN THE CLOUDS.
SAVAGE WITH NO ETHICS. KILLS ANYONE IN HIS WAY.
BAD GUY.
WE SHOULD GO.
HOW MANY NAILS YOU GOT?
ONE. BUT I'VE STILL GOT THE WHITE LADY'S LANTERN. I CAN CHARGE DIRECTLY FROM THE WELL--
DON'T EVEN THINK ABOUT THAT.
YOU'D OPEN THE LIBRARY, BUT HAVE NO CONTROL OVER WHAT YOUR HAMMER PULLED IN.
WORSE THINGS LIVE IN THE WELL THAN YOU KNOW.

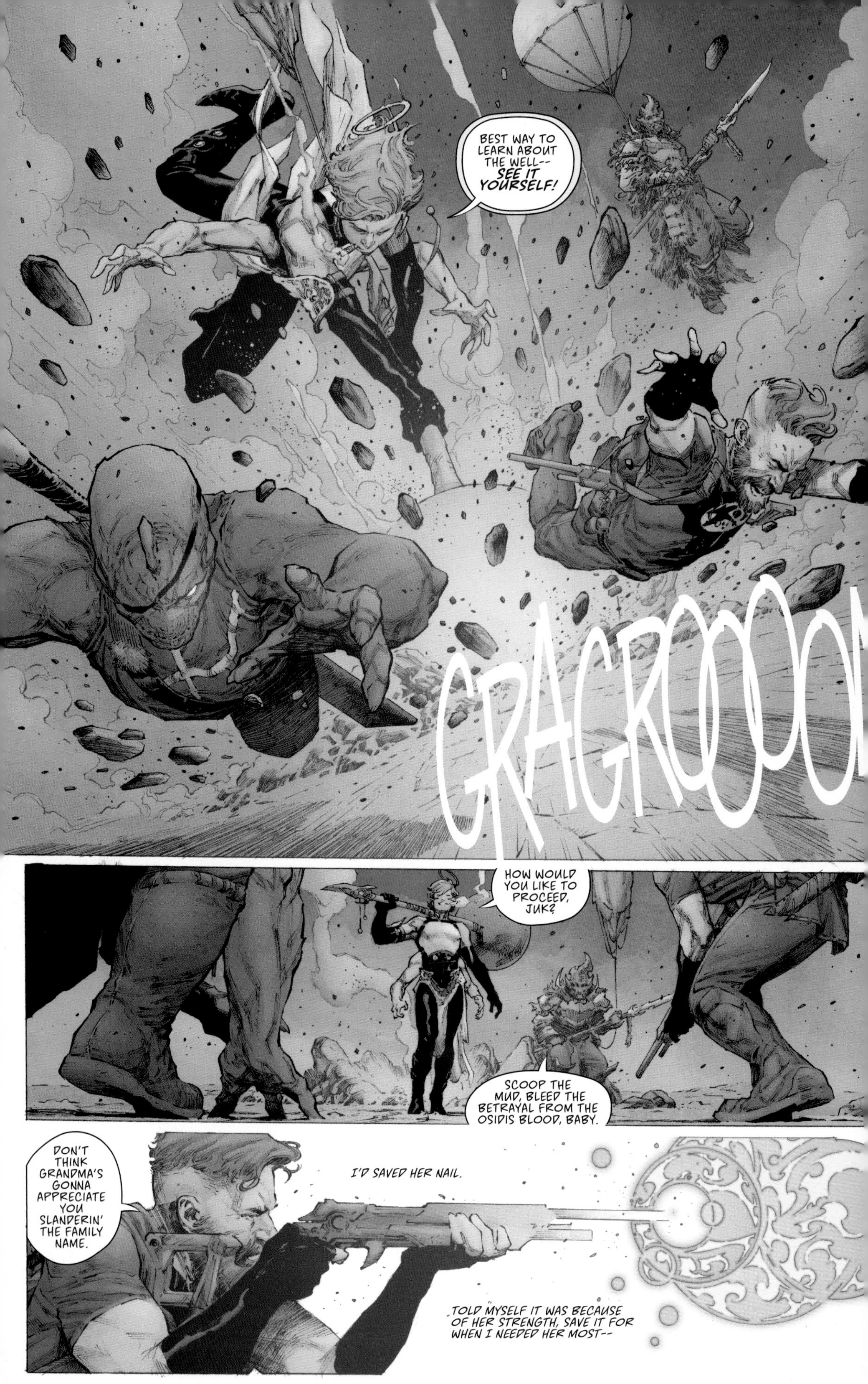
BEST WAY TO LEARN ABOUT THE WELL-- *SEE IT YOURSELF!*
GRAGROOOOO
HOW WOULD YOU LIKE TO PROCEED, JUK?
SCOOP THE MUD, BLEED THE BETRAYAL FROM THE OSIDIS BLOOD, BABY.
DON'T THINK GRANDMA'S GONNA APPRECIATE YOU SLANDERIN' THE FAMILY NAME.
I'D SAVED HER NAIL.
TOLD MYSELF IT WAS BECAUSE OF HER STRENGTH, SAVE IT FOR WHEN I NEEDED HER MOST--

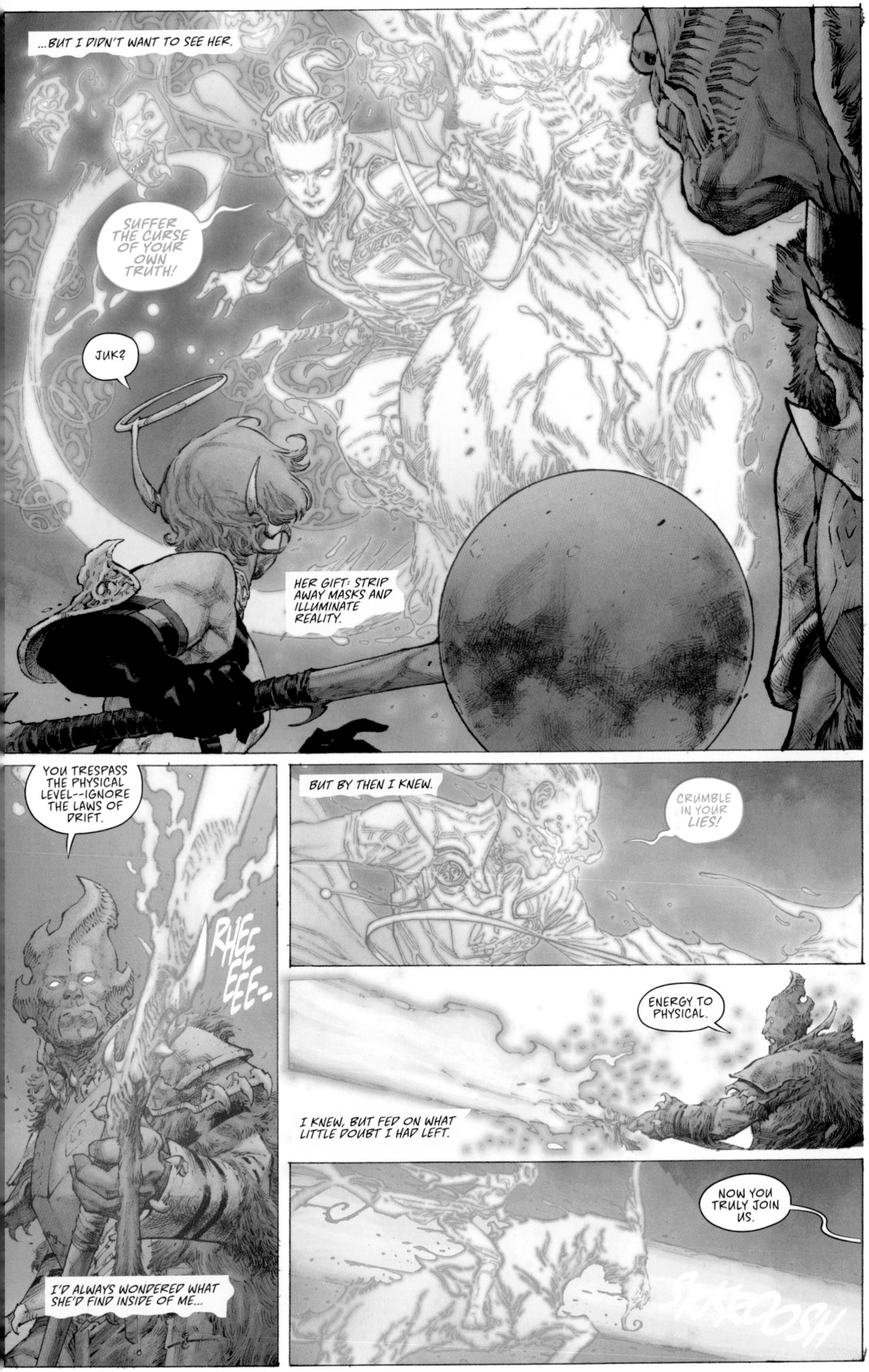
...BUT I DIDN'T WANT TO SEE HER.
SUFFER THE CURSE OF YOUR OWN TRUTH!
JUK?
HER GIFT: STRIP AWAY MASKS AND ILLUMINATE REALITY.
YOU TRESPASS THE PHYSICAL LEVEL--IGNORE THE LAWS OF DRIFT.
RHEE EEE--
I'D ALWAYS WONDERED WHAT SHE'D FIND INSIDE OF ME...
BUT BY THEN I KNEW.
CRUMBLE IN YOUR LIES!
ENERGY TO PHYSICAL.
I KNEW, BUT FED ON WHAT LITTLE DOUBT I HAD LEFT.
NOW YOU TRULY JOIN US.

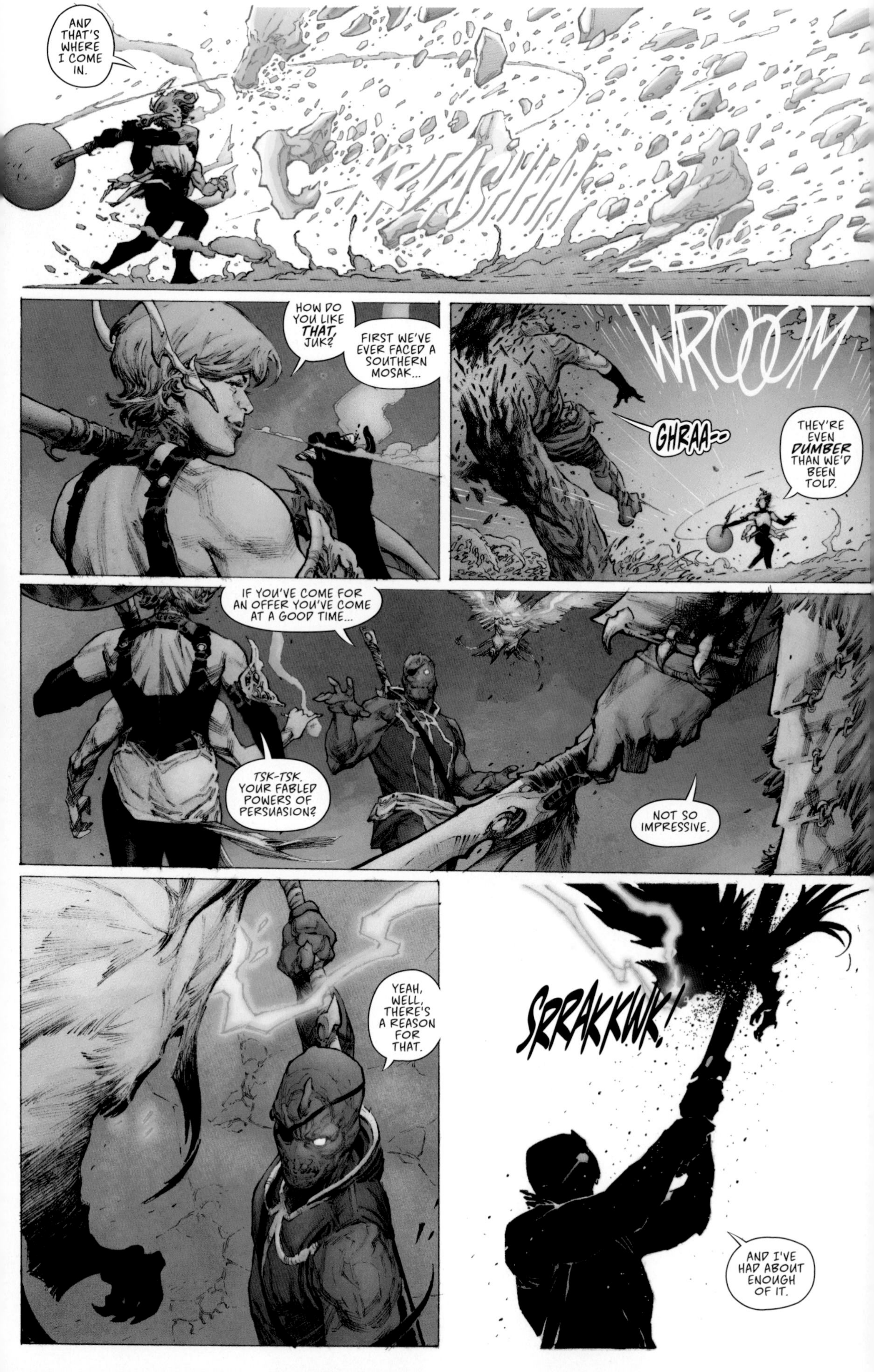
AND THAT'S WHERE I COME IN.
CRRASHHH
HOW DO YOU LIKE THAT, JUK?
FIRST WE'VE EVER FACED A SOUTHERN MOSAK...
WROOOM
GHRAA--
THEY'RE EVEN DUMBER THAN WE'D BEEN TOLD.
IF YOU'VE COME FOR AN OFFER YOU'VE COME AT A GOOD TIME...
TSK-TSK. YOUR FABLED POWERS OF PERSUASION?
NOT SO IMPRESSIVE.
YEAH, WELL, THERE'S A REASON FOR THAT.
SKRAKKWK!
AND I'VE HAD ABOUT ENOUGH OF IT.

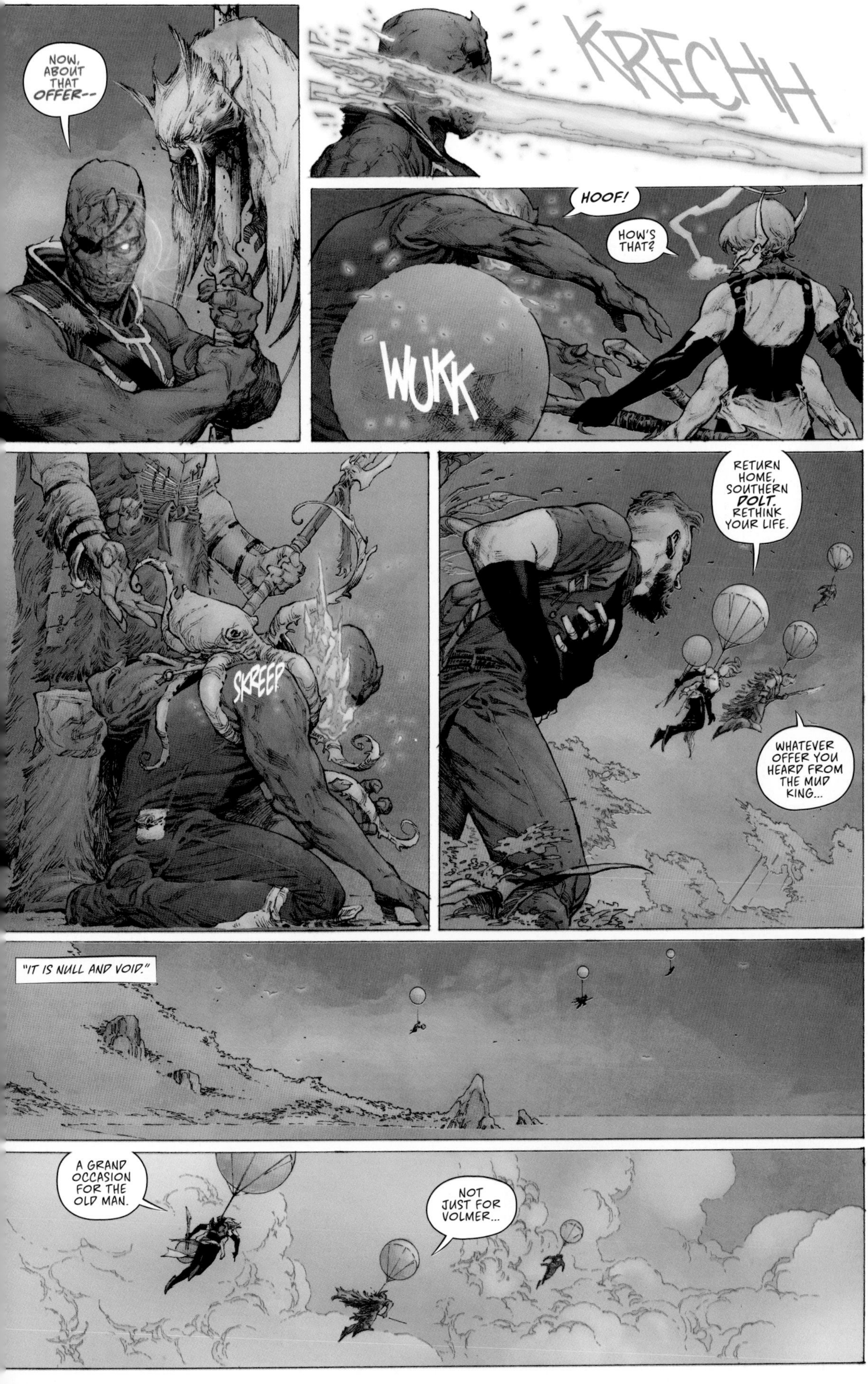
NOW, ABOUT THAT OFFER--
KRECHH
HOOF!
HOW'S THAT?
WUKK
SKREEP
RETURN HOME, SOUTHERN DOLT. RETHINK YOUR LIFE.
WHATEVER OFFER YOU HEARD FROM THE MUD KING...
"IT IS NULL AND VOID."
A GRAND OCCASION FOR THE OLD MAN.
NOT JUST FOR VOLMER...

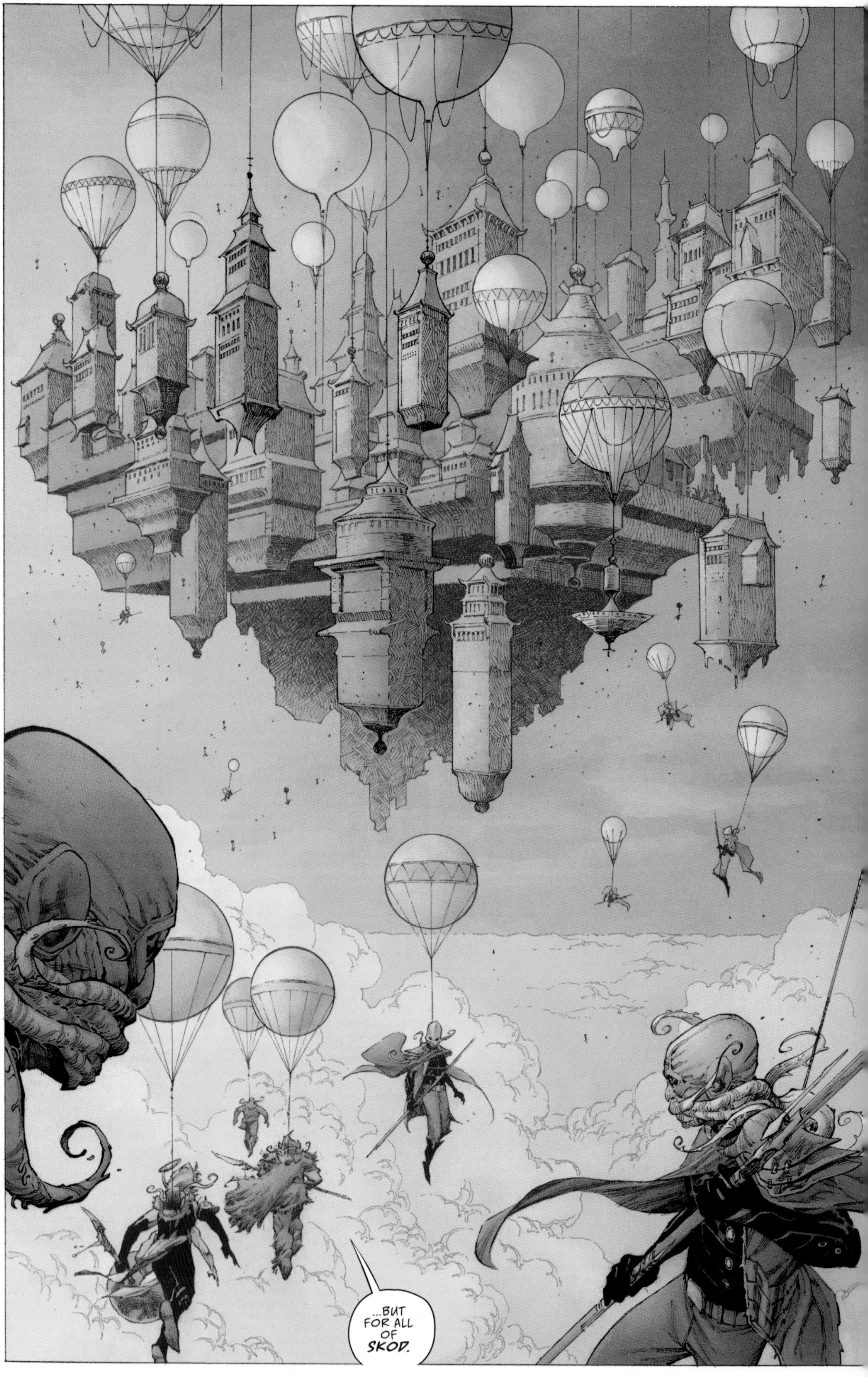
...BUT FOR ALL OF SKOD.

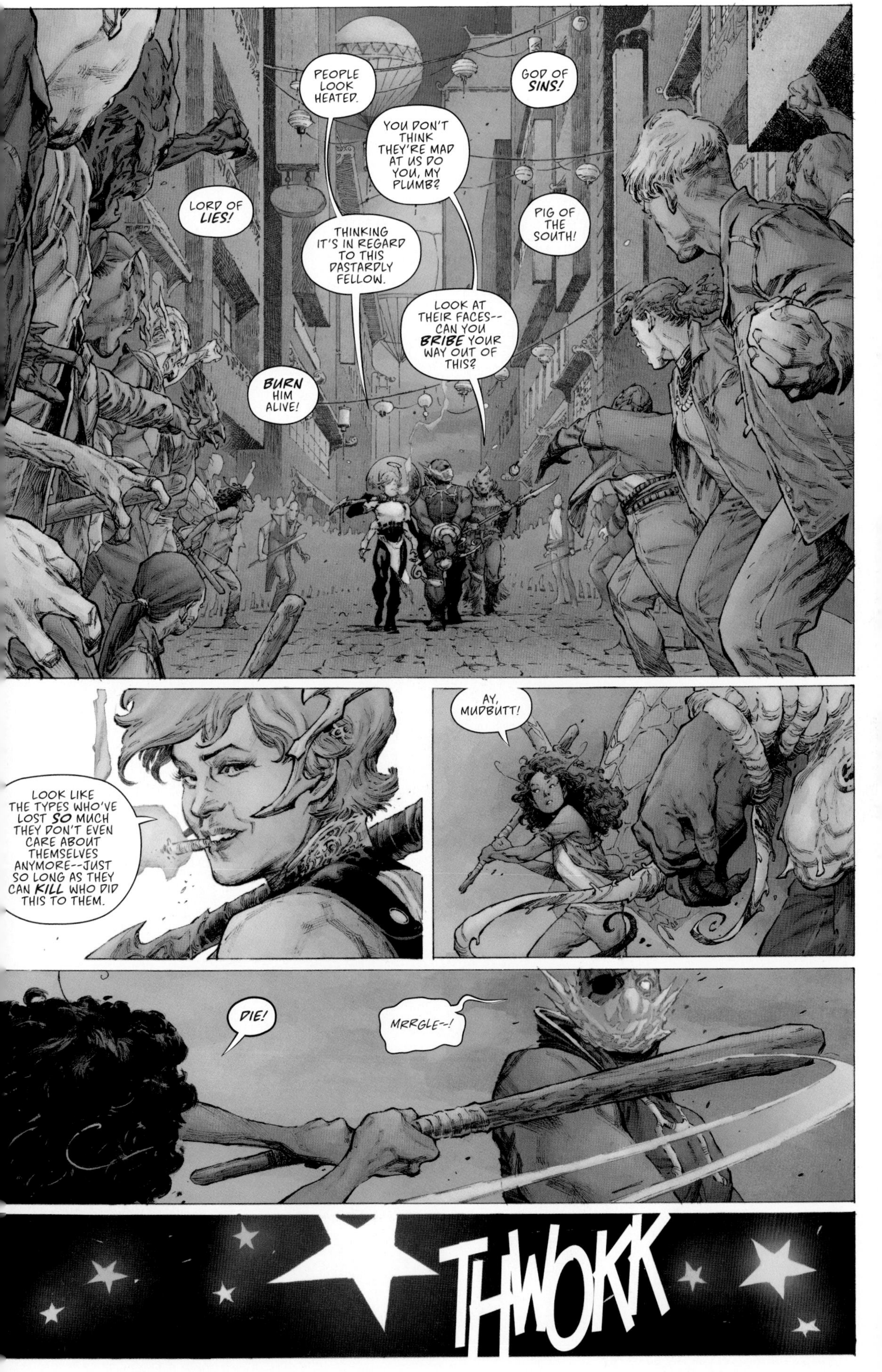
PEOPLE LOOK HEATED.
GOD OF SINS!
YOU DON'T THINK THEY'RE MAD AT US DO YOU, MY PLUMB?
LORD OF LIES!
PIG OF THE SOUTH!
THINKING IT'S IN REGARD TO THIS DASTARDLY FELLOW.
LOOK AT THEIR FACES--CAN YOU BRIBE YOUR WAY OUT OF THIS?
BURN HIM ALIVE!
LOOK LIKE THE TYPES WHO'VE LOST SO MUCH THEY DON'T EVEN CARE ABOUT THEMSELVES ANYMORE--JUST SO LONG AS THEY CAN KILL WHO DID THIS TO THEM.
AY, MUDBUTT!
DIE!
MRRGLE--!
THWOKK

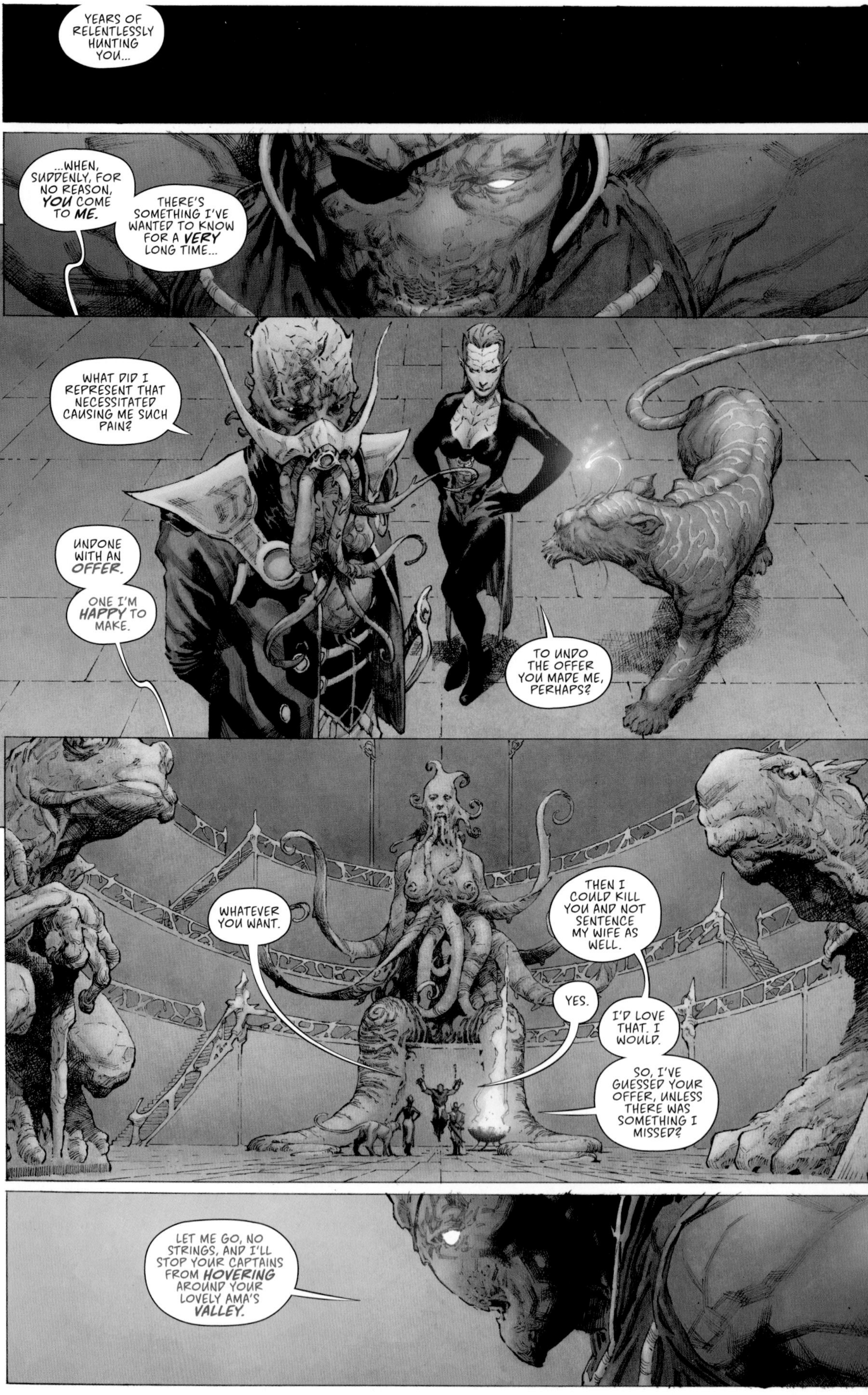
YEARS OF RELENTLESSLY HUNTING YOU...
...WHEN, SUDDENLY, FOR NO REASON, YOU COME TO ME.
THERE'S SOMETHING I'VE WANTED TO KNOW FOR A VERY LONG TIME...
WHAT DID I REPRESENT THAT NECESSITATED CAUSING ME SUCH PAIN?
UNDONE WITH AN OFFER.
ONE I'M HAPPY TO MAKE.
TO UNDO THE OFFER YOU MADE ME, PERHAPS?
WHATEVER YOU WANT.
THEN I COULD KILL YOU AND NOT SENTENCE MY WIFE AS WELL.
YES.
I'D LOVE THAT. I WOULD.
SO, I'VE GUESSED YOUR OFFER, UNLESS THERE WAS SOMETHING I MISSED?
LET ME GO, NO STRINGS, AND I'LL STOP YOUR CAPTAINS FROM HOVERING AROUND YOUR LOVELY AMA'S VALLEY.

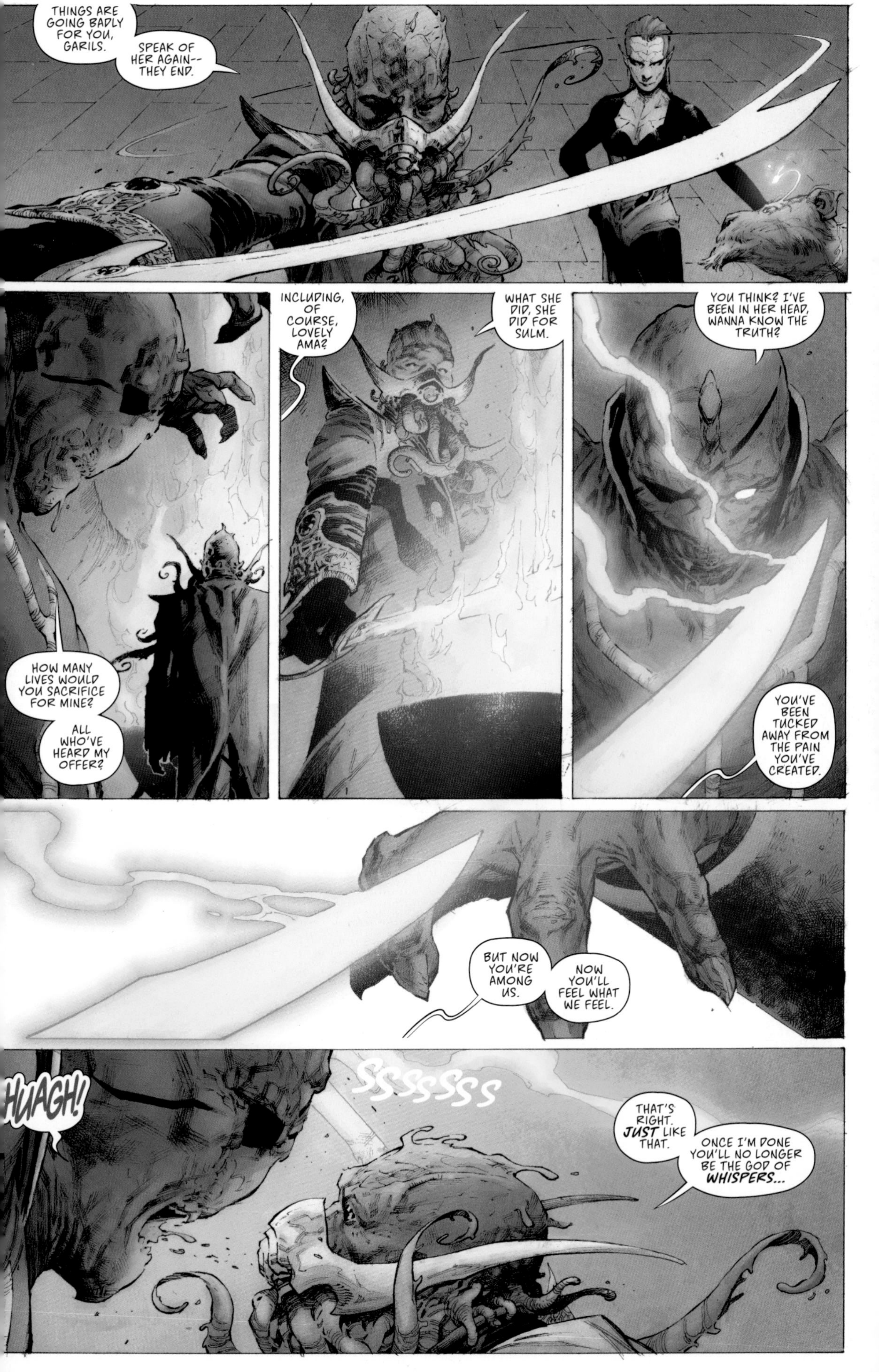
THINGS ARE GOING BADLY FOR YOU, GARILS.
SPEAK OF HER AGAIN-- THEY END.
INCLUDING, OF COURSE, LOVELY AMA?
WHAT SHE DID, SHE DID FOR SULM.
YOU THINK? I'VE BEEN IN HER HEAD, WANNA KNOW THE TRUTH?
HOW MANY LIVES WOULD YOU SACRIFICE FOR MINE?
ALL WHO'VE HEARD MY OFFER?
YOU'VE BEEN TUCKED AWAY FROM THE PAIN YOU'VE CREATED.
BUT NOW YOU'RE AMONG US.
NOW YOU'LL FEEL WHAT WE FEEL.
HUAGH!
SSSSSS
THAT'S RIGHT. JUST LIKE THAT.
ONCE I'M DONE YOU'LL NO LONGER BE THE GOD OF WHISPERS...

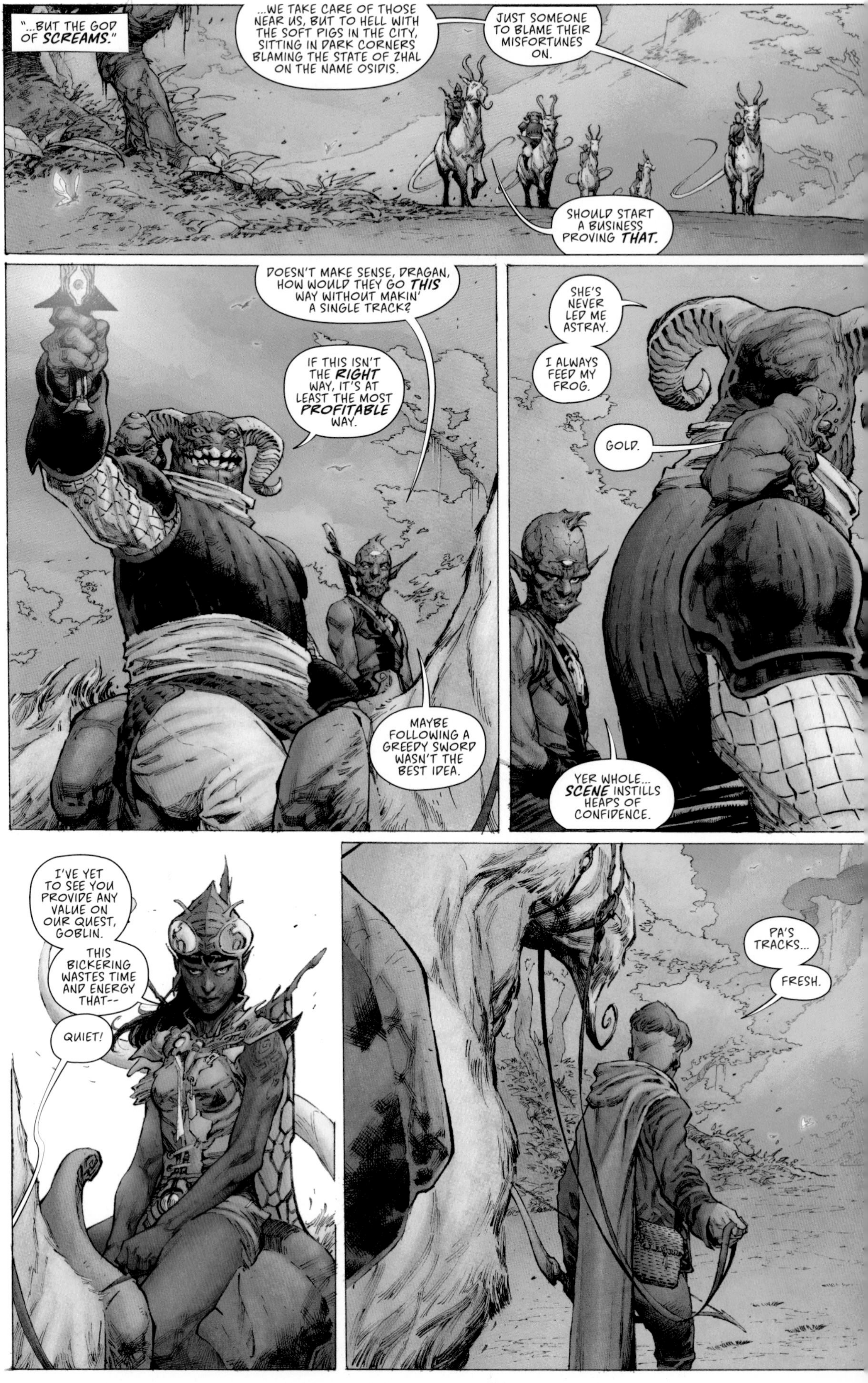
"...BUT THE GOD OF SCREAMS."
...WE TAKE CARE OF THOSE NEAR US, BUT TO HELL WITH THE SOFT PIGS IN THE CITY, SITTING IN DARK CORNERS BLAMING THE STATE OF ZHAL ON THE NAME OSIDIS.
JUST SOMEONE TO BLAME THEIR MISFORTUNES ON.
SHOULD START A BUSINESS PROVING THAT.
DOESN'T MAKE SENSE, DRAGAN, HOW WOULD THEY GO THIS WAY WITHOUT MAKIN' A SINGLE TRACK?
IF THIS ISN'T THE RIGHT WAY, IT'S AT LEAST THE MOST PROFITABLE WAY.
MAYBE FOLLOWING A GREEDY SWORD WASN'T THE BEST IDEA.
SHE'S NEVER LED ME ASTRAY.
I ALWAYS FEED MY FROG.
GOLD.
YER WHOLE... SCENE INSTILLS HEAPS OF CONFIDENCE.
I'VE YET TO SEE YOU PROVIDE ANY VALUE ON OUR QUEST, GOBLIN.
THIS BICKERING WASTES TIME AND ENERGY THAT--
QUIET!
PA'S TRACKS...
FRESH.

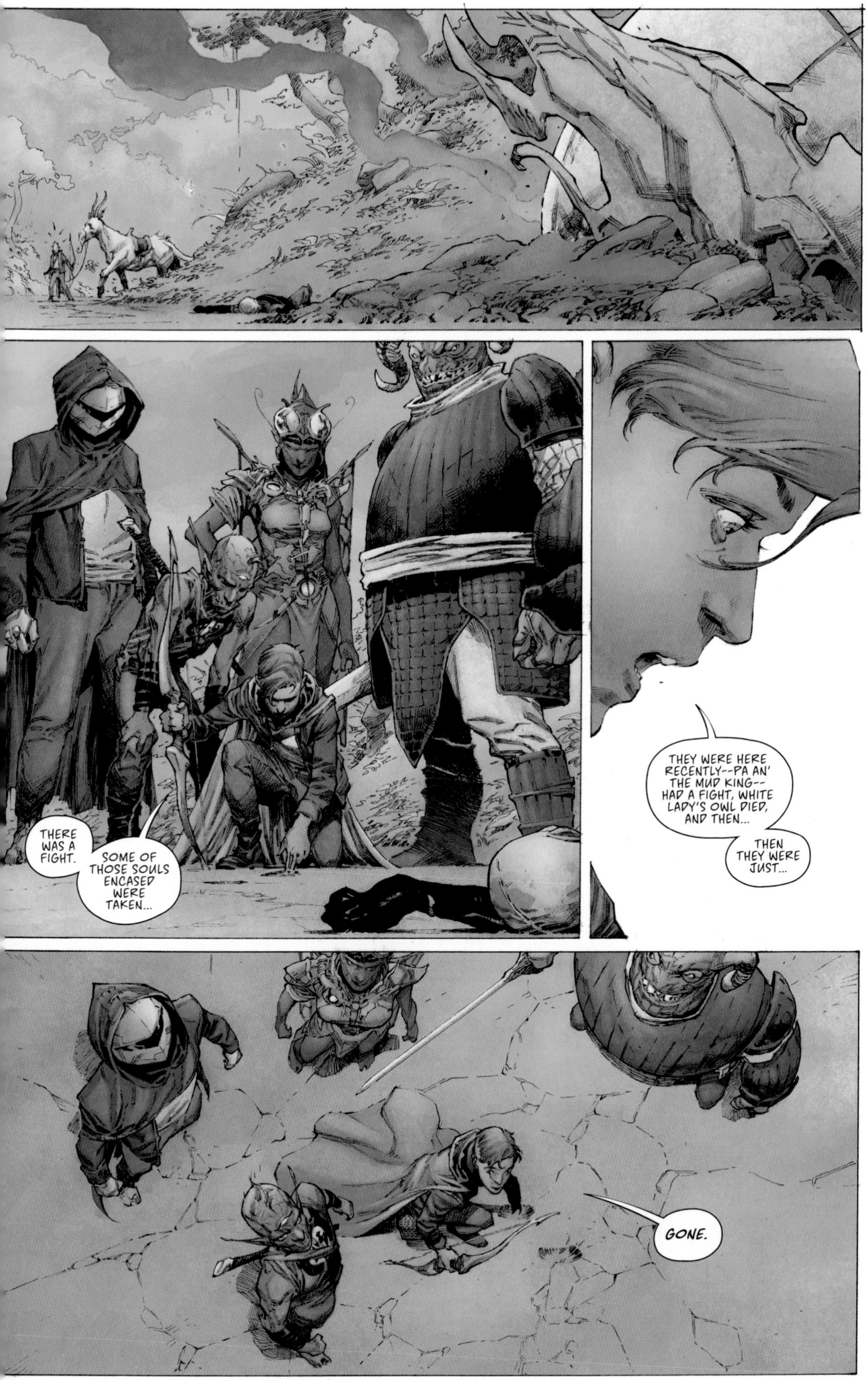
THERE WAS A FIGHT.
SOME OF THOSE SOULS ENCASED WERE TAKEN...
THEY WERE HERE RECENTLY--PA AN' THE MUD KING--HAD A FIGHT, WHITE LADY'S OWL DIED, AND THEN...
THEN THEY WERE JUST...
GONE.

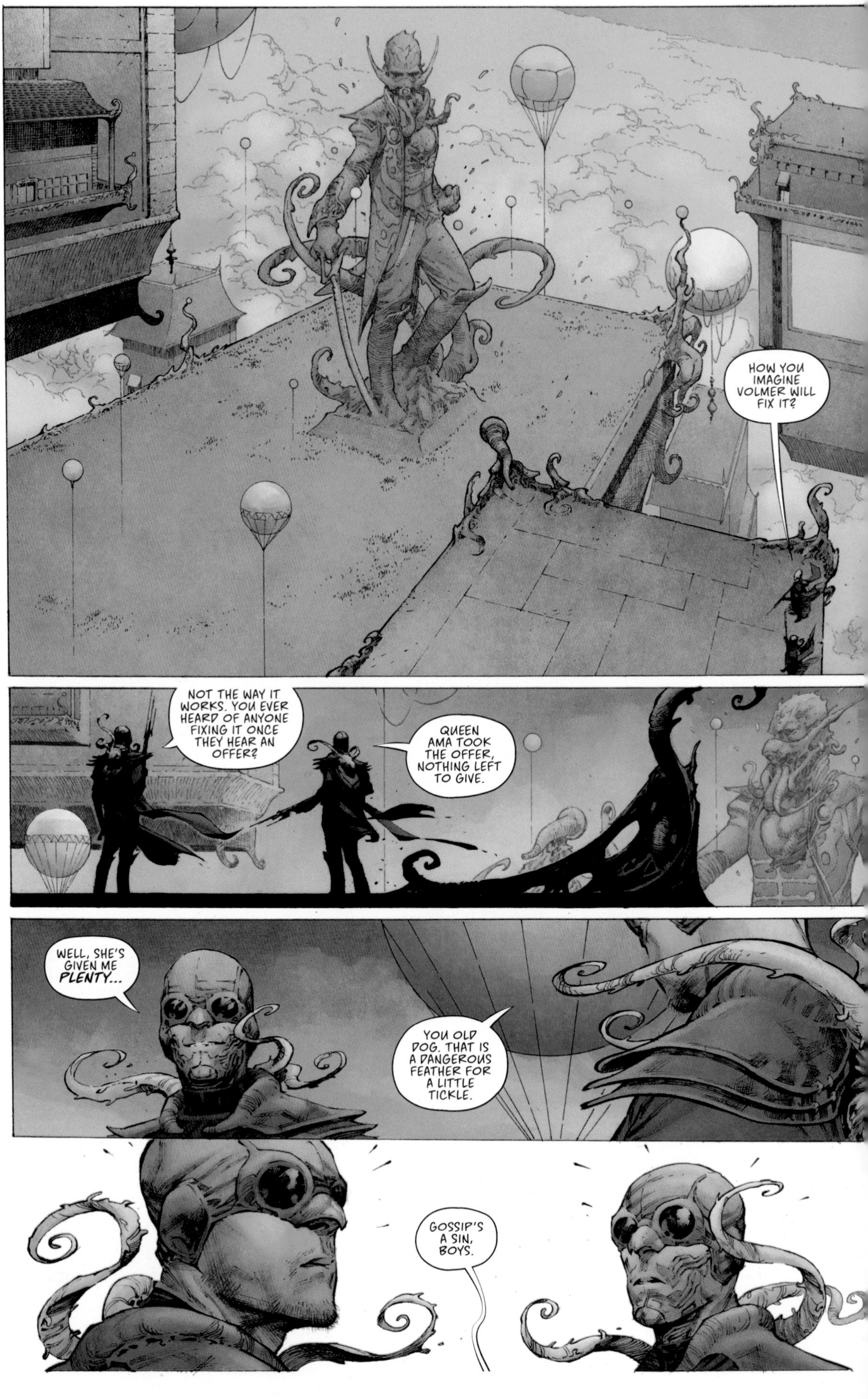
HOW YOU IMAGINE VOLMER WILL FIX IT?
NOT THE WAY IT WORKS. YOU EVER HEARD OF ANYONE FIXING IT ONCE THEY HEAR AN OFFER?
QUEEN AMA TOOK THE OFFER, NOTHING LEFT TO GIVE.
WELL, SHE'S GIVEN ME *PLENTY*...
YOU OLD DOG. THAT IS A DANGEROUS FEATHER FOR A LITTLE TICKLE.
GOSSIP'S A SIN, BOYS.

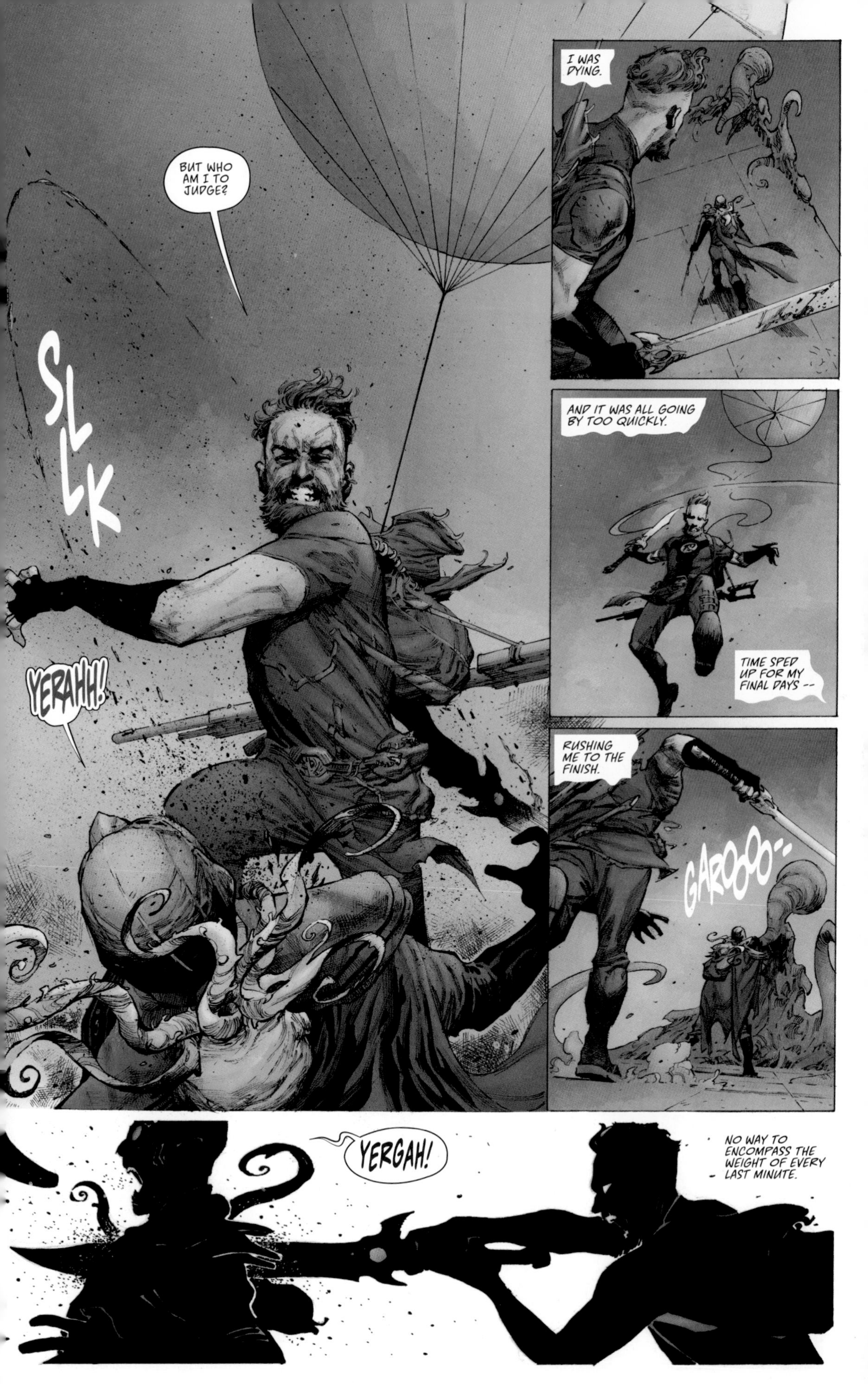
BUT WHO AM I TO JUDGE?
SLLK
YERAHH!
I WAS DYING.
AND IT WAS ALL GOING BY TOO QUICKLY.
TIME SPED UP FOR MY FINAL DAYS --
RUSHING ME TO THE FINISH.
GAROOOO--
YERGAH!
NO WAY TO ENCOMPASS THE WEIGHT OF EVERY LAST MINUTE.

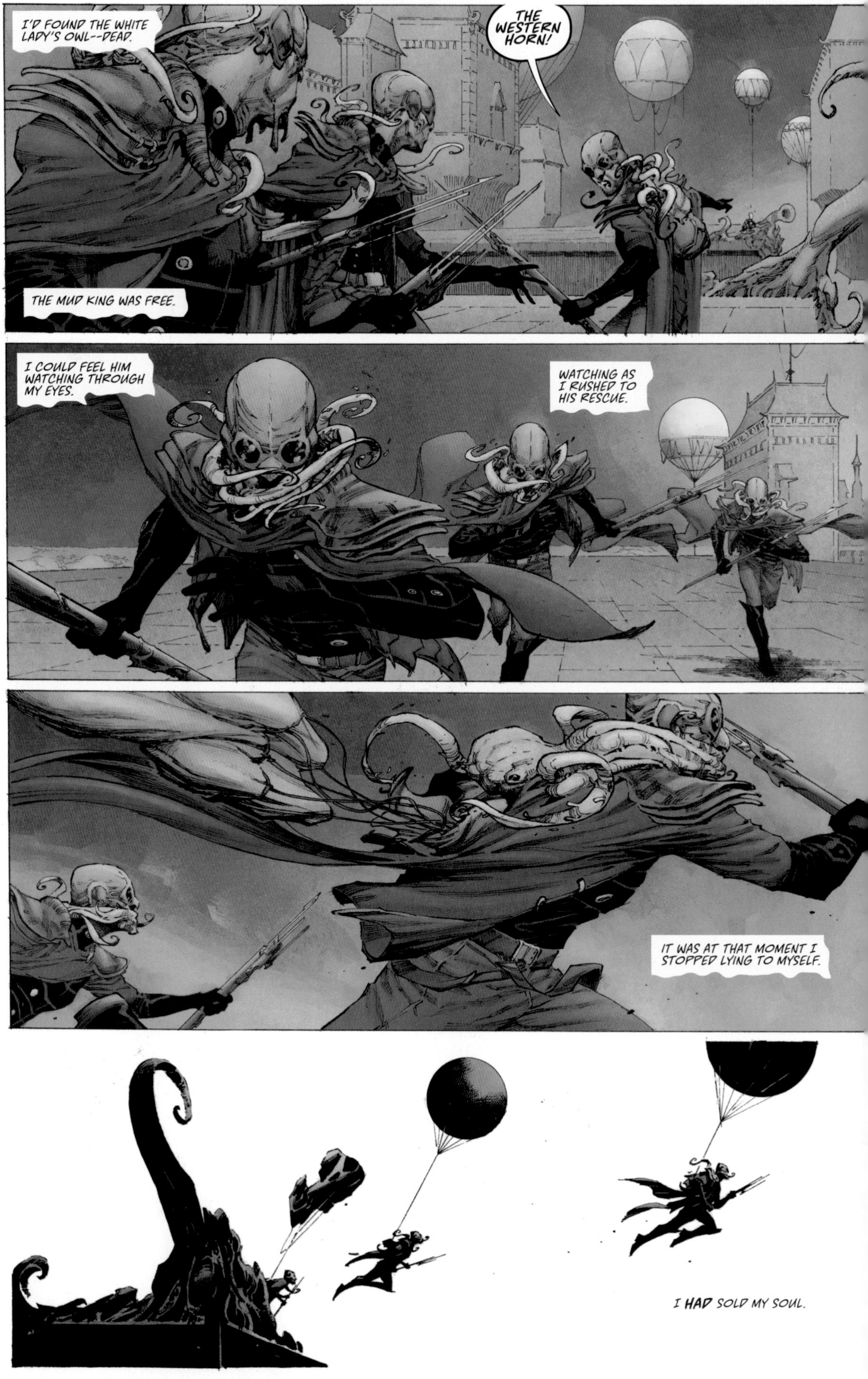
I'D FOUND THE WHITE LADY'S OWL--DEAD.
THE WESTERN HORN!
THE MUD KING WAS FREE.
I COULD FEEL HIM WATCHING THROUGH MY EYES.
WATCHING AS I RUSHED TO HIS RESCUE.
IT WAS AT THAT MOMENT I STOPPED LYING TO MYSELF.
I HAD SOLD MY SOUL.

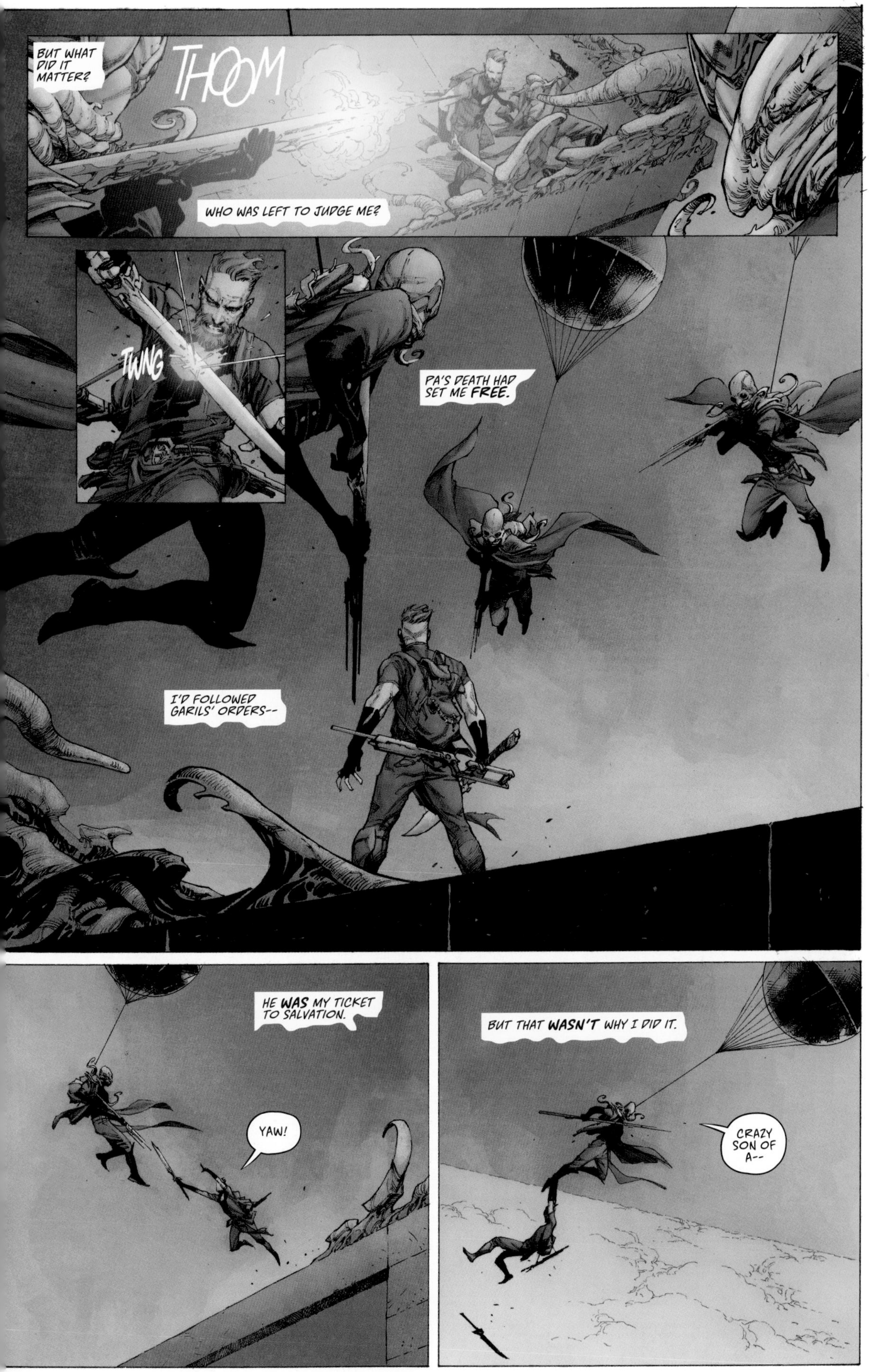
BUT WHAT DID IT MATTER?
THOOM
WHO WAS LEFT TO JUDGE ME?
TWNG
PA'S DEATH HAD SET ME FREE.
I'D FOLLOWED GARILS' ORDERS--
HE WAS MY TICKET TO SALVATION.
YAW!
BUT THAT WASN'T WHY I DID IT.
CRAZY SON OF A--

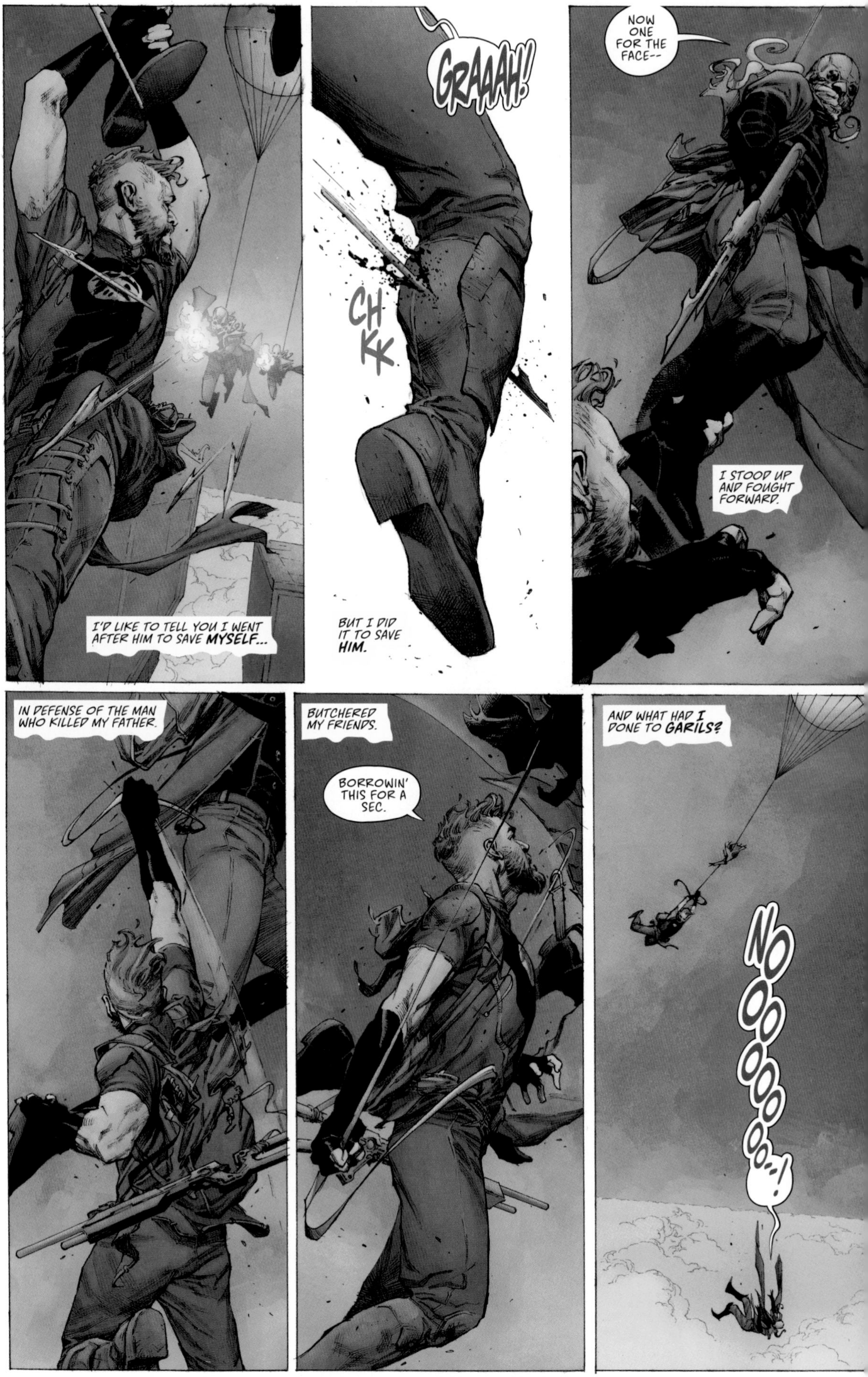
I'D LIKE TO TELL YOU I WENT AFTER HIM TO SAVE MYSELF...
GRAAAH!
CHKK
BUT I DID IT TO SAVE HIM.
NOW ONE FOR THE FACE--
I STOOD UP AND FOUGHT FORWARD.
IN DEFENSE OF THE MAN WHO KILLED MY FATHER.
BUTCHERED MY FRIENDS.
BORROWIN' THIS FOR A SEC.
AND WHAT HAD I DONE TO GARILS?
NOOOOOOOO--!

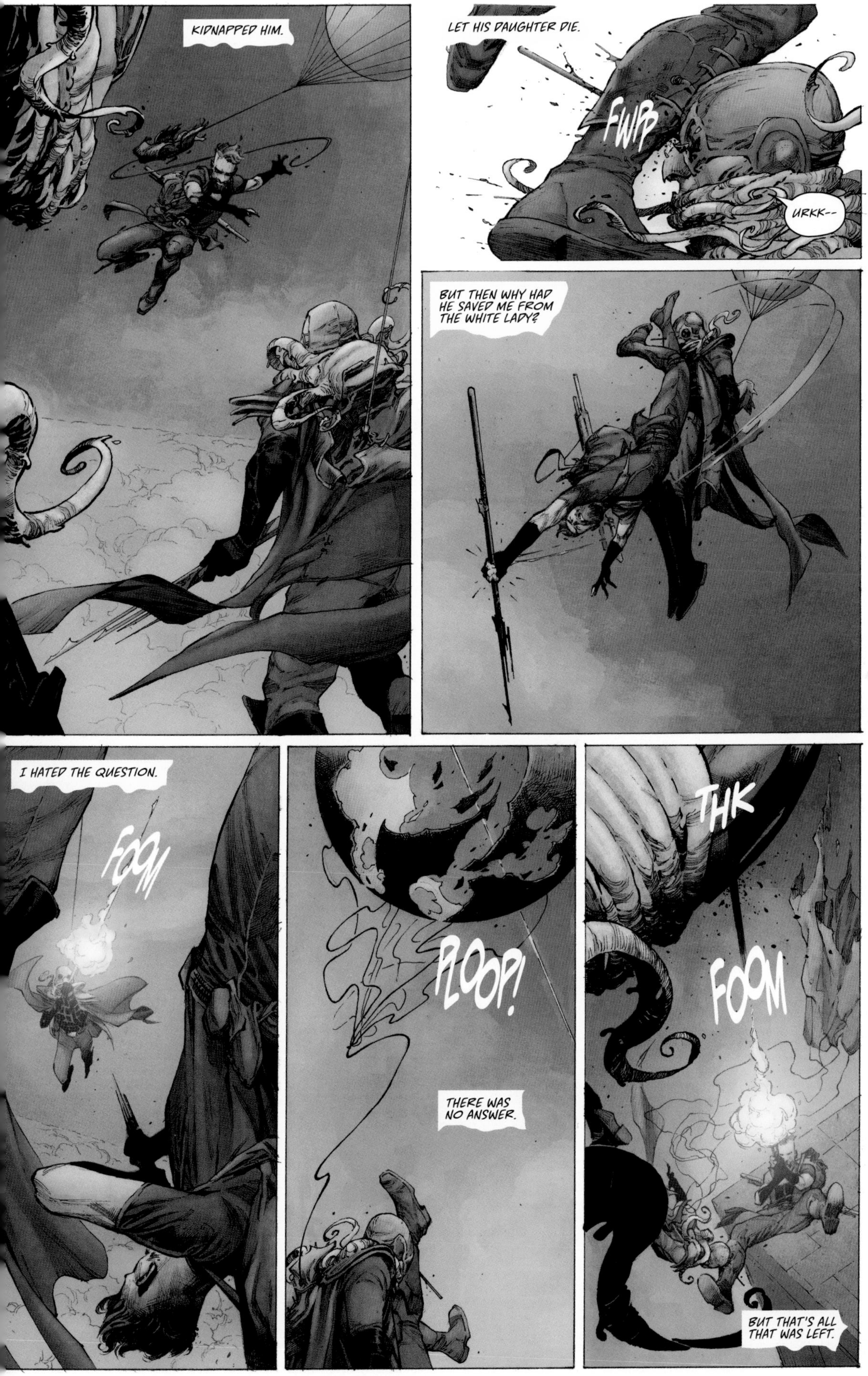
KIDNAPPED HIM.
LET HIS DAUGHTER DIE.
FWIP
URKK--
BUT THEN WHY HAD HE SAVED ME FROM THE WHITE LADY?
I HATED THE QUESTION.
FOOM
PLOOP!
THERE WAS NO ANSWER.
THK
FOOM
BUT THAT'S ALL THAT WAS LEFT.

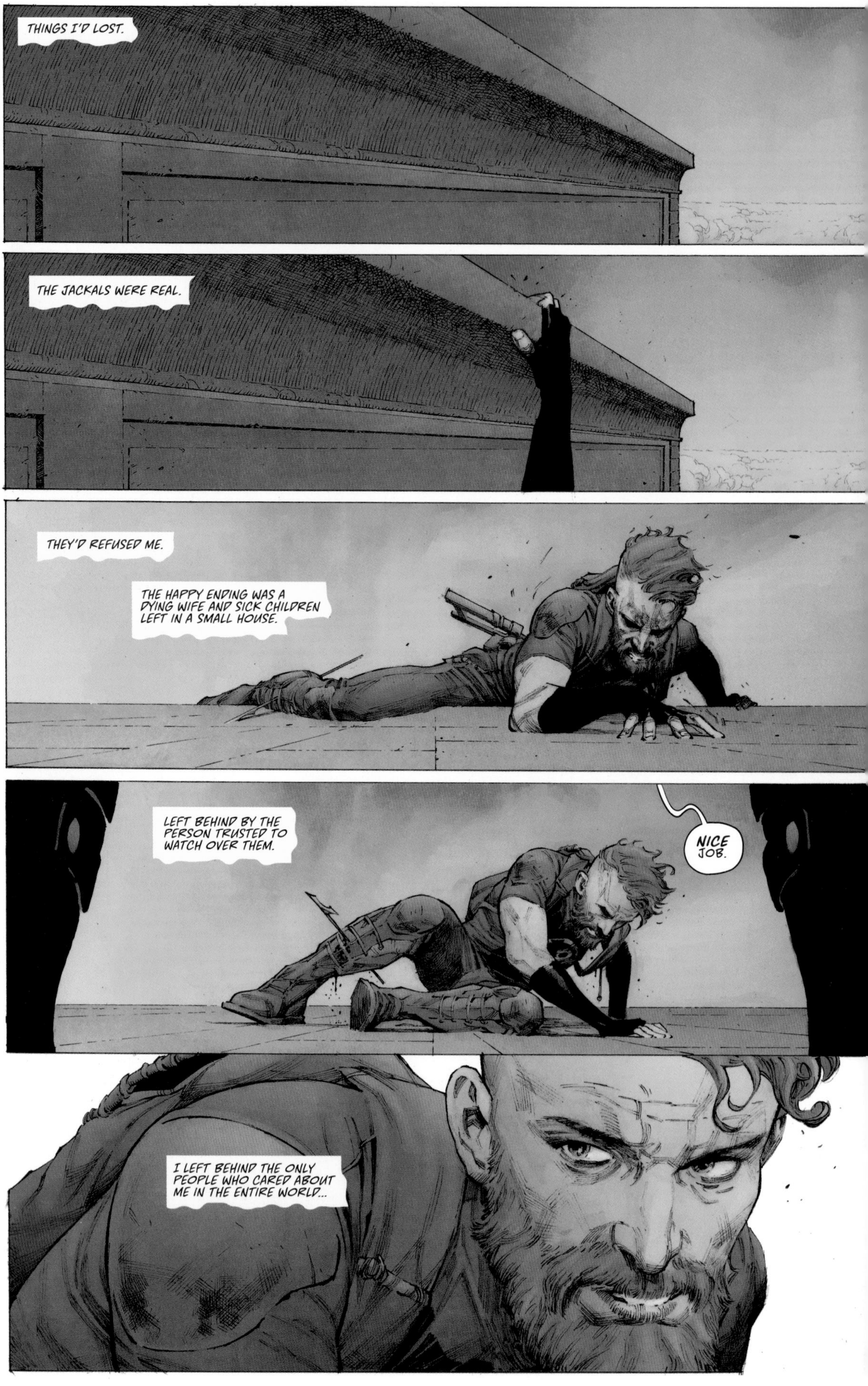
THINGS I'D LOST.
THE JACKALS WERE REAL.
THEY'D REFUSED ME.
THE HAPPY ENDING WAS A DYING WIFE AND SICK CHILDREN LEFT IN A SMALL HOUSE.
LEFT BEHIND BY THE PERSON TRUSTED TO WATCH OVER THEM.
NICE JOB.
I LEFT BEHIND THE ONLY PEOPLE WHO CARED ABOUT ME IN THE ENTIRE WORLD...

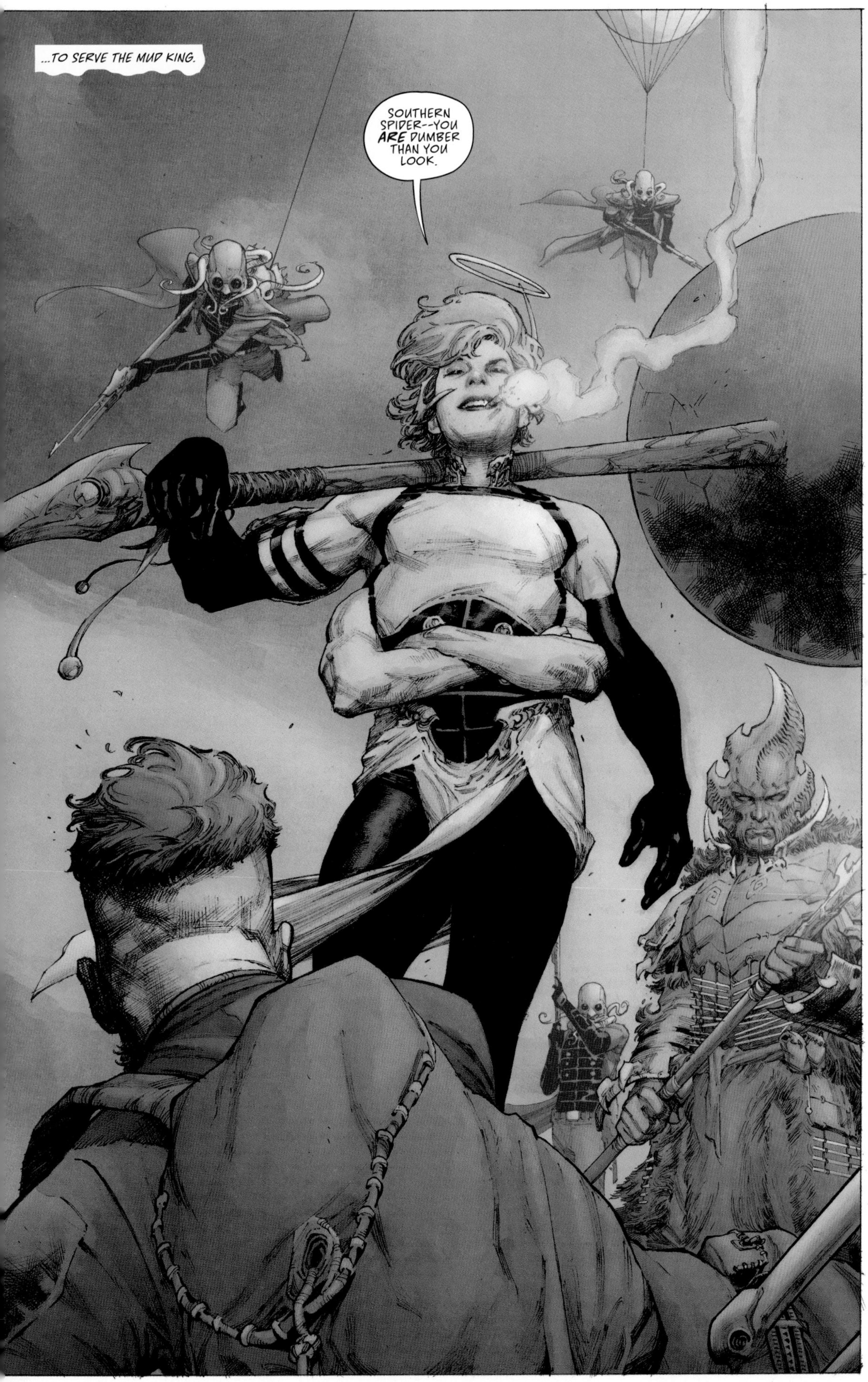
...TO SERVE THE MUD KING.
SOUTHERN SPIDER--YOU ARE DUMBER THAN YOU LOOK.

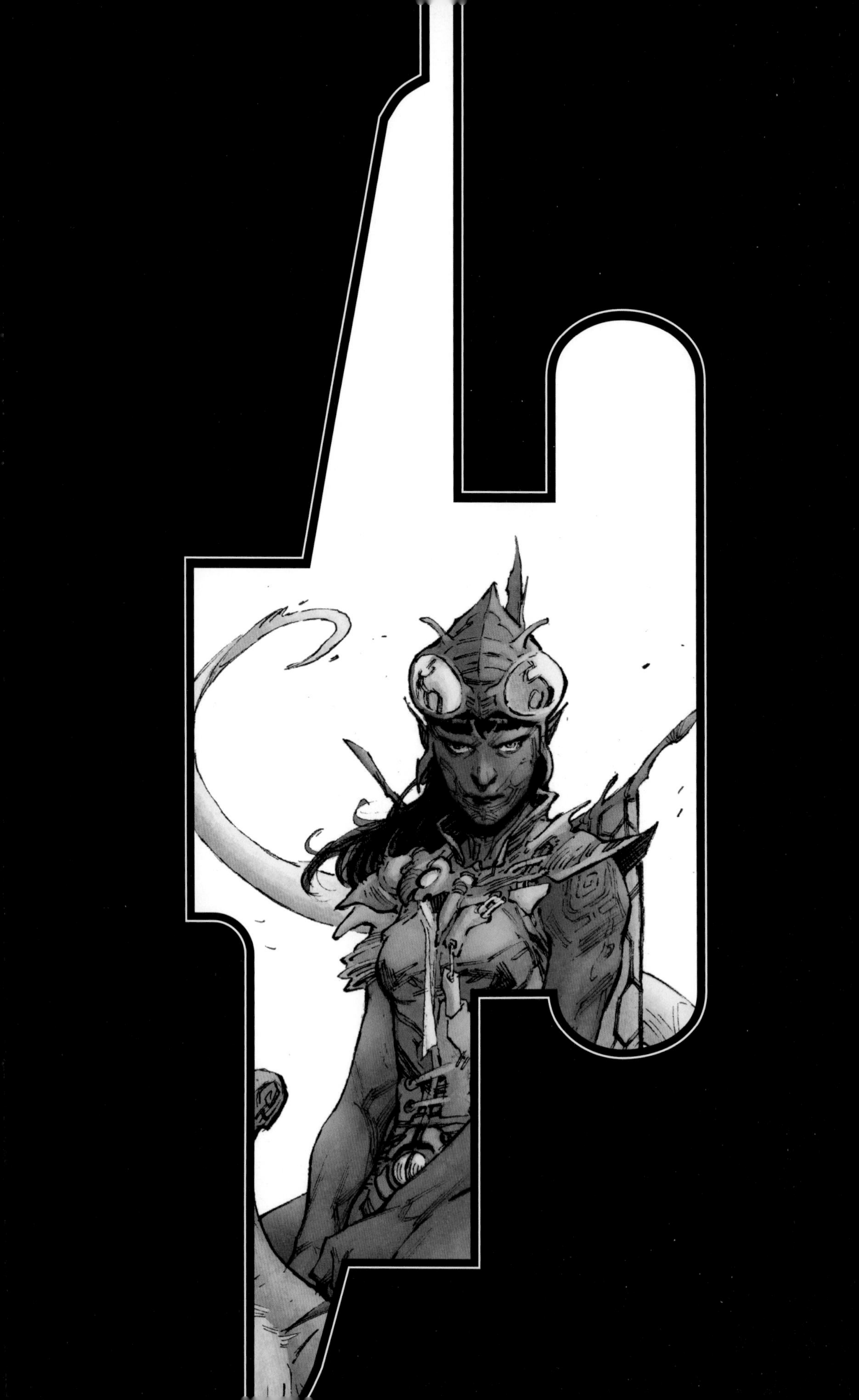

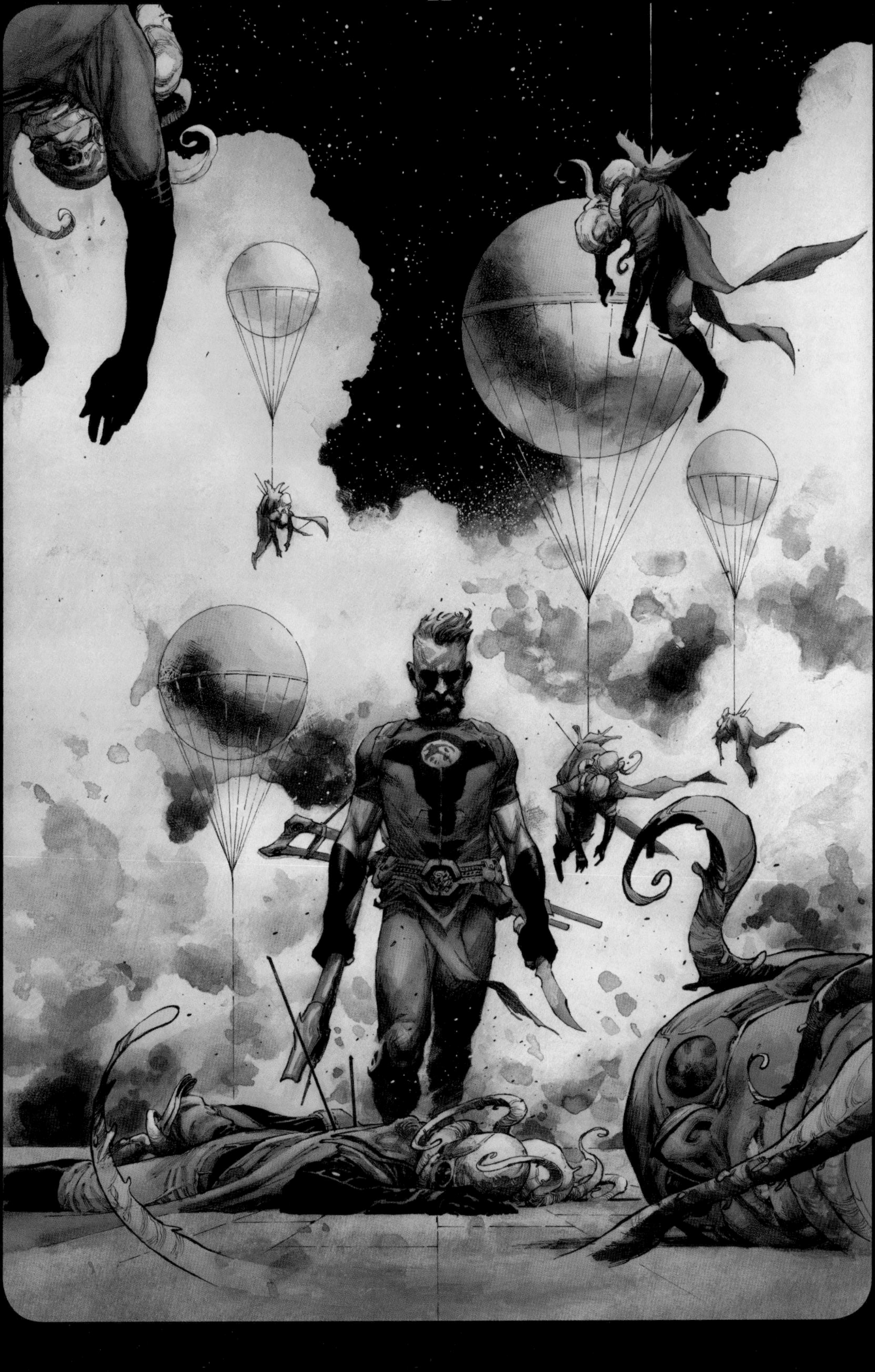

FROM THE JOURNAL OF ADAM OSIDIS

Existence is a compromise. Life discovers us without our consent and leaves us in a similar fashion. There's no negotiation. Though some of us do try.

As children, our parents help us tread the stream of existence, but eventually, we realize they're also sinking. Concealing it all along for our sake. And when you graduate, when you take that same role on for your own kids, well, that's the death of the child, and the birth of the adult.

"The rot of all principles begins with a single compromise." While drowning, the irony of the Osidis' credo was especially sour. What do we have without compromise? Inflexible walls inevitably become cages.

They say courage is putting the overwhelmingly human sense of self-preservation on hold—to do the right thing—mindless of personal harm, or the fact it may be futile. When you are powerless, lost, and facing your end, the truth of your convictions is fully shown.

Everyone has haughty ideals until they face the dark choice themselves, when everything is on the line. Then they all turn to the lifeline of compromise. They do the thing they swore they'd never do. They turn into one of us.

Zeb came to the conclusion that most of life's problems could be solved by isolating oneself from that which challenged this principle. What he overlooked is that isolation just creates a new set of problems.

Garils loved isolation as well. He promoted it. He'd secluded the tribes of Zhal, cut off lines of communication to other tribes, other points of view. Allowing each tribe to become overly self-confident and certain that their ways were right...

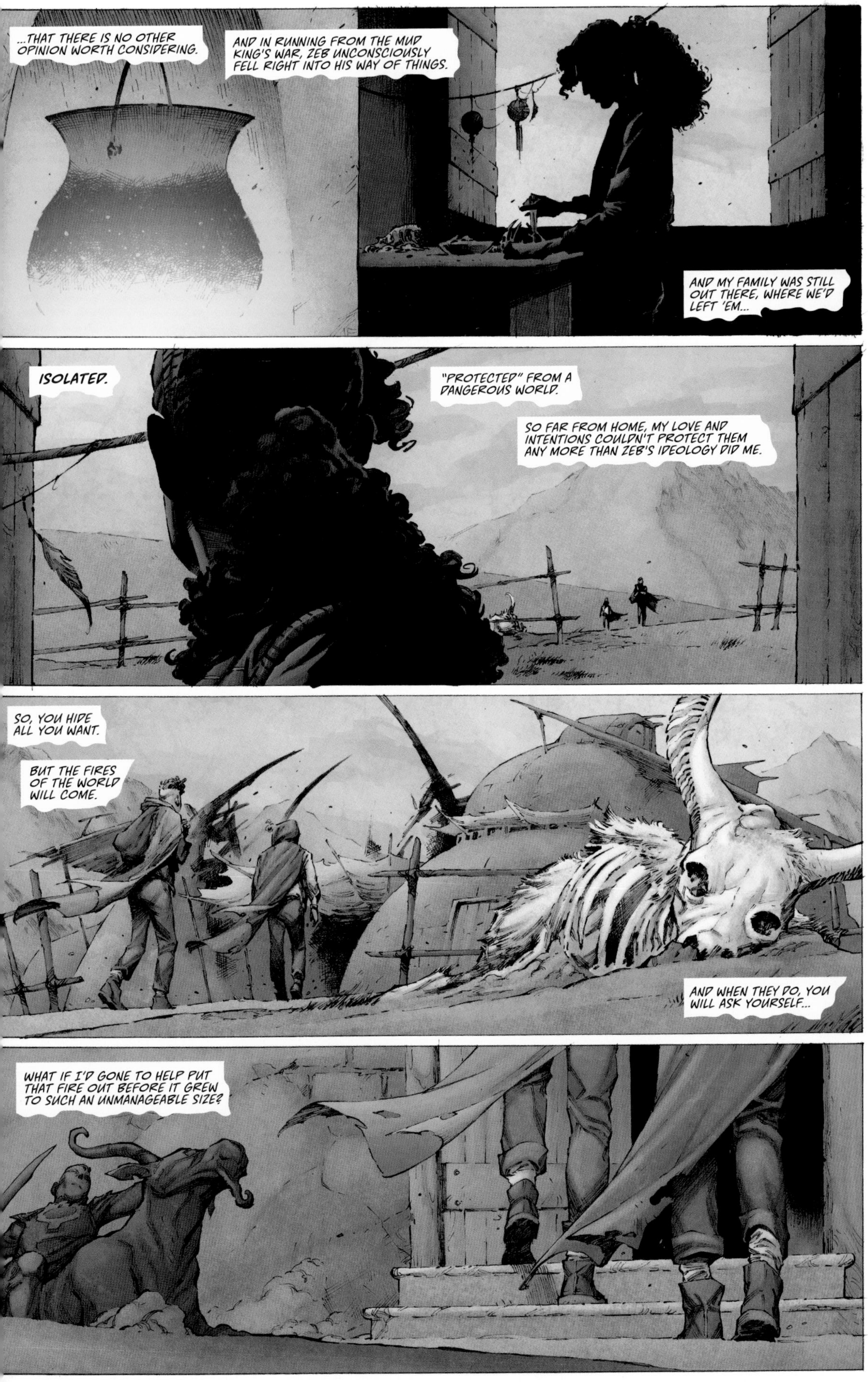
...THAT THERE IS NO OTHER OPINION WORTH CONSIDERING.
AND IN RUNNING FROM THE MUD KING'S WAR, ZEB UNCONSCIOUSLY FELL RIGHT INTO HIS WAY OF THINGS.
AND MY FAMILY WAS STILL OUT THERE, WHERE WE'D LEFT 'EM...
ISOLATED.
"PROTECTED" FROM A DANGEROUS WORLD.
SO FAR FROM HOME, MY LOVE AND INTENTIONS COULDN'T PROTECT THEM ANY MORE THAN ZEB'S IDEOLOGY DID ME.
SO, YOU HIDE ALL YOU WANT.
BUT THE FIRES OF THE WORLD WILL COME.
AND WHEN THEY DO, YOU WILL ASK YOURSELF...
WHAT IF I'D GONE TO HELP PUT THAT FIRE OUT BEFORE IT GREW TO SUCH AN UNMANAGEABLE SIZE?

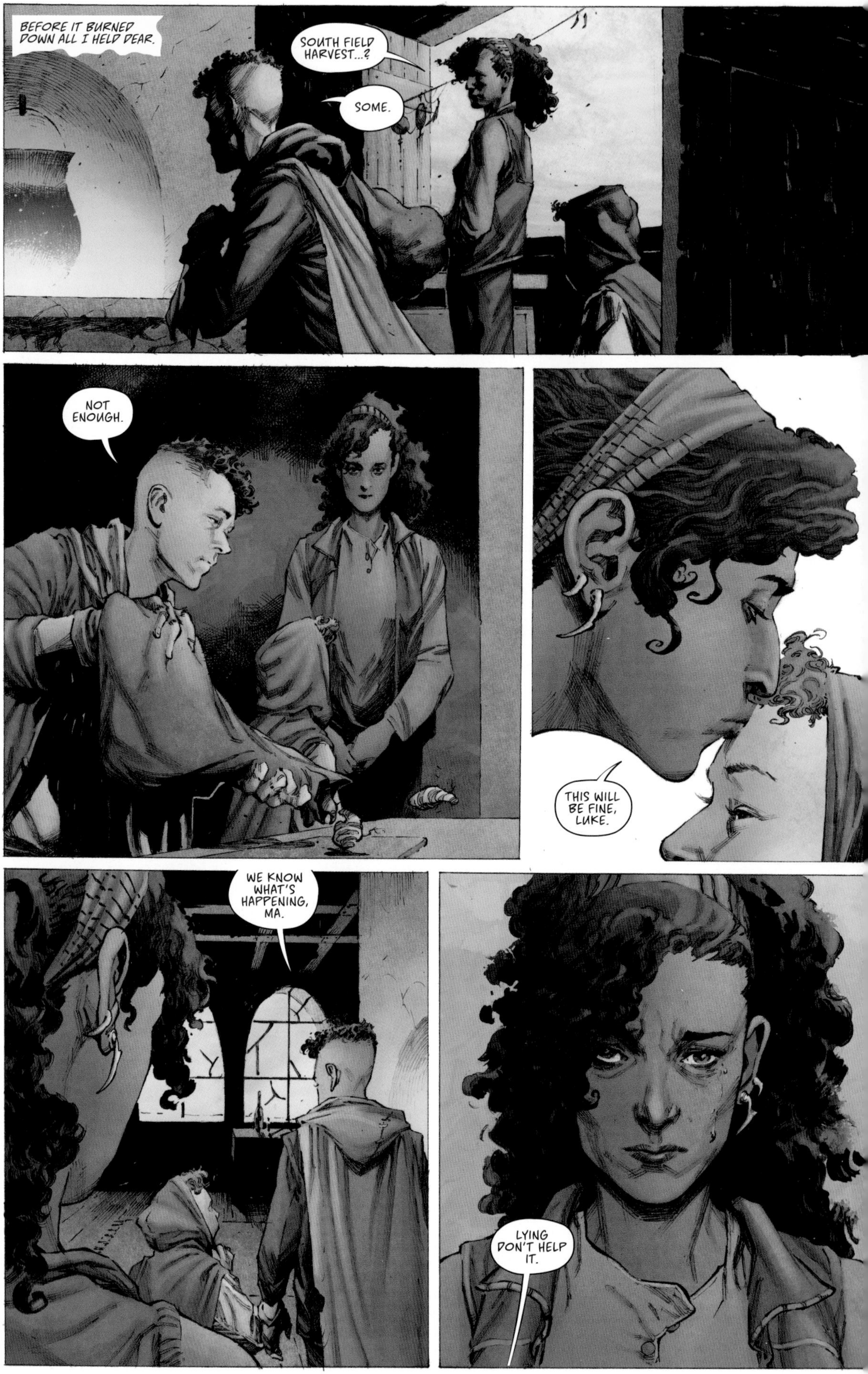
BEFORE IT BURNED DOWN ALL I HELD DEAR.
SOUTH FIELD HARVEST...?
SOME.
NOT ENOUGH.
THIS WILL BE FINE, LUKE.
WE KNOW WHAT'S HAPPENING, MA.
LYING DON'T HELP IT.

UGH... TASTES LIKE DIRT.

MAMA, THE ROOTS ARE DYING.

YET THEY PROVIDE.

DON'T FOCUS ON WHAT WE LACK, THANK THE WELL FOR WHAT WE HAVE.

AND WHILE WE DON'T HAVE MUCH, WE HAVE EACH OTHER.

YOUR FATHER IS PART OF THIS BOND...

HE'S OUT THERE, FIGHTING FOR OUR TOMORROW.

CAN'T YOU FEEL HIS LOVE FROM ACROSS THE HORIZON?

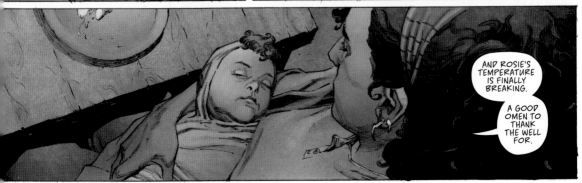

AND ROSIE'S TEMPERATURE IS FINALLY BREAKING.

A GOOD OMEN TO THANK THE WELL FOR.

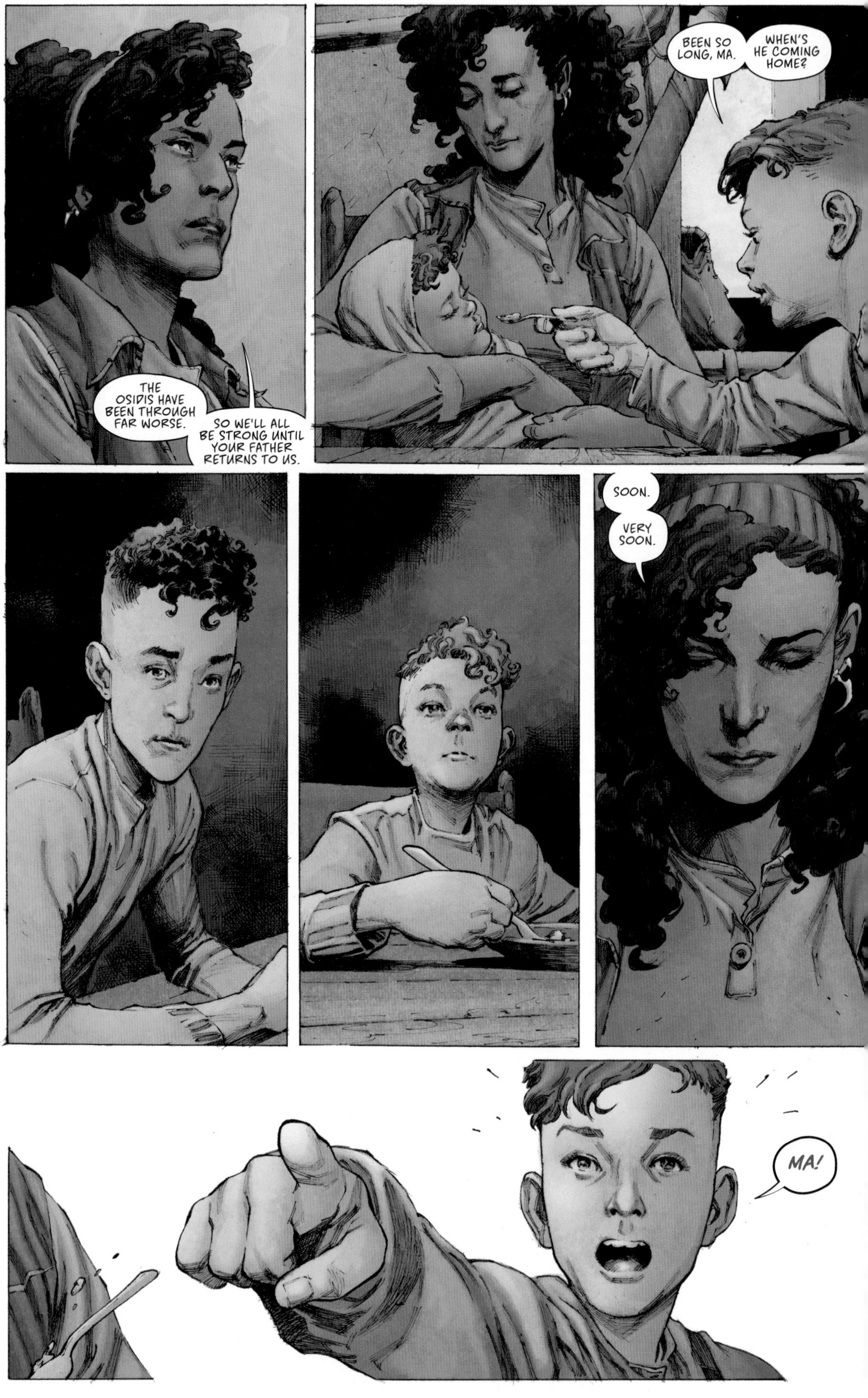
THE OSIDIS HAVE BEEN THROUGH FAR WORSE.
SO WE'LL ALL BE STRONG UNTIL YOUR FATHER RETURNS TO US.
BEEN SO LONG, MA.
WHEN'S HE COMING HOME?
SOON.
VERY SOON.
MA!

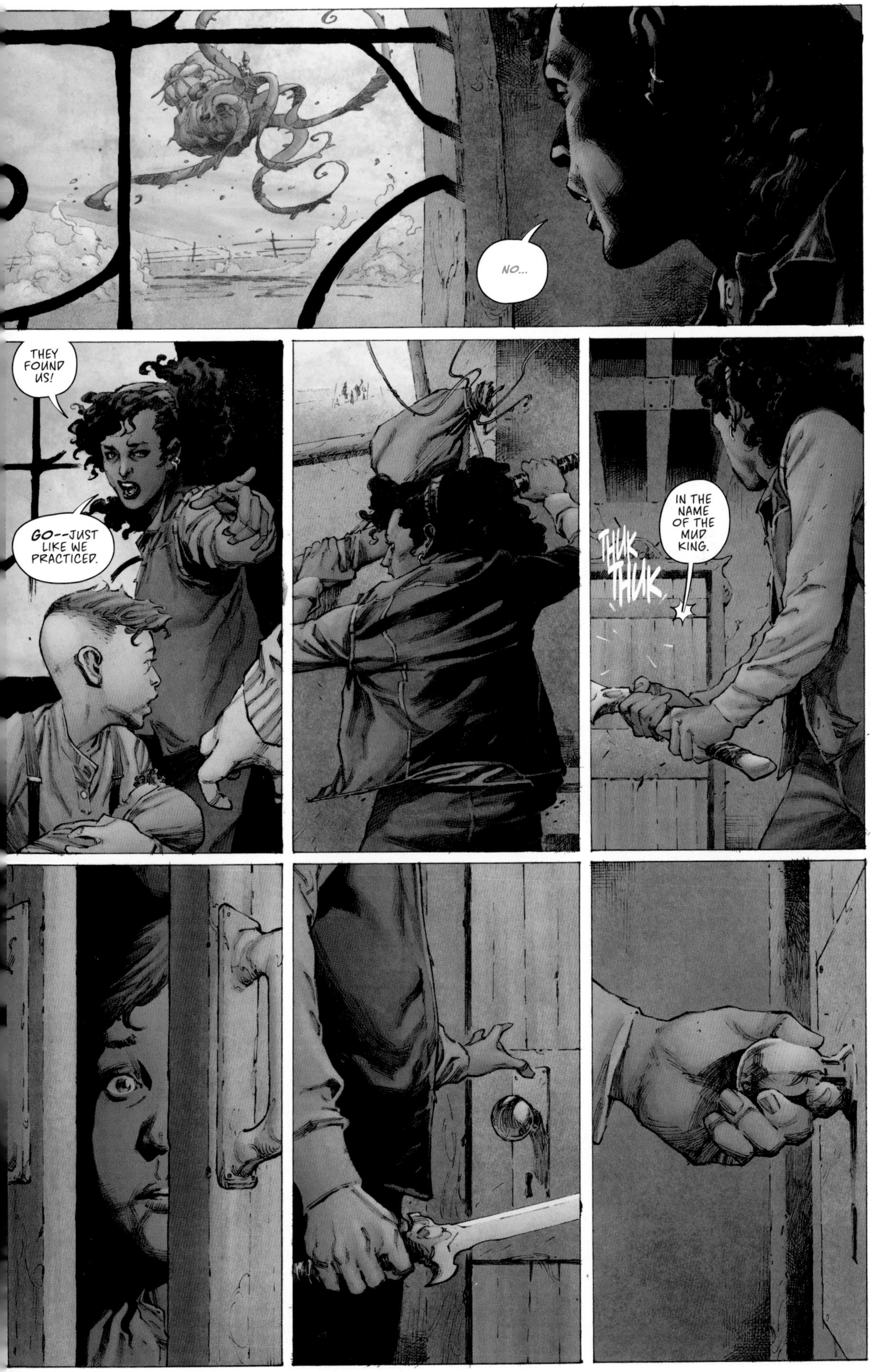
NO...
THEY FOUND US!
GO--JUST LIKE WE PRACTICED.
THUK THUK
IN THE NAME OF THE MUD KING.

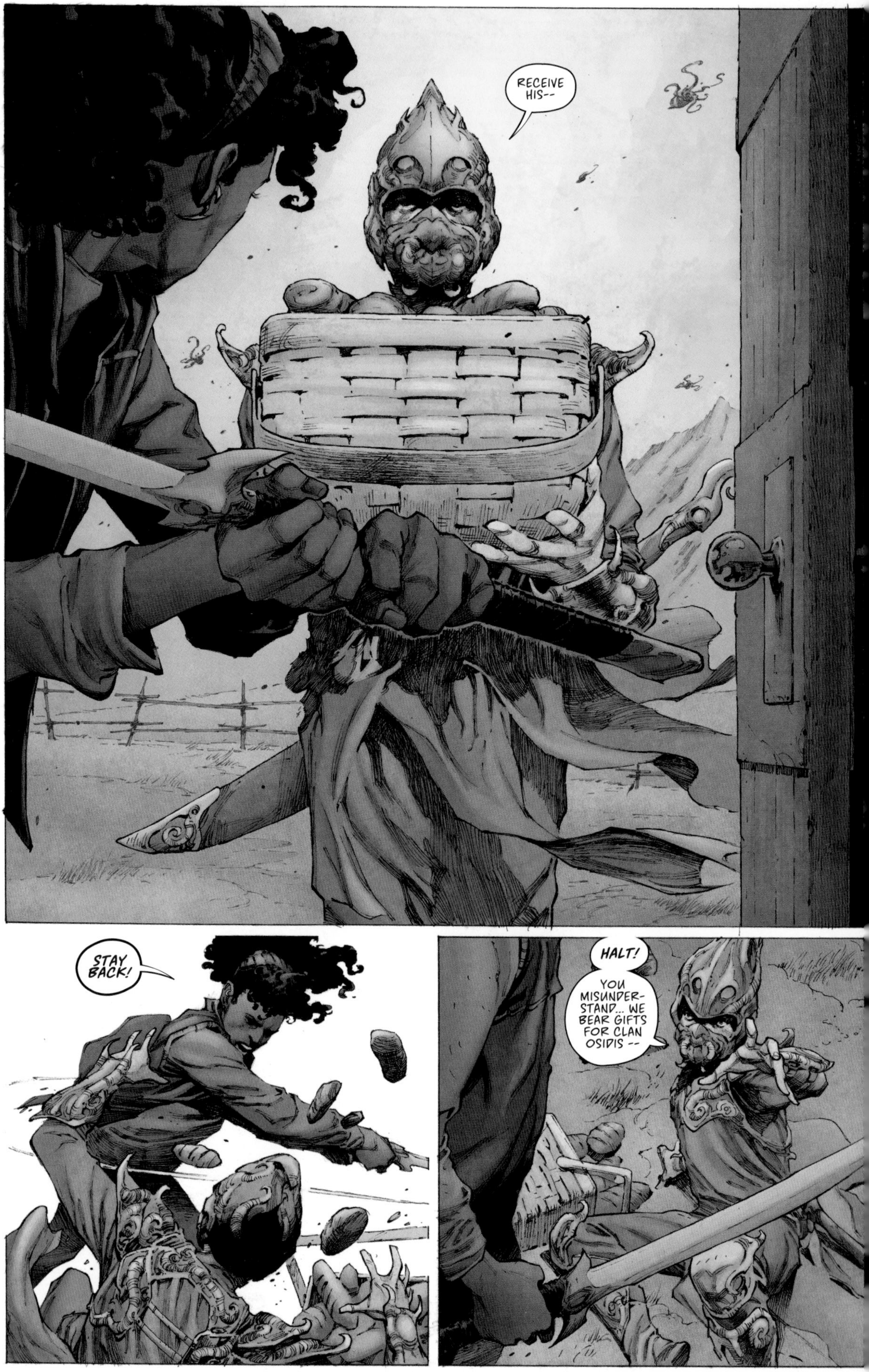
RECEIVE HIS--
STAY BACK!
HALT!
YOU MISUNDER-STAND... WE BEAR GIFTS FOR CLAN OSIDIS --

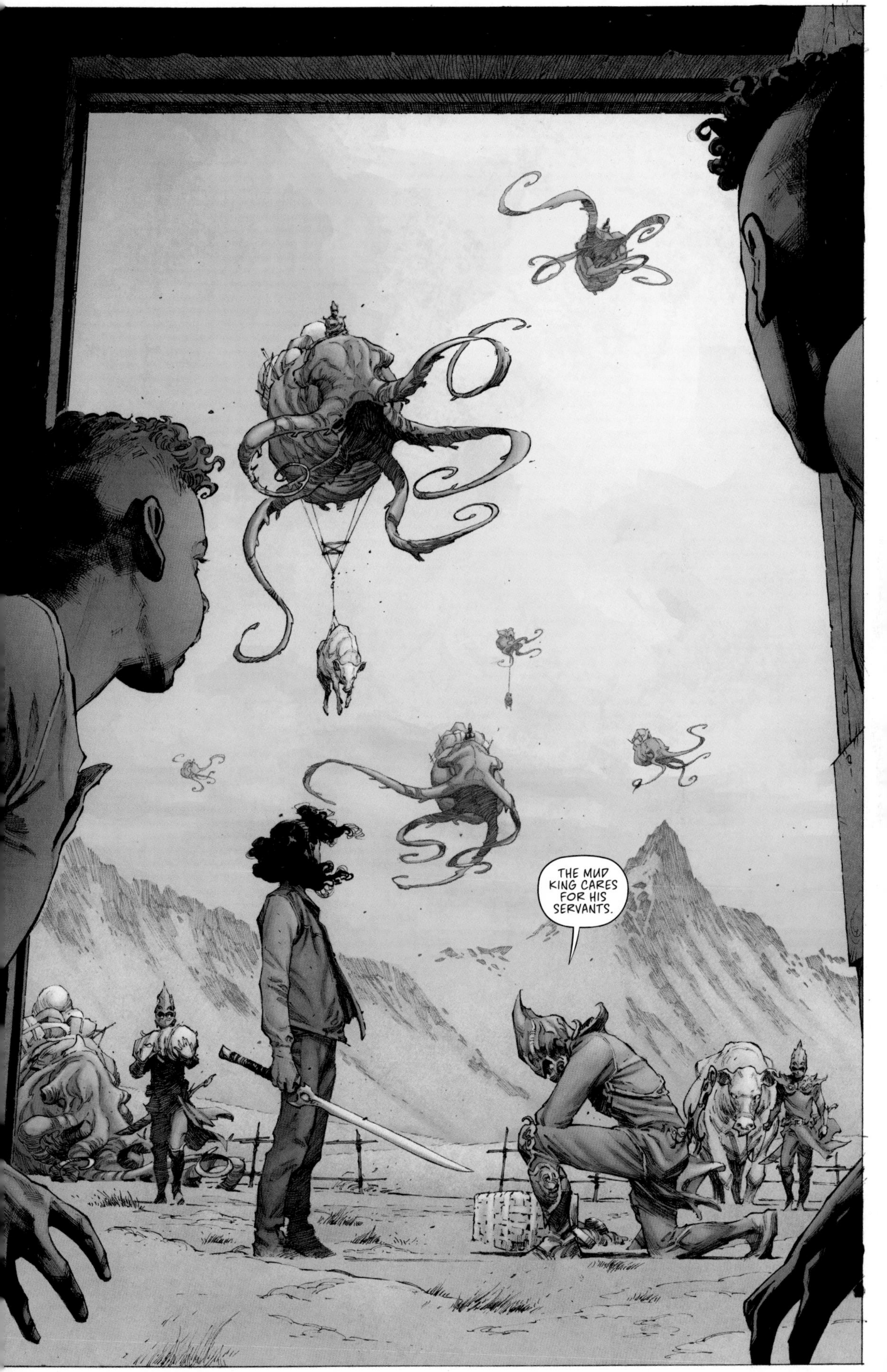
THE MUD KING CARES FOR HIS SERVANTS.

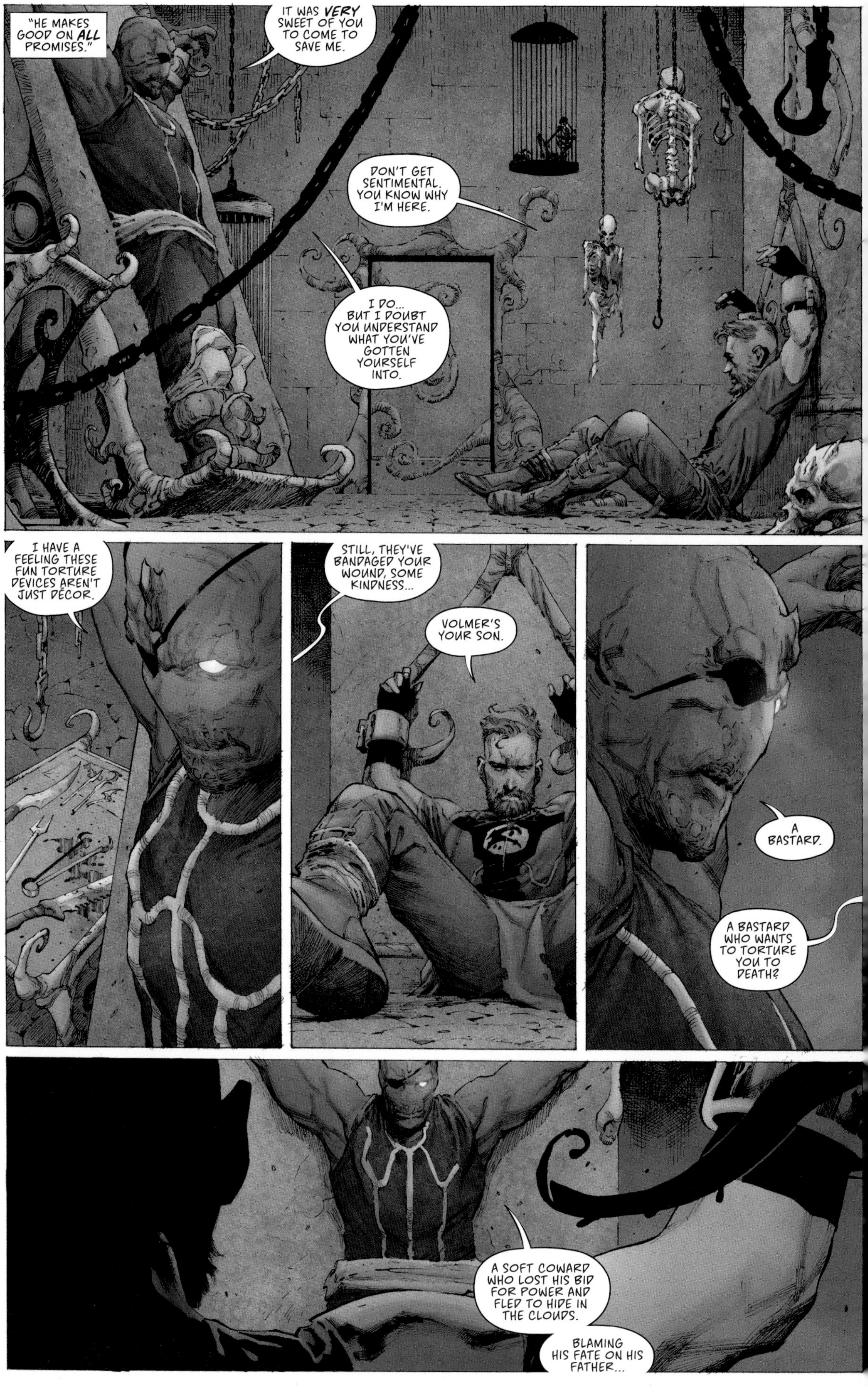
"HE MAKES GOOD ON ALL PROMISES."
IT WAS VERY SWEET OF YOU TO COME TO SAVE ME.
DON'T GET SENTIMENTAL. YOU KNOW WHY I'M HERE.
I DO... BUT I DOUBT YOU UNDERSTAND WHAT YOU'VE GOTTEN YOURSELF INTO.
I HAVE A FEELING THESE FUN TORTURE DEVICES AREN'T JUST DÉCOR.
STILL, THEY'VE BANDAGED YOUR WOUND, SOME KINDNESS...
VOLMER'S YOUR SON.
A BASTARD.
A BASTARD WHO WANTS TO TORTURE YOU TO DEATH?
A SOFT COWARD WHO LOST HIS BID FOR POWER AND FLED TO HIDE IN THE CLOUDS.
BLAMING HIS FATE ON HIS FATHER...

...AS SO MANY FAILURES DO.

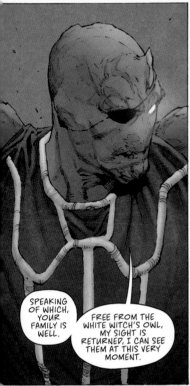

SPEAKING OF WHICH, YOUR FAMILY IS WELL.

FREE FROM THE WHITE WITCH'S OWL, MY SIGHT IS RETURNED, I CAN SEE THEM AT THIS VERY MOMENT.

YOUR SONS ARE EXCITED TO HAVE BREAD FOR THE FIRST TIME IN--

HOW DO YOU SEE 'EM?

WHO DID YOU SEND TO MY HOME?!

MY ELITE GUARD.

THEY WERE NEAR DEAD, ADAM. I'M FEEDING AND PROTECTING THEM.

AS PER OUR BARTER.

YOU CAN SEE AGAIN--SO YOU'RE IN MY HEAD, TOO?!

AND WHEN VOLMER *KILLS* YOU--WHAT OF THOSE WHO'VE HEARD YOUR OFFER?

VOLMER BELIEVES THEY ALL DESERVE TO DIE.

AND, OF COURSE, ONCE I DO...

YOU BREAK YOUR PROMISE TO ME.

DON'T FRET, MY BOY. I'VE SEEN TO OUR RESCUE.

VOLMER ISN'T MY *ONLY* SON, YOU KNOW.

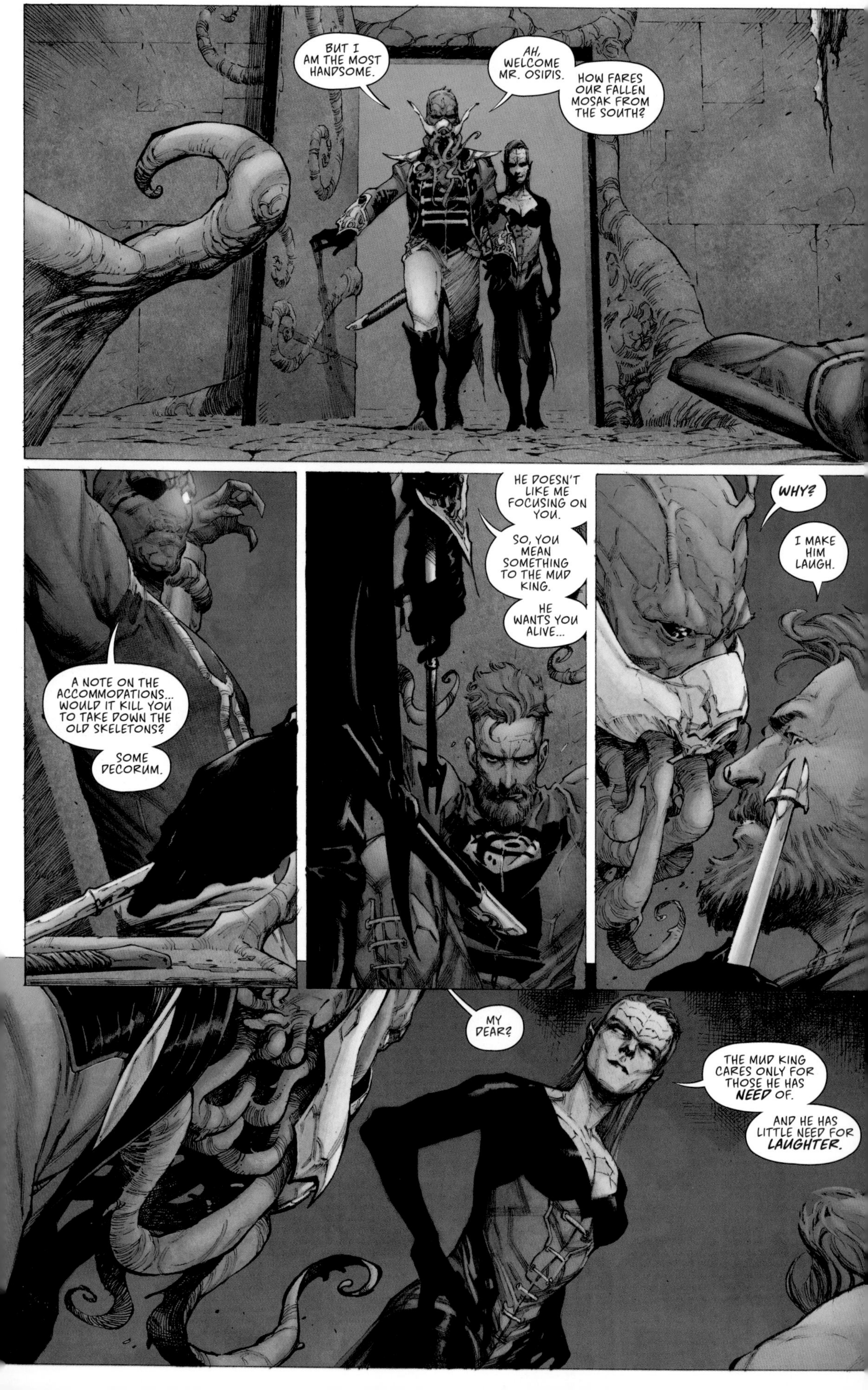
BUT I AM THE MOST HANDSOME.
AH, WELCOME MR. OSIDIS.
HOW FARES OUR FALLEN MOSAK FROM THE SOUTH?
A NOTE ON THE ACCOMMODATIONS... WOULD IT KILL YOU TO TAKE DOWN THE OLD SKELETONS?
SOME DECORUM.
HE DOESN'T LIKE ME FOCUSING ON YOU.
SO, YOU MEAN SOMETHING TO THE MUD KING.
HE WANTS YOU ALIVE...
WHY?
I MAKE HIM LAUGH.
MY DEAR?
THE MUD KING CARES ONLY FOR THOSE HE HAS NEED OF.
AND HE HAS LITTLE NEED FOR LAUGHTER.

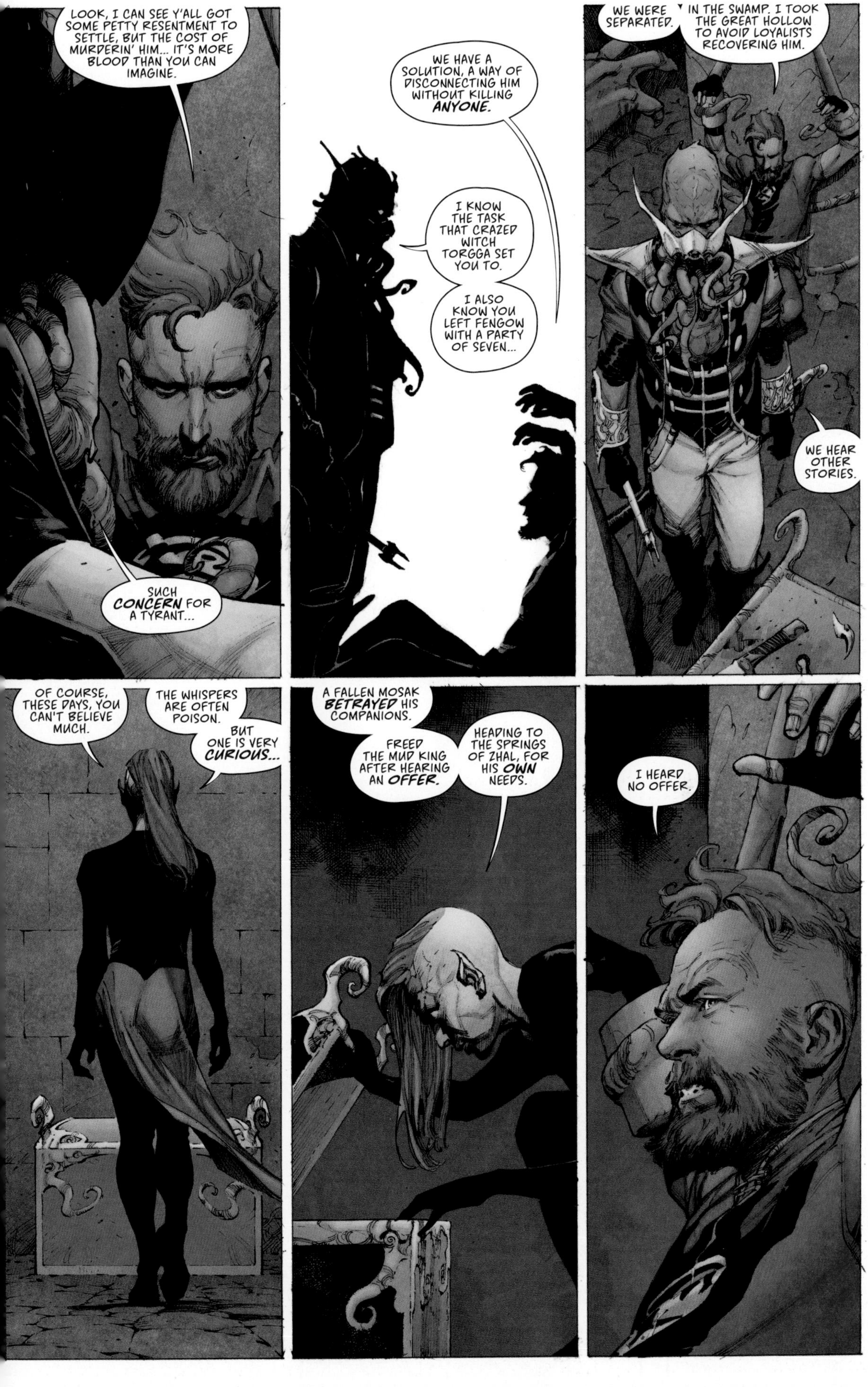
LOOK, I CAN SEE Y'ALL GOT SOME PETTY RESENTMENT TO SETTLE, BUT THE COST OF MURDERIN' HIM... IT'S MORE BLOOD THAN YOU CAN IMAGINE.
SUCH CONCERN FOR A TYRANT...
WE HAVE A SOLUTION, A WAY OF DISCONNECTING HIM WITHOUT KILLING ANYONE.
I KNOW THE TASK THAT CRAZED WITCH TORGGA SET YOU TO.
I ALSO KNOW YOU LEFT FENGOW WITH A PARTY OF SEVEN...
WE WERE SEPARATED.
IN THE SWAMP. I TOOK THE GREAT HOLLOW TO AVOID LOYALISTS RECOVERING HIM.
WE HEAR OTHER STORIES.
OF COURSE, THESE DAYS, YOU CAN'T BELIEVE MUCH.
THE WHISPERS ARE OFTEN POISON.
BUT ONE IS VERY CURIOUS...
A FALLEN MOSAK BETRAYED HIS COMPANIONS.
FREED THE MUD KING AFTER HEARING AN OFFER.
HEADING TO THE SPRINGS OF ZHAL, FOR HIS OWN NEEDS.
I HEARD NO OFFER.

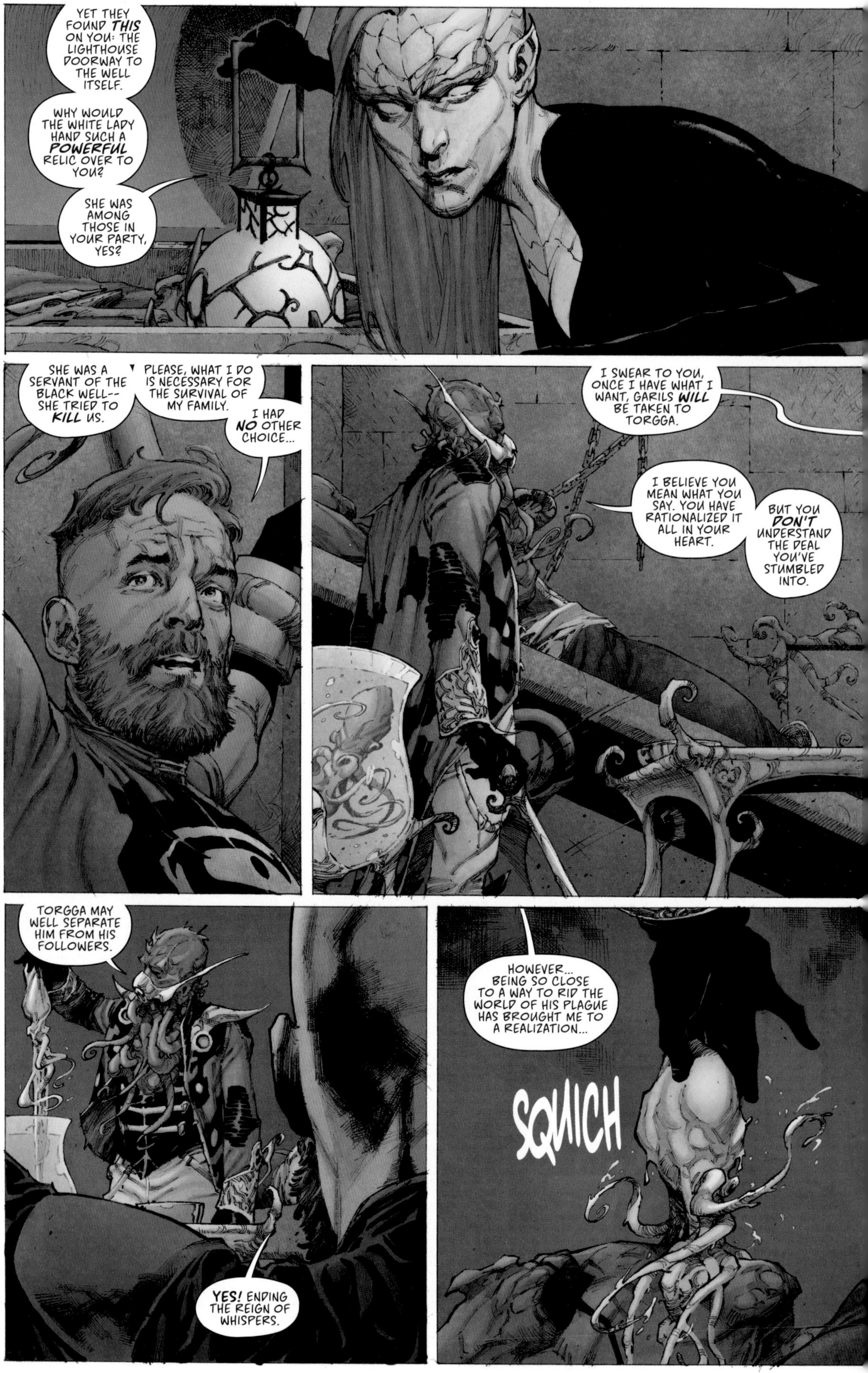
YET THEY FOUND THIS ON YOU: THE LIGHTHOUSE DOORWAY TO THE WELL ITSELF.
WHY WOULD THE WHITE LADY HAND SUCH A POWERFUL RELIC OVER TO YOU?
SHE WAS AMONG THOSE IN YOUR PARTY, YES?
SHE WAS A SERVANT OF THE BLACK WELL-- SHE TRIED TO KILL US.
PLEASE, WHAT I DO IS NECESSARY FOR THE SURVIVAL OF MY FAMILY.
I HAD NO OTHER CHOICE...
I SWEAR TO YOU, ONCE I HAVE WHAT I WANT, GARILS WILL BE TAKEN TO TORGGA.
I BELIEVE YOU MEAN WHAT YOU SAY. YOU HAVE RATIONALIZED IT ALL IN YOUR HEART.
BUT YOU DON'T UNDERSTAND THE DEAL YOU'VE STUMBLED INTO.
TORGGA MAY WELL SEPARATE HIM FROM HIS FOLLOWERS.
YES! ENDING THE REIGN OF WHISPERS.
HOWEVER... BEING SO CLOSE TO A WAY TO RID THE WORLD OF HIS PLAGUE HAS BROUGHT ME TO A REALIZATION...
SQUICH

...MY WINDOW OF OPPORTUNITY CLOSES.

MY *LAST* CHANCE TO SPEND TIME WITH MY FATHER.

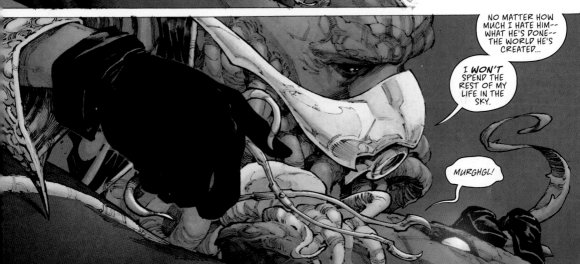

NO MATTER HOW MUCH I HATE HIM-- WHAT HE'S DONE-- THE WORLD HE'S CREATED...

I *WON'T* SPEND THE REST OF MY LIFE IN THE SKY.

MURGHGL!

GHUGHHGGH~!

SHLKK

FOR ONCE, I'LL PRIORITIZE MY NEEDS.

SO, YOU *WIN* FATHER.

I WILL HEAR YOUR OFFER...

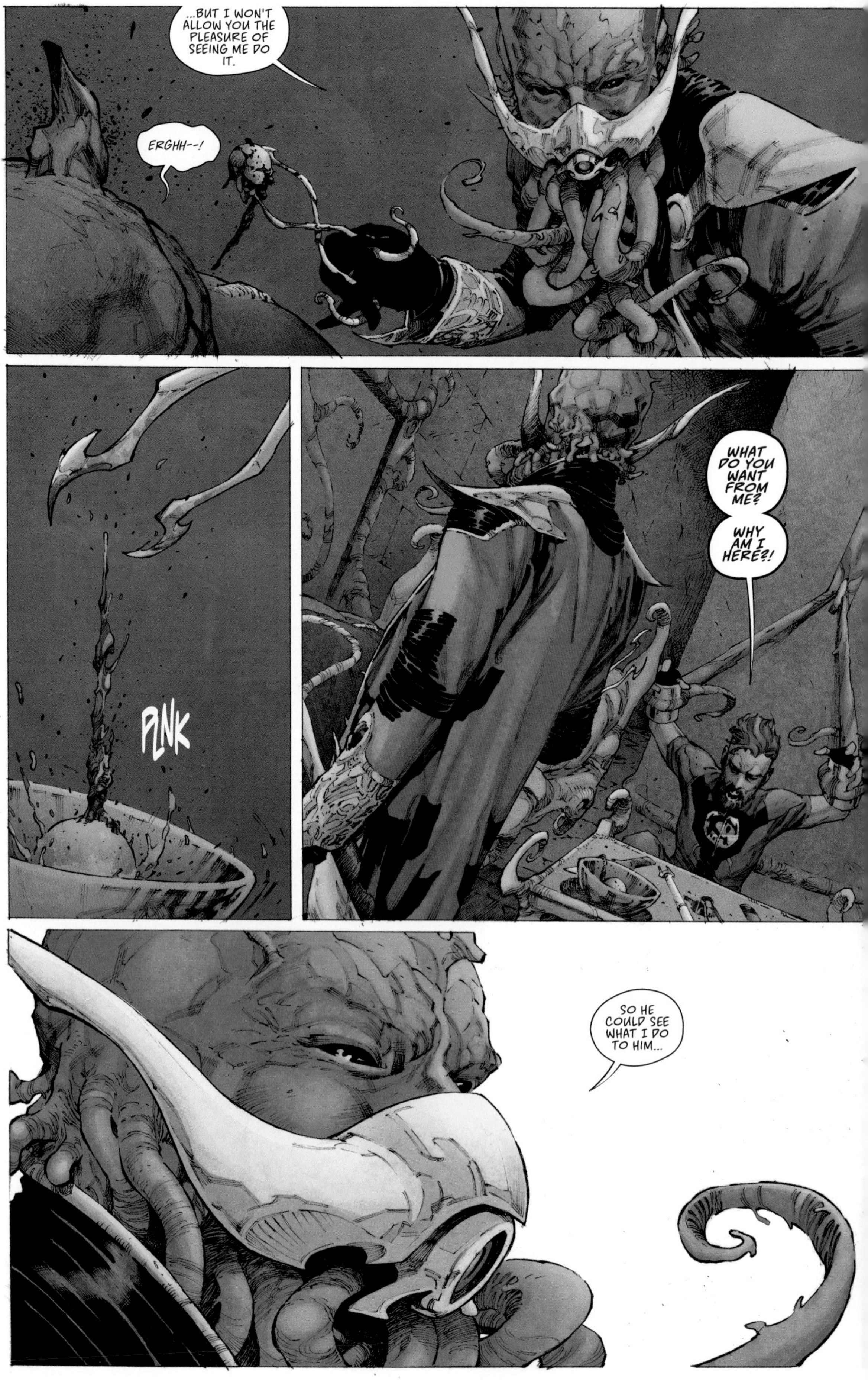
...BUT I WON'T ALLOW YOU THE PLEASURE OF SEEING ME DO IT.
ERGHH--!
PLNK
WHAT DO YOU WANT FROM ME?
WHY AM I HERE?!
SO HE COULD SEE WHAT I DO TO HIM...

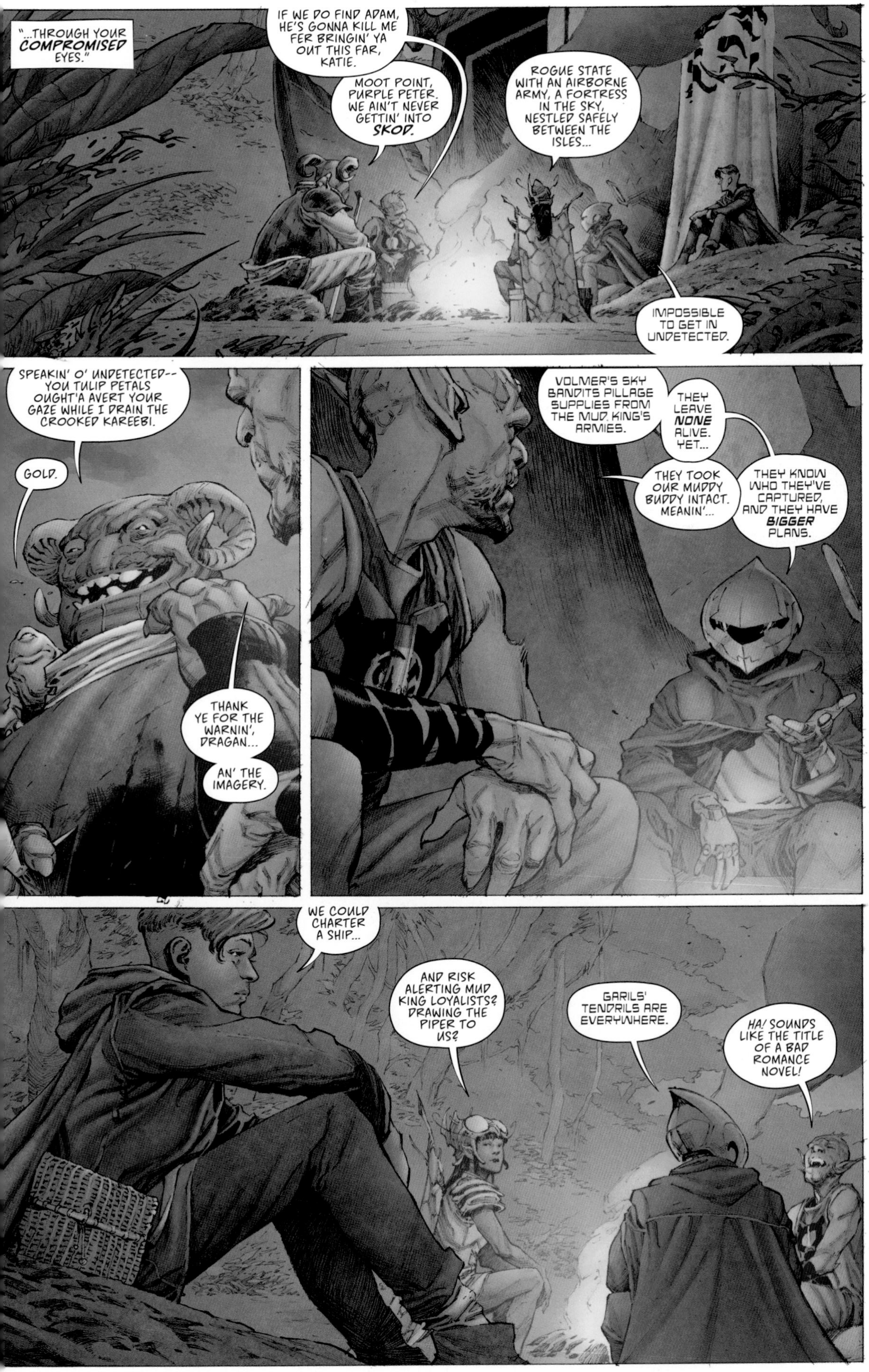
"...THROUGH YOUR COMPROMISED EYES."
IF WE DO FIND ADAM, HE'S GONNA KILL ME FER BRINGIN' YA OUT THIS FAR, KATIE.
MOOT POINT, PURPLE PETER. WE AIN'T NEVER GETTIN' INTO SKOD.
ROGUE STATE WITH AN AIRBORNE ARMY, A FORTRESS IN THE SKY, NESTLED SAFELY BETWEEN THE ISLES...
IMPOSSIBLE TO GET IN UNDETECTED.
SPEAKIN' O' UNDETECTED-- YOU TULIP PETALS OUGHT'A AVERT YOUR GAZE WHILE I DRAIN THE CROOKED KAREEBI.
GOLD.
THANK YE FOR THE WARNIN', DRAGAN...
AN' THE IMAGERY.
VOLMER'S SKY BANDITS PILLAGE SUPPLIES FROM THE MUD KING'S ARMIES.
THEY LEAVE NONE ALIVE. YET...
THEY TOOK OUR MUDDY BUDDY INTACT. MEANIN'...
THEY KNOW WHO THEY'VE CAPTURED, AND THEY HAVE BIGGER PLANS.
WE COULD CHARTER A SHIP...
AND RISK ALERTING MUD KING LOYALISTS? DRAWING THE PIPER TO US?
GARILS' TENDRILS ARE EVERYWHERE.
HA! SOUNDS LIKE THE TITLE OF A BAD ROMANCE NOVEL!

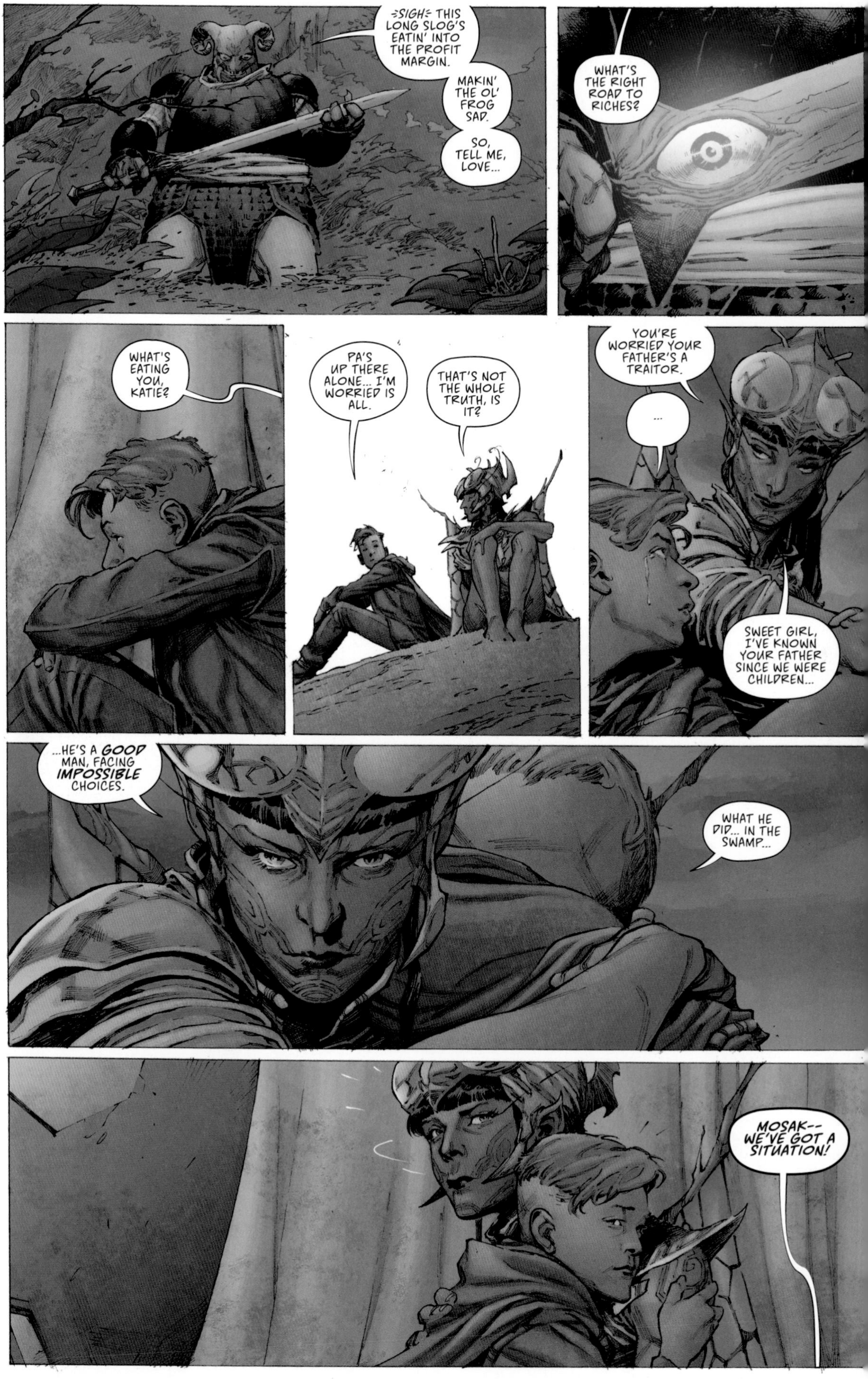
=SIGH= THIS LONG SLOG'S EATIN' INTO THE PROFIT MARGIN.
MAKIN' THE OL' FROG SAD.
SO, TELL ME, LOVE...
WHAT'S THE RIGHT ROAD TO RICHES?
WHAT'S EATING YOU, KATIE?
PA'S UP THERE ALONE... I'M WORRIED IS ALL.
THAT'S NOT THE WHOLE TRUTH, IS IT?
YOU'RE WORRIED YOUR FATHER'S A TRAITOR.
...
SWEET GIRL, I'VE KNOWN YOUR FATHER SINCE WE WERE CHILDREN...
...HE'S A GOOD MAN, FACING IMPOSSIBLE CHOICES.
WHAT HE DID... IN THE SWAMP...
MOSAK-- WE'VE GOT A SITUATION!

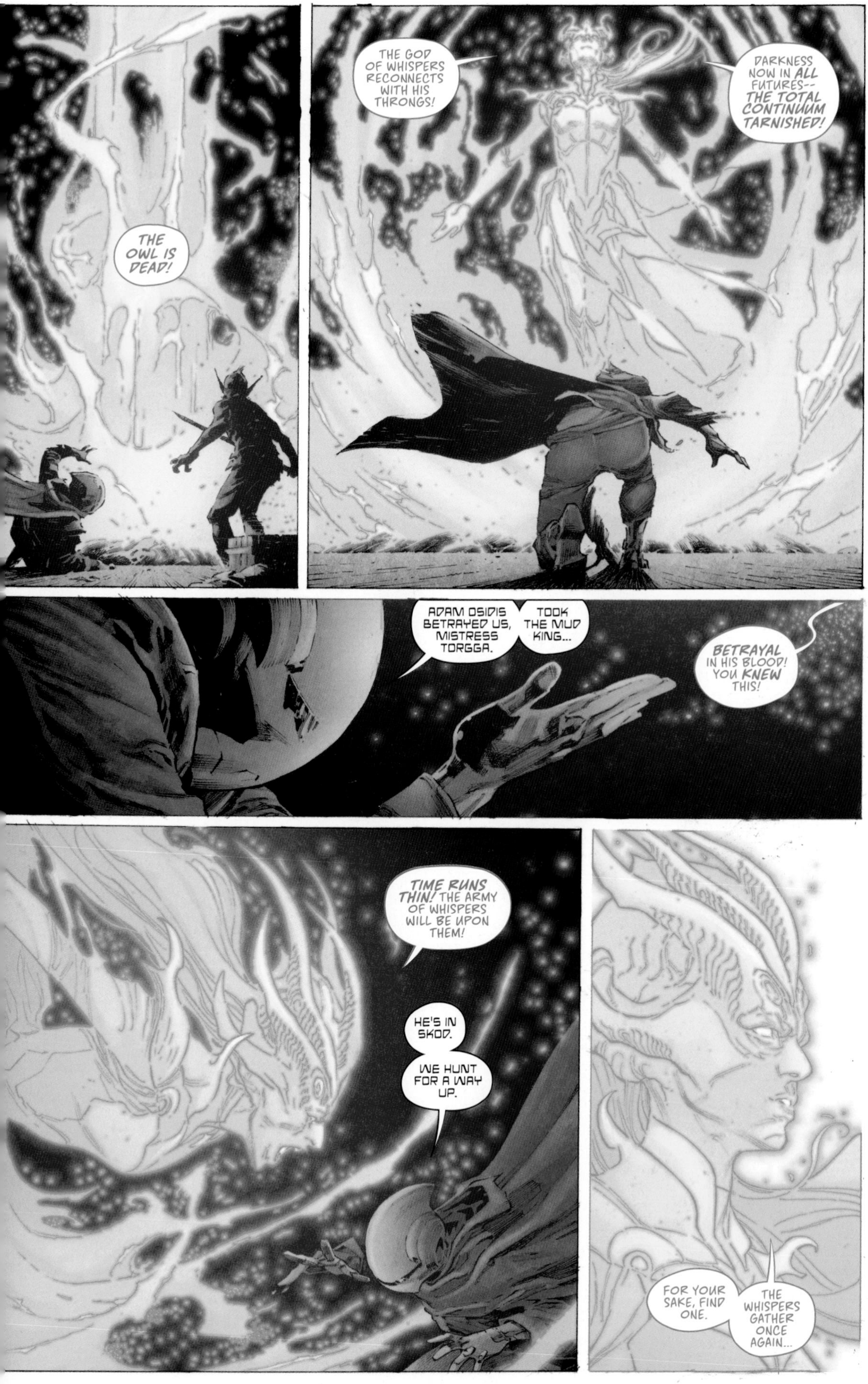
THE OWL IS DEAD!
THE GOD OF WHISPERS RECONNECTS WITH HIS THRONGS!
DARKNESS NOW IN ALL FUTURES-- THE TOTAL CONTINUUM TARNISHED!
ADAM OSIDIS BETRAYED US, MISTRESS TORGGA.
TOOK THE MUD KING...
BETRAYAL IN HIS BLOOD! YOU KNEW THIS!
TIME RUNS THIN! THE ARMY OF WHISPERS WILL BE UPON THEM!
HE'S IN SKOD.
WE HUNT FOR A WAY UP.
FOR YOUR SAKE, FIND ONE.
THE WHISPERS GATHER ONCE AGAIN...

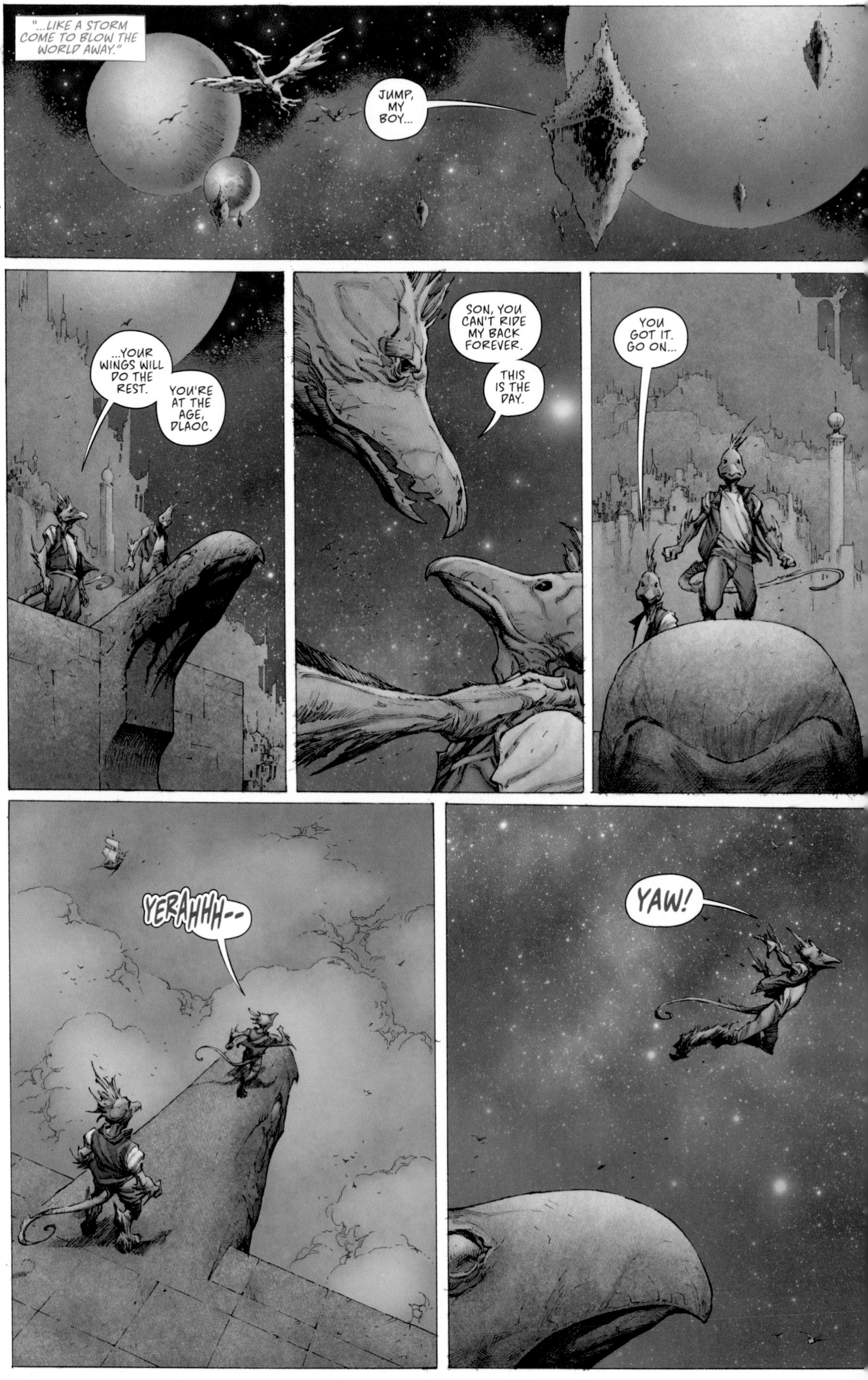
"...LIKE A STORM COME TO BLOW THE WORLD AWAY."
JUMP, MY BOY...
...YOUR WINGS WILL DO THE REST.
YOU'RE AT THE AGE, DLAOC.
SON, YOU CAN'T RIDE MY BACK FOREVER.
THIS IS THE DAY.
YOU GOT IT. GO ON...
YERAHHH--
YAW!

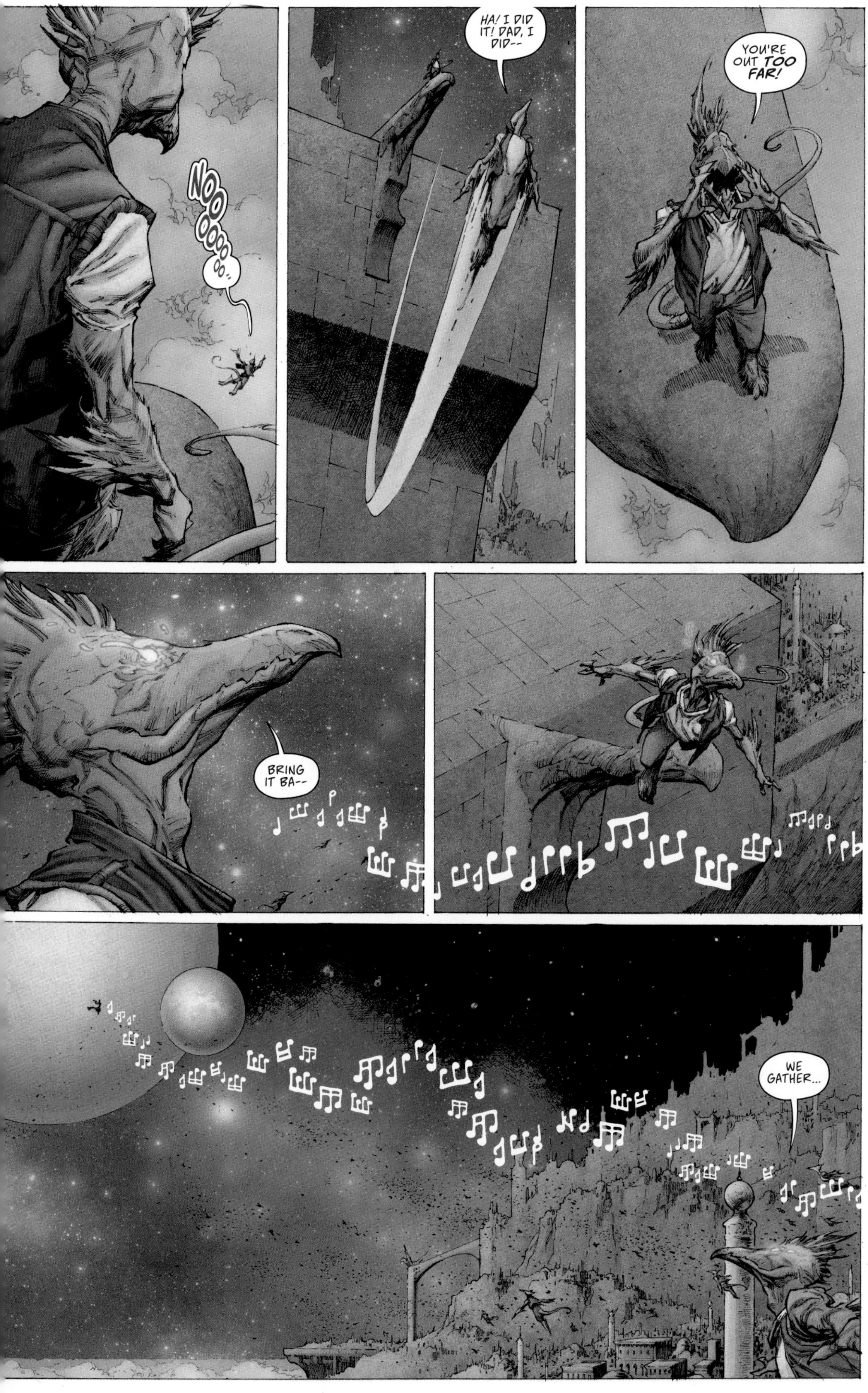
NOOOOOOOO..
HA! I DID IT! DAD, I DID--
YOU'RE OUT TOO FAR!
BRING IT BA--
WE GATHER...

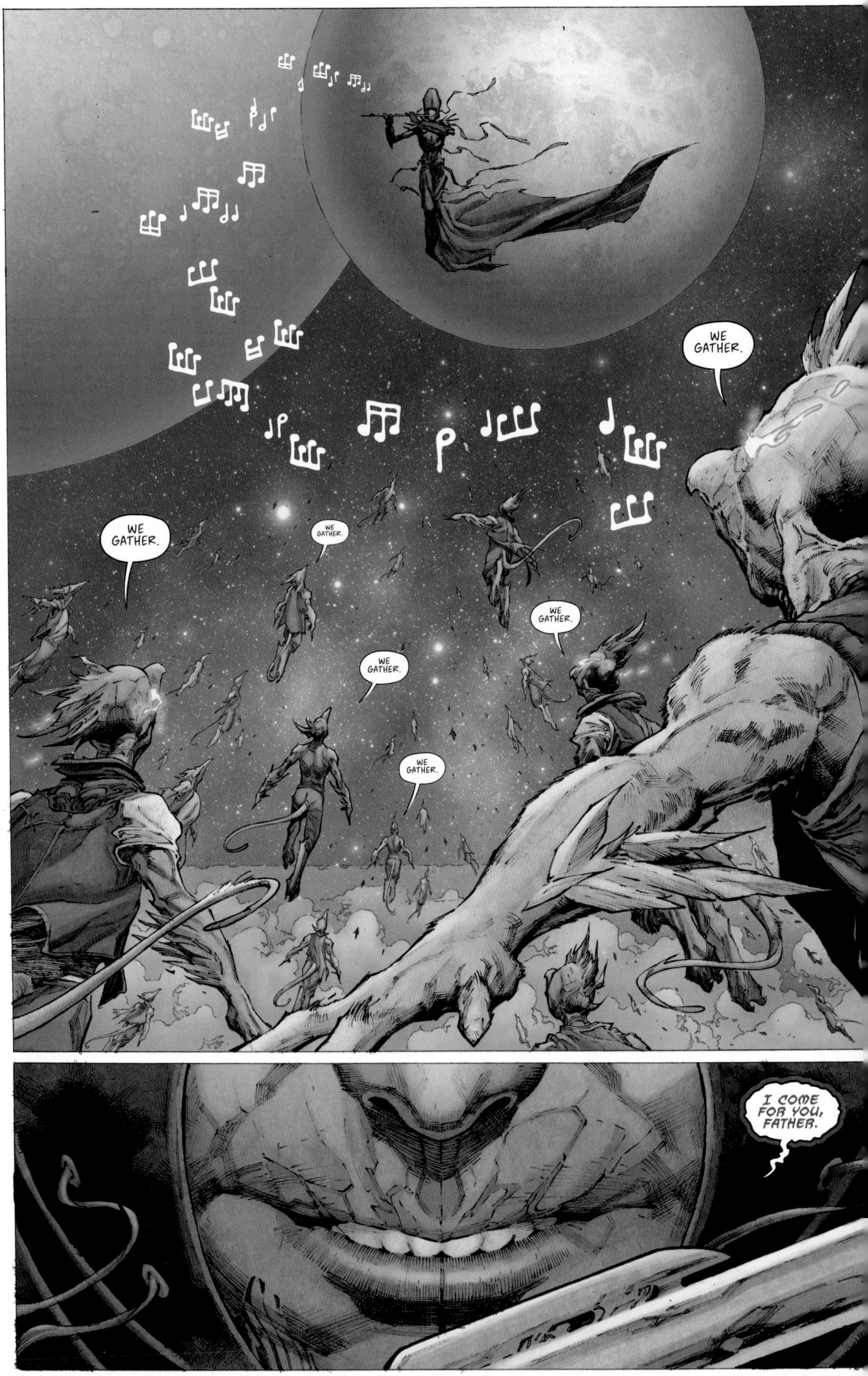
WE GATHER.
WE GATHER.
WE GATHER.
WE GATHER.
WE GATHER.
WE GATHER.
I COME FOR YOU, FATHER.

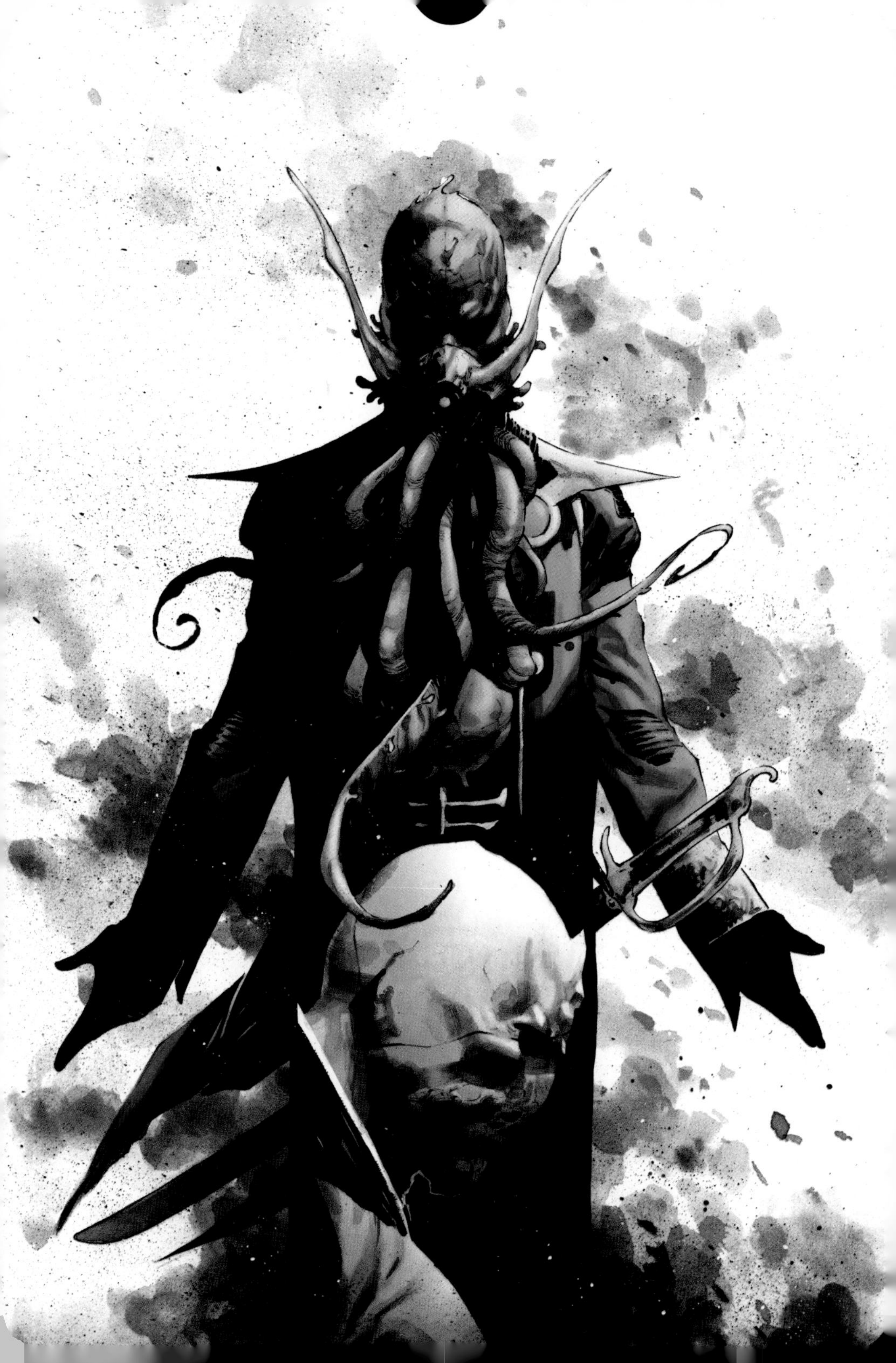

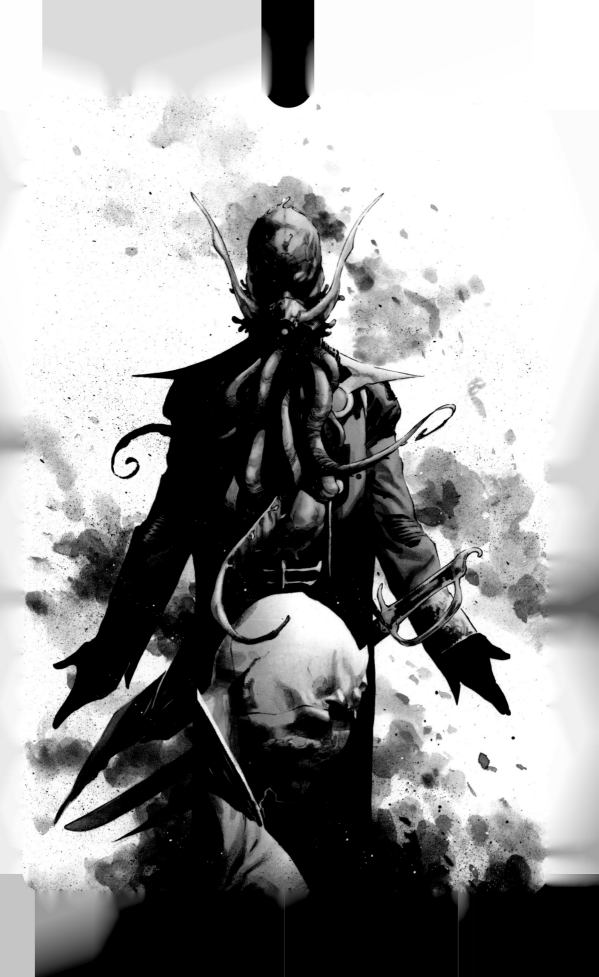

FROM THE JOURNAL OF ADAM OSIDIS

When I first met Volmer, I was nearly dead and desperate to make it to the Springs of Zhal for my salvation. Volmer played an intimidating figure, I remember that much. He was determined to sell the notion. But looking back on it, what I remember the most clearly is what I saw a reflected in his eyes:

An unloved child screaming at a wall.

I could see an ever-present anger that he still felt so wounded, all this time later, as a grown man. He was lord commander of an entire city, with endless responsibilities met, trials bested, and yet his father's cruelty and low estimation of him still echoed, still haunted.

Volmer marched into that prison posing as if he was in control, but it was clear to everyone in the room that he wasn't. He was reacting to the presence of the man he blamed for his circumstance. Volmer was a child in a man's form, intent to redistribute his pain to the one who caused it as if that would somehow undo it.

But that's not how pain works.

I could see it in that face, something in those eyes: Nothing he did would ever soothe the pain. Exacting his revenge only made it that much worse, that much more apparent that he'd never overcome the hurt.

And on the face of the Mud King, before he was blinded by his son, I saw something that brought back a terrible recollection: the look I saw on my own father's face when we last parted. Before he turned his back to me and left me forever...

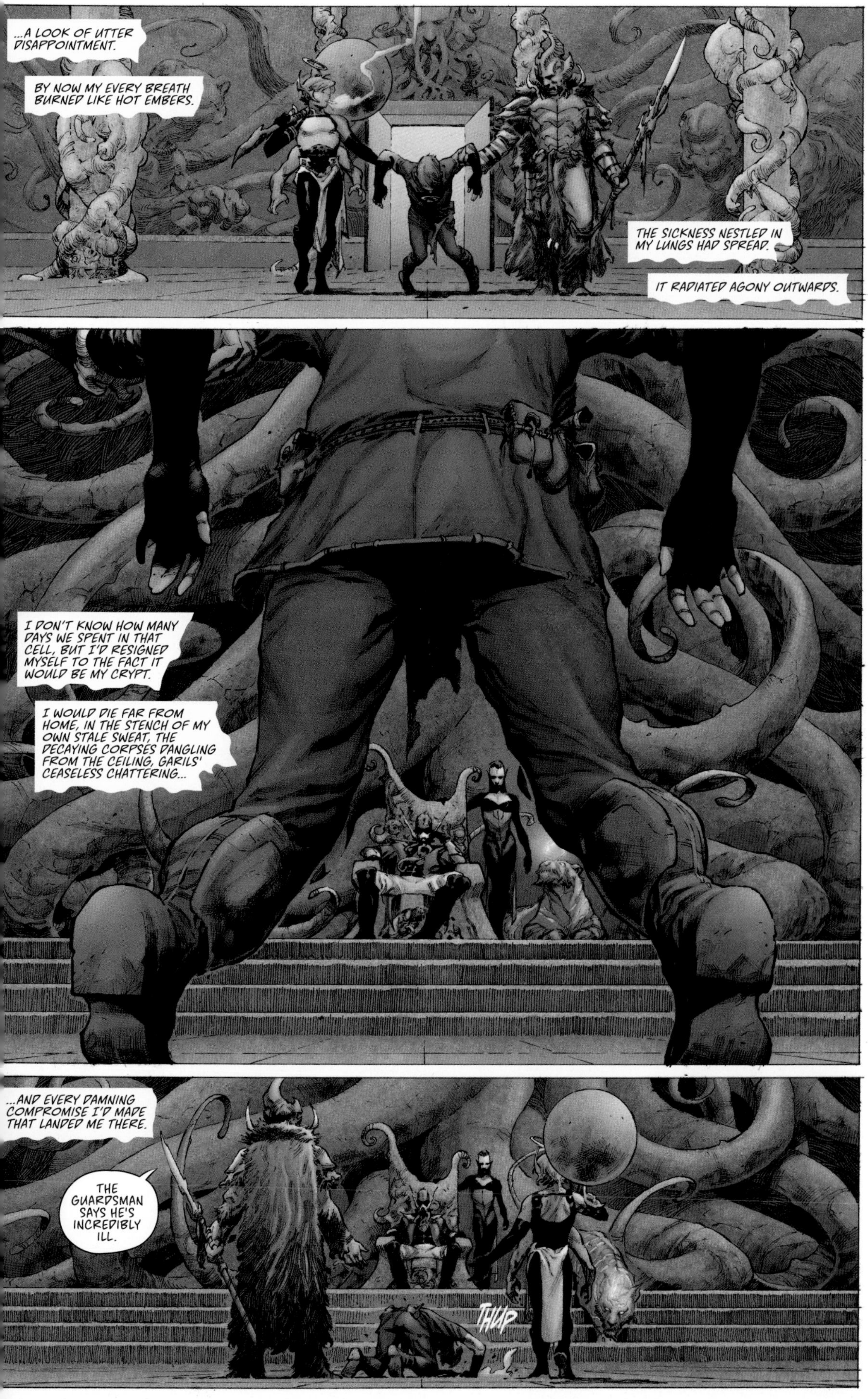
...A LOOK OF UTTER DISAPPOINTMENT.
BY NOW MY EVERY BREATH BURNED LIKE HOT EMBERS.
THE SICKNESS NESTLED IN MY LUNGS HAD SPREAD.
IT RADIATED AGONY OUTWARDS.
I DON'T KNOW HOW MANY DAYS WE SPENT IN THAT CELL, BUT I'D RESIGNED MYSELF TO THE FACT IT WOULD BE MY CRYPT.
I WOULD DIE FAR FROM HOME, IN THE STENCH OF MY OWN STALE SWEAT, THE DECAYING CORPSES DANGLING FROM THE CEILING, GARILS' CEASELESS CHATTERING...
...AND EVERY DAMNING COMPROMISE I'D MADE THAT LANDED ME THERE.
THE GUARDSMAN SAYS HE'S INCREDIBLY ILL.
THUP

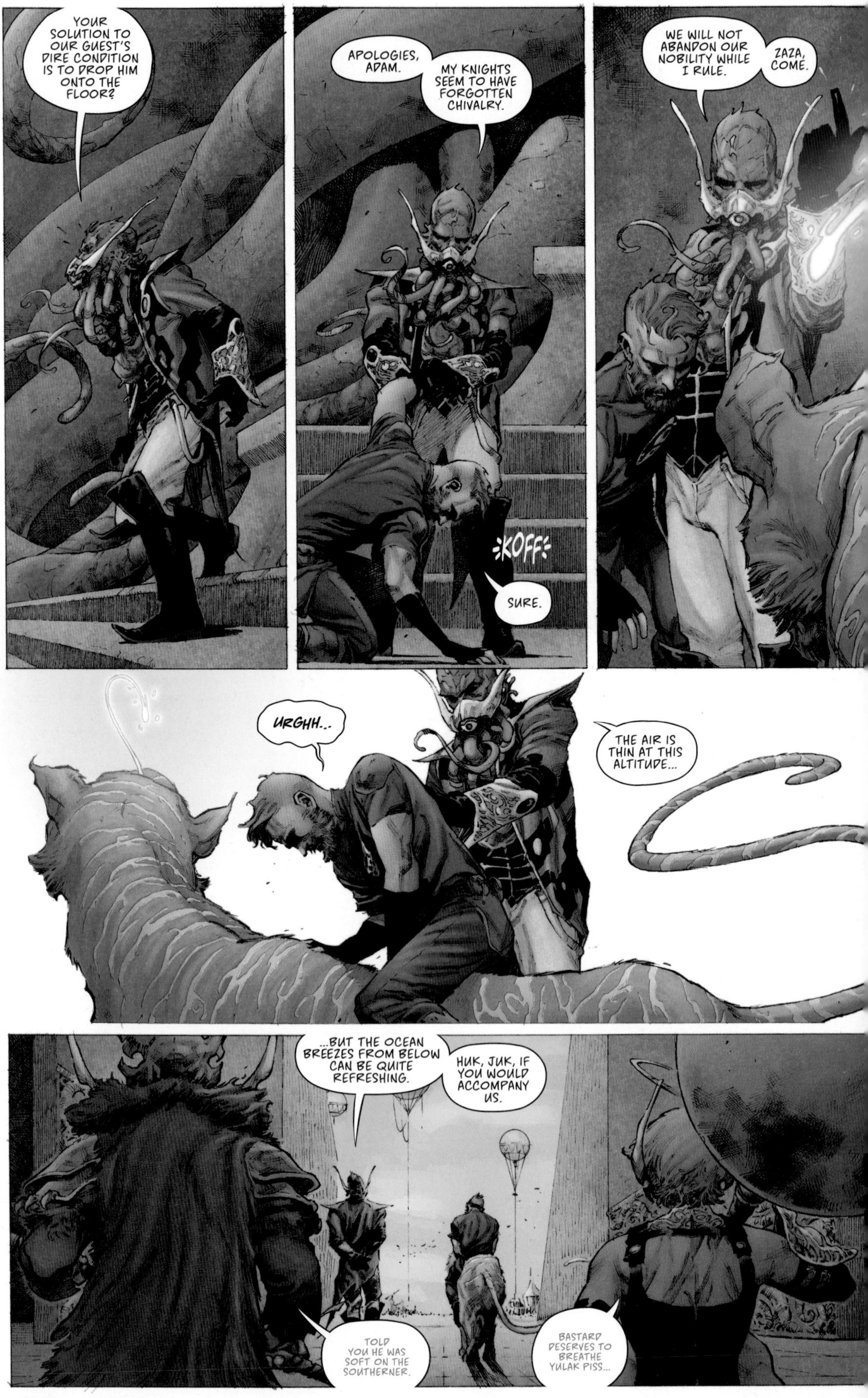
YOUR SOLUTION TO OUR GUEST'S DIRE CONDITION IS TO DROP HIM ONTO THE FLOOR?
APOLOGIES, ADAM.
MY KNIGHTS SEEM TO HAVE FORGOTTEN CHIVALRY.
KOFF
SURE.
WE WILL NOT ABANDON OUR NOBILITY WHILE I RULE.
ZAZA, COME.
URGHH...
THE AIR IS THIN AT THIS ALTITUDE...
...BUT THE OCEAN BREEZES FROM BELOW CAN BE QUITE REFRESHING.
HUK, JUK, IF YOU WOULD ACCOMPANY US.
TOLD YOU HE WAS SOFT ON THE SOUTHERNER.
BASTARD DESERVES TO BREATHE YULAK PISS...

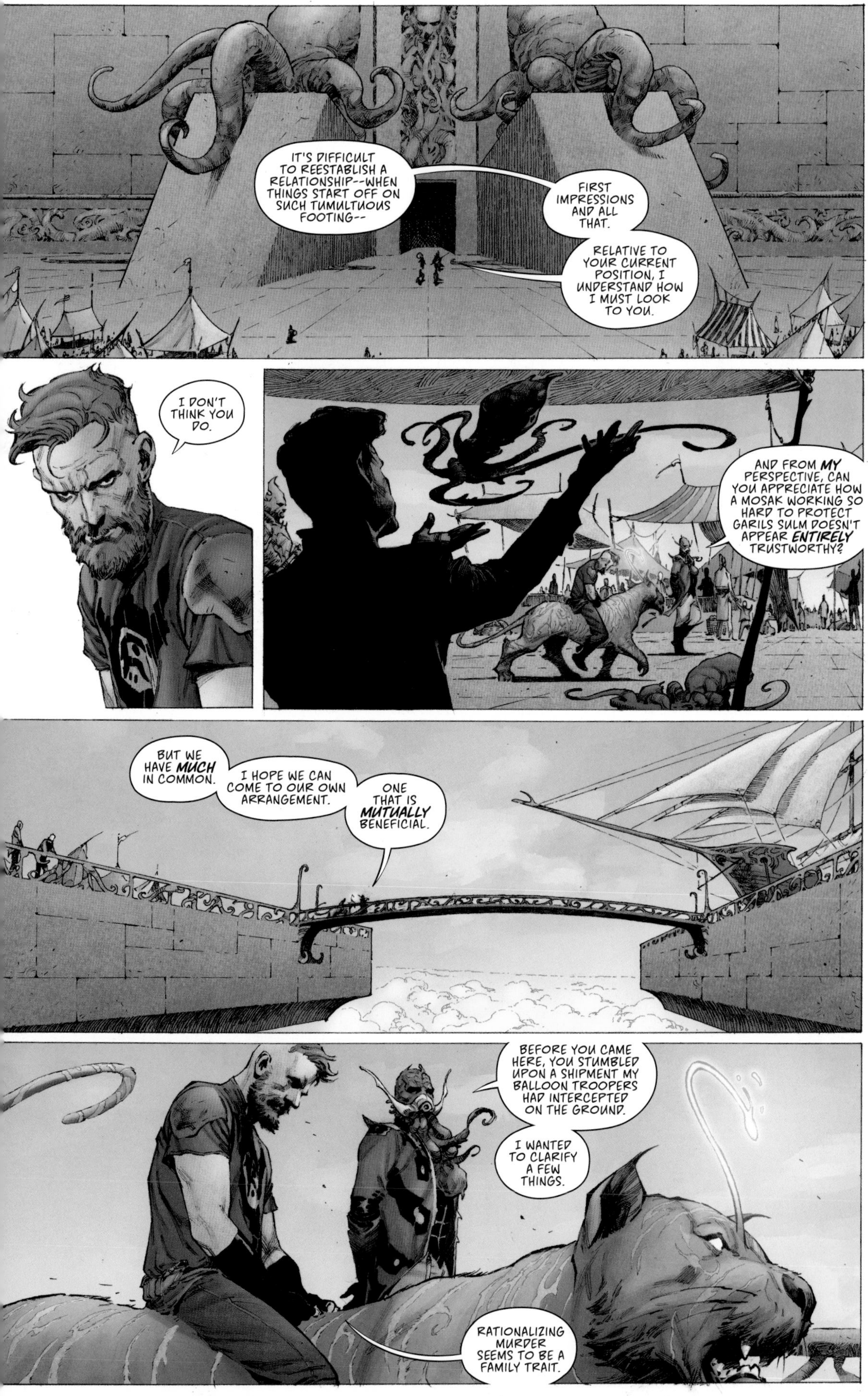
IT'S DIFFICULT TO REESTABLISH A RELATIONSHIP--WHEN THINGS START OFF ON SUCH TUMULTUOUS FOOTING--
FIRST IMPRESSIONS AND ALL THAT.
RELATIVE TO YOUR CURRENT POSITION, I UNDERSTAND HOW I MUST LOOK TO YOU.
I DON'T THINK YOU DO.
AND FROM MY PERSPECTIVE, CAN YOU APPRECIATE HOW A MOSAK WORKING SO HARD TO PROTECT GARILS SULM DOESN'T APPEAR ENTIRELY TRUSTWORTHY?
BUT WE HAVE MUCH IN COMMON.
I HOPE WE CAN COME TO OUR OWN ARRANGEMENT.
ONE THAT IS MUTUALLY BENEFICIAL.
BEFORE YOU CAME HERE, YOU STUMBLED UPON A SHIPMENT MY BALLOON TROOPERS HAD INTERCEPTED ON THE GROUND.
I WANTED TO CLARIFY A FEW THINGS.
RATIONALIZING MURDER SEEMS TO BE A FAMILY TRAIT.

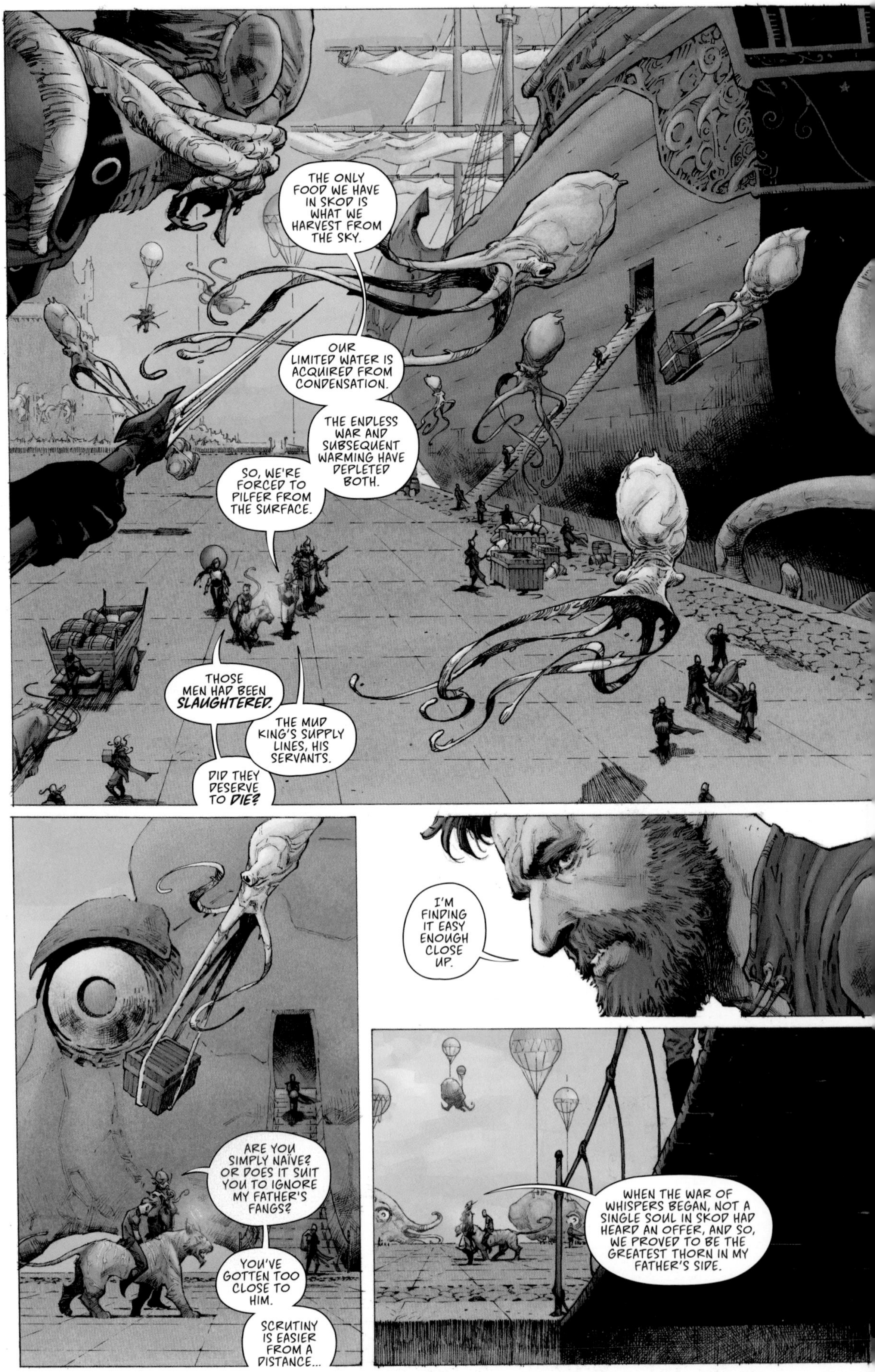
THE ONLY FOOD WE HAVE IN SKOD IS WHAT WE HARVEST FROM THE SKY.
OUR LIMITED WATER IS ACQUIRED FROM CONDENSATION.
THE ENDLESS WAR AND SUBSEQUENT WARMING HAVE DEPLETED BOTH.
SO, WE'RE FORCED TO PILFER FROM THE SURFACE.
THOSE MEN HAD BEEN SLAUGHTERED.
THE MUD KING'S SUPPLY LINES, HIS SERVANTS.
DID THEY DESERVE TO DIE?
ARE YOU SIMPLY NAÏVE? OR DOES IT SUIT YOU TO IGNORE MY FATHER'S FANGS?
YOU'VE GOTTEN TOO CLOSE TO HIM.
SCRUTINY IS EASIER FROM A DISTANCE...
I'M FINDING IT EASY ENOUGH CLOSE UP.
WHEN THE WAR OF WHISPERS BEGAN, NOT A SINGLE SOUL IN SKOD HAD HEARD AN OFFER, AND SO, WE PROVED TO BE THE GREATEST THORN IN MY FATHER'S SIDE.

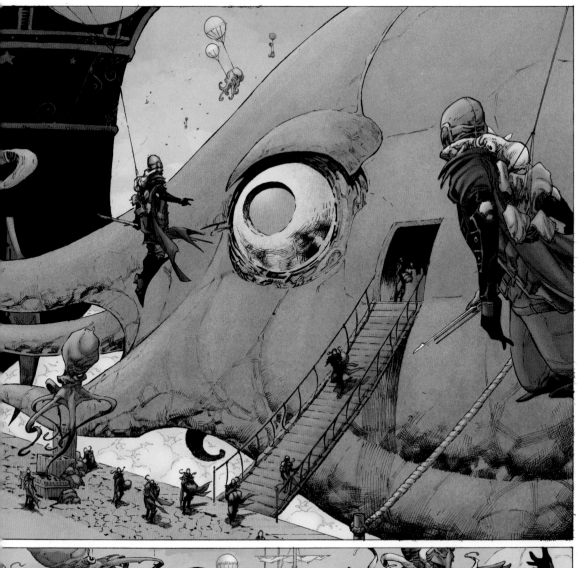

BUT, EVENTUALLY, WE WERE ENCIRCLED BY KINGDOMS LOYAL TO HIM.

IN TRYING TO EARN OUR REPRIEVE, MY LOVING WIFE, AMA, MADE A *TERRIBLE* MISTAKE.

WE WOULD NOT JOIN HIM, WOULD NOT BEND, AND SO WE WERE PUNISHED.

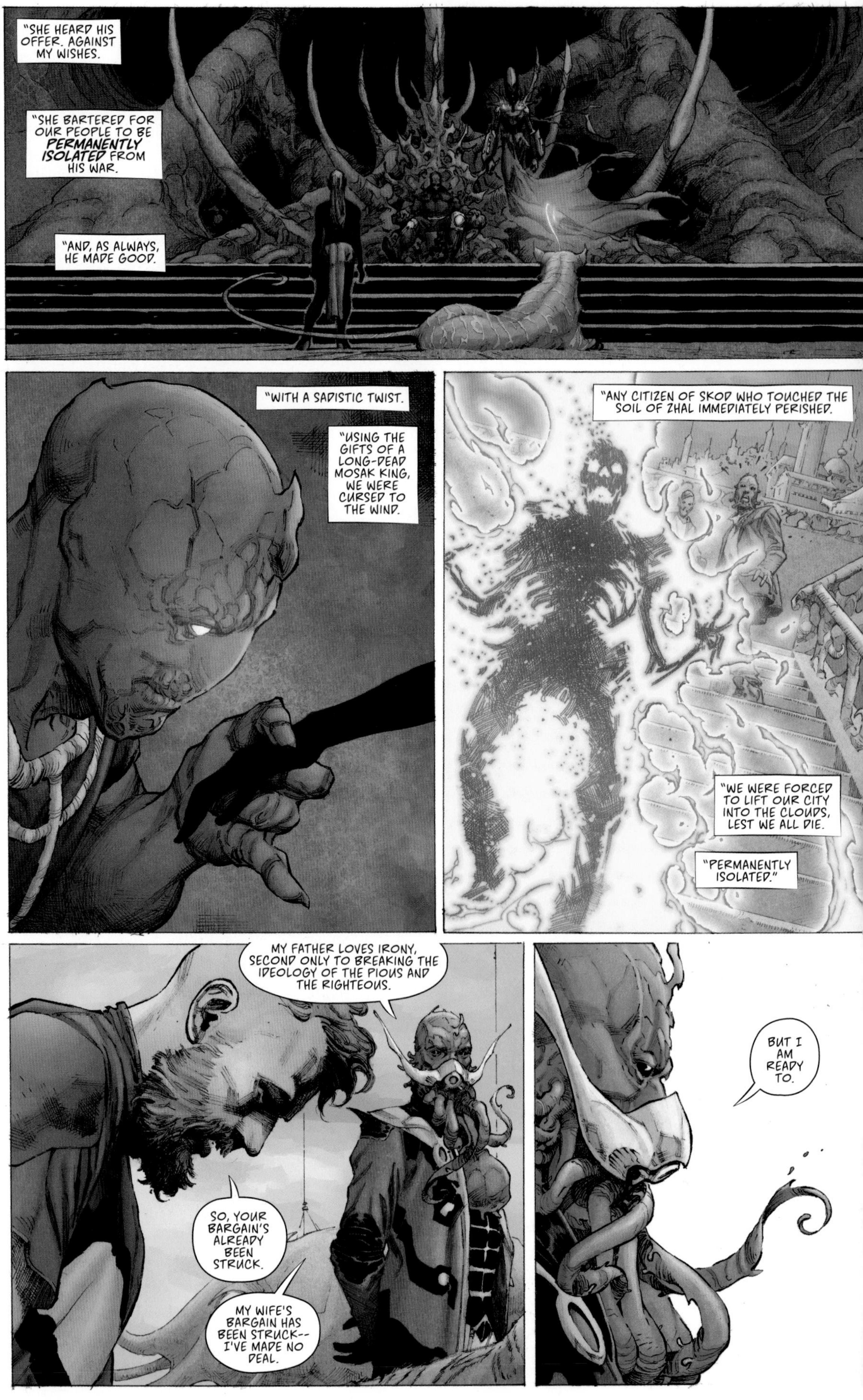
"SHE HEARD HIS OFFER. AGAINST MY WISHES.
"SHE BARTERED FOR OUR PEOPLE TO BE PERMANENTLY ISOLATED FROM HIS WAR.
"AND, AS ALWAYS, HE MADE GOOD.
"WITH A SADISTIC TWIST.
"USING THE GIFTS OF A LONG-DEAD MOSAK KING, WE WERE CURSED TO THE WIND.
"ANY CITIZEN OF SKOD WHO TOUCHED THE SOIL OF ZHAL IMMEDIATELY PERISHED.
"WE WERE FORCED TO LIFT OUR CITY INTO THE CLOUDS, LEST WE ALL DIE.
"PERMANENTLY ISOLATED."
MY FATHER LOVES IRONY, SECOND ONLY TO BREAKING THE IDEOLOGY OF THE PIOUS AND THE RIGHTEOUS.
SO, YOUR BARGAIN'S ALREADY BEEN STRUCK.
MY WIFE'S BARGAIN HAS BEEN STRUCK-- I'VE MADE NO DEAL.
BUT I AM READY TO.

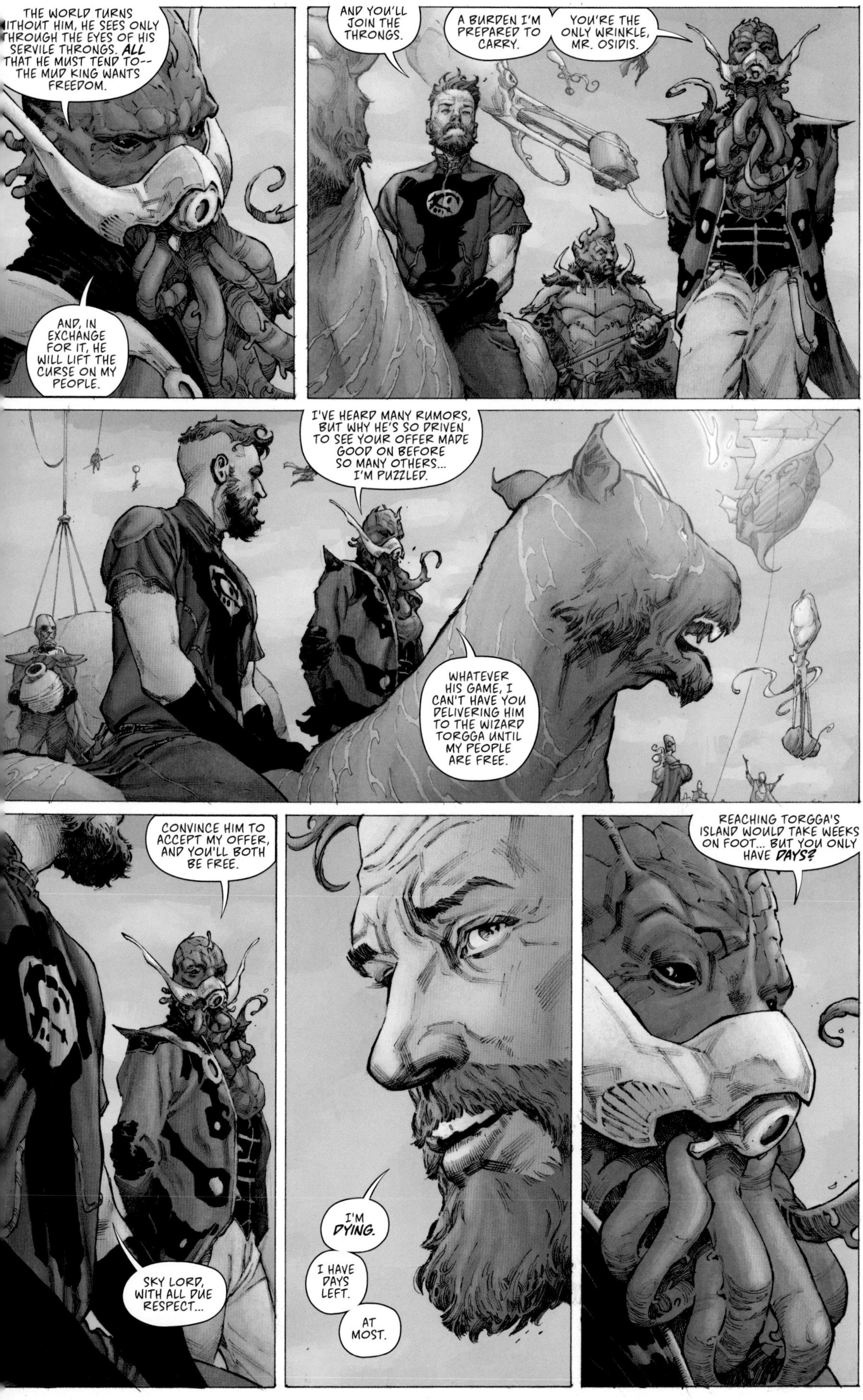
THE WORLD TURNS WITHOUT HIM, HE SEES ONLY THROUGH THE EYES OF HIS SERVILE THRONGS. ALL THAT HE MUST TEND TO-- THE MUD KING WANTS FREEDOM.
AND, IN EXCHANGE FOR IT, HE WILL LIFT THE CURSE ON MY PEOPLE.
AND YOU'LL JOIN THE THRONGS.
A BURDEN I'M PREPARED TO CARRY.
YOU'RE THE ONLY WRINKLE, MR. OSIDIS.
I'VE HEARD MANY RUMORS, BUT WHY HE'S SO DRIVEN TO SEE YOUR OFFER MADE GOOD ON BEFORE SO MANY OTHERS... I'M PUZZLED.
WHATEVER HIS GAME, I CAN'T HAVE YOU DELIVERING HIM TO THE WIZARD TORGGA UNTIL MY PEOPLE ARE FREE.
CONVINCE HIM TO ACCEPT MY OFFER, AND YOU'LL BOTH BE FREE.
SKY LORD, WITH ALL DUE RESPECT...
I'M DYING.
I HAVE DAYS LEFT.
AT MOST.
REACHING TORGGA'S ISLAND WOULD TAKE WEEKS ON FOOT... BUT YOU ONLY HAVE DAYS?

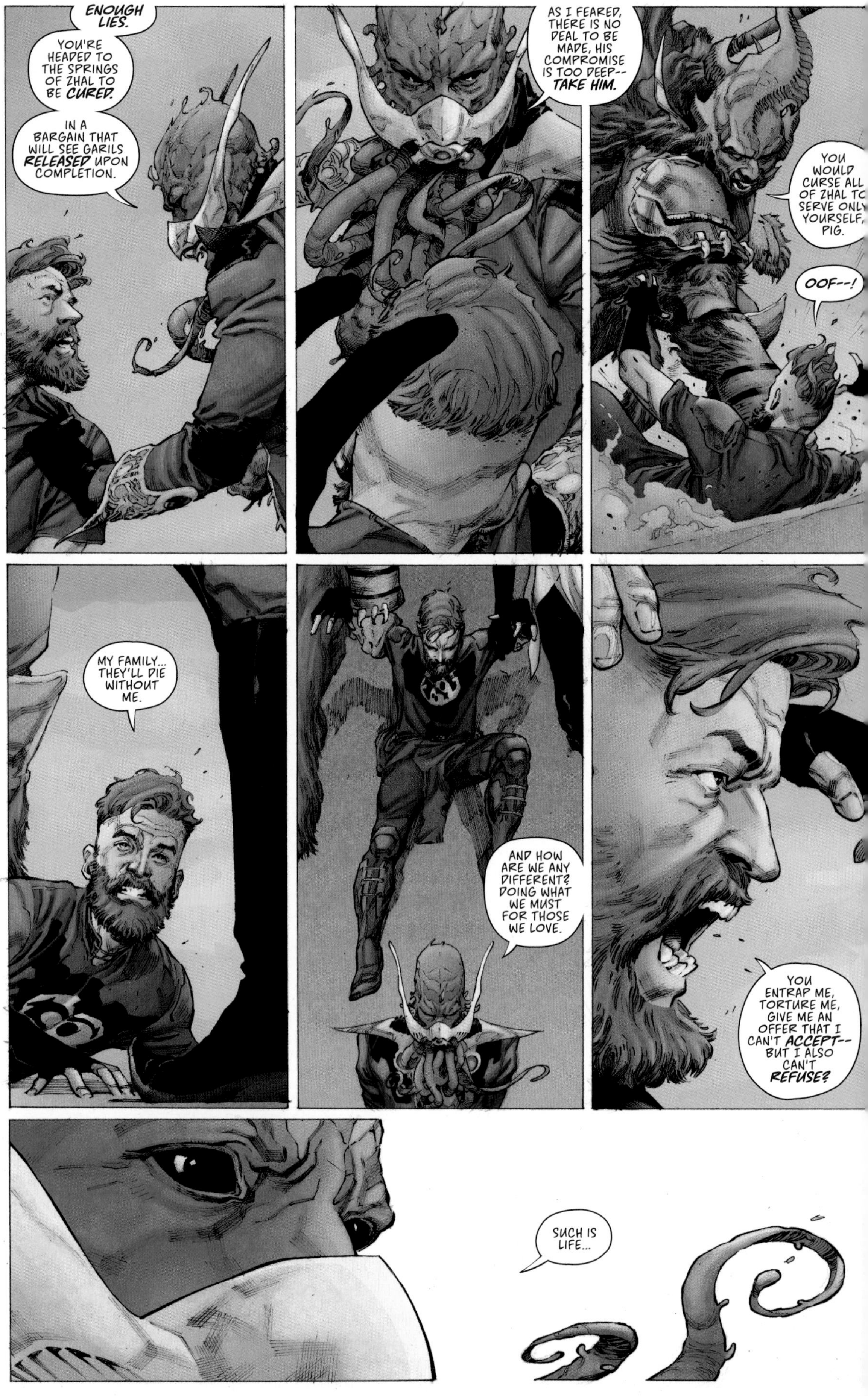
ENOUGH LIES.
YOU'RE HEADED TO THE SPRINGS OF ZHAL TO BE CURED.
IN A BARGAIN THAT WILL SEE GARILS RELEASED UPON COMPLETION.
AS I FEARED, THERE IS NO DEAL TO BE MADE, HIS COMPROMISE IS TOO DEEP-- TAKE HIM.
YOU WOULD CURSE ALL OF ZHAL TO SERVE ONLY YOURSELF, PIG.
OOF--!
MY FAMILY... THEY'LL DIE WITHOUT ME.
AND HOW ARE WE ANY DIFFERENT? DOING WHAT WE MUST FOR THOSE WE LOVE.
YOU ENTRAP ME, TORTURE ME, GIVE ME AN OFFER THAT I CAN'T ACCEPT-- BUT I ALSO CAN'T REFUSE?
SUCH IS LIFE...

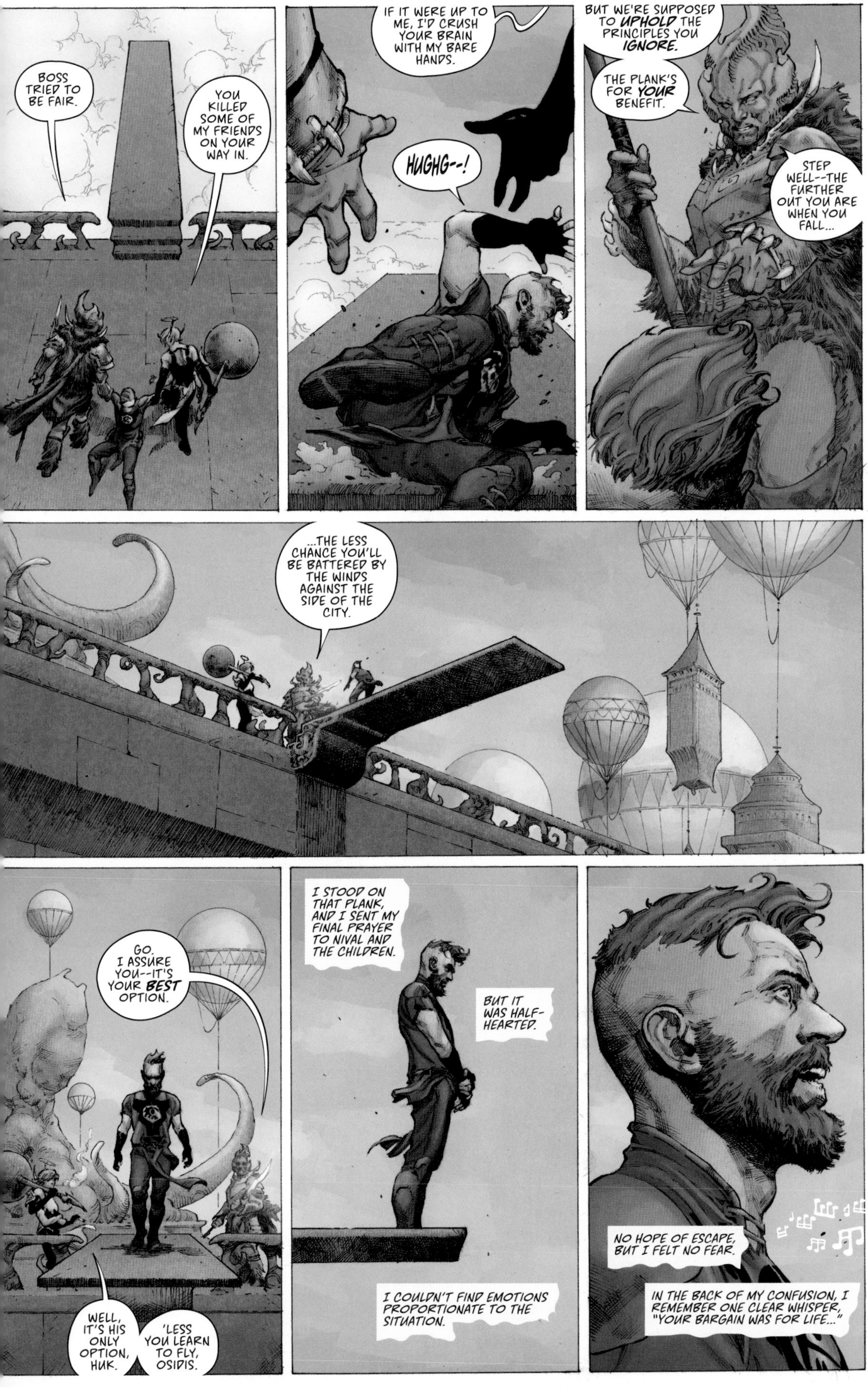

BOSS TRIED TO BE FAIR.
YOU KILLED SOME OF MY FRIENDS ON YOUR WAY IN.
IF IT WERE UP TO ME, I'D CRUSH YOUR BRAIN WITH MY BARE HANDS.
HUGHG--!
BUT WE'RE SUPPOSED TO UPHOLD THE PRINCIPLES YOU IGNORE.
THE PLANK'S FOR YOUR BENEFIT.
STEP WELL--THE FURTHER OUT YOU ARE WHEN YOU FALL...
...THE LESS CHANCE YOU'LL BE BATTERED BY THE WINDS AGAINST THE SIDE OF THE CITY.
GO. I ASSURE YOU--IT'S YOUR BEST OPTION.
WELL, IT'S HIS ONLY OPTION, HUK.
'LESS YOU LEARN TO FLY, OSIDIS.
I STOOD ON THAT PLANK, AND I SENT MY FINAL PRAYER TO NIVAL AND THE CHILDREN.
BUT IT WAS HALF-HEARTED.
I COULDN'T FIND EMOTIONS PROPORTIONATE TO THE SITUATION.
NO HOPE OF ESCAPE, BUT I FELT NO FEAR.
IN THE BACK OF MY CONFUSION, I REMEMBER ONE CLEAR WHISPER, "YOUR BARGAIN WAS FOR LIFE..."

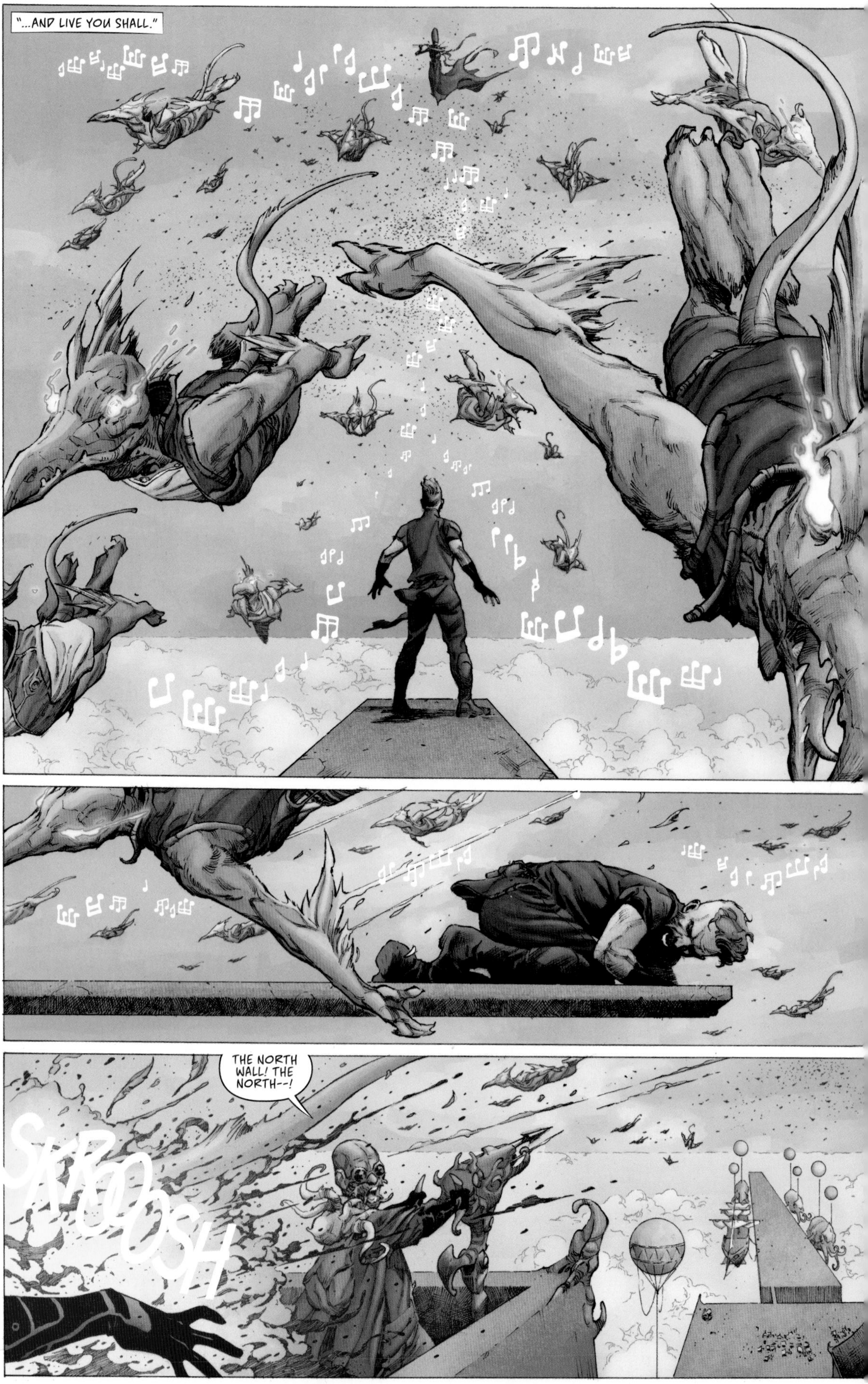
"...AND LIVE YOU SHALL."
THE NORTH WALL! THE NORTH--!
SKROOSH

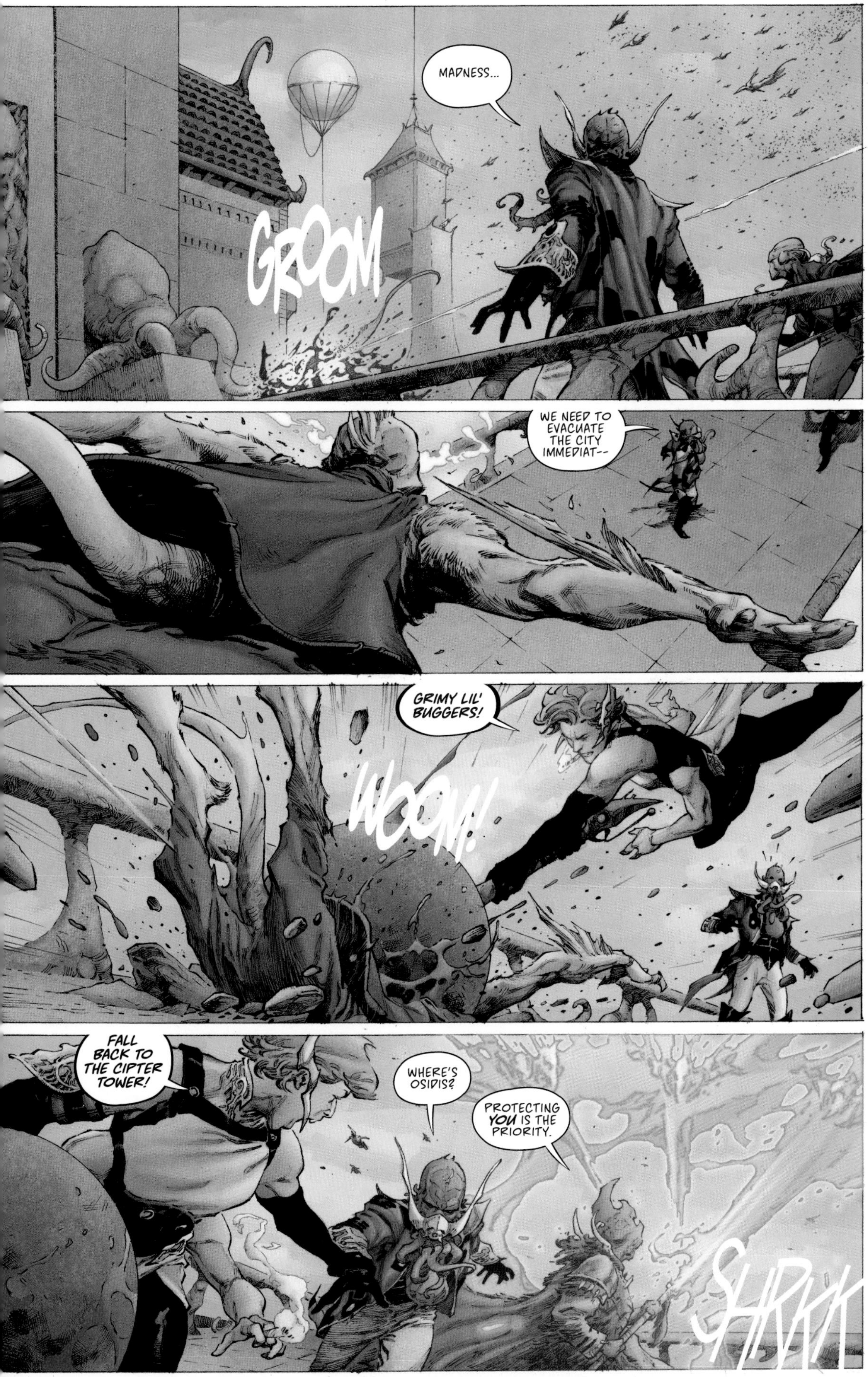
MADNESS...
GROOM
WE NEED TO EVACUATE THE CITY IMMEDIAT--
GRIMY LIL' BUGGERS!
WOOM!
FALL BACK TO THE CIPTER TOWER!
WHERE'S OSIDIS?
PROTECTING YOU IS THE PRIORITY.
SHRKK

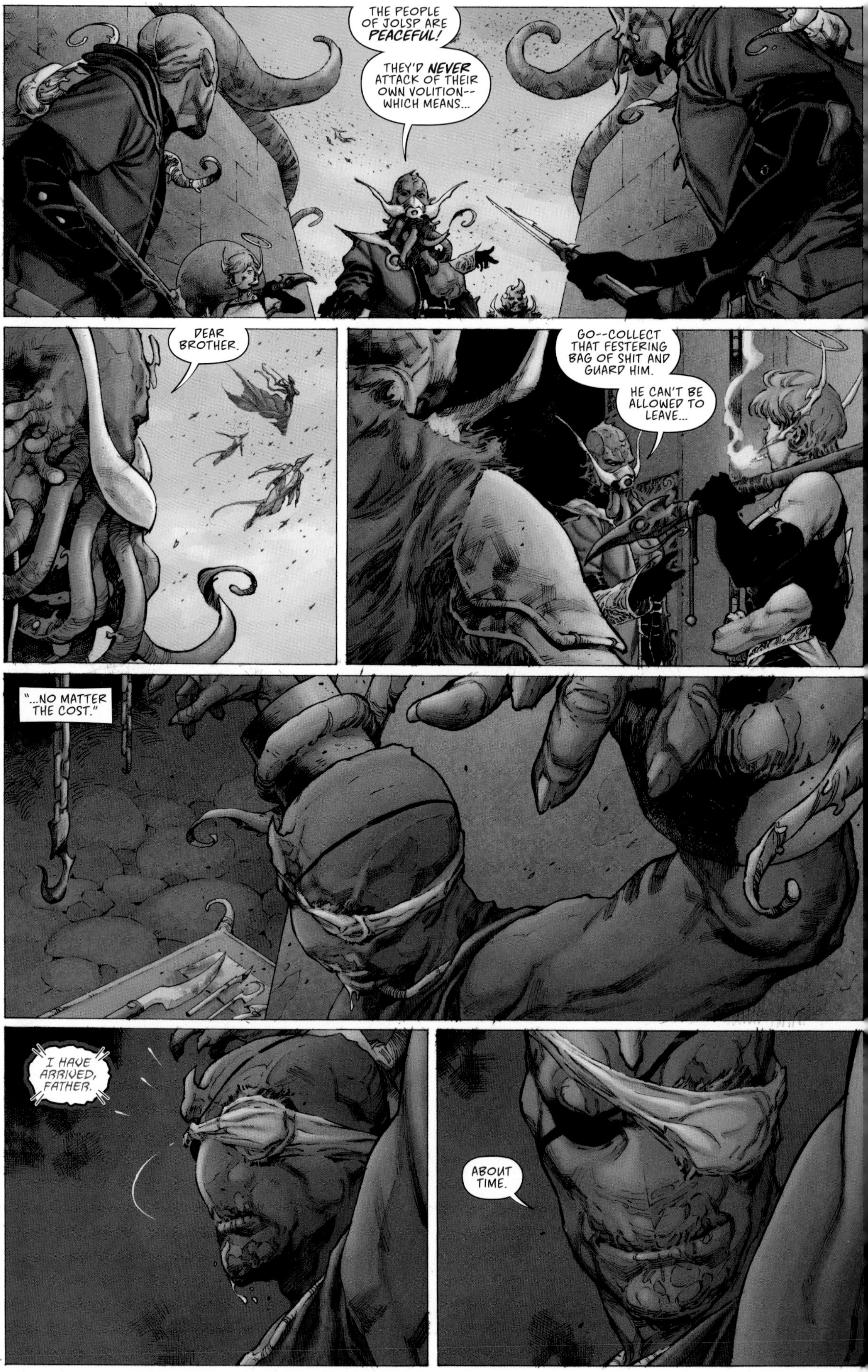
THE PEOPLE OF JOLSP ARE PEACEFUL!
THEY'D NEVER ATTACK OF THEIR OWN VOLITION-- WHICH MEANS...
DEAR BROTHER.
GO--COLLECT THAT FESTERING BAG OF SHIT AND GUARD HIM.
HE CAN'T BE ALLOWED TO LEAVE...
"...NO MATTER THE COST."
I HAVE ARRIVED, FATHER.
ABOUT TIME.

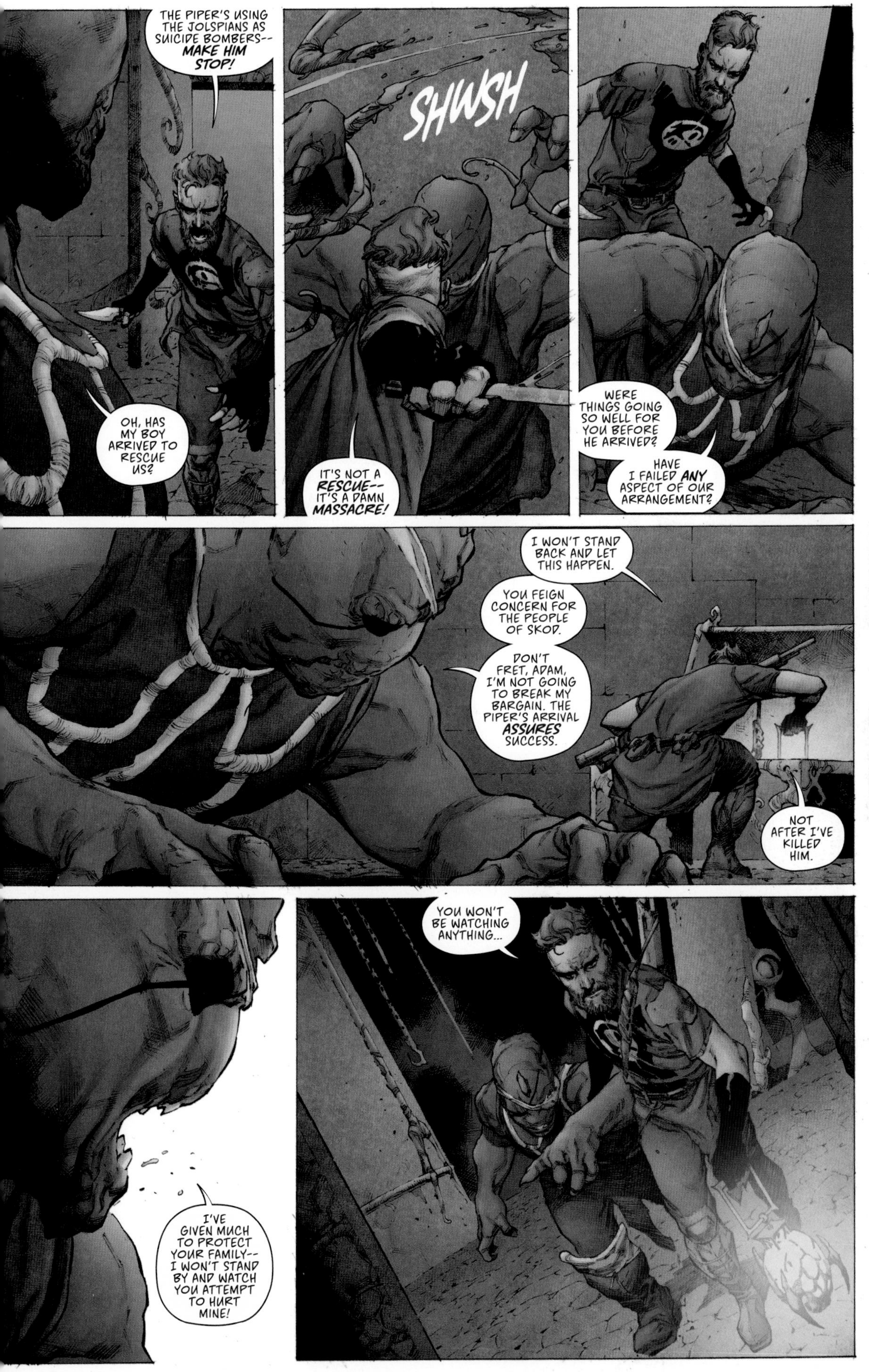
THE PIPER'S USING THE JOLSPIANS AS SUICIDE BOMBERS-- MAKE HIM STOP!
OH, HAS MY BOY ARRIVED TO RESCUE US?
SHWSH
IT'S NOT A RESCUE-- IT'S A DAMN MASSACRE!
WERE THINGS GOING SO WELL FOR YOU BEFORE HE ARRIVED?
HAVE I FAILED ANY ASPECT OF OUR ARRANGEMENT?
I WON'T STAND BACK AND LET THIS HAPPEN.
YOU FEIGN CONCERN FOR THE PEOPLE OF SKOD.
DON'T FRET, ADAM, I'M NOT GOING TO BREAK MY BARGAIN. THE PIPER'S ARRIVAL ASSURES SUCCESS.
NOT AFTER I'VE KILLED HIM.
I'VE GIVEN MUCH TO PROTECT YOUR FAMILY-- I WON'T STAND BY AND WATCH YOU ATTEMPT TO HURT MINE!
YOU WON'T BE WATCHING ANYTHING...

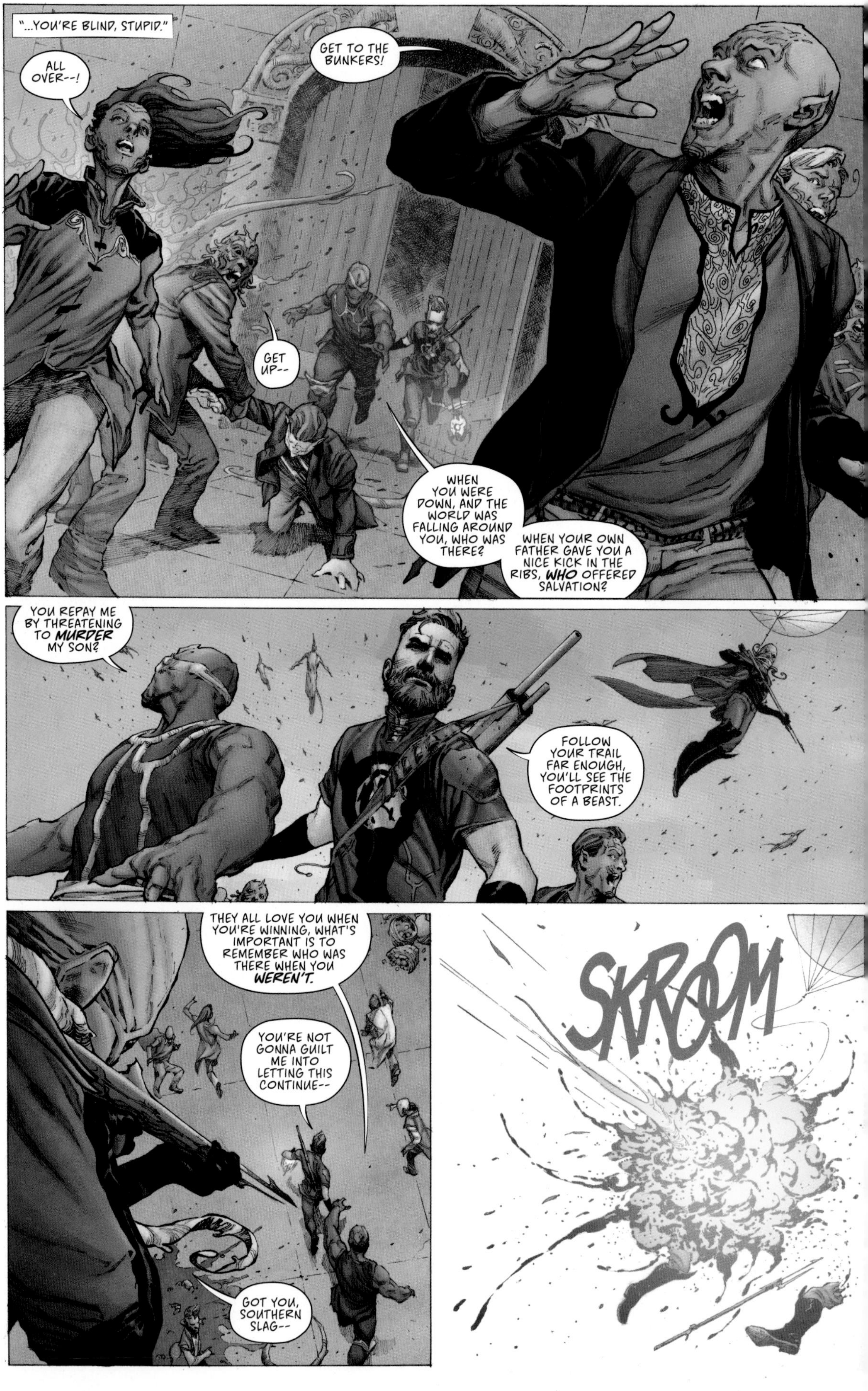
"...YOU'RE BLIND, STUPID."
ALL OVER--!
GET TO THE BUNKERS!
GET UP--
WHEN YOU WERE DOWN, AND THE WORLD WAS FALLING AROUND YOU, WHO WAS THERE?
WHEN YOUR OWN FATHER GAVE YOU A NICE KICK IN THE RIBS, WHO OFFERED SALVATION?
YOU REPAY ME BY THREATENING TO MURDER MY SON?
FOLLOW YOUR TRAIL FAR ENOUGH, YOU'LL SEE THE FOOTPRINTS OF A BEAST.
THEY ALL LOVE YOU WHEN YOU'RE WINNING, WHAT'S IMPORTANT IS TO REMEMBER WHO WAS THERE WHEN YOU WEREN'T.
YOU'RE NOT GONNA GUILT ME INTO LETTING THIS CONTINUE--
GOT YOU, SOUTHERN SLAG--
SKROOM

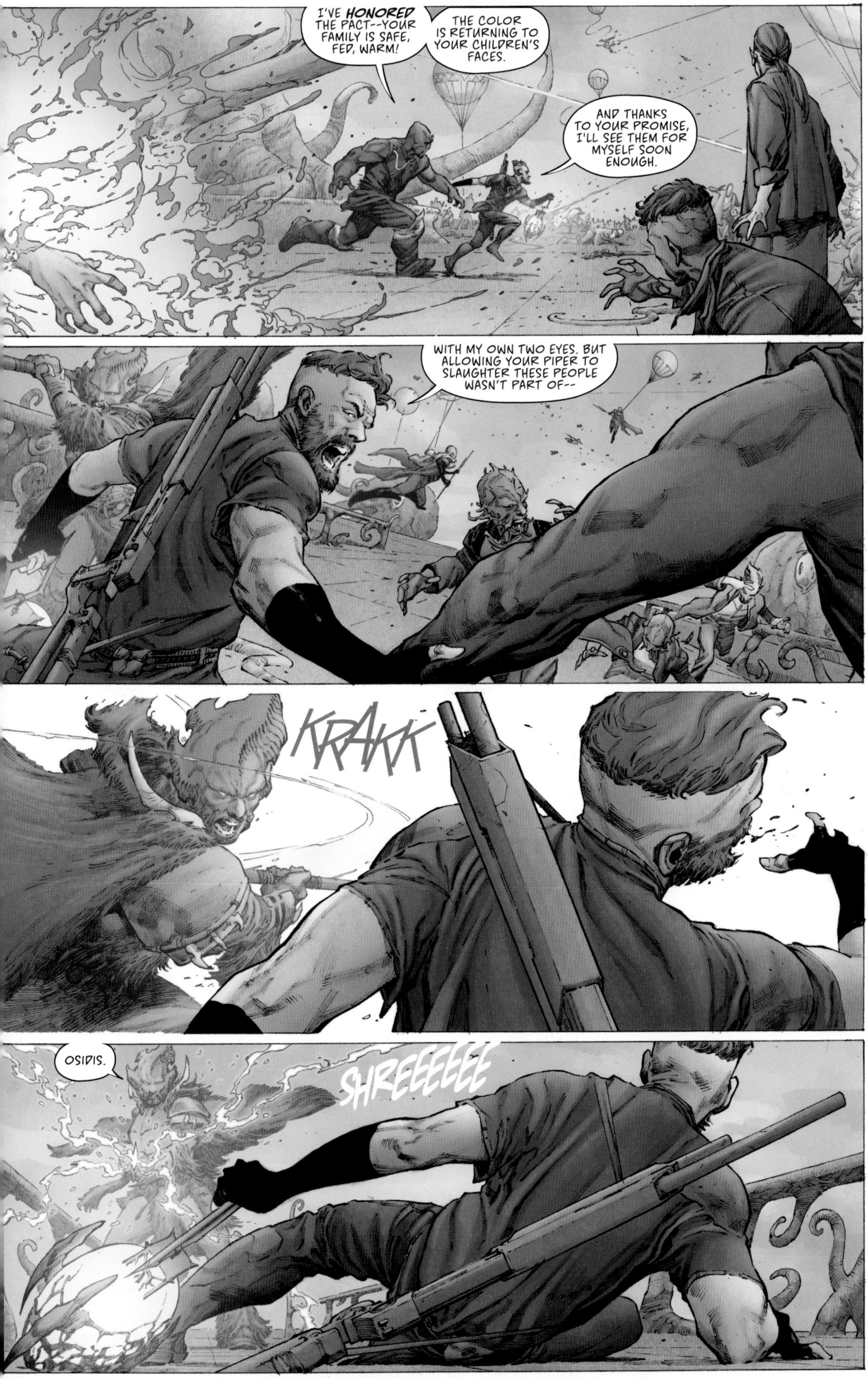
I'VE HONORED THE PACT--YOUR FAMILY IS SAFE, FED, WARM!
THE COLOR IS RETURNING TO YOUR CHILDREN'S FACES.
AND THANKS TO YOUR PROMISE, I'LL SEE THEM FOR MYSELF SOON ENOUGH.
WITH MY OWN TWO EYES. BUT ALLOWING YOUR PIPER TO SLAUGHTER THESE PEOPLE WASN'T PART OF--
KRAKK
OSIDIS.
SHREEEEEE

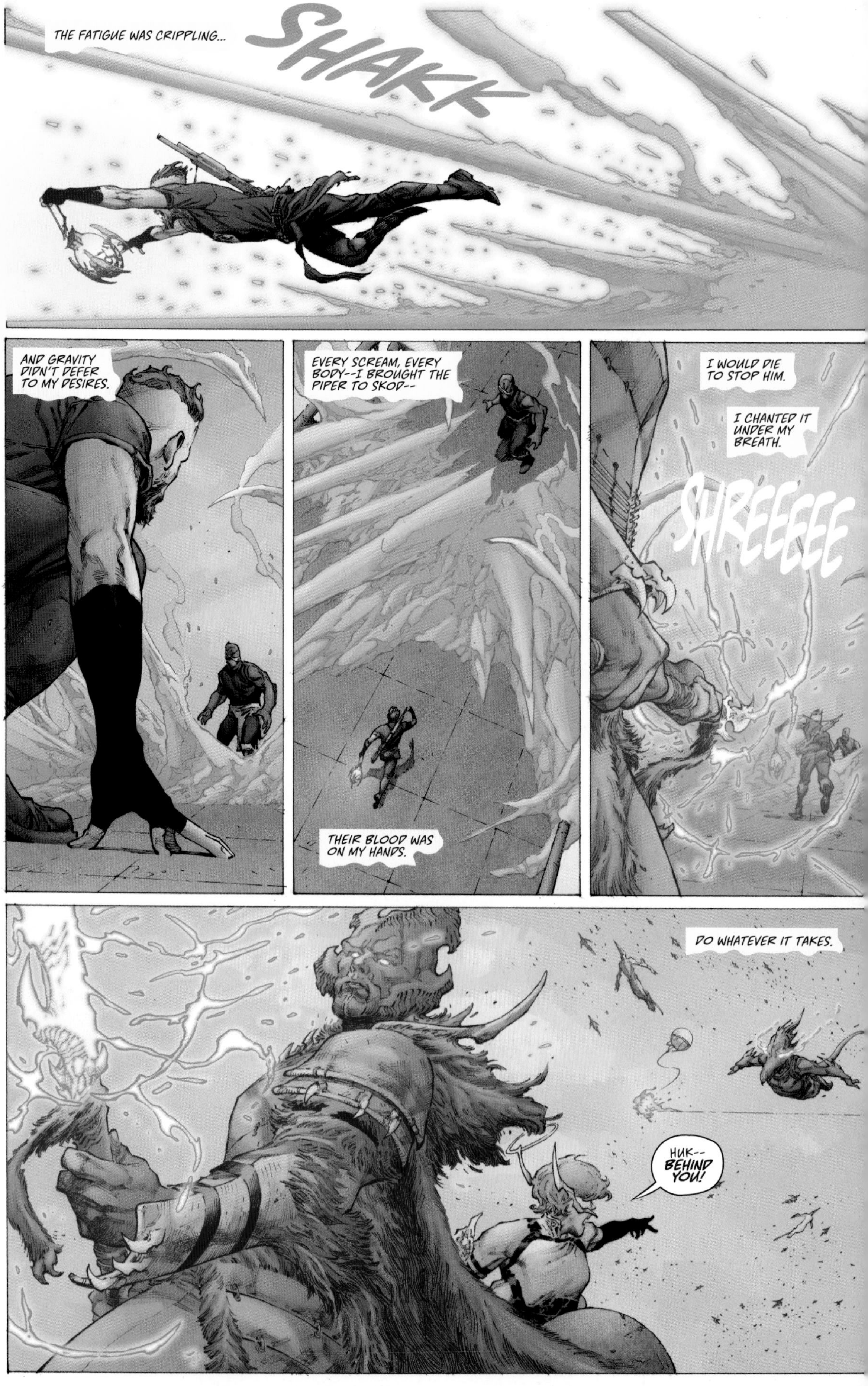
THE FATIGUE WAS CRIPPLING...
SHAKK
AND GRAVITY DIDN'T DEFER TO MY DESIRES.
EVERY SCREAM, EVERY BODY--I BROUGHT THE PIPER TO SKOD--
THEIR BLOOD WAS ON MY HANDS.
I WOULD DIE TO STOP HIM.
I CHANTED IT UNDER MY BREATH.
SHREEEEEE
DO WHATEVER IT TAKES.
HUK-- BEHIND YOU!

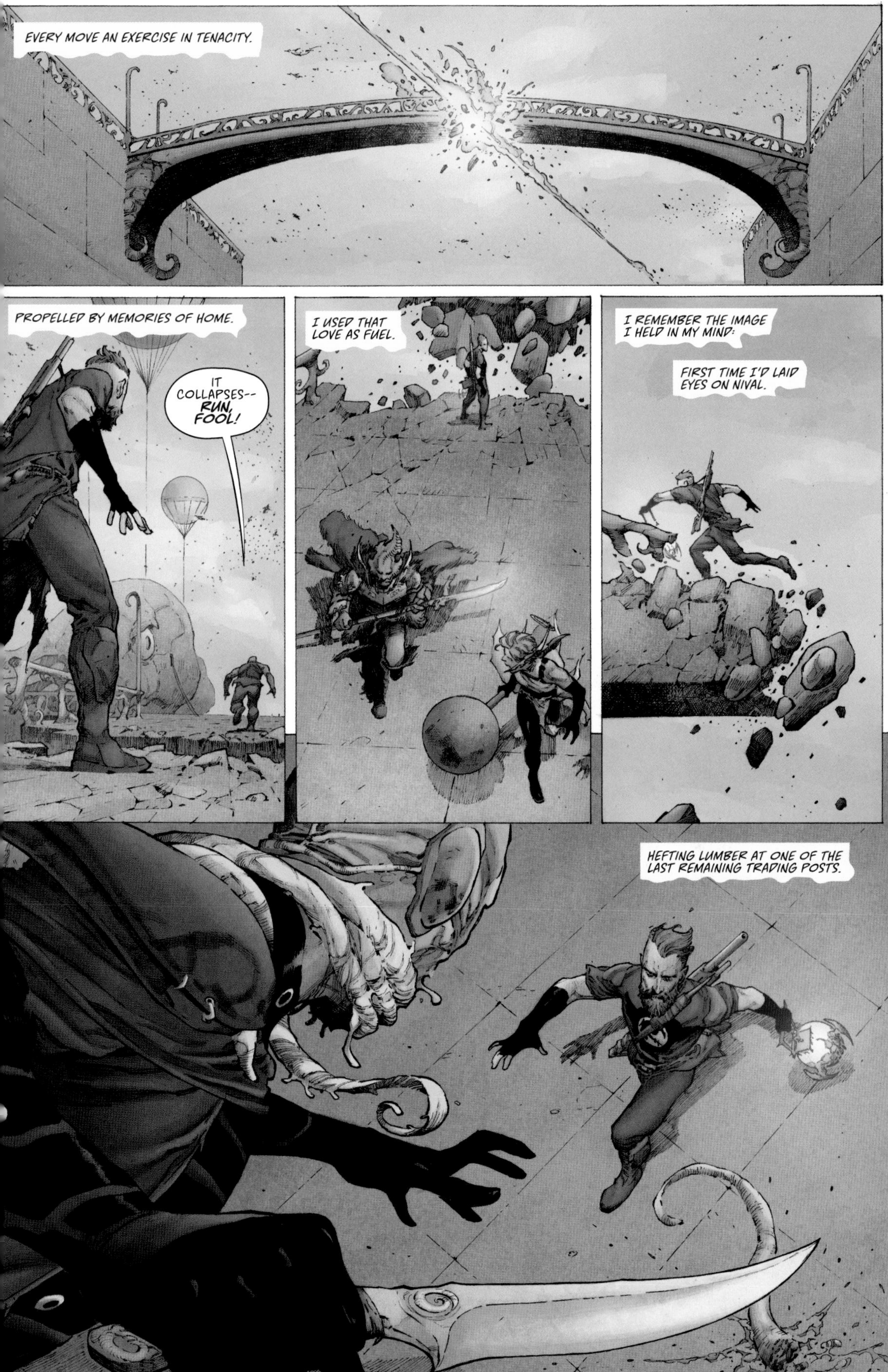
EVERY MOVE AN EXERCISE IN TENACITY.
PROPELLED BY MEMORIES OF HOME.
IT COLLAPSES-- RUN, FOOL!
I USED THAT LOVE AS FUEL.
I REMEMBER THE IMAGE I HELD IN MY MIND:
FIRST TIME I'D LAID EYES ON NIVAL.
HEFTING LUMBER AT ONE OF THE LAST REMAINING TRADING POSTS.

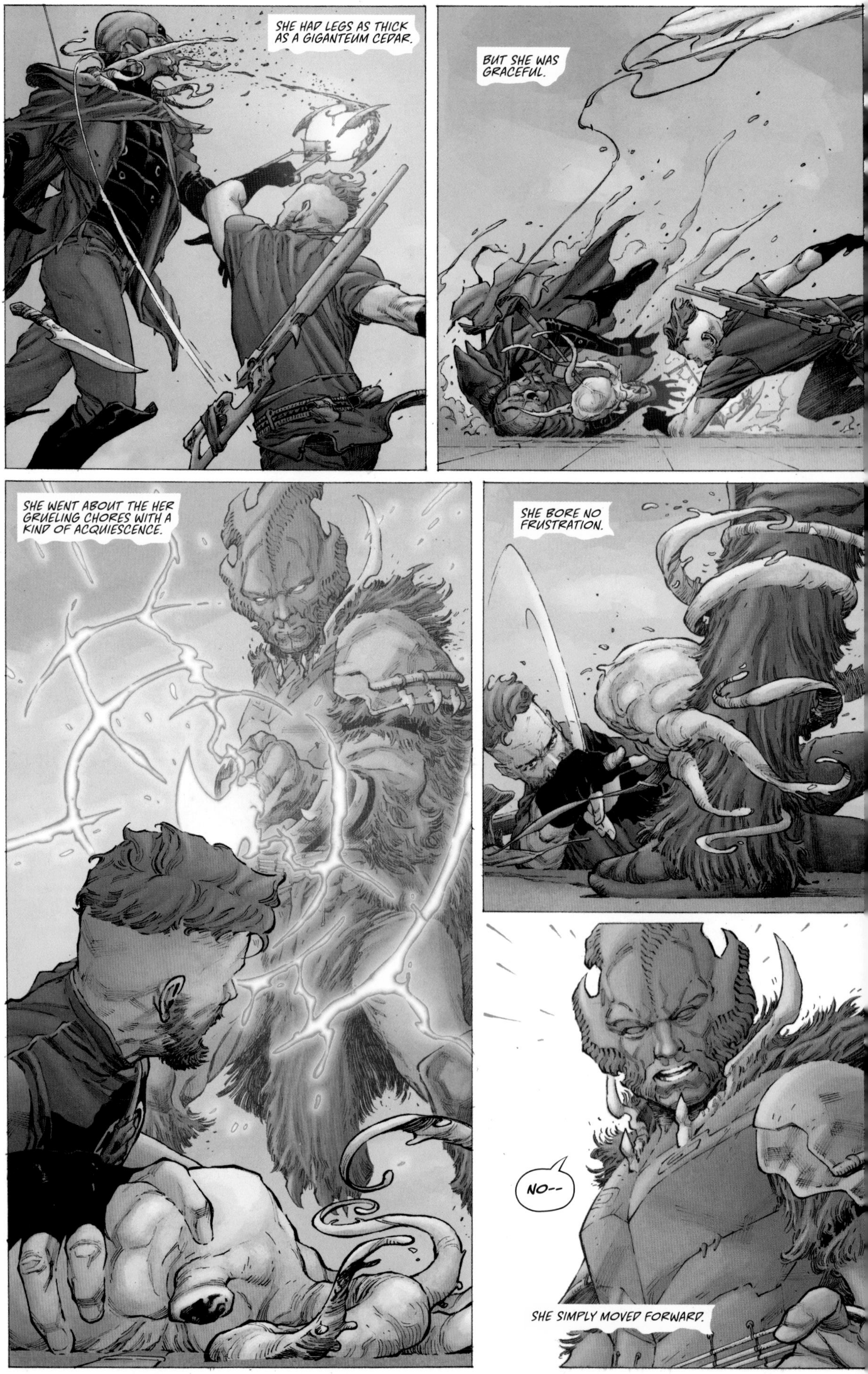
SHE HAD LEGS AS THICK AS A GIGANTEUM CEDAR.
BUT SHE WAS GRACEFUL.
SHE WENT ABOUT THE HER GRUELING CHORES WITH A KIND OF ACQUIESCENCE.
SHE BORE NO FRUSTRATION.
NO--
SHE SIMPLY MOVED FORWARD.

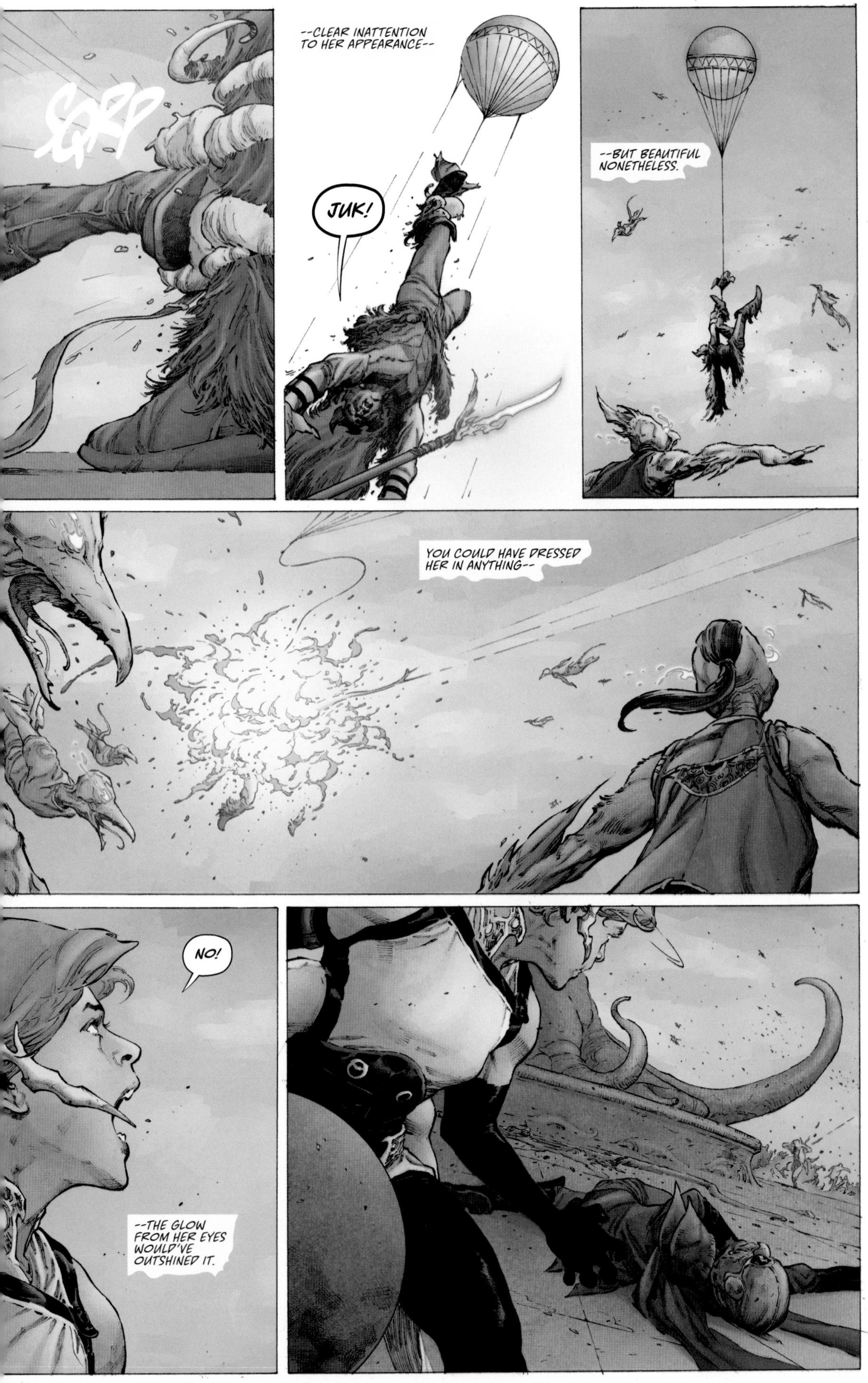

SQRP
--CLEAR INATTENTION TO HER APPEARANCE--
JUK!
--BUT BEAUTIFUL NONETHELESS.
YOU COULD HAVE DRESSED HER IN ANYTHING--
NO!
--THE GLOW FROM HER EYES WOULD'VE OUTSHINED IT.

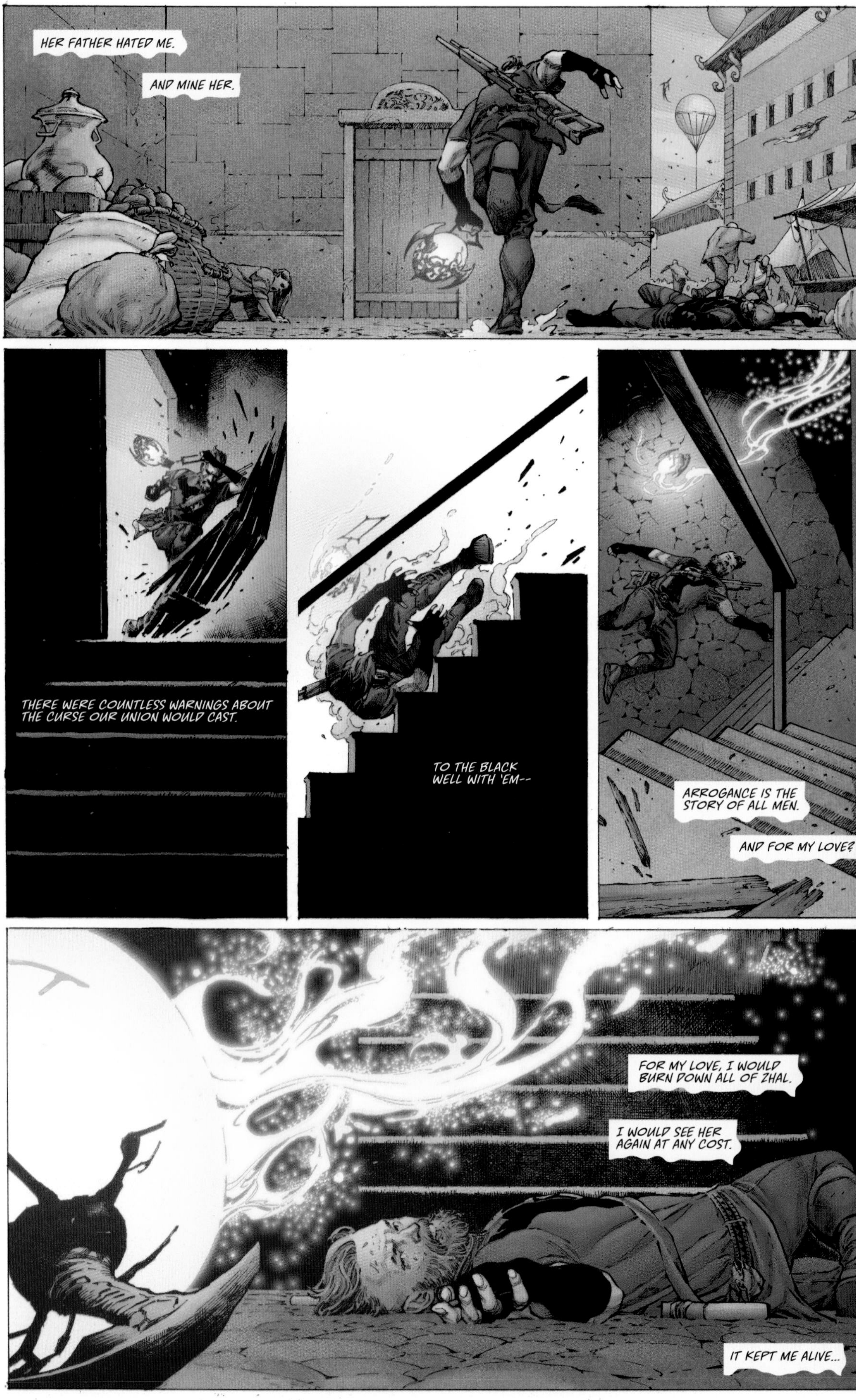
HER FATHER HATED ME.
AND MINE HER.
THERE WERE COUNTLESS WARNINGS ABOUT THE CURSE OUR UNION WOULD CAST.
TO THE BLACK WELL WITH 'EM--
ARROGANCE IS THE STORY OF ALL MEN.
AND FOR MY LOVE?
FOR MY LOVE, I WOULD BURN DOWN ALL OF ZHAL.
I WOULD SEE HER AGAIN AT ANY COST.
IT KEPT ME ALIVE...

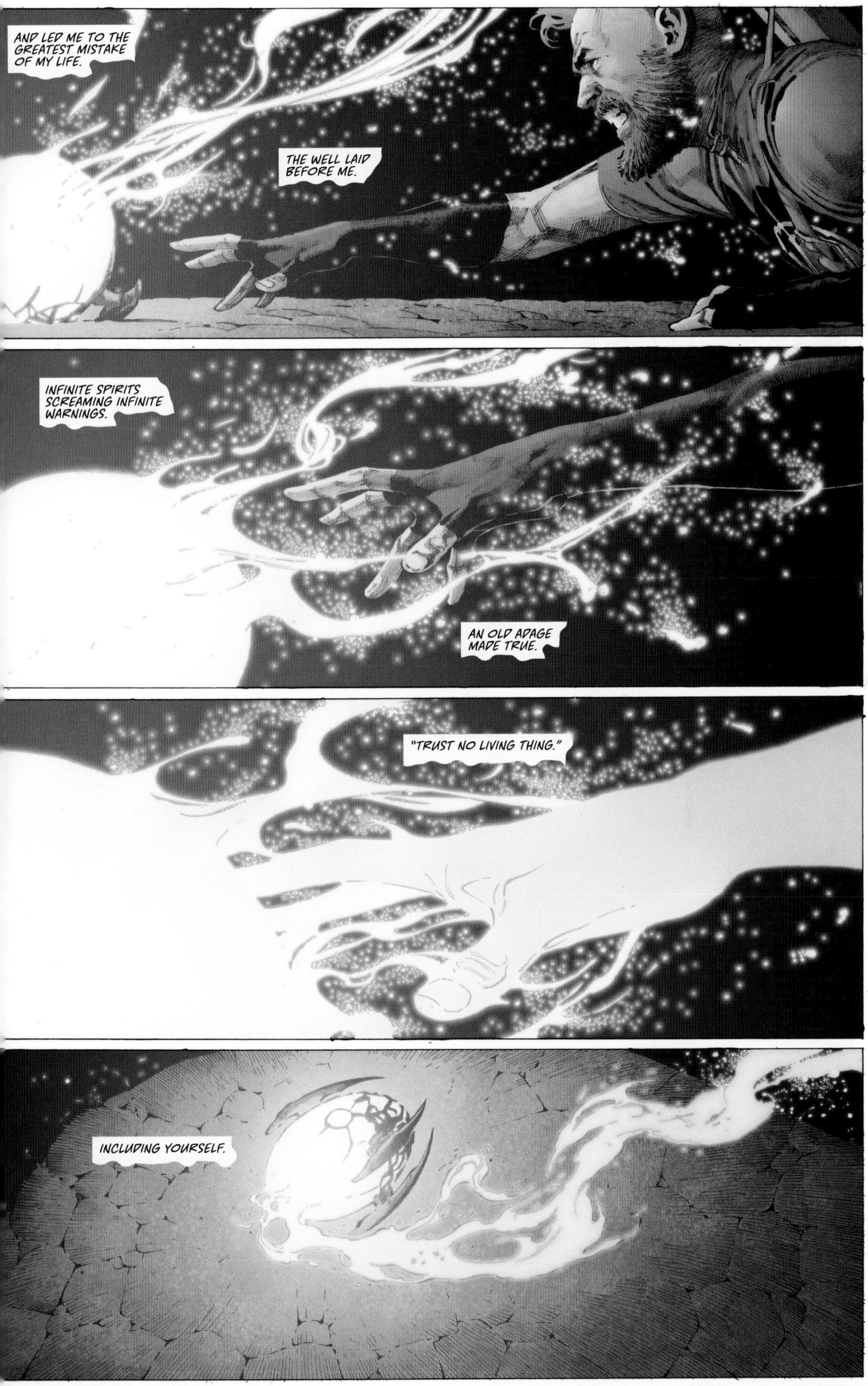
AND LED ME TO THE GREATEST MISTAKE OF MY LIFE.
THE WELL LAID BEFORE ME.
INFINITE SPIRITS SCREAMING INFINITE WARNINGS.
AN OLD ADAGE MADE TRUE.
"TRUST NO LIVING THING."
INCLUDING YOURSELF.

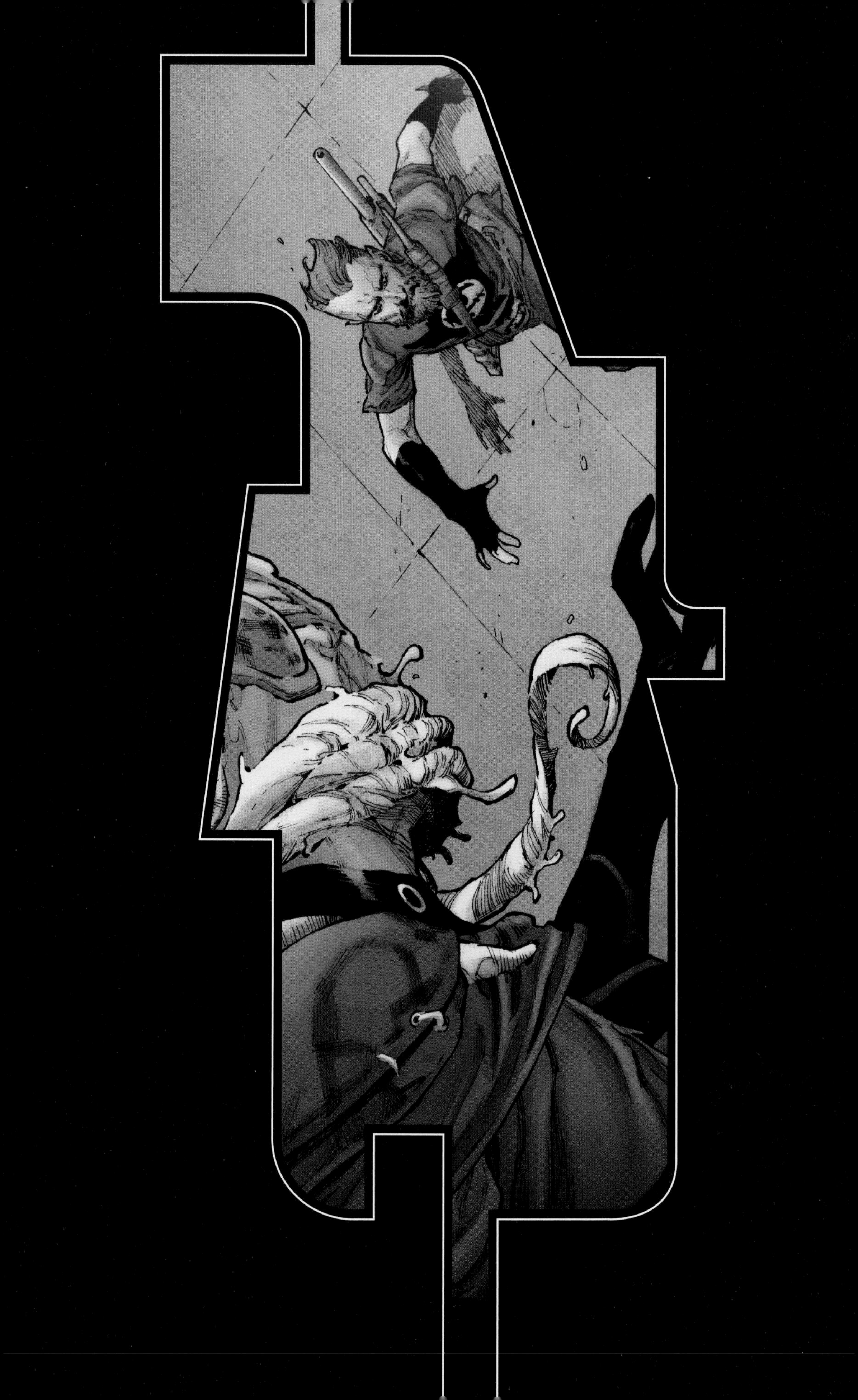

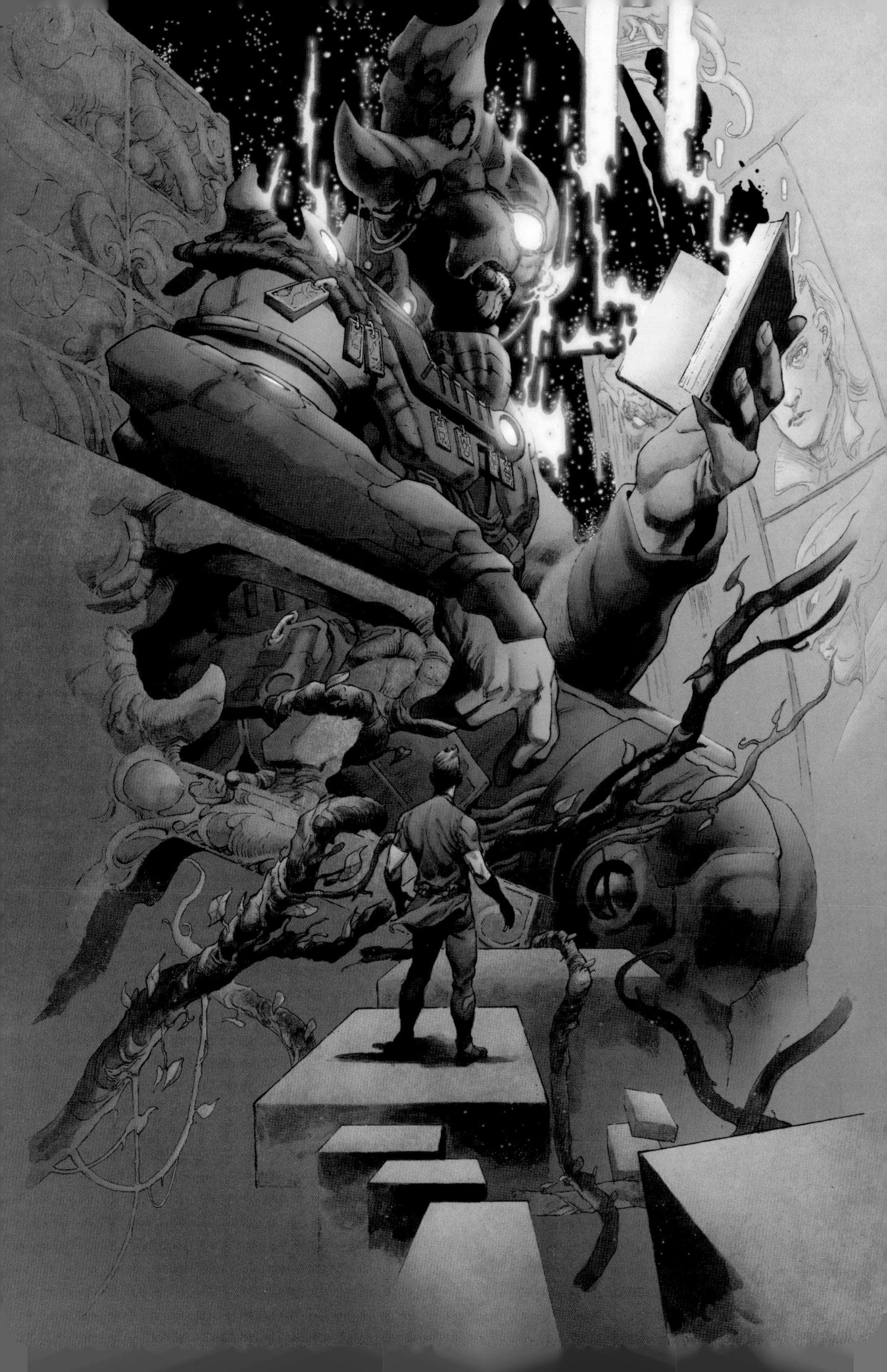

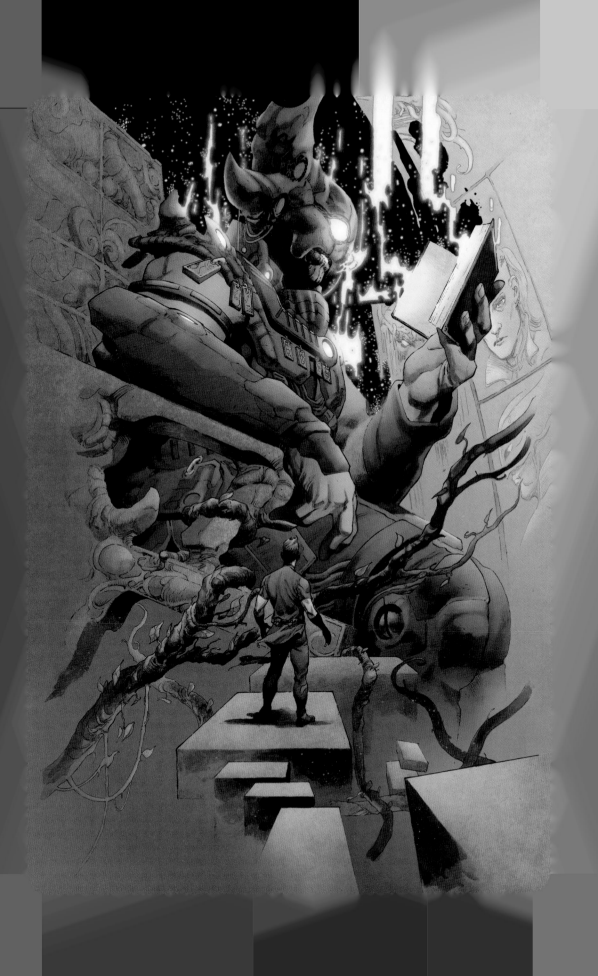

FROM THE JOURNAL OF ADAM OSIDIS

I'm aware that everything I've written to this point stands as a preface to the tale you've been waiting to hear.

The day that I changed it all, set in motion the freedom of Zhal and the liberation of her children from the whispers.

Now, mind you, I was no deluded fool set out to change history. I was a father and husband. People needed me, counted on me to be there for them. Takes a special type of mental disorder to imagine yourself having any impact on that chaos outside while also holding together a family.

I never suffered such delusions. Never imagined myself any kind of nobleman.

But, then—that's how it works—how you get yourself pulled along into the sort of affairs that change things. But that day in the skylands of Skod, the day of deliverance, I never set out to do anything like what I'm given credit for.

Now, I'm not the type to sell a dream of optimism to get you to lower your guard, but there was finally hope of ending the war burning Zhal. A war not imposed on us by an all-powerful God of Whispers, but a war that we chose and, upon not finding it much to our liking, blamed on him.

Garils was not the problem with the world—we were.

And when I look back on those days, one thing is irrefutable: our world had lost its mind...

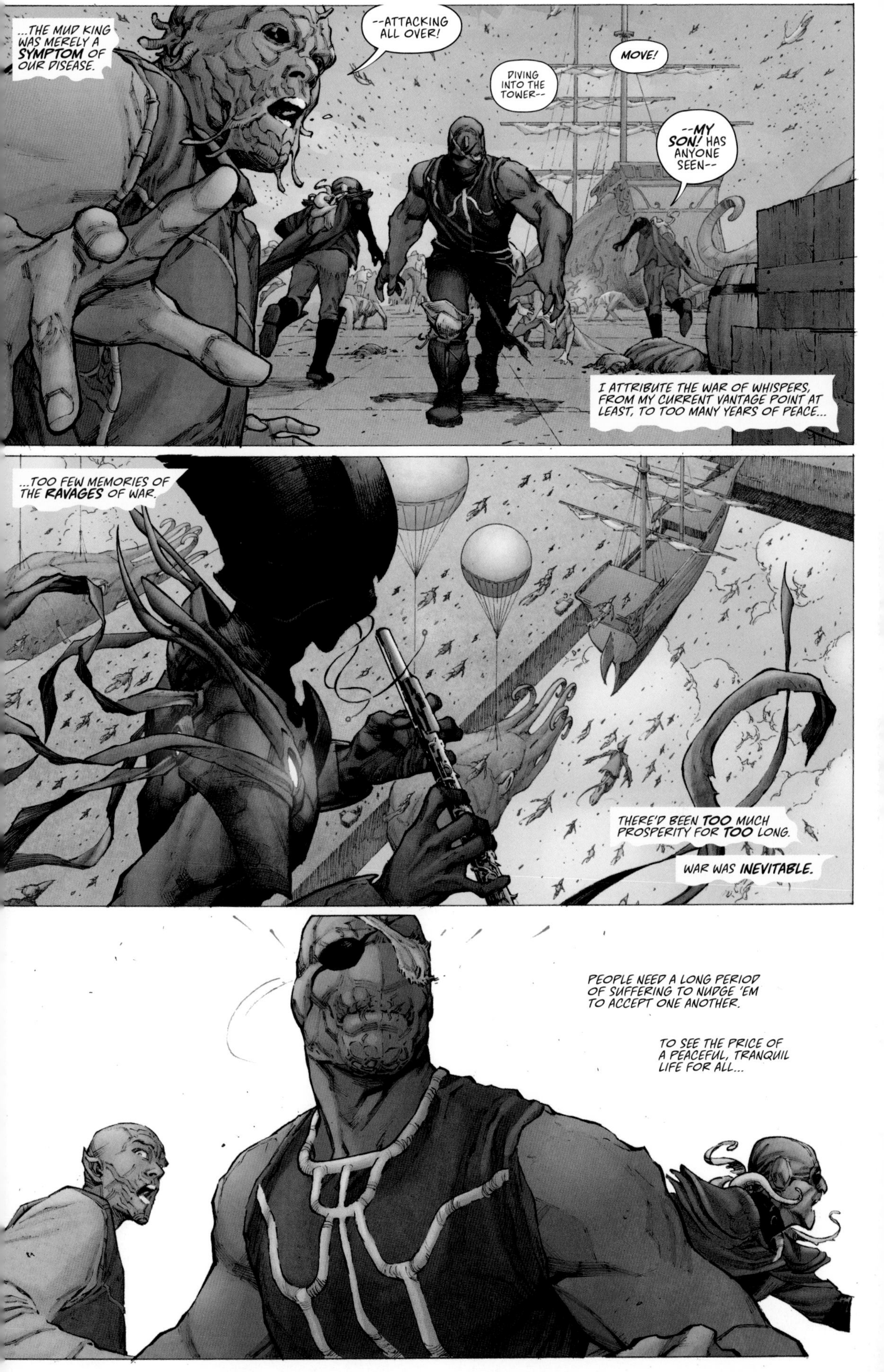
...THE MUD KING WAS MERELY A SYMPTOM OF OUR DISEASE.
--ATTACKING ALL OVER!
DIVING INTO THE TOWER--
MOVE!
--MY SON! HAS ANYONE SEEN--
I ATTRIBUTE THE WAR OF WHISPERS, FROM MY CURRENT VANTAGE POINT AT LEAST, TO TOO MANY YEARS OF PEACE...
...TOO FEW MEMORIES OF THE RAVAGES OF WAR.
THERE'D BEEN TOO MUCH PROSPERITY FOR TOO LONG.
WAR WAS INEVITABLE.
PEOPLE NEED A LONG PERIOD OF SUFFERING TO NUDGE 'EM TO ACCEPT ONE ANOTHER.
TO SEE THE PRICE OF A PEACEFUL, TRANQUIL LIFE FOR ALL...

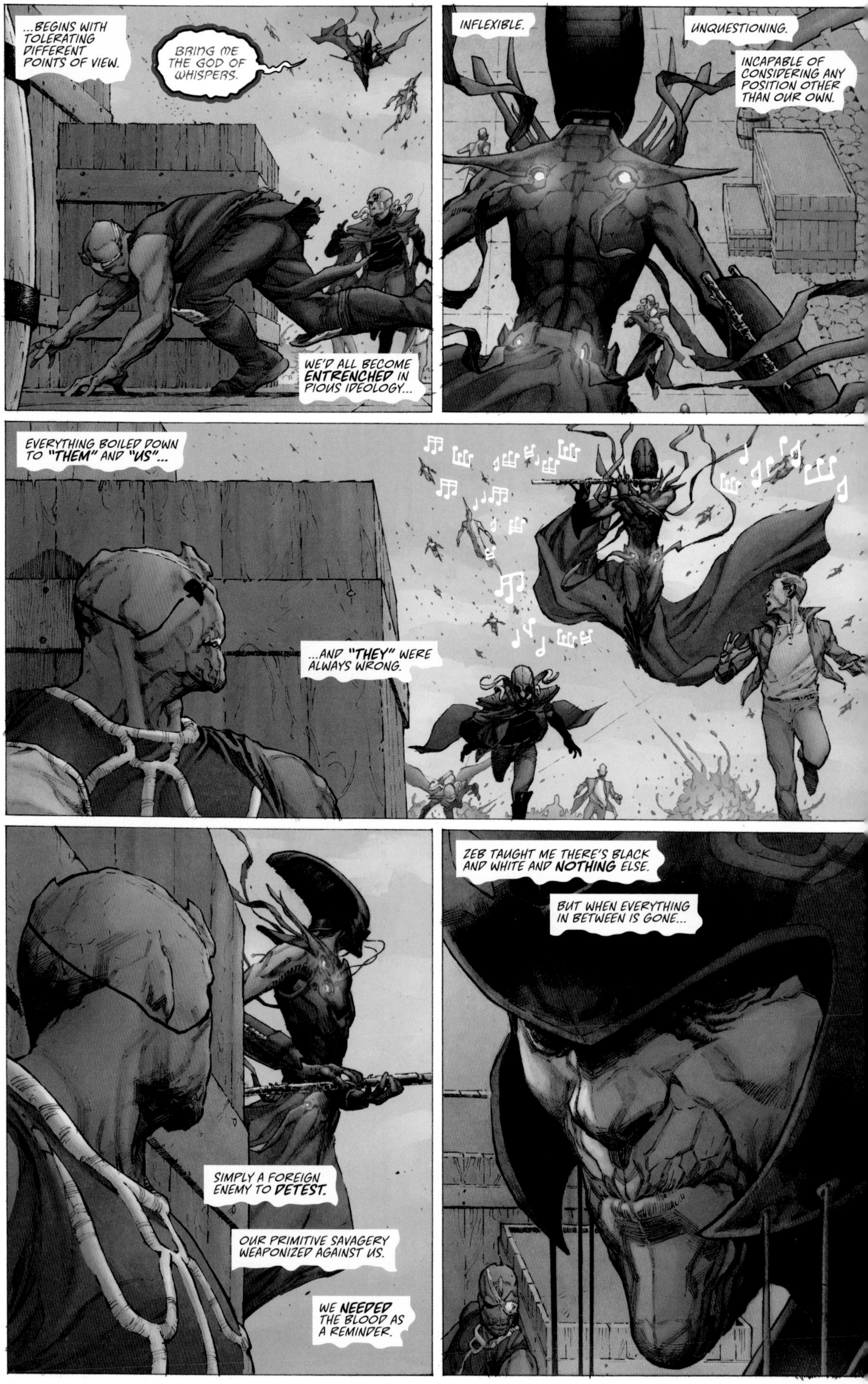

...BEGINS WITH TOLERATING DIFFERENT POINTS OF VIEW.
BRING ME THE GOD OF WHISPERS.
WE'D ALL BECOME ENTRENCHED IN PIOUS IDEOLOGY...
INFLEXIBLE.
UNQUESTIONING.
INCAPABLE OF CONSIDERING ANY POSITION OTHER THAN OUR OWN.
EVERYTHING BOILED DOWN TO "THEM" AND "US"...
...AND "THEY" WERE ALWAYS WRONG.
SIMPLY A FOREIGN ENEMY TO DETEST.
OUR PRIMITIVE SAVAGERY WEAPONIZED AGAINST US.
WE NEEDED THE BLOOD AS A REMINDER.
ZEB TAUGHT ME THERE'S BLACK AND WHITE AND NOTHING ELSE.
BUT WHEN EVERYTHING IN BETWEEN IS GONE...

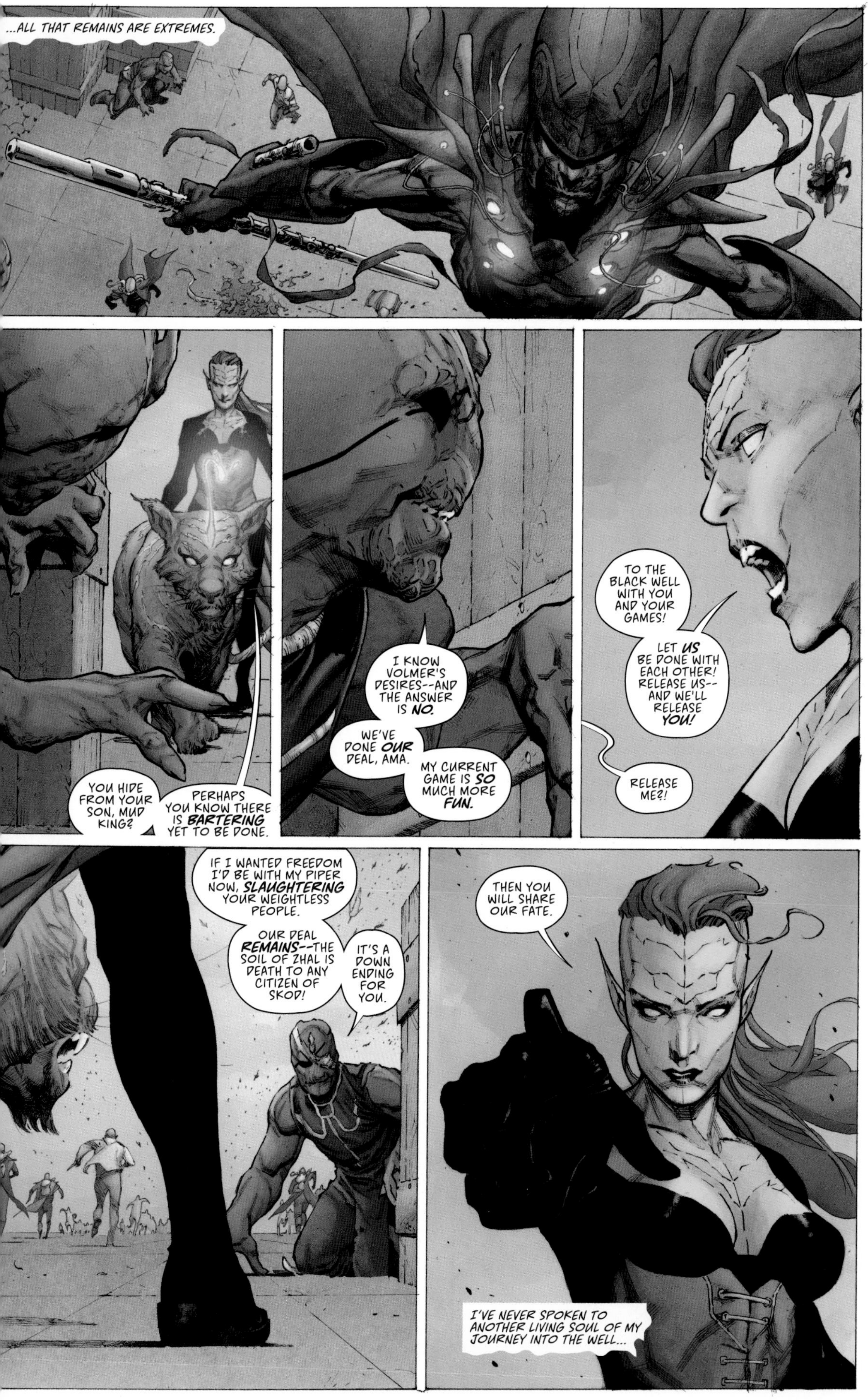
...ALL THAT REMAINS ARE EXTREMES.
YOU HIDE FROM YOUR SON, MUD KING?
PERHAPS YOU KNOW THERE IS BARTERING YET TO BE DONE.
I KNOW VOLMER'S DESIRES--AND THE ANSWER IS NO.
WE'VE DONE OUR DEAL, AMA.
MY CURRENT GAME IS SO MUCH MORE FUN.
TO THE BLACK WELL WITH YOU AND YOUR GAMES!
LET US BE DONE WITH EACH OTHER! RELEASE US--AND WE'LL RELEASE YOU!
RELEASE ME?!
IF I WANTED FREEDOM I'D BE WITH MY PIPER NOW, SLAUGHTERING YOUR WEIGHTLESS PEOPLE.
OUR DEAL REMAINS--THE SOIL OF ZHAL IS DEATH TO ANY CITIZEN OF SKOD!
IT'S A DOWN ENDING FOR YOU.
THEN YOU WILL SHARE OUR FATE.
I'VE NEVER SPOKEN TO ANOTHER LIVING SOUL OF MY JOURNEY INTO THE WELL...

...OR THE TRUTH BEHIND THE BURNING CLARITY IT FORCED ON ME.

THE WEIGHT OF HAVING ALL DELUSION AND RATIONALIZATION TORN AWAY IS HARD TO EXPRESS.

OUR FANTASIES RUN **TOO** DEEP TO BE PULLED OUT SO QUICKLY.

WITH THE CURTAIN PULLED BACK...

IT **ALL** SNAPPED INTO FOCUS AT ONCE:

WHAT IS ESSENTIAL TO LIFE IS **INVISIBLE** TO THE NAKED EYE.

MOTIVELESS HOURS WITH MY FAMILY.

JAMES: IN THE READING ROOM, NAPS IN THE SUNLIGHT.

ETHAN: POURS WATER FROM ONE GLASS TO ANOTHER FOR HOURS.

LUKE: A JOYFUL SMILE AS HE WATCHES, ABSORBED BY THE SIMPLE MOTION, THE LIQUID TRICKLE.

KATIE: DANCES IN THE LIVING ROOM, THROWS HERSELF INTO IT AS IF PERFORMIN' FOR A QUEEN.

ZEB: READS AN OLD LETTER OF HIS UNDYING LOVE TO MOM.

DIDN'T WANT IT TO REMAIN UNSAID.

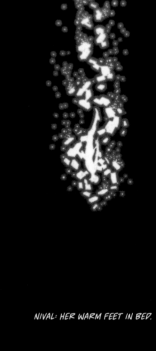

NIVAL: HER WARM FEET IN BED.

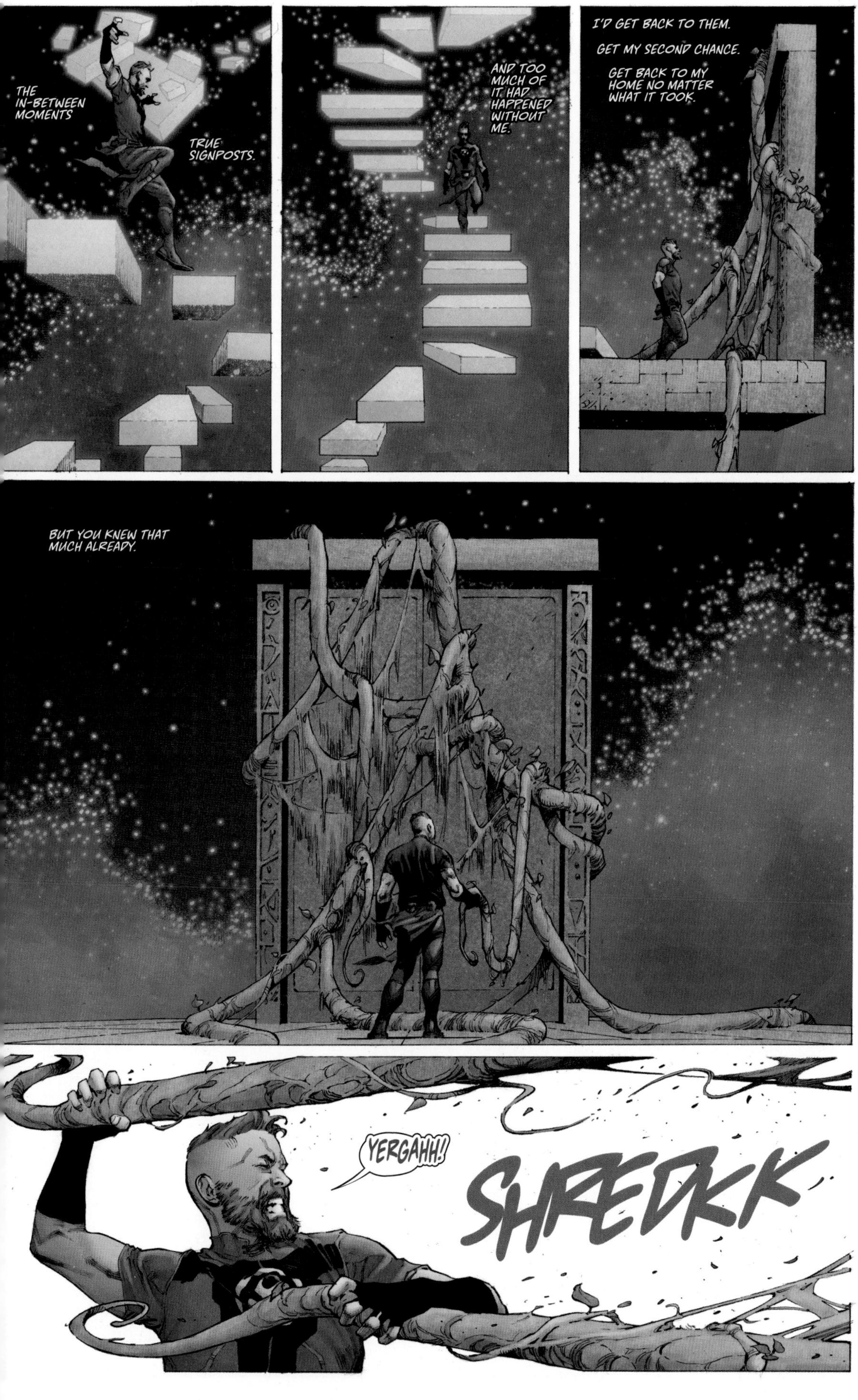
THE IN-BETWEEN MOMENTS
TRUE SIGNPOSTS.
AND TOO MUCH OF IT HAD HAPPENED WITHOUT ME.
I'D GET BACK TO THEM.
GET MY SECOND CHANCE.
GET BACK TO MY HOME NO MATTER WHAT IT TOOK.
BUT YOU KNEW THAT MUCH ALREADY.
YERGAHH!
SHREDKK

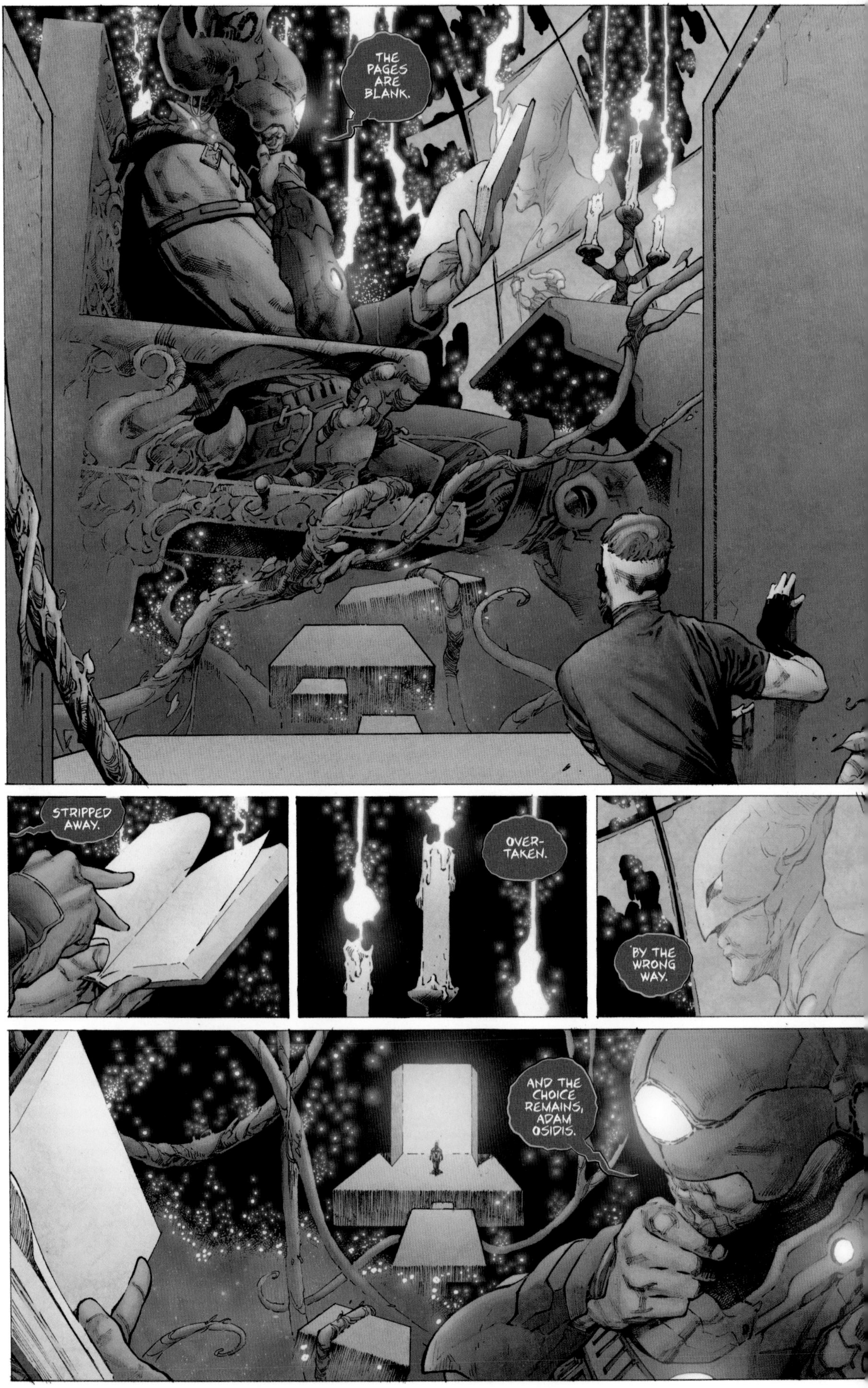
THE PAGES ARE BLANK.
STRIPPED AWAY.
OVER-TAKEN.
BY THE WRONG WAY.
AND THE CHOICE REMAINS, ADAM OSIDIS.

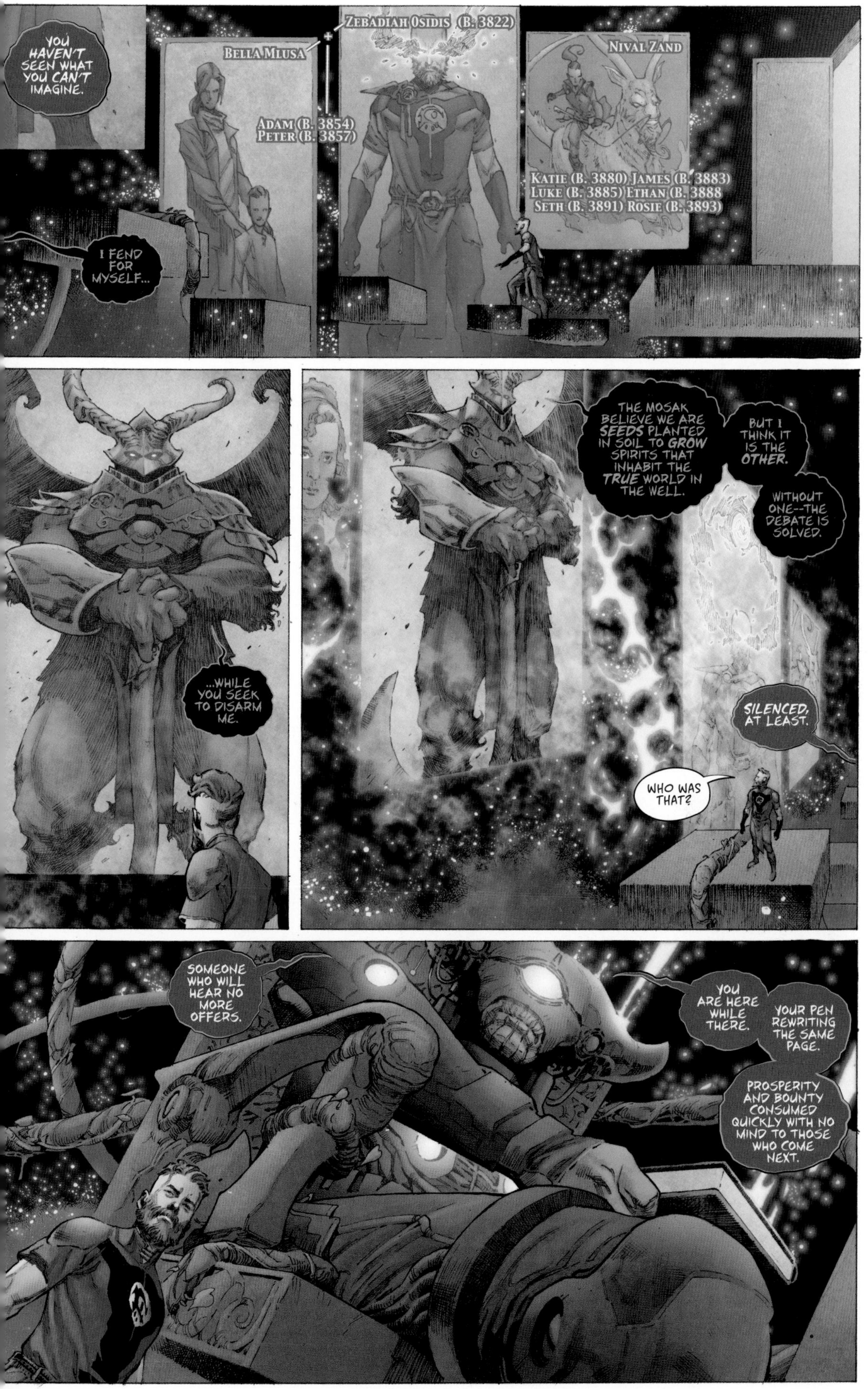
YOU HAVEN'T SEEN WHAT YOU CAN'T IMAGINE.
BELLA MLUSA
ZEBADIAH OSIDIS (B. 3822)
ADAM (B. 3854)
PETER (B. 3857)
NIVAL ZAND
KATIE (B. 3880) JAMES (B. 3883)
LUKE (B. 3885) ETHAN (B. 3888
SETH (B. 3891) ROSIE (B. 3893)
I FEND FOR MYSELF...
...WHILE YOU SEEK TO DISARM ME.
THE MOSAK BELIEVE WE ARE SEEDS PLANTED IN SOIL TO GROW SPIRITS THAT INHABIT THE TRUE WORLD IN THE WELL.
BUT I THINK IT IS THE OTHER.
WITHOUT ONE--THE DEBATE IS SOLVED.
SILENCED, AT LEAST.
WHO WAS THAT?
SOMEONE WHO WILL HEAR NO MORE OFFERS.
YOU ARE HERE WHILE THERE.
YOUR PEN REWRITING THE SAME PAGE.
PROSPERITY AND BOUNTY CONSUMED QUICKLY WITH NO MIND TO THOSE WHO COME NEXT.

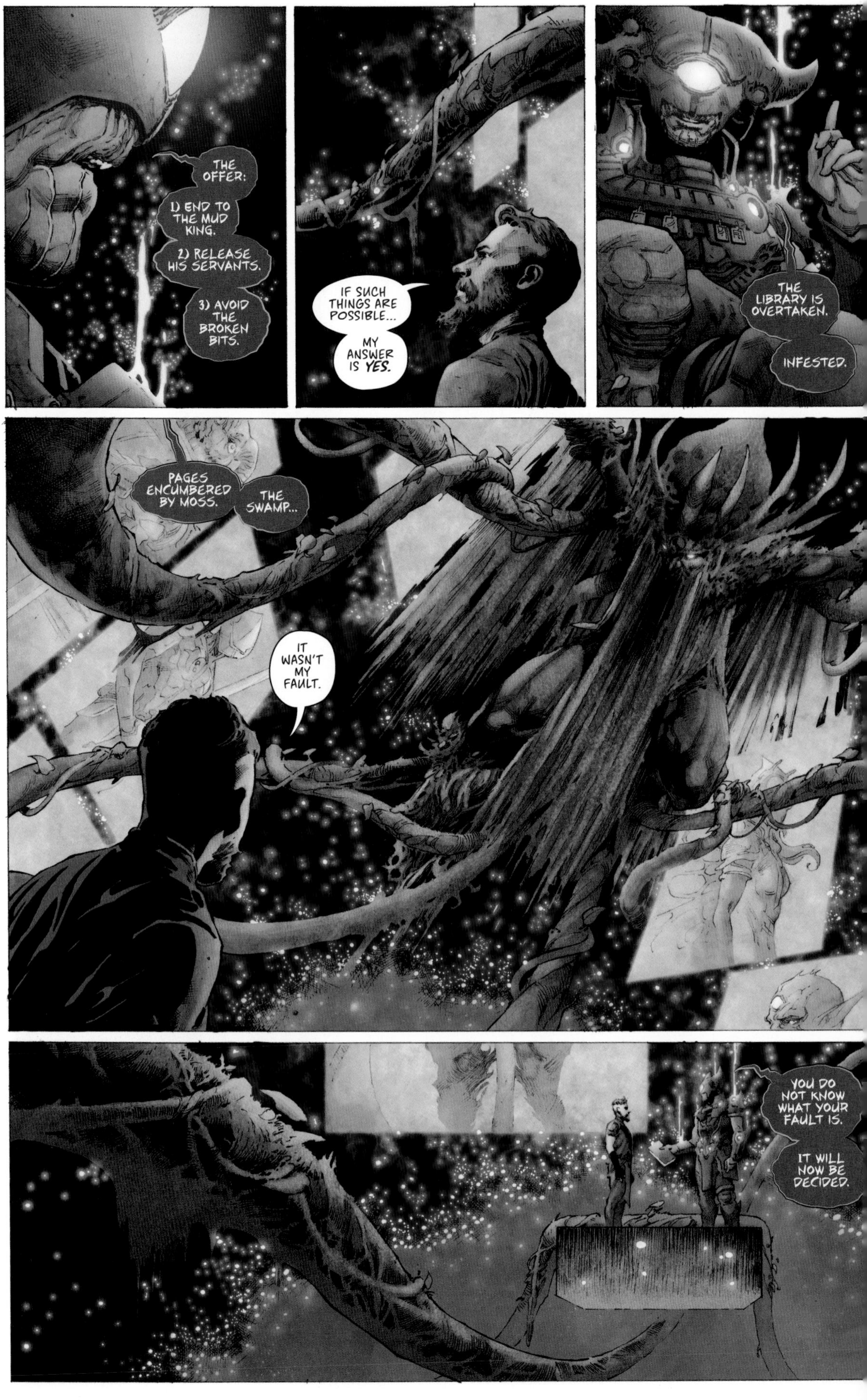
THE OFFER:
1) END TO THE MUD KING.
2) RELEASE HIS SERVANTS.
3) AVOID THE BROKEN BITS.
IF SUCH THINGS ARE POSSIBLE...
MY ANSWER IS *YES.*
THE LIBRARY IS OVERTAKEN.
INFESTED.
PAGES ENCUMBERED BY MOSS.
THE SWAMP...
IT WASN'T MY FAULT.
YOU DO NOT KNOW WHAT YOUR FAULT IS.
IT WILL NOW BE DECIDED.

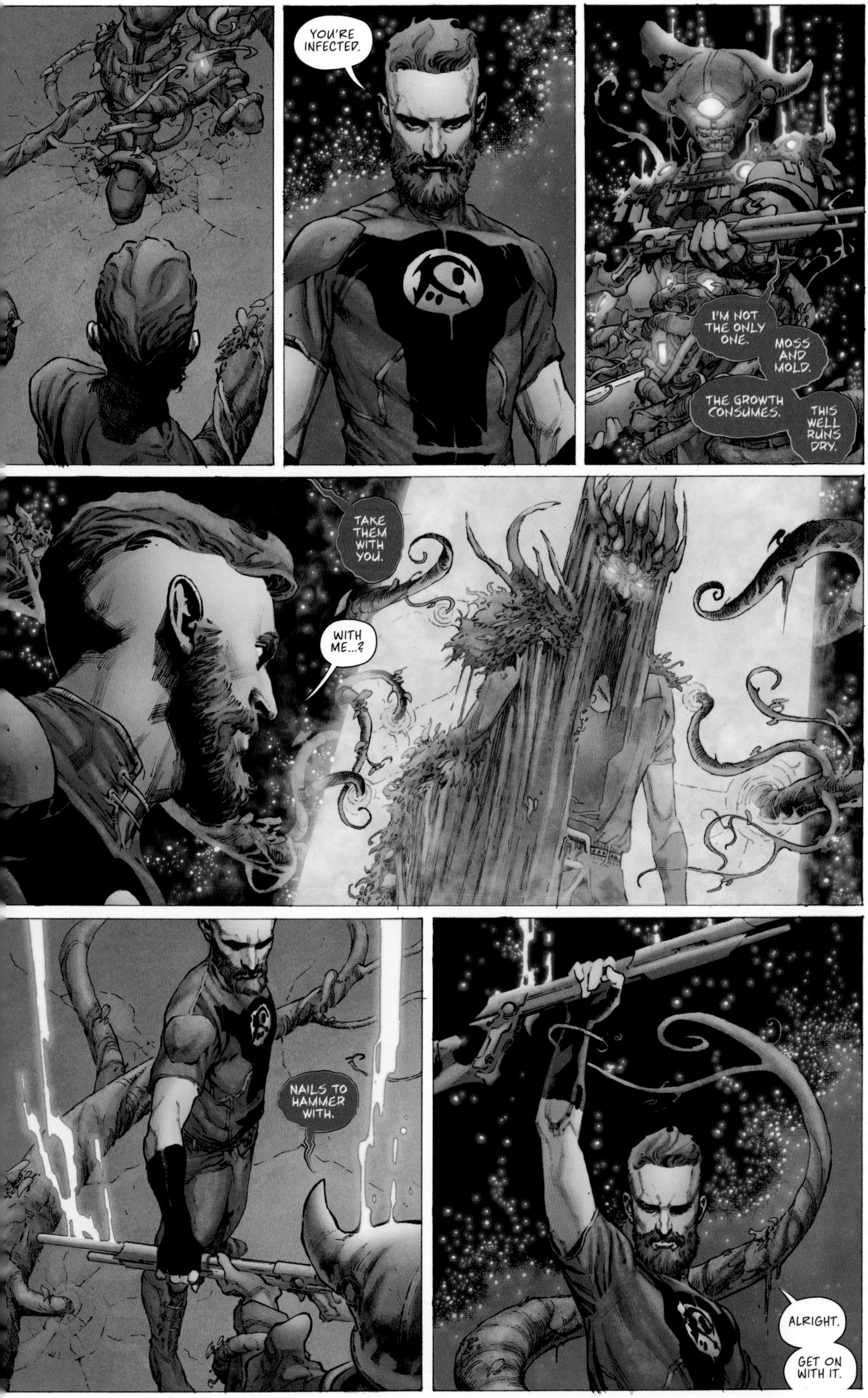
YOU'RE INFECTED.
I'M NOT THE ONLY ONE.
MOSS AND MOLD.
THE GROWTH CONSUMES.
THIS WELL RUNS DRY.
TAKE THEM WITH YOU.
WITH ME...?
NAILS TO HAMMER WITH.
ALRIGHT.
GET ON WITH IT.

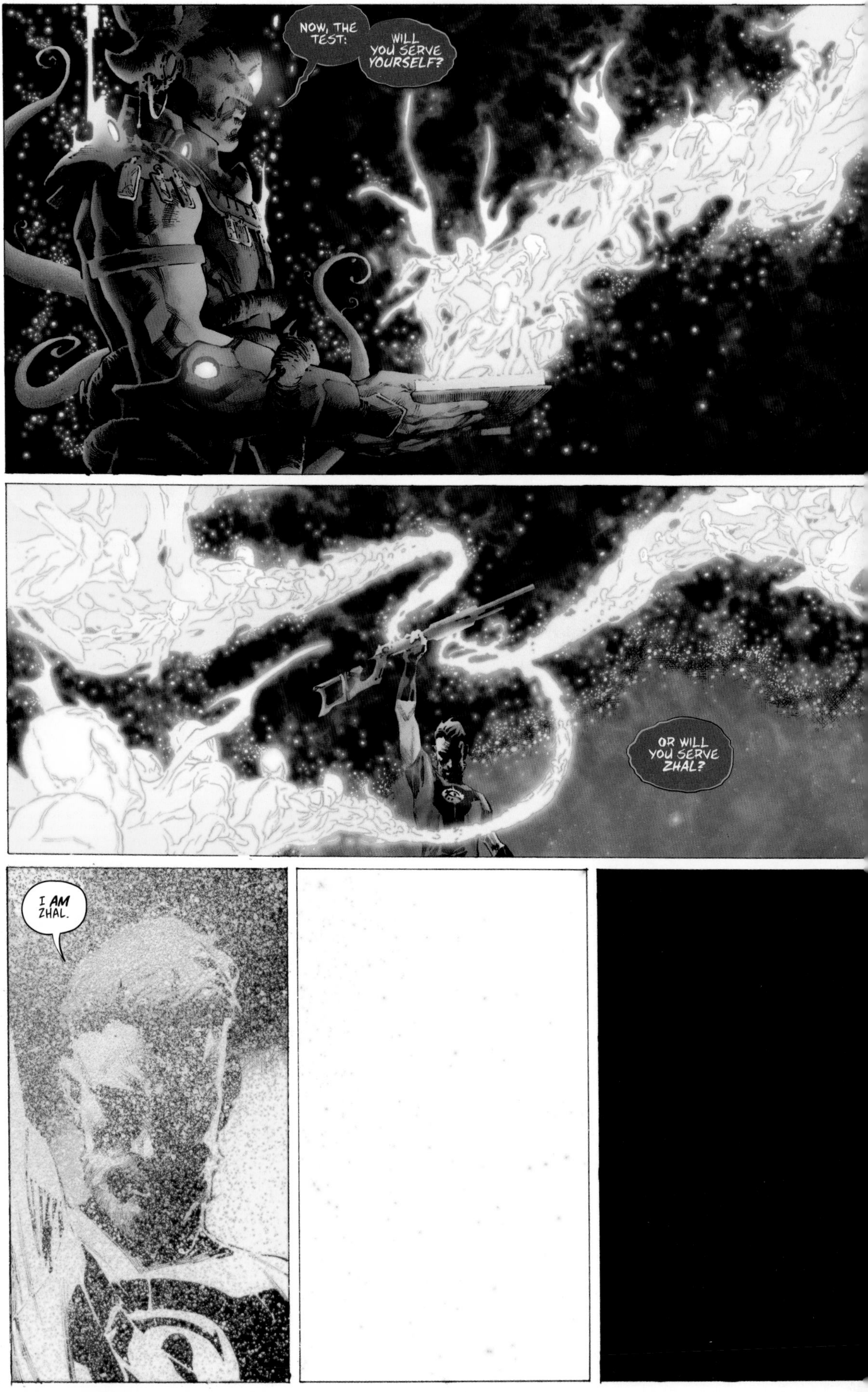
NOW, THE TEST:
WILL YOU SERVE YOURSELF?
OR WILL YOU SERVE ZHAL?
I AM ZHAL.

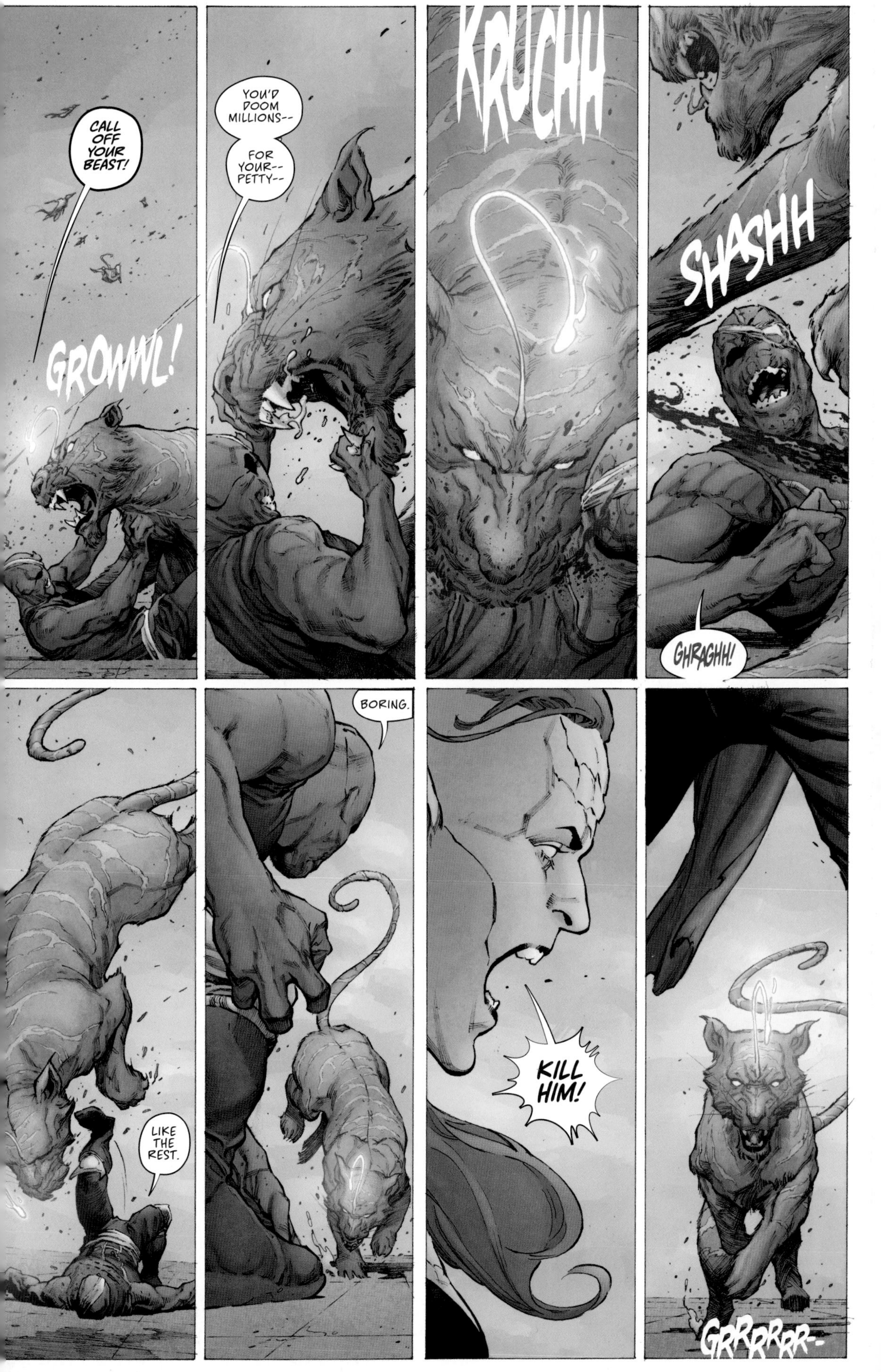
CALL OFF YOUR BEAST!
GROWWL!
YOU'D DOOM MILLIONS--
FOR YOUR--PETTY--
KRUCHH
SHASHH
GHRAGHH!
LIKE THE REST.
BORING.
KILL HIM!
GRRRRRR-

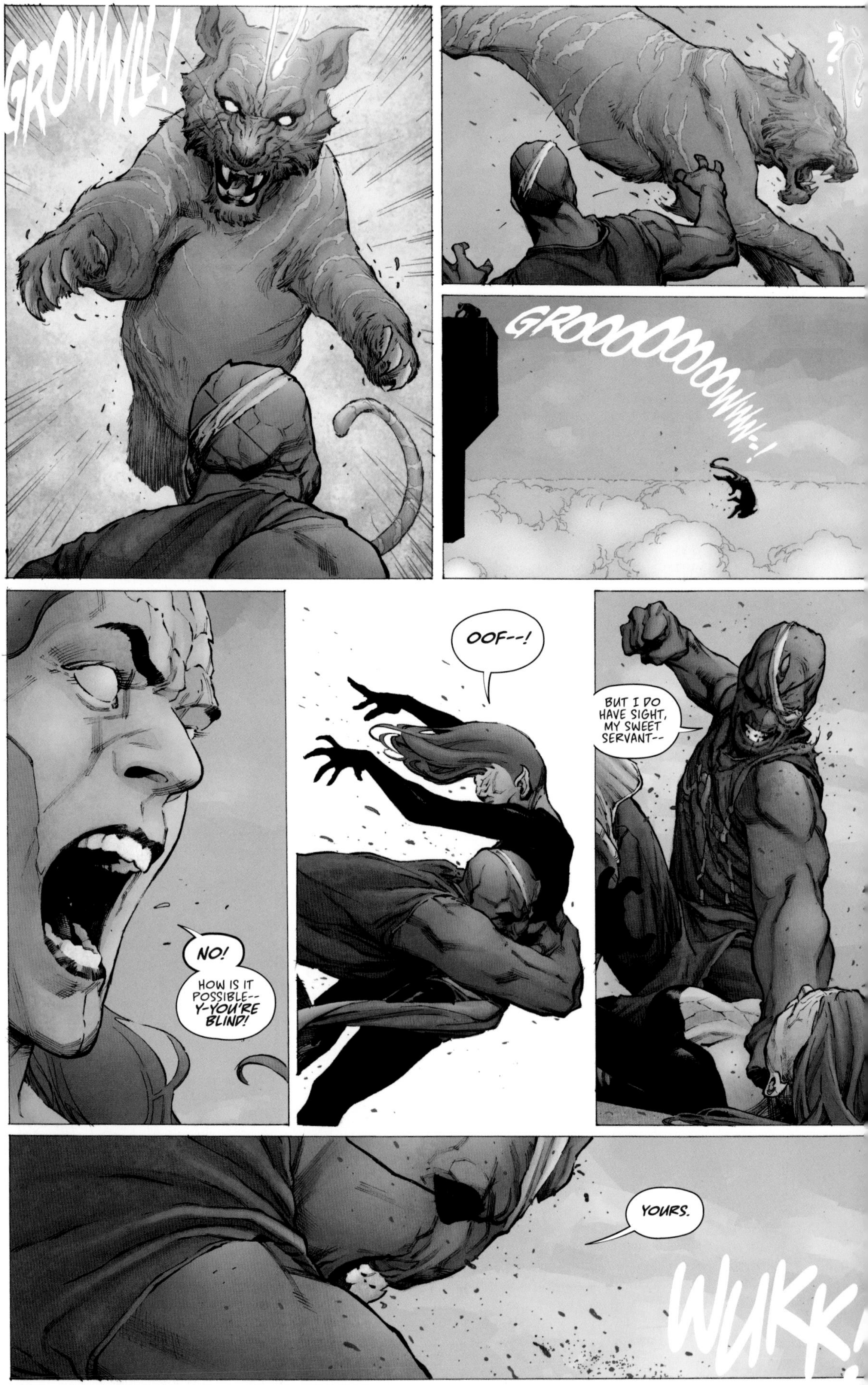
GROWWLL!
?
GROOOOOOOWWW--!
NO!
HOW IS IT POSSIBLE-- Y-YOU'RE BLIND!
OOF--!
BUT I DO HAVE SIGHT, MY SWEET SERVANT--
YOURS.
WUKK!

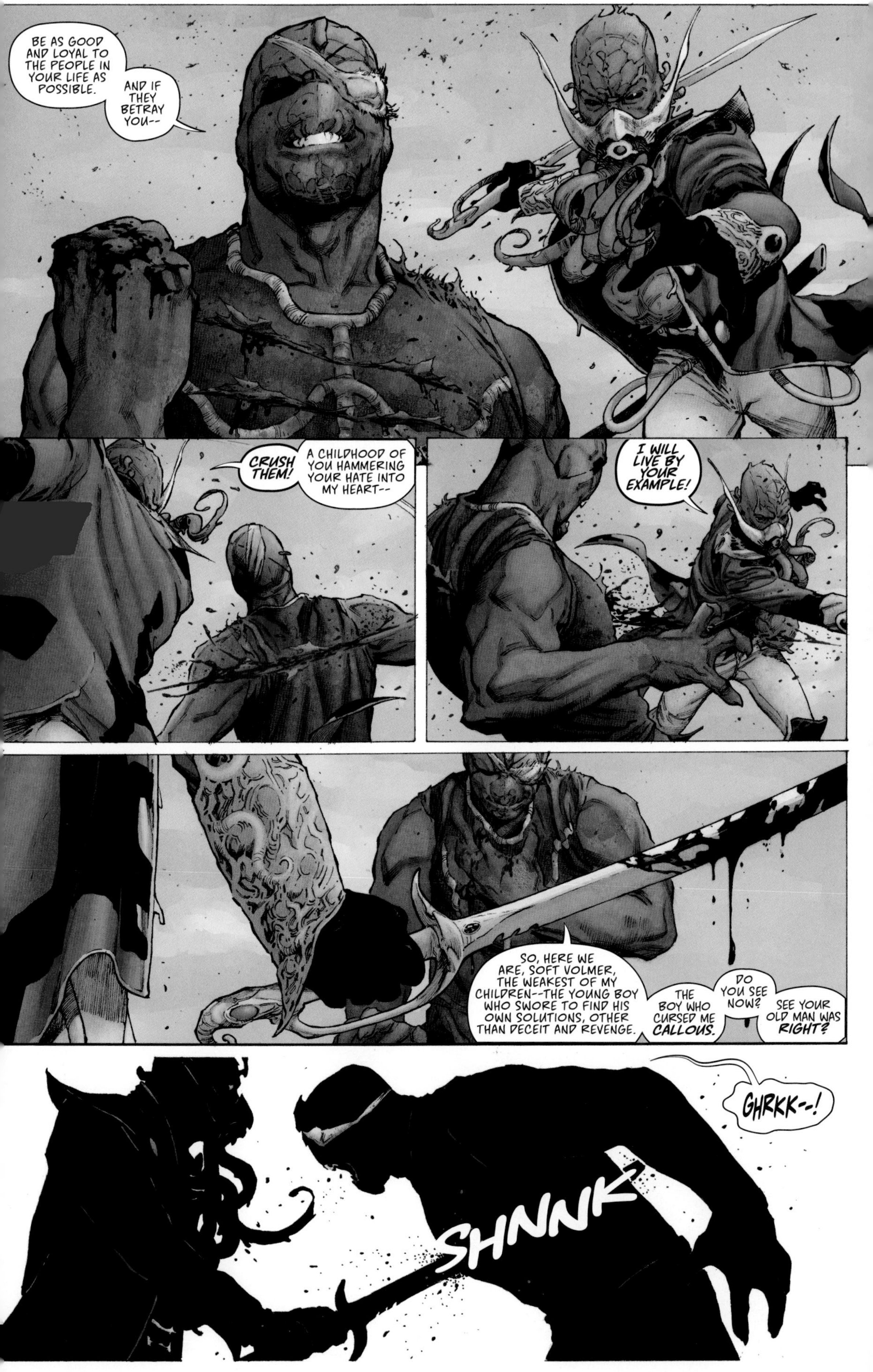

BE AS GOOD AND LOYAL TO THE PEOPLE IN YOUR LIFE AS POSSIBLE.
AND IF THEY BETRAY YOU--
CRUSH THEM!
A CHILDHOOD OF YOU HAMMERING YOUR HATE INTO MY HEART--
I WILL LIVE BY YOUR EXAMPLE!
SO, HERE WE ARE, SOFT VOLMER, THE WEAKEST OF MY CHILDREN--THE YOUNG BOY WHO SWORE TO FIND HIS OWN SOLUTIONS, OTHER THAN DECEIT AND REVENGE.
THE BOY WHO CURSED ME CALLOUS.
DO YOU SEE NOW?
SEE YOUR OLD MAN WAS RIGHT?
GHRKK--!
SHNNK

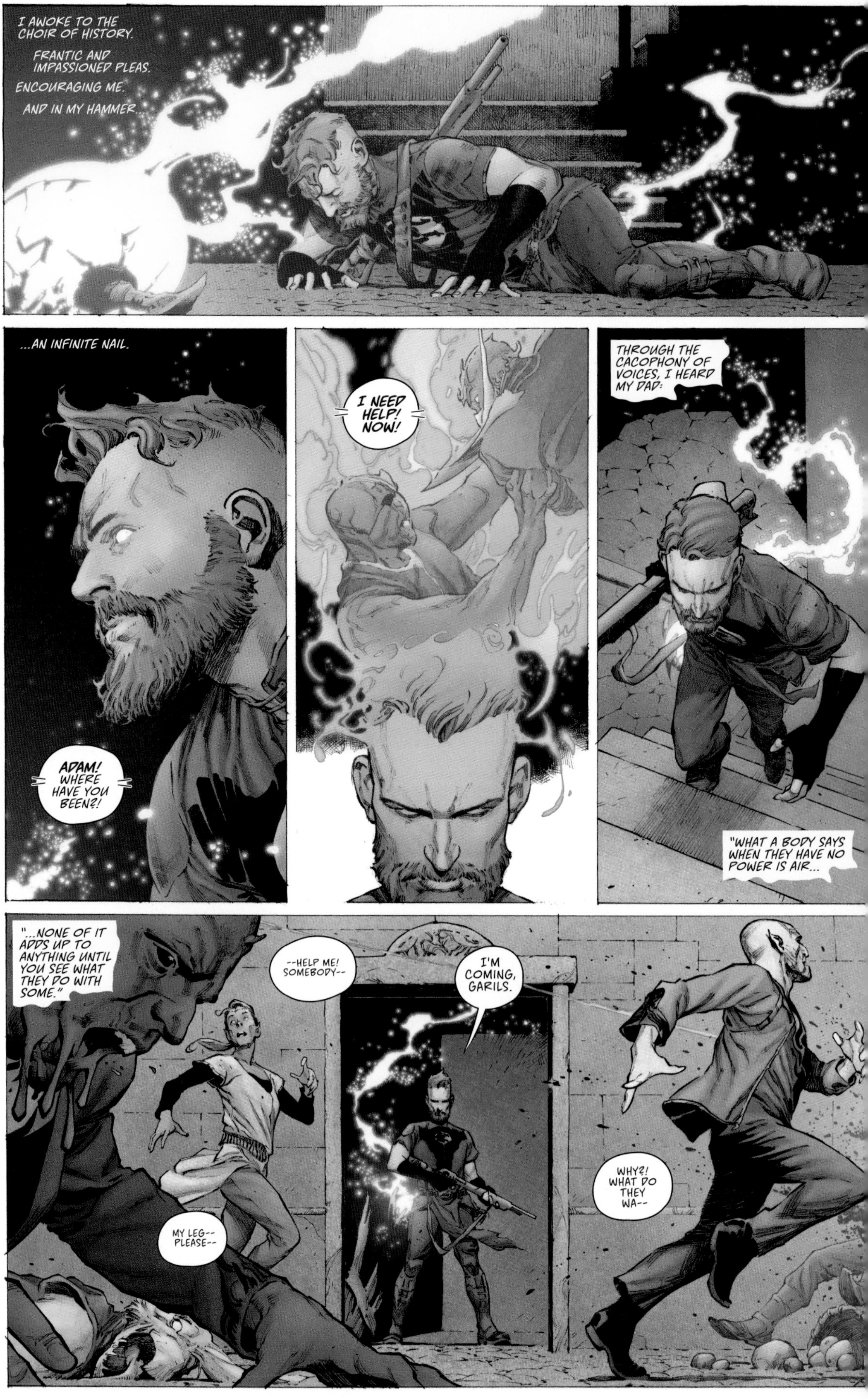

I AWOKE TO THE CHOIR OF HISTORY.
FRANTIC AND IMPASSIONED PLEAS.
ENCOURAGING ME.
AND IN MY HAMMER...
...AN INFINITE NAIL.
ADAM! WHERE HAVE YOU BEEN?!
I NEED HELP! NOW!
THROUGH THE CACOPHONY OF VOICES, I HEARD MY DAD:
"WHAT A BODY SAYS WHEN THEY HAVE NO POWER IS AIR...
"...NONE OF IT ADDS UP TO ANYTHING UNTIL YOU SEE WHAT THEY DO WITH SOME."
--HELP ME! SOMEBODY--
I'M COMING, GARILS.
MY LEG-- PLEASE--
WHY?! WHAT DO THEY WA--

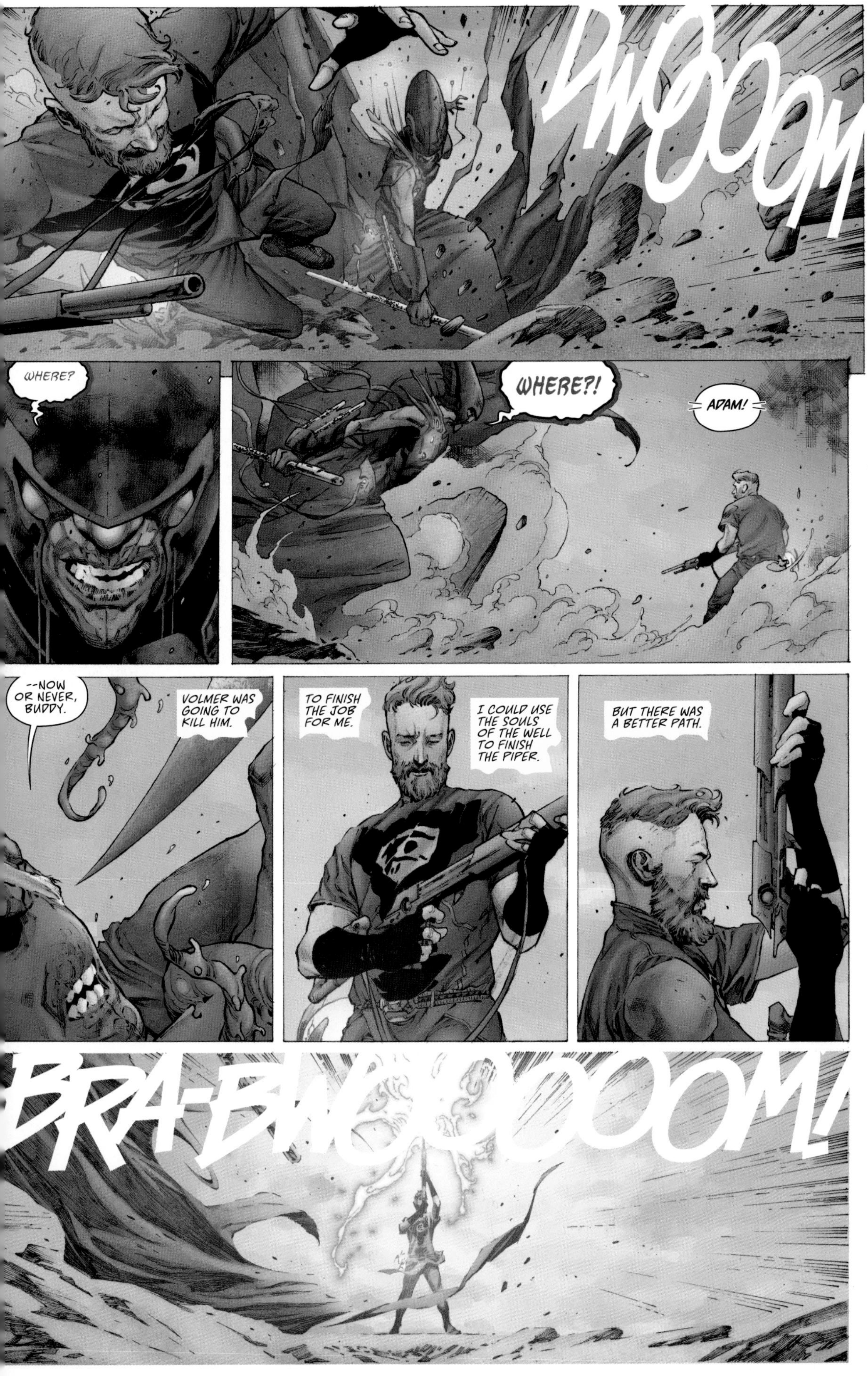
DWOOOOM
WHERE?
WHERE?!
ADAM!
--NOW OR NEVER, BUDDY.
VOLMER WAS GOING TO KILL HIM.
TO FINISH THE JOB FOR ME.
I COULD USE THE SOULS OF THE WELL TO FINISH THE PIPER.
BUT THERE WAS A BETTER PATH.
BRA-BWOOOOOOM!

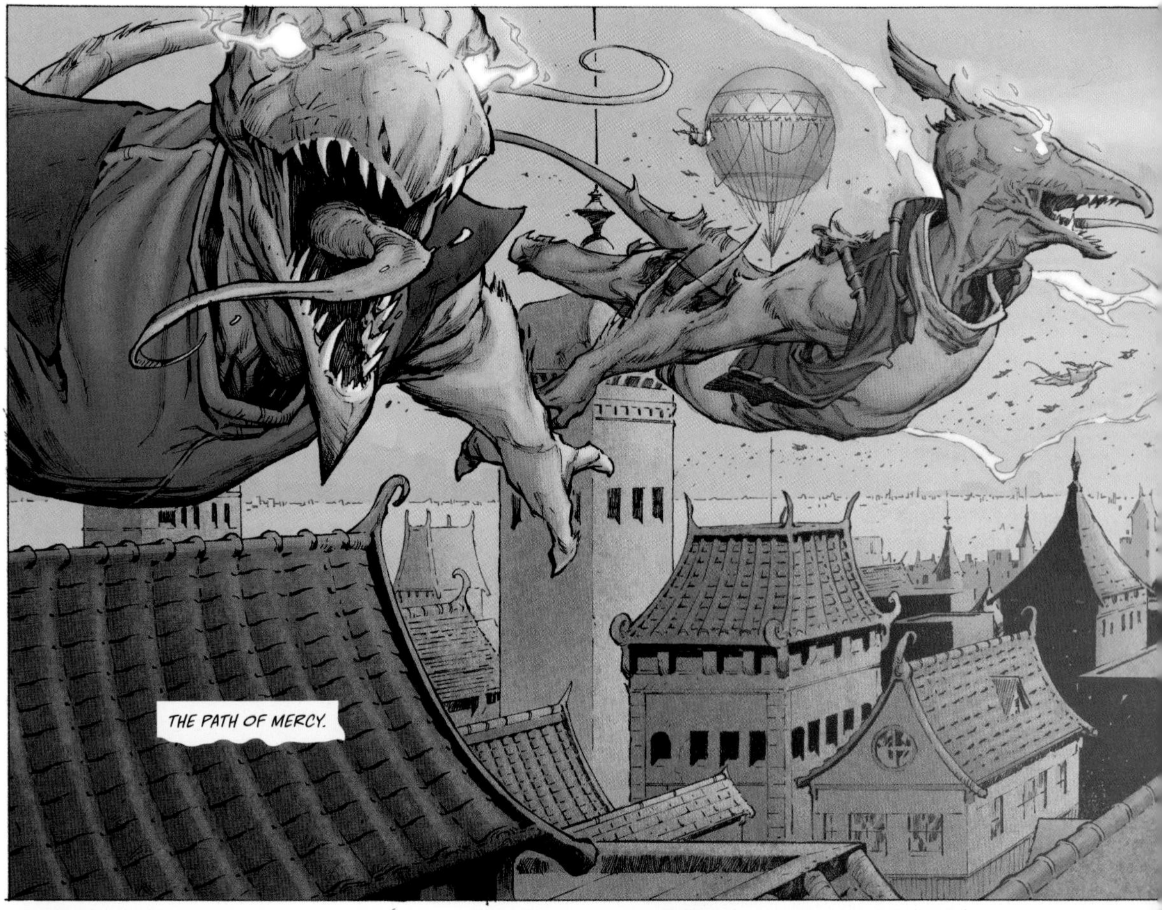
THE PATH OF MERCY.

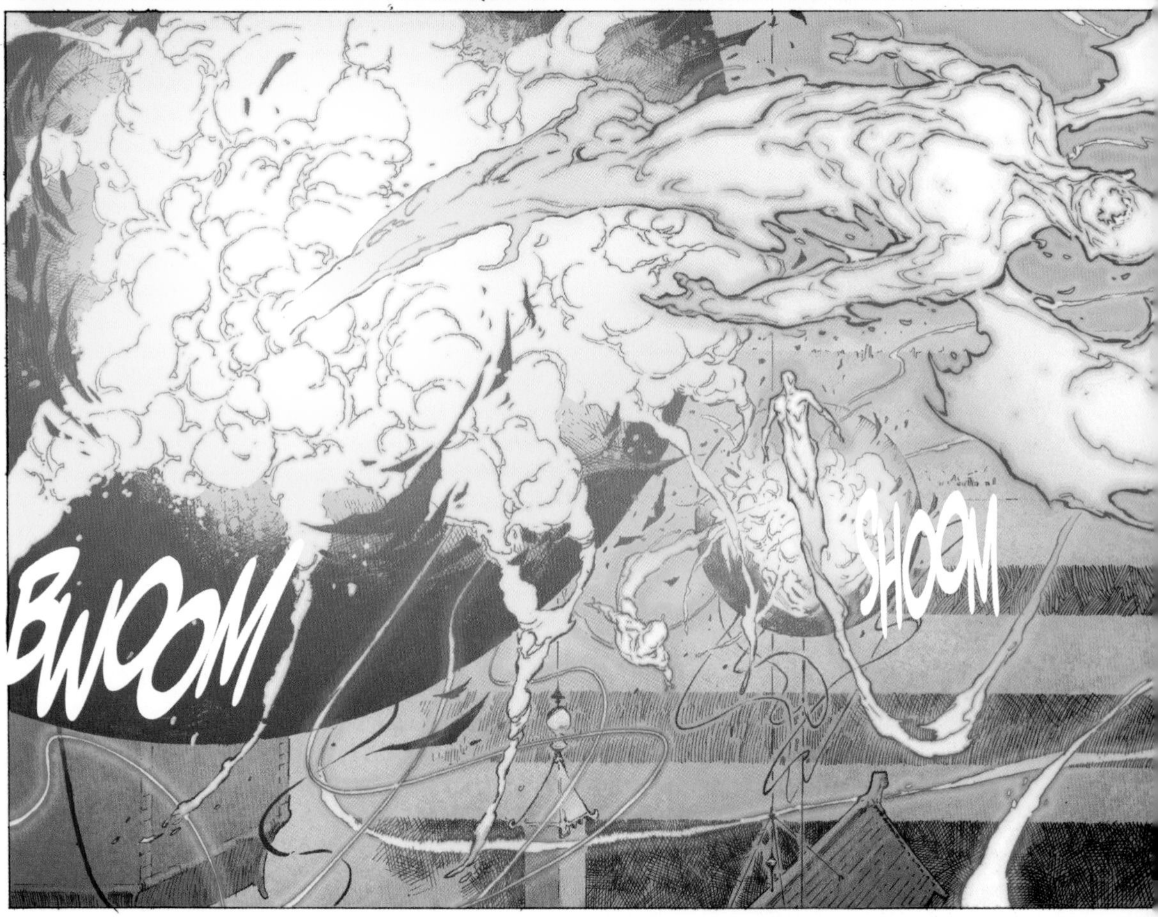
BWOOM
SHOOM

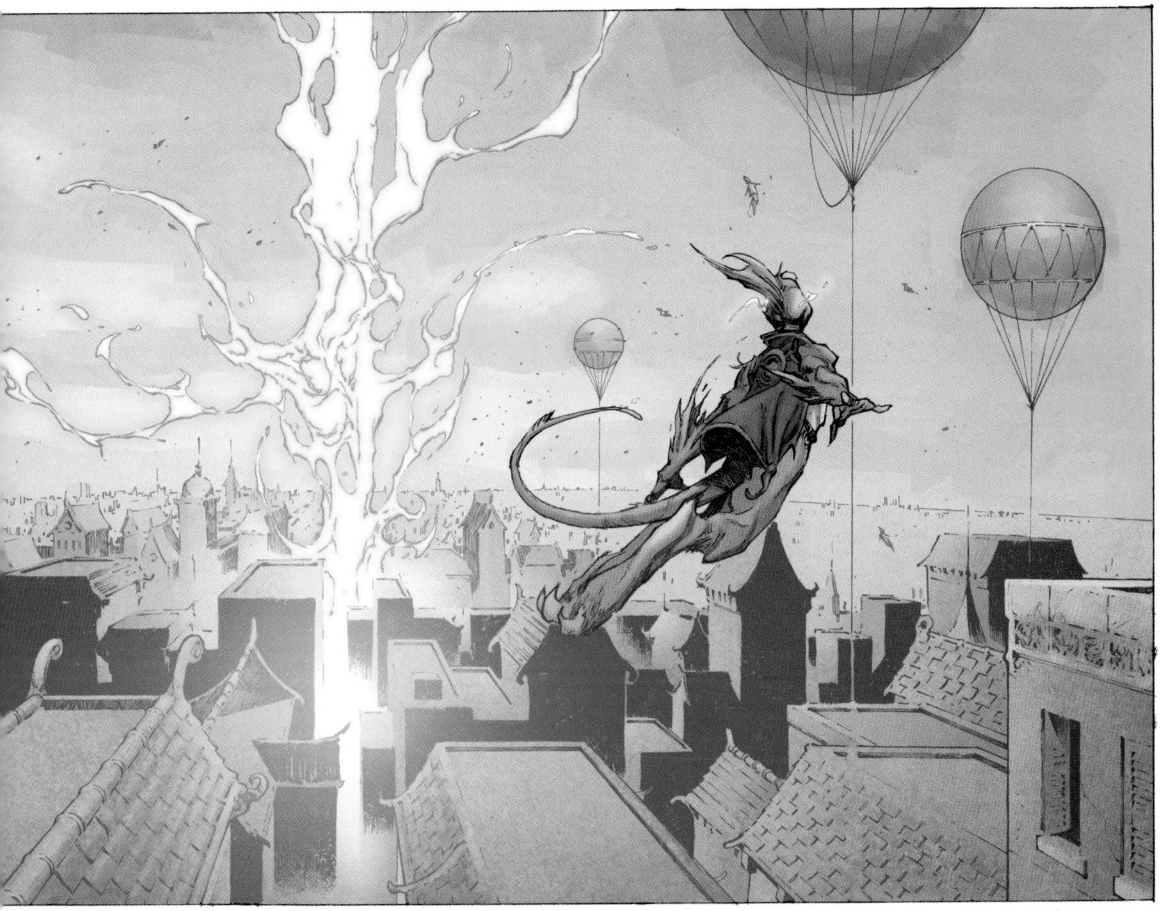

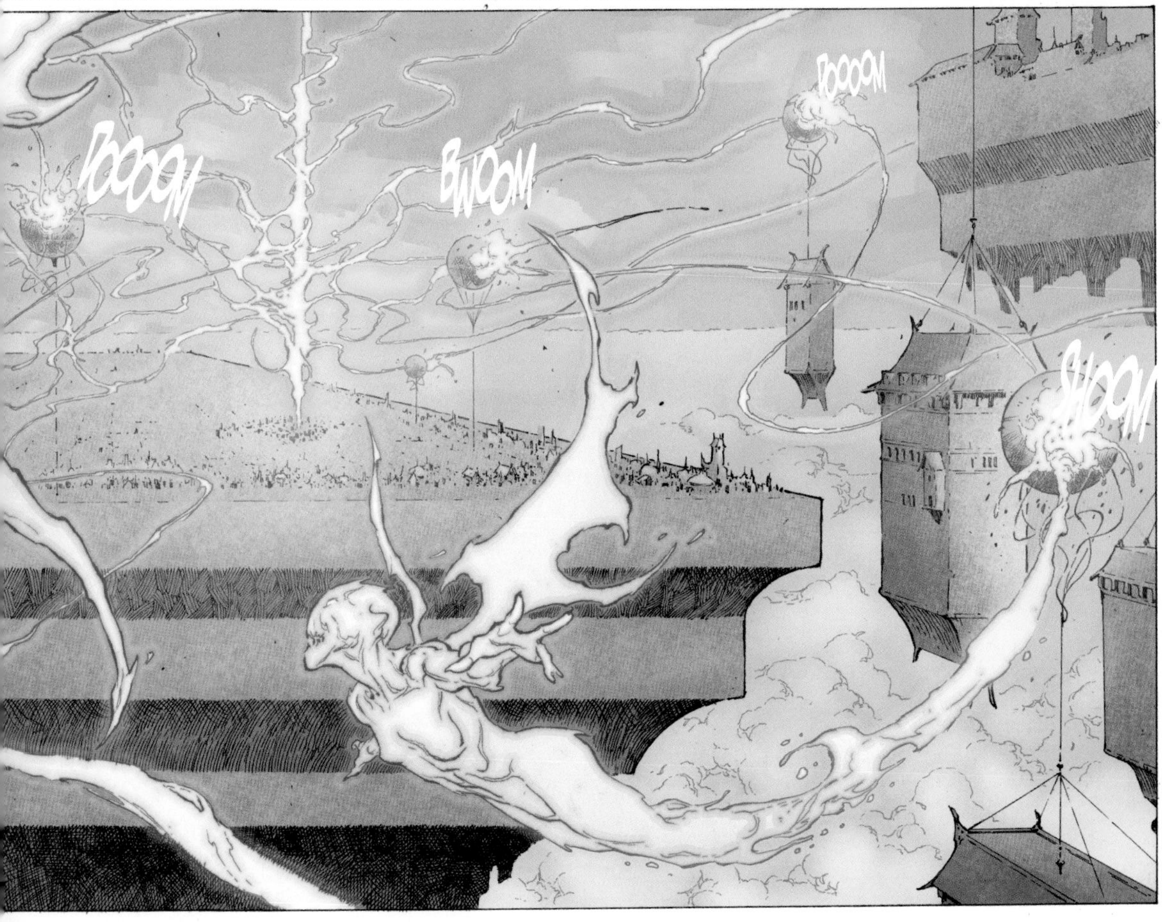
DOOOOM
BWOOM!
DOOOOM
SHOOM

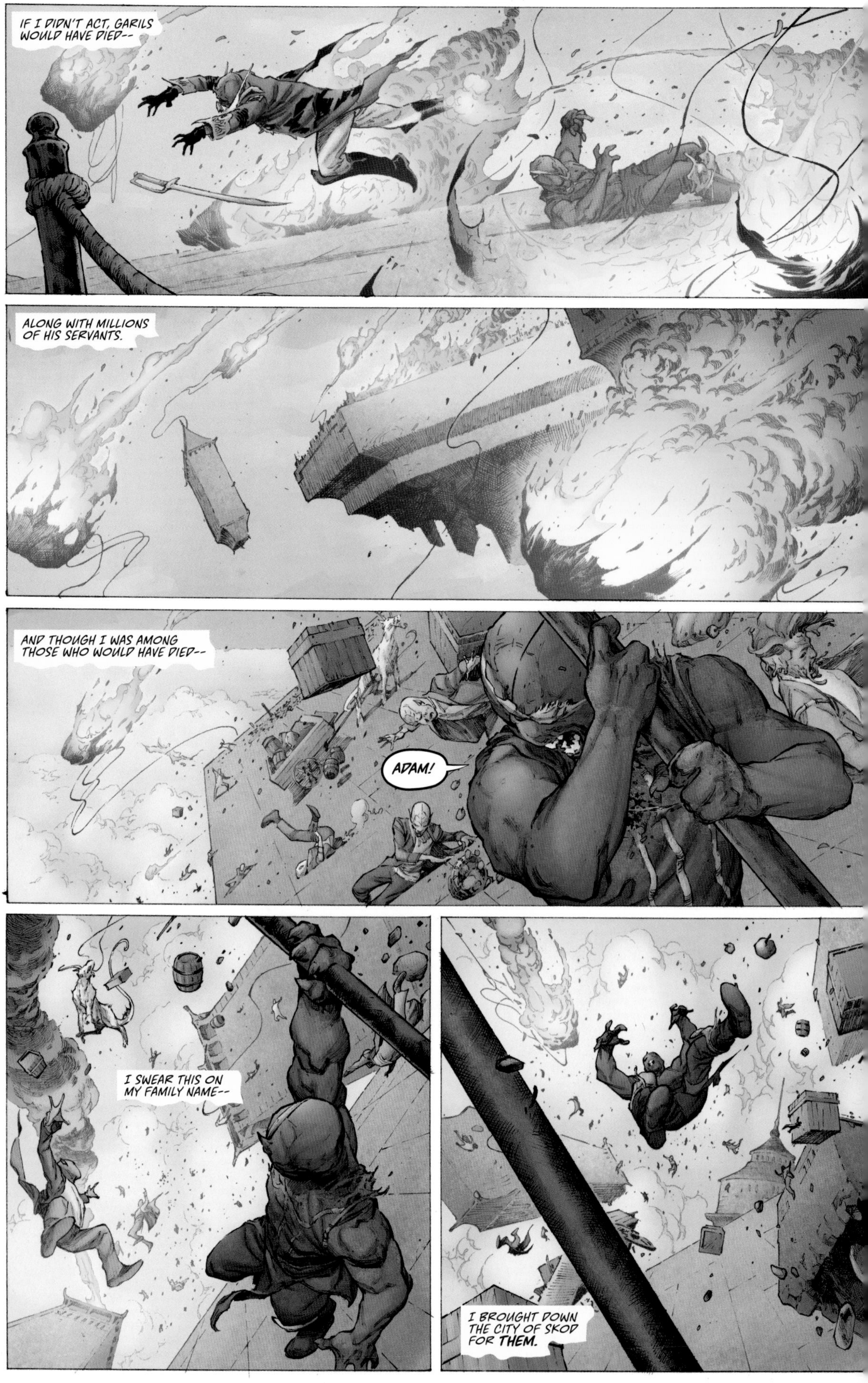
IF I DIDN'T ACT, GARILS WOULD HAVE DIED--
ALONG WITH MILLIONS OF HIS SERVANTS.
AND THOUGH I WAS AMONG THOSE WHO WOULD HAVE DIED--
ADAM!
I SWEAR THIS ON MY FAMILY NAME--
I BROUGHT DOWN THE CITY OF SKOD FOR THEM.

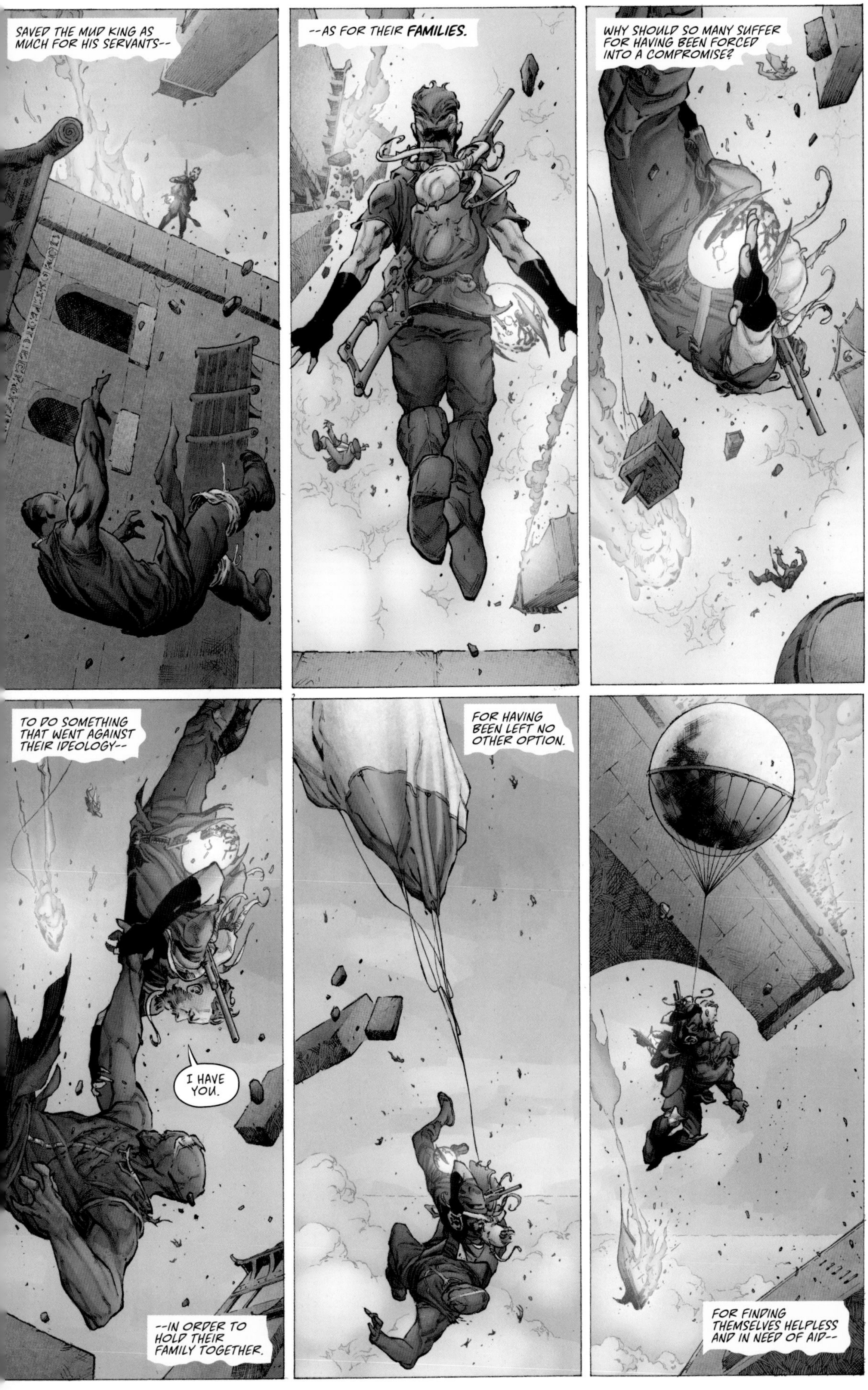
SAVED THE MUD KING AS MUCH FOR HIS SERVANTS--
--AS FOR THEIR FAMILIES.
WHY SHOULD SO MANY SUFFER FOR HAVING BEEN FORCED INTO A COMPROMISE?
TO DO SOMETHING THAT WENT AGAINST THEIR IDEOLOGY--
I HAVE YOU.
--IN ORDER TO HOLD THEIR FAMILY TOGETHER.
FOR HAVING BEEN LEFT NO OTHER OPTION.
FOR FINDING THEMSELVES HELPLESS AND IN NEED OF AID--

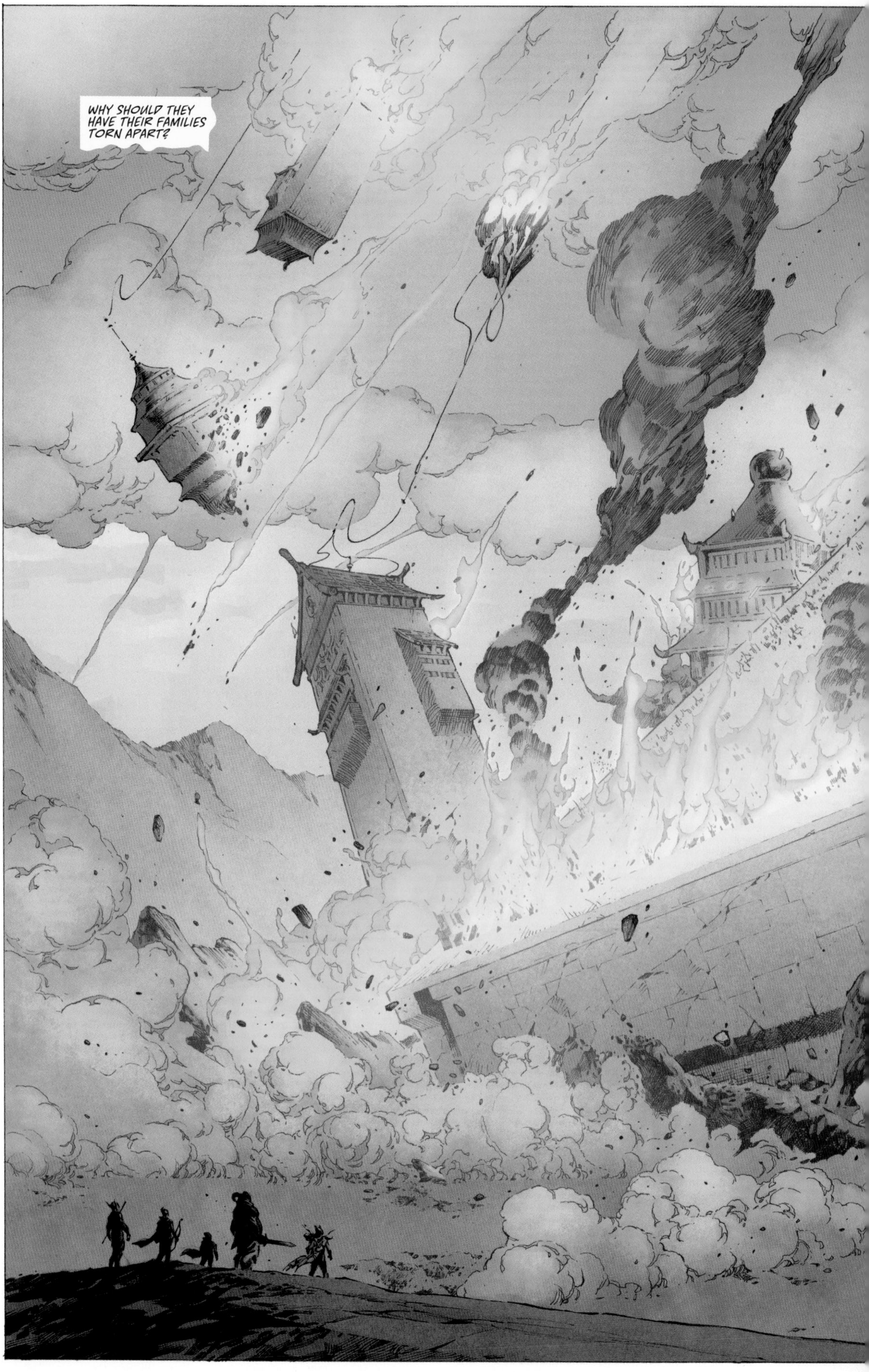
WHY SHOULD THEY HAVE THEIR FAMILIES TORN APART?

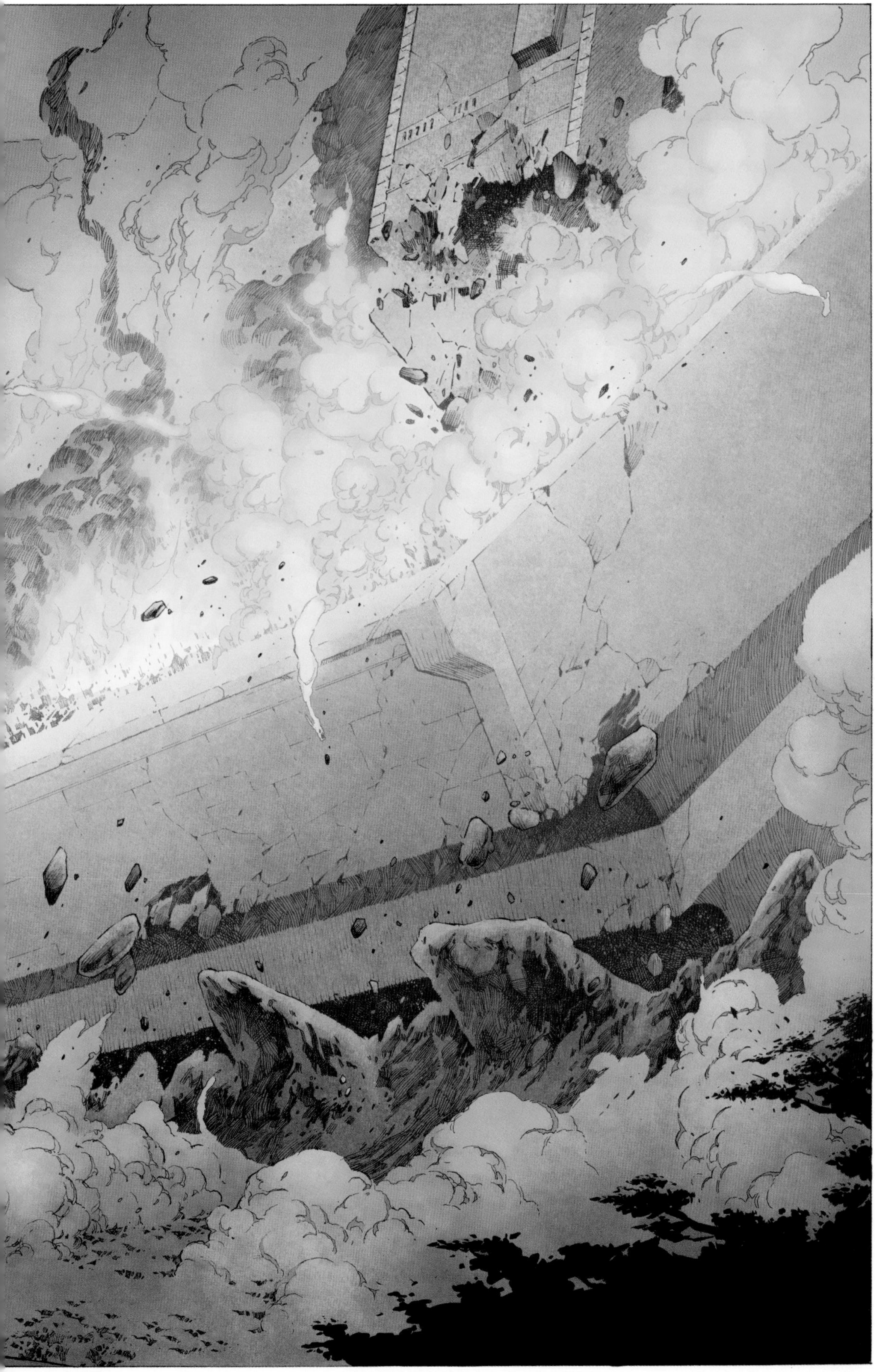

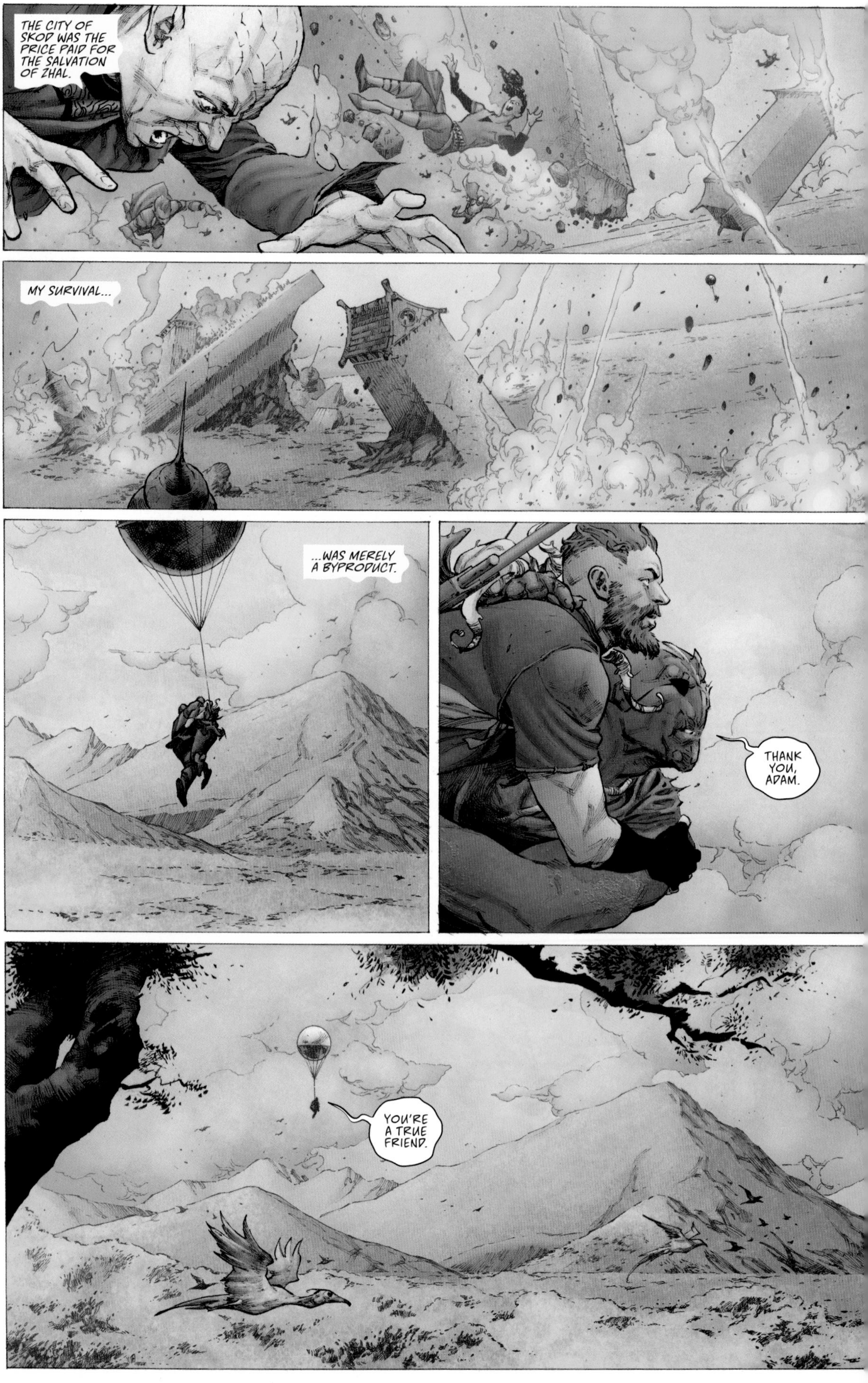
THE CITY OF SKOD WAS THE PRICE PAID FOR THE SALVATION OF ZHAL.
MY SURVIVAL...
...WAS MERELY A BYPRODUCT.
THANK YOU, ADAM.
YOU'RE A TRUE FRIEND.

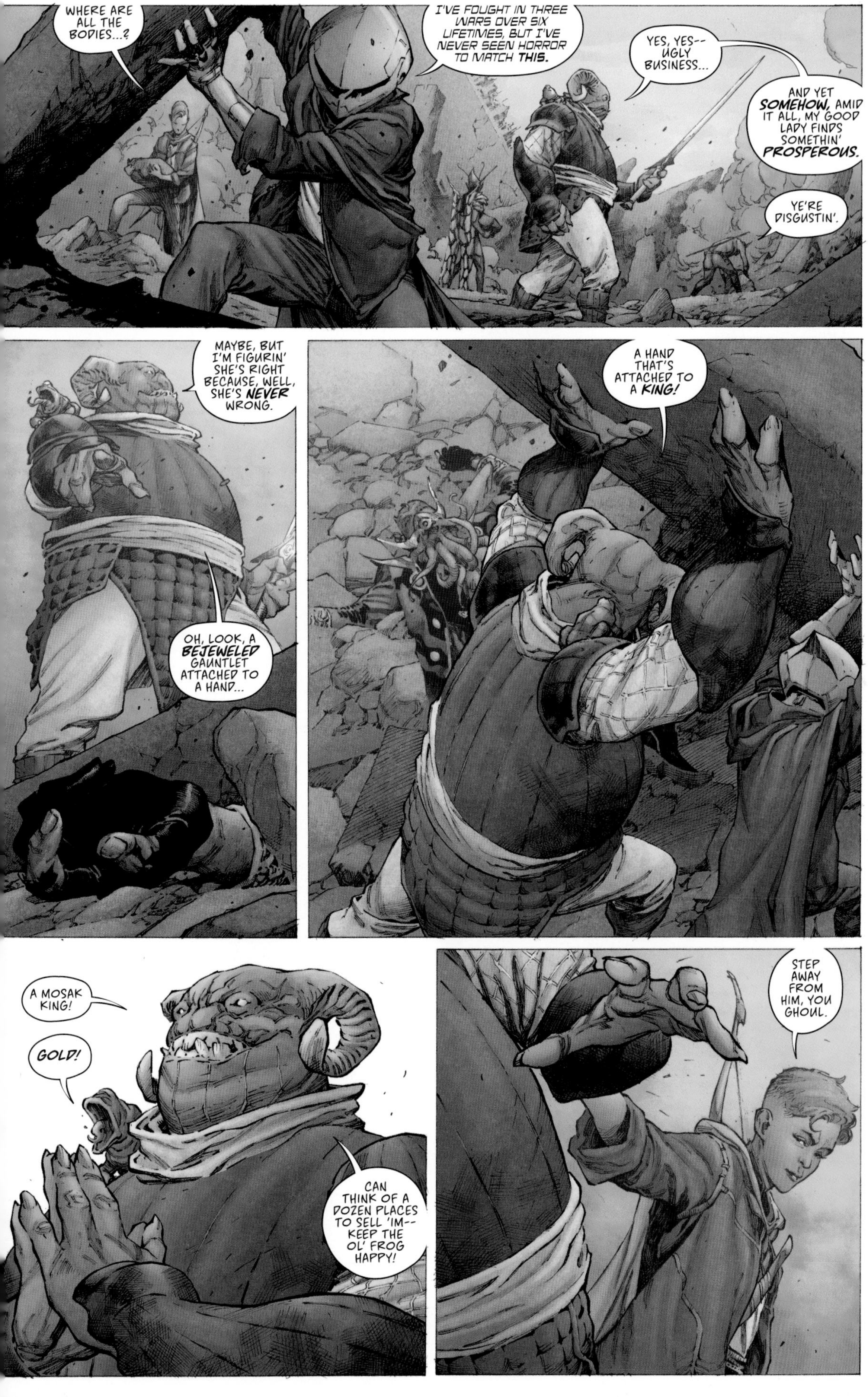
WHERE ARE ALL THE BODIES...?
I'VE FOUGHT IN THREE WARS OVER SIX LIFETIMES, BUT I'VE NEVER SEEN HORROR TO MATCH **THIS.**
YES, YES-- UGLY BUSINESS...
AND YET **SOMEHOW,** AMID IT ALL, MY GOOD LADY FINDS SOMETHIN' **PROSPEROUS.**
YE'RE DISGUSTIN'.
MAYBE, BUT I'M FIGURIN' SHE'S RIGHT BECAUSE, WELL, SHE'S **NEVER** WRONG.
OH, LOOK, A **BEJEWELED** GAUNTLET ATTACHED TO A HAND...
A HAND THAT'S ATTACHED TO A **KING!**
A MOSAK KING!
GOLD!
CAN THINK OF A DOZEN PLACES TO SELL 'IM-- KEEP THE OL' FROG HAPPY!
STEP AWAY FROM HIM, YOU GHOUL.

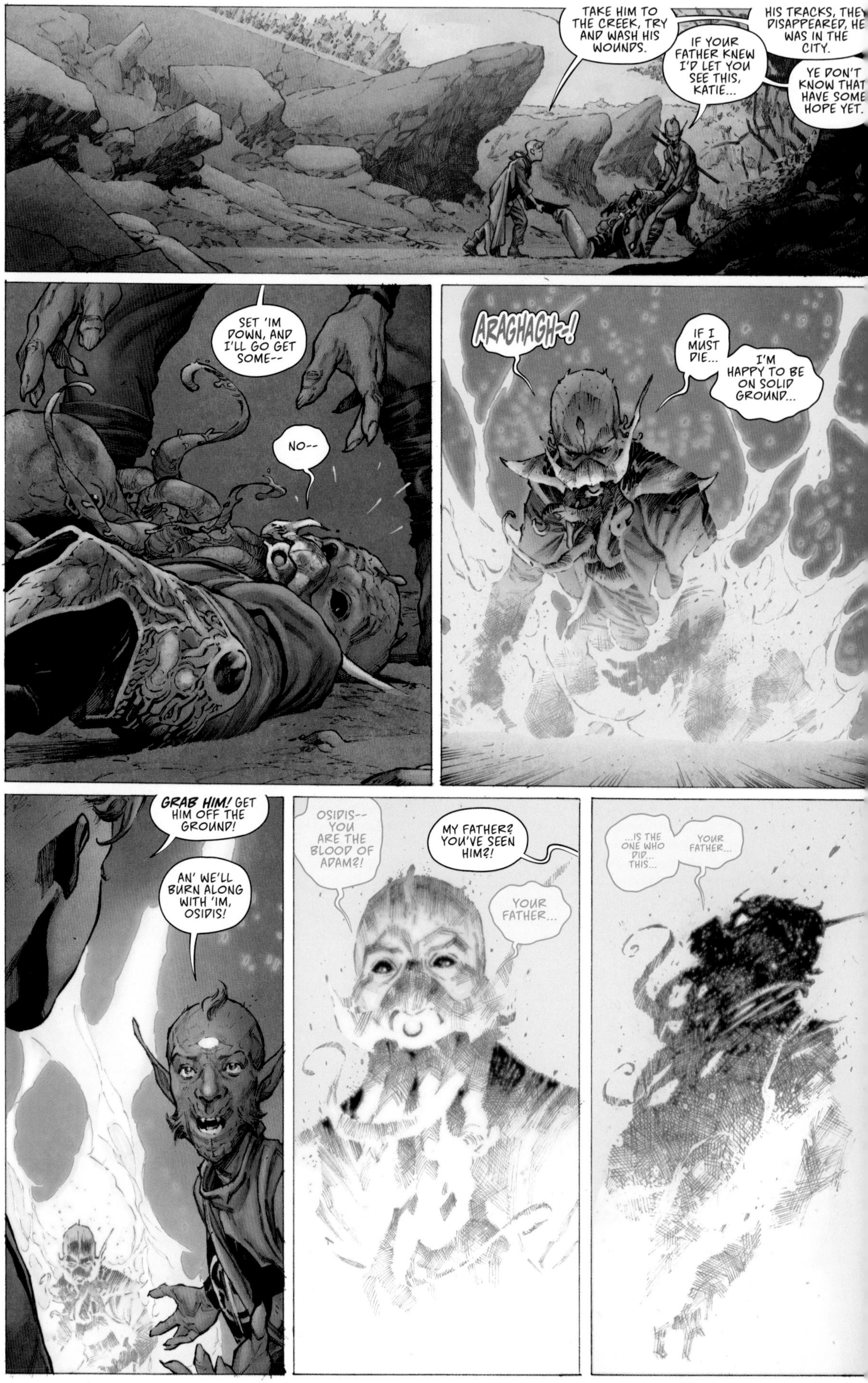
TAKE HIM TO THE CREEK, TRY AND WASH HIS WOUNDS.
IF YOUR FATHER KNEW I'D LET YOU SEE THIS, KATIE...
HIS TRACKS, THEY DISAPPEARED, HE WAS IN THE CITY.
YE DON'T KNOW THAT HAVE SOME HOPE YET.
SET 'IM DOWN, AND I'LL GO GET SOME--
NO--
ARAGHAGH--!
IF I MUST DIE...
I'M HAPPY TO BE ON SOLID GROUND...
GRAB HIM! GET HIM OFF THE GROUND!
AN' WE'LL BURN ALONG WITH 'IM, OSIDIS!
OSIDIS-- YOU ARE THE BLOOD OF ADAM?!
MY FATHER? YOU'VE SEEN HIM?!
YOUR FATHER...
YOUR FATHER...
...IS THE ONE WHO DID THIS...

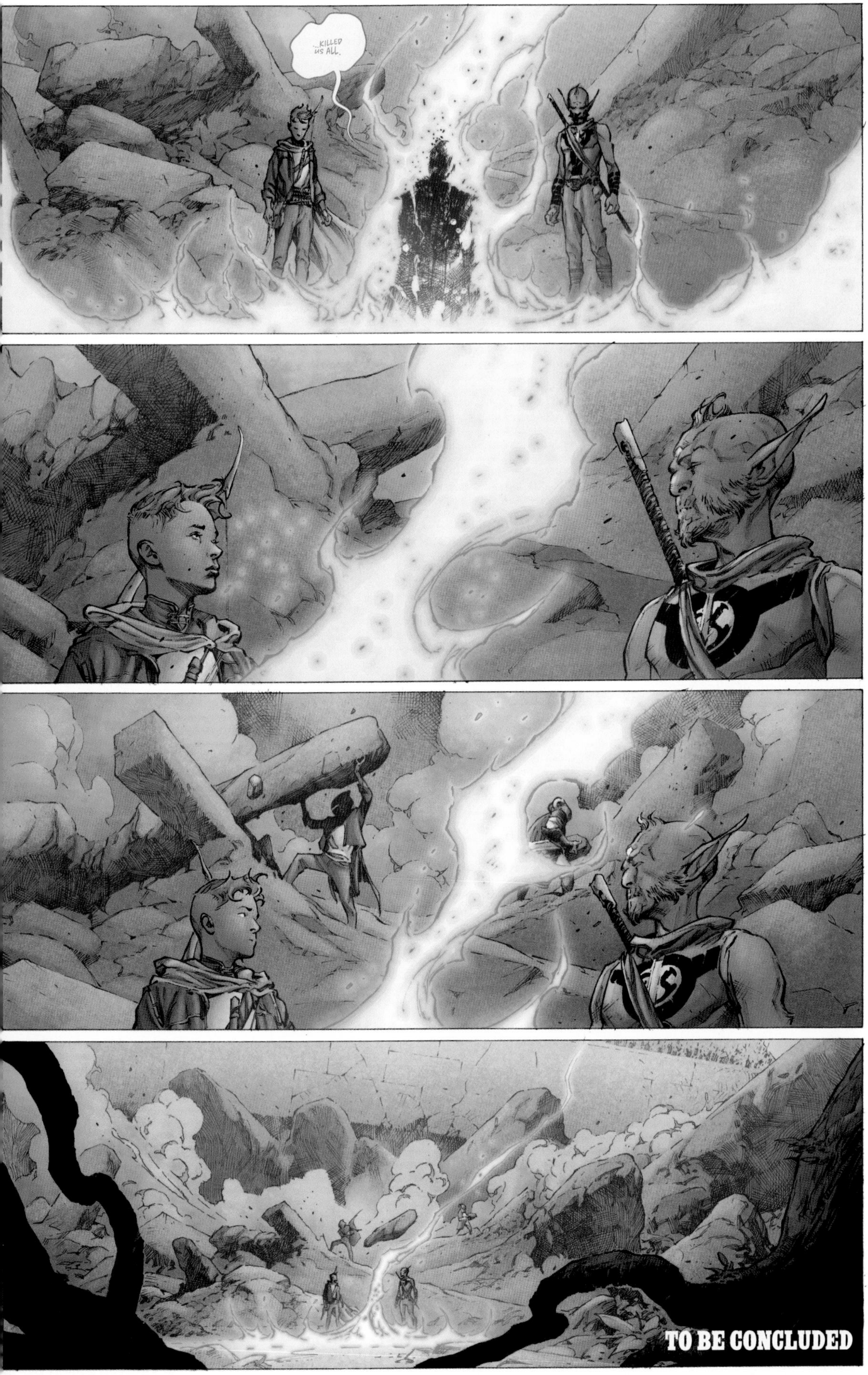
...KILLED US ALL.
TO BE CONCLUDED

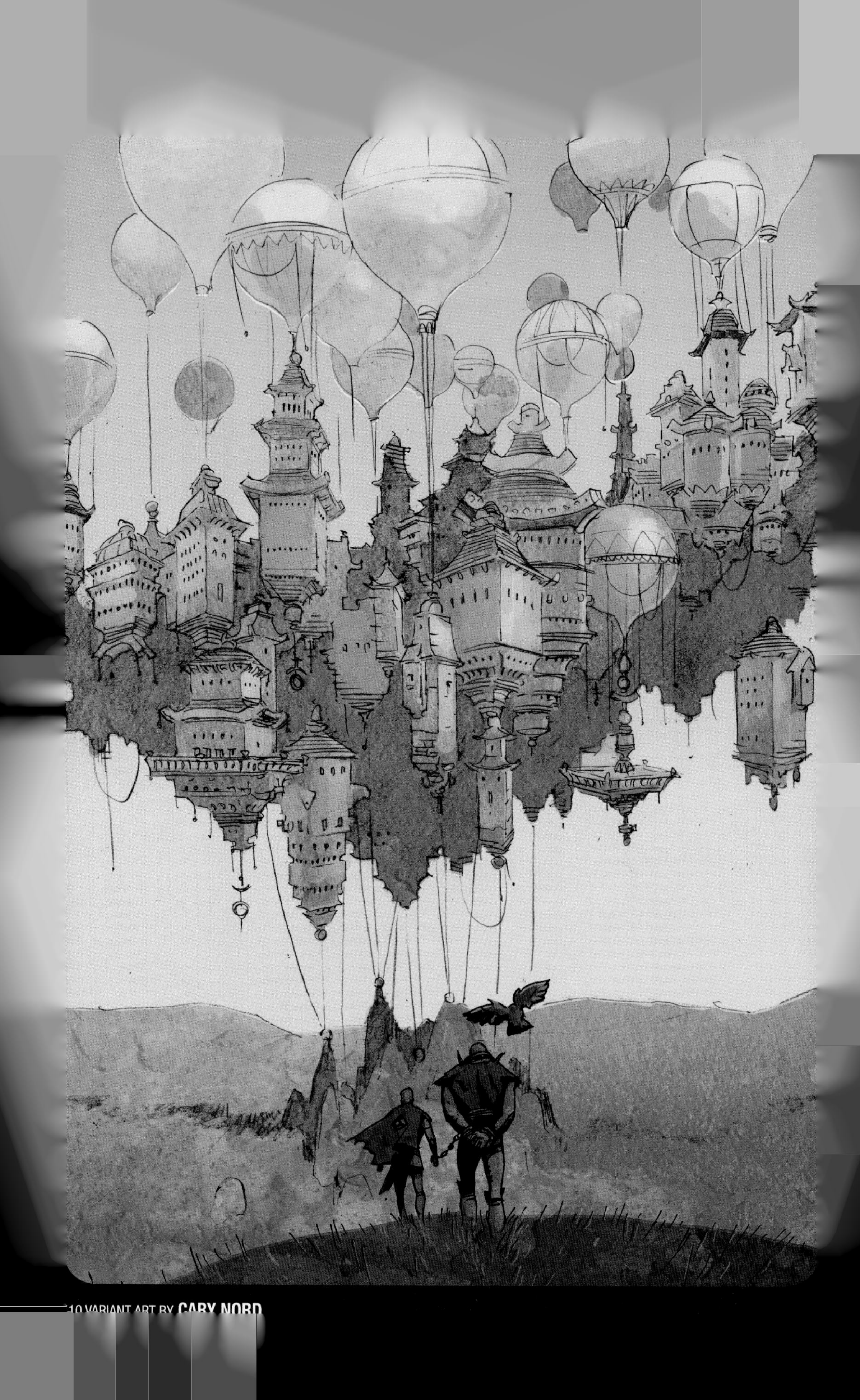

10 VARIANT ART BY GARY NORD

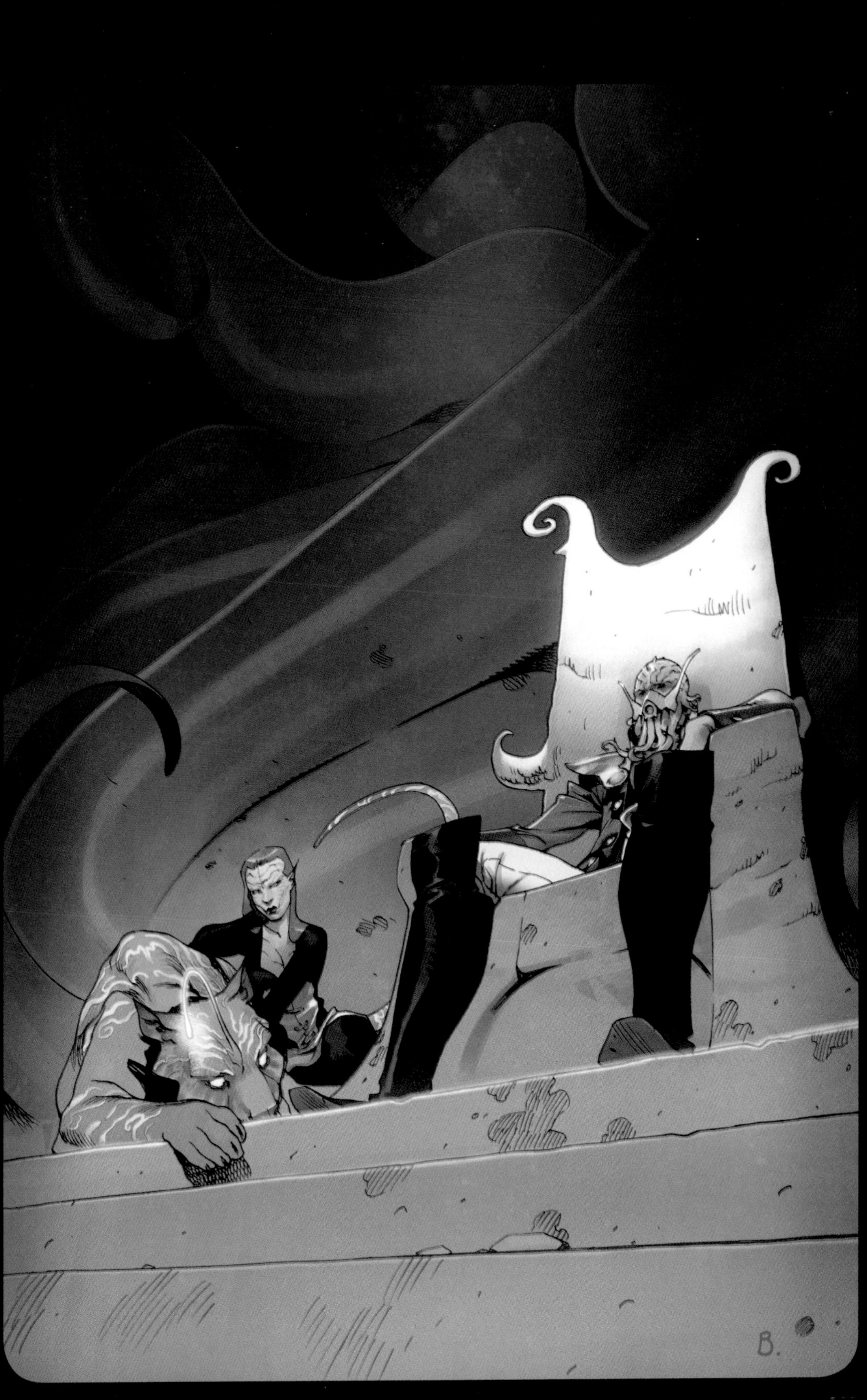
B.

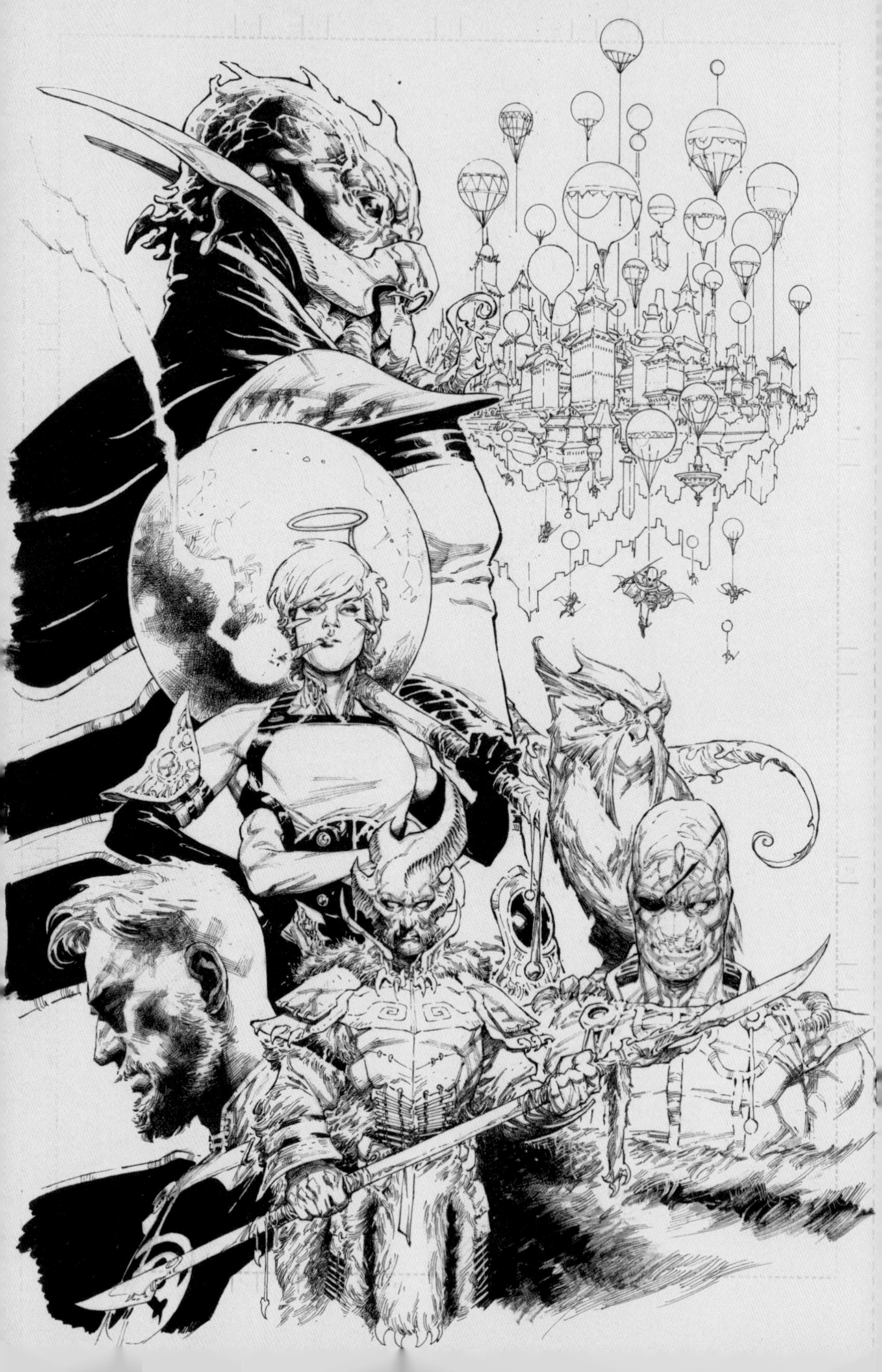

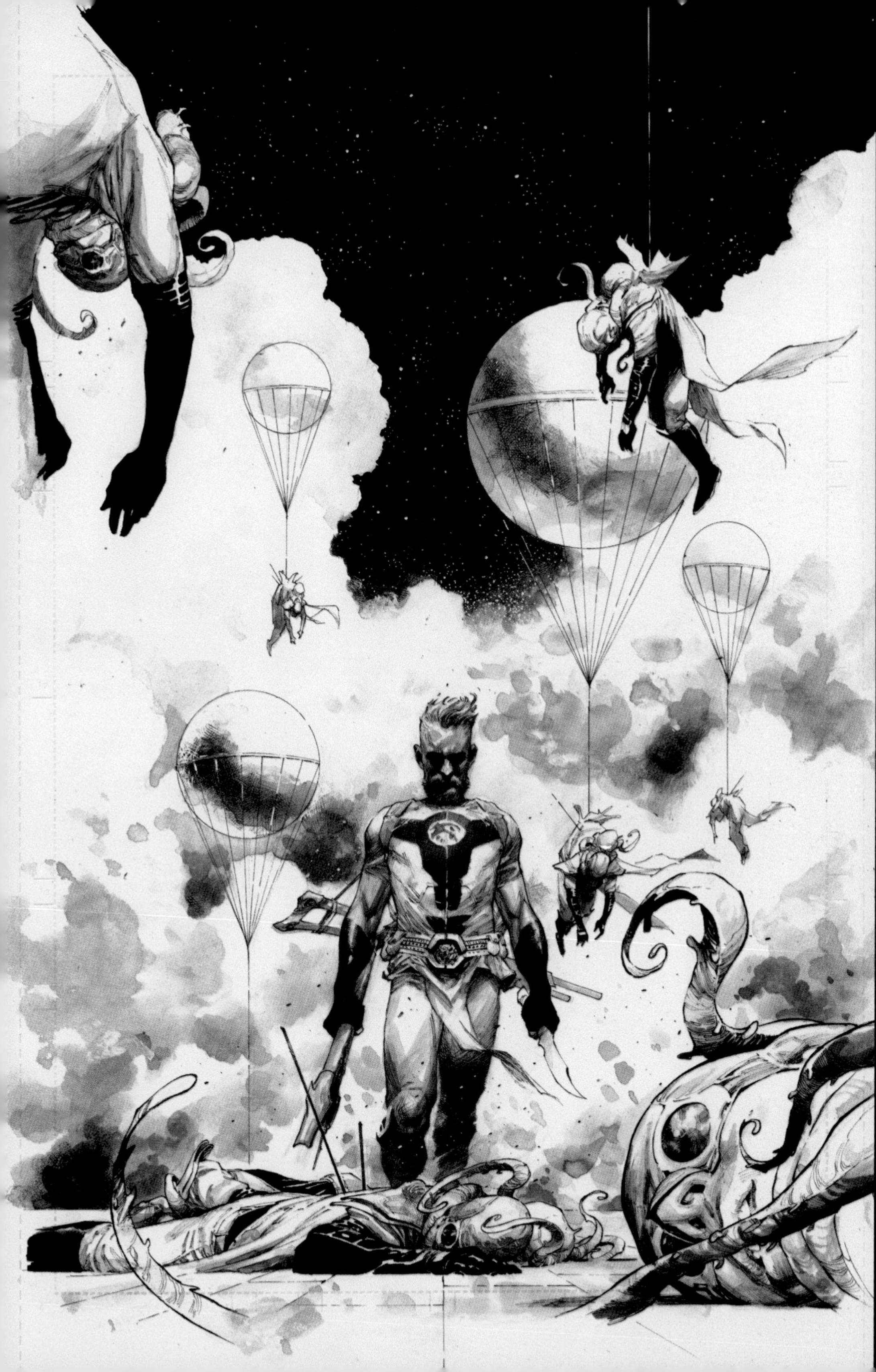

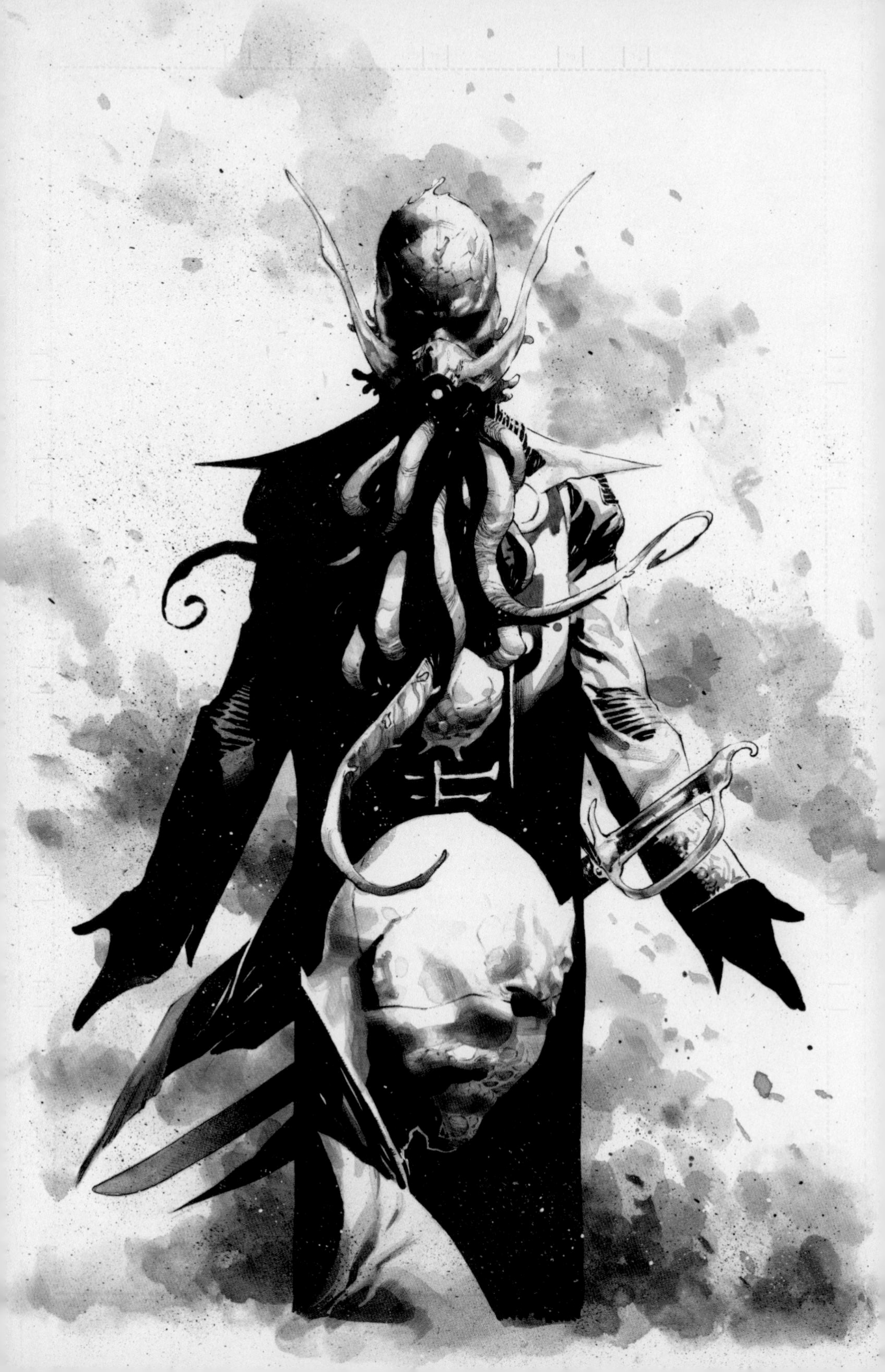

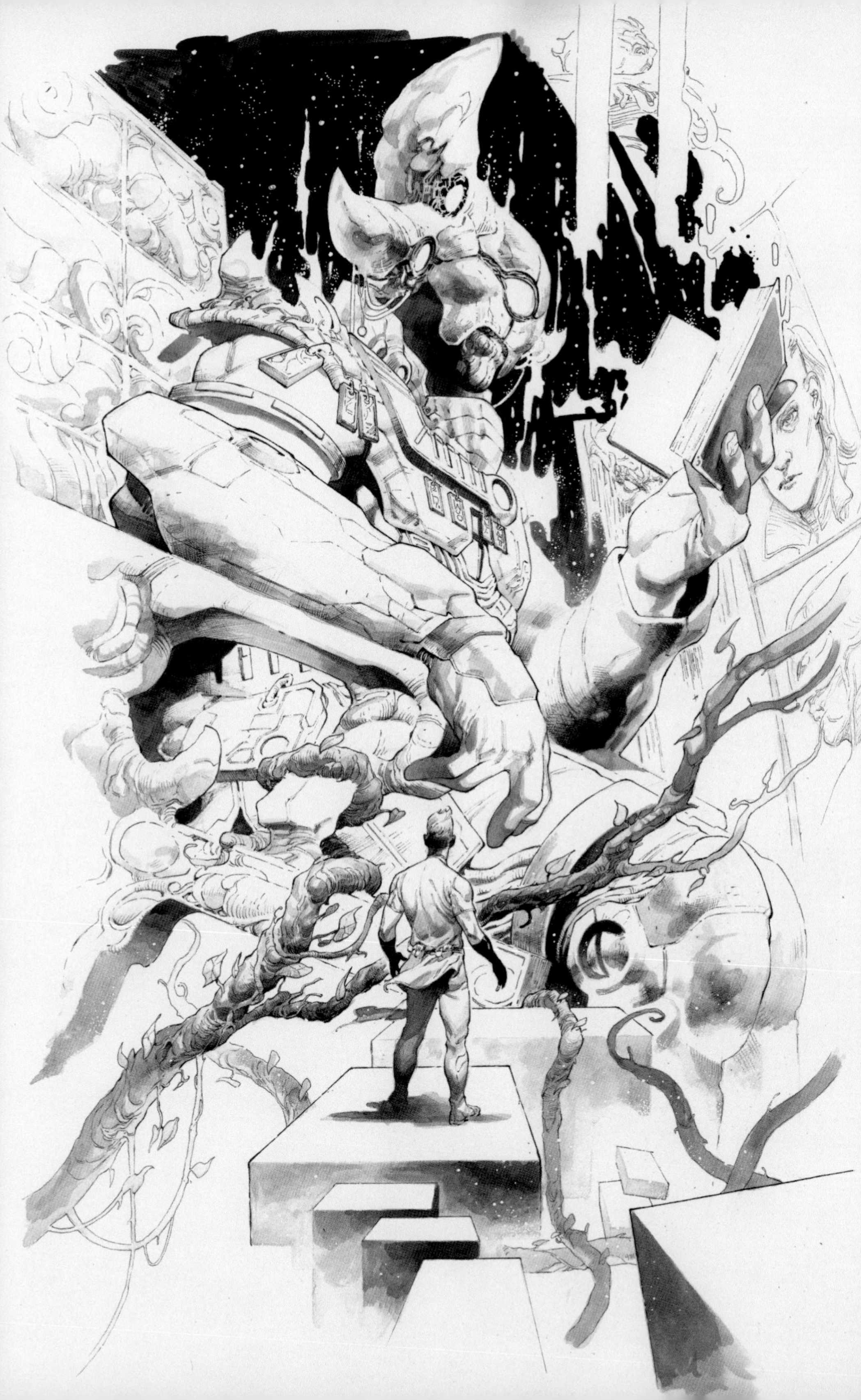

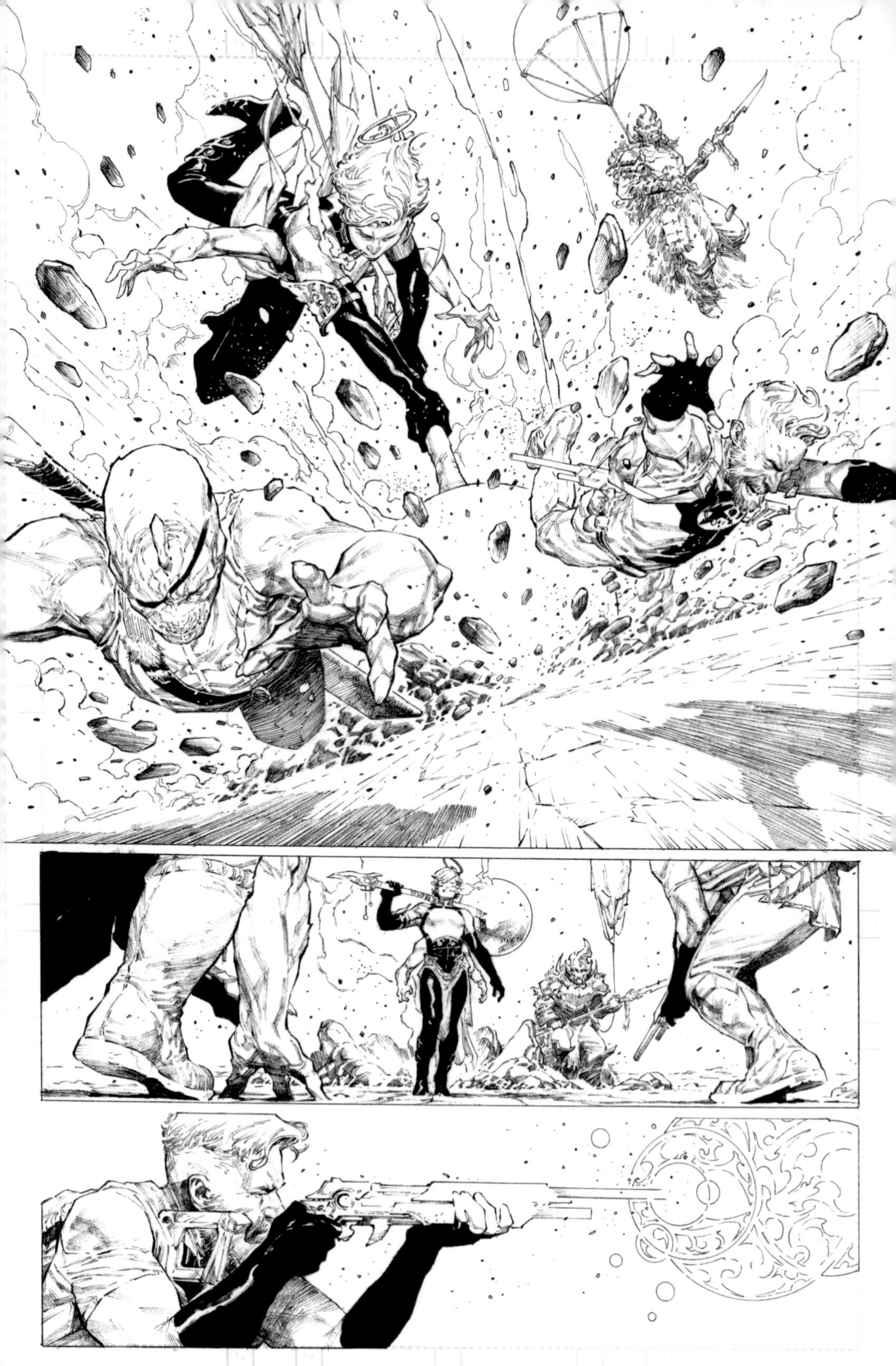

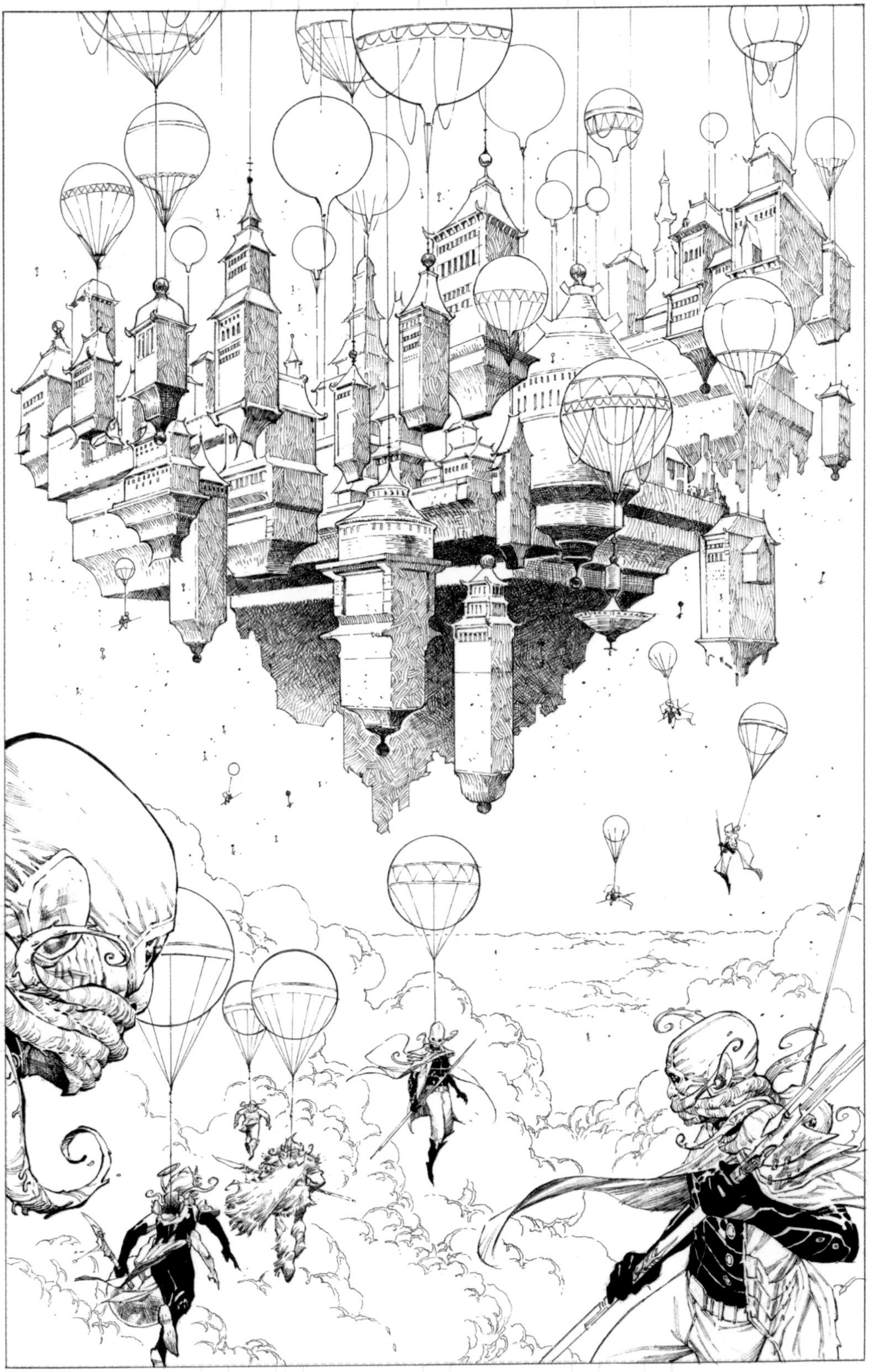

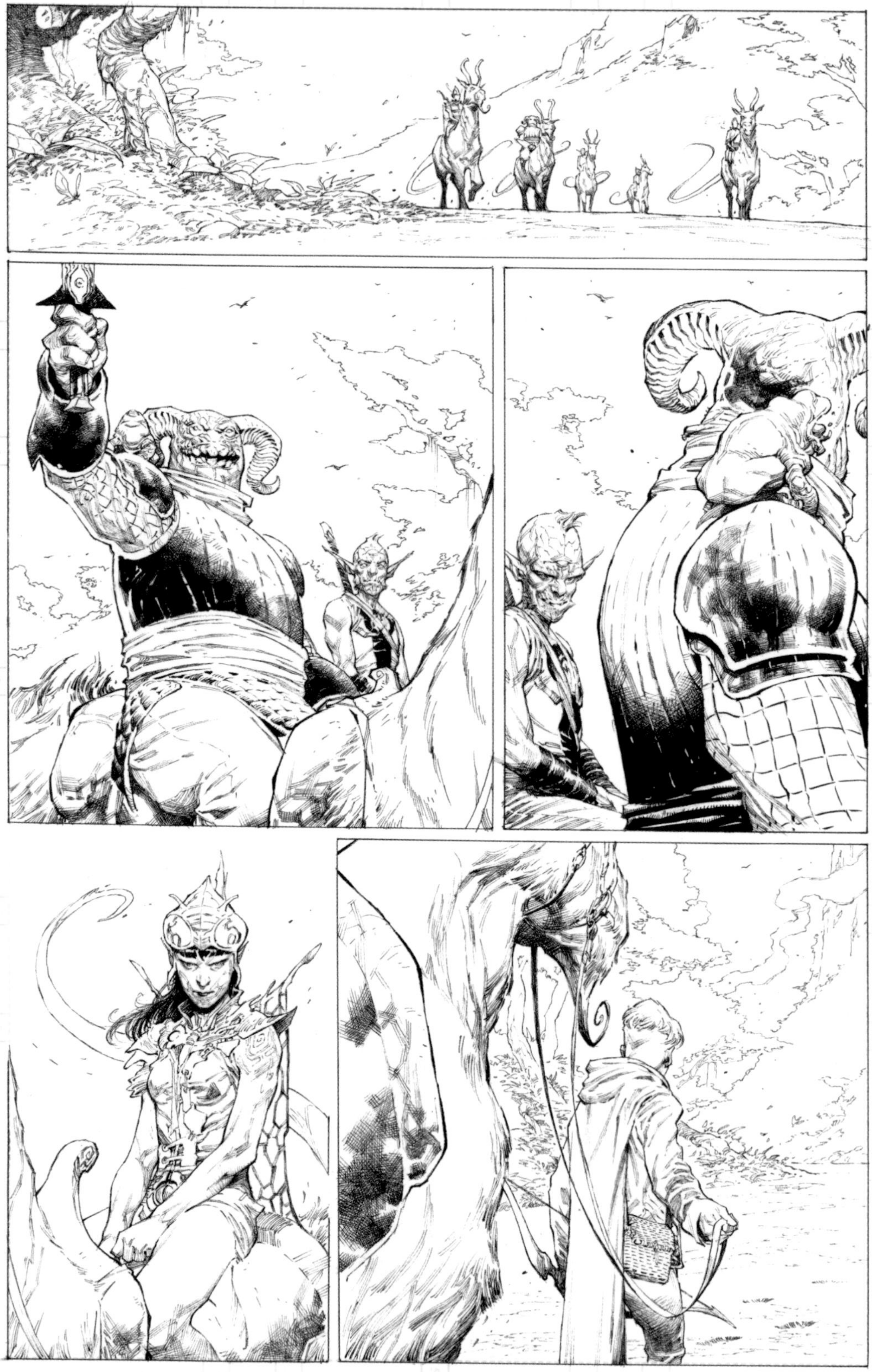

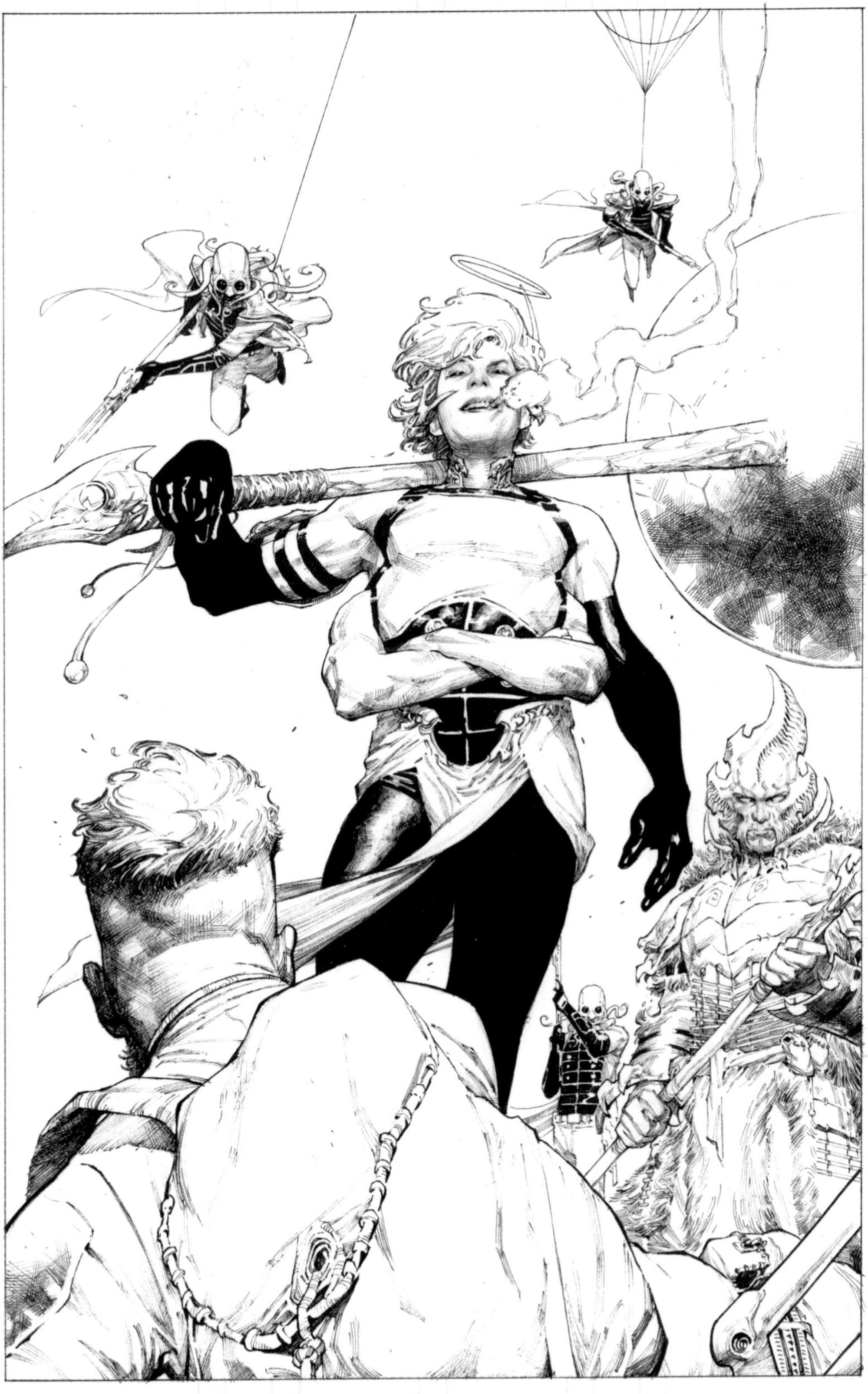

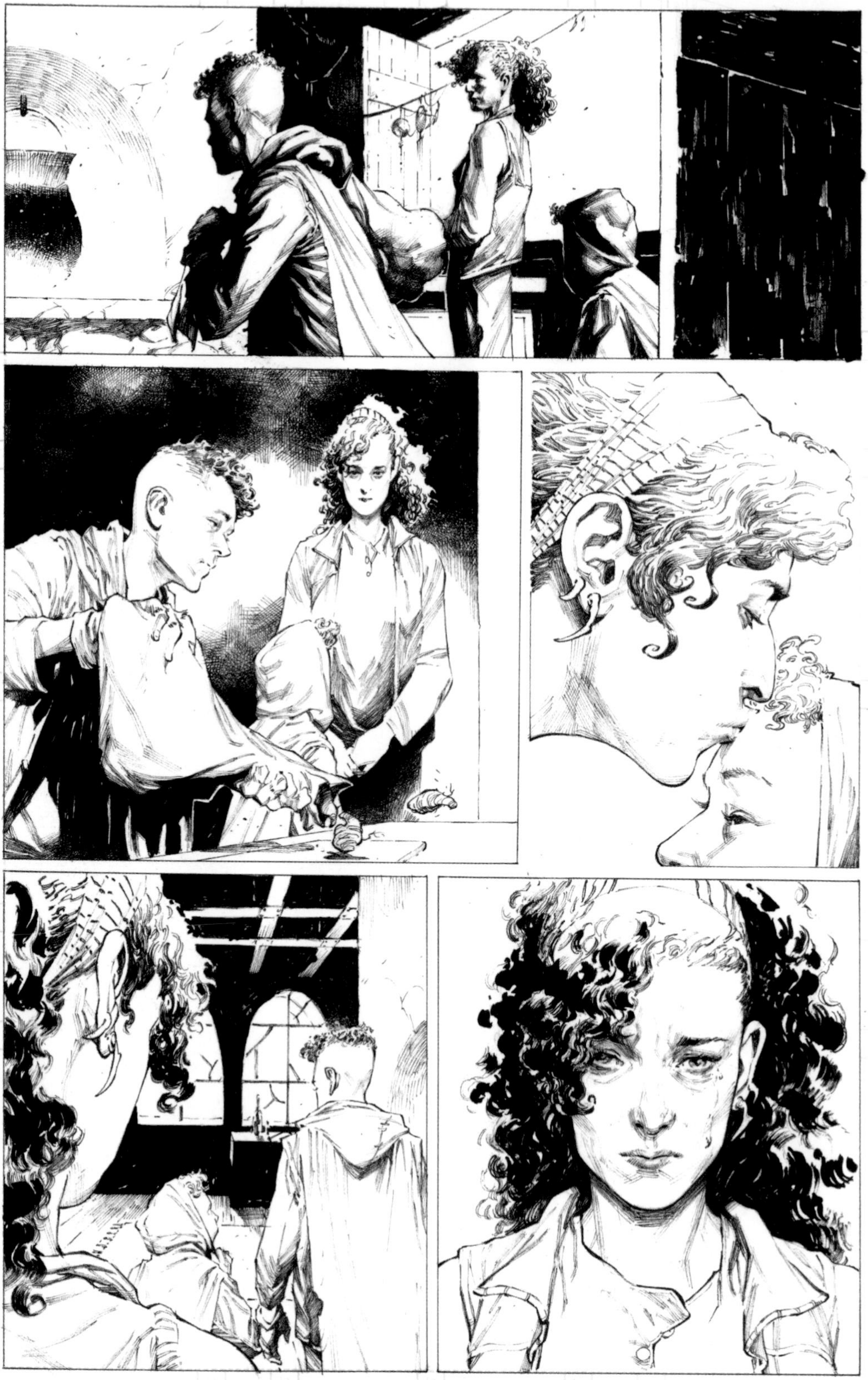

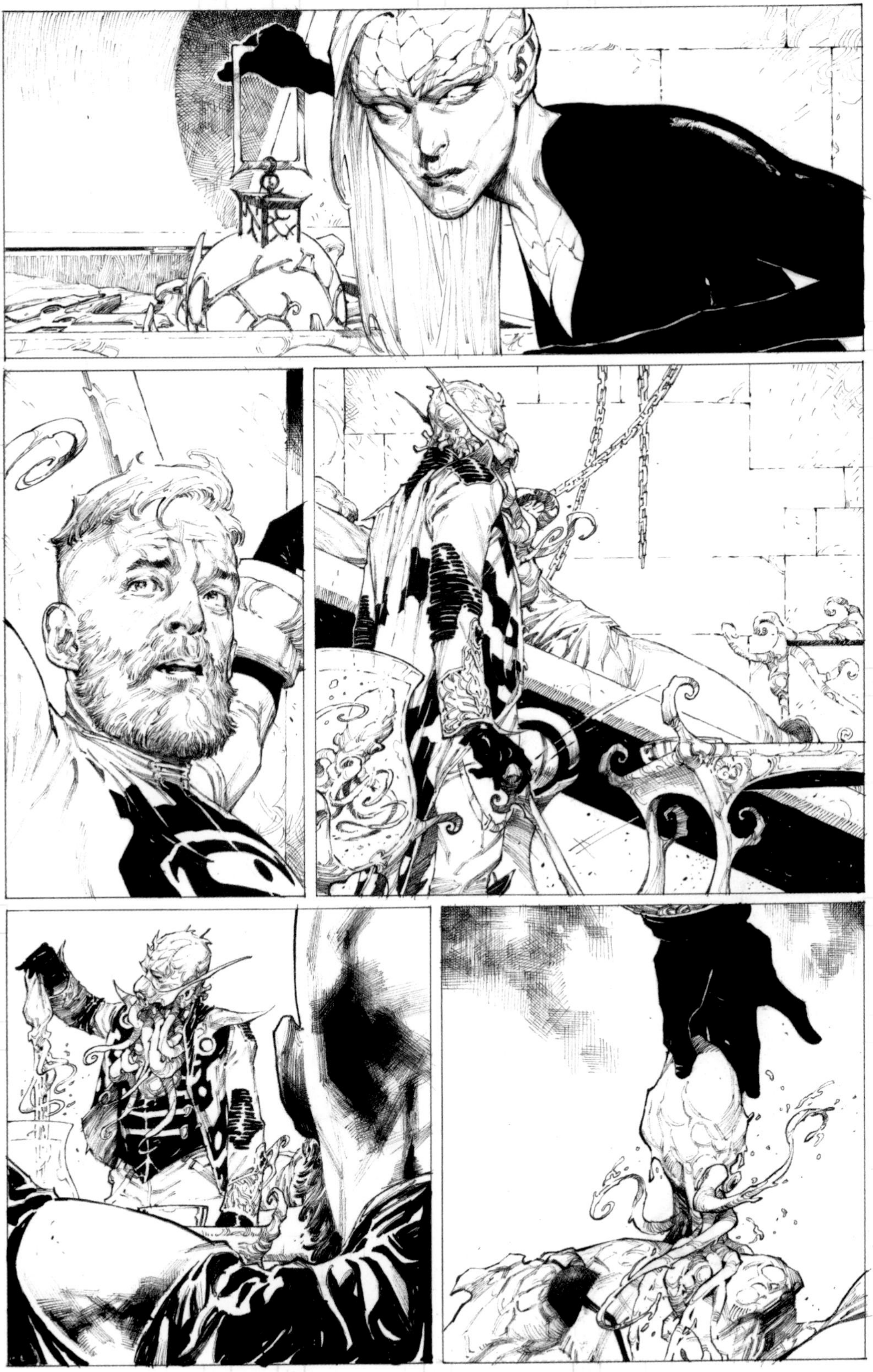

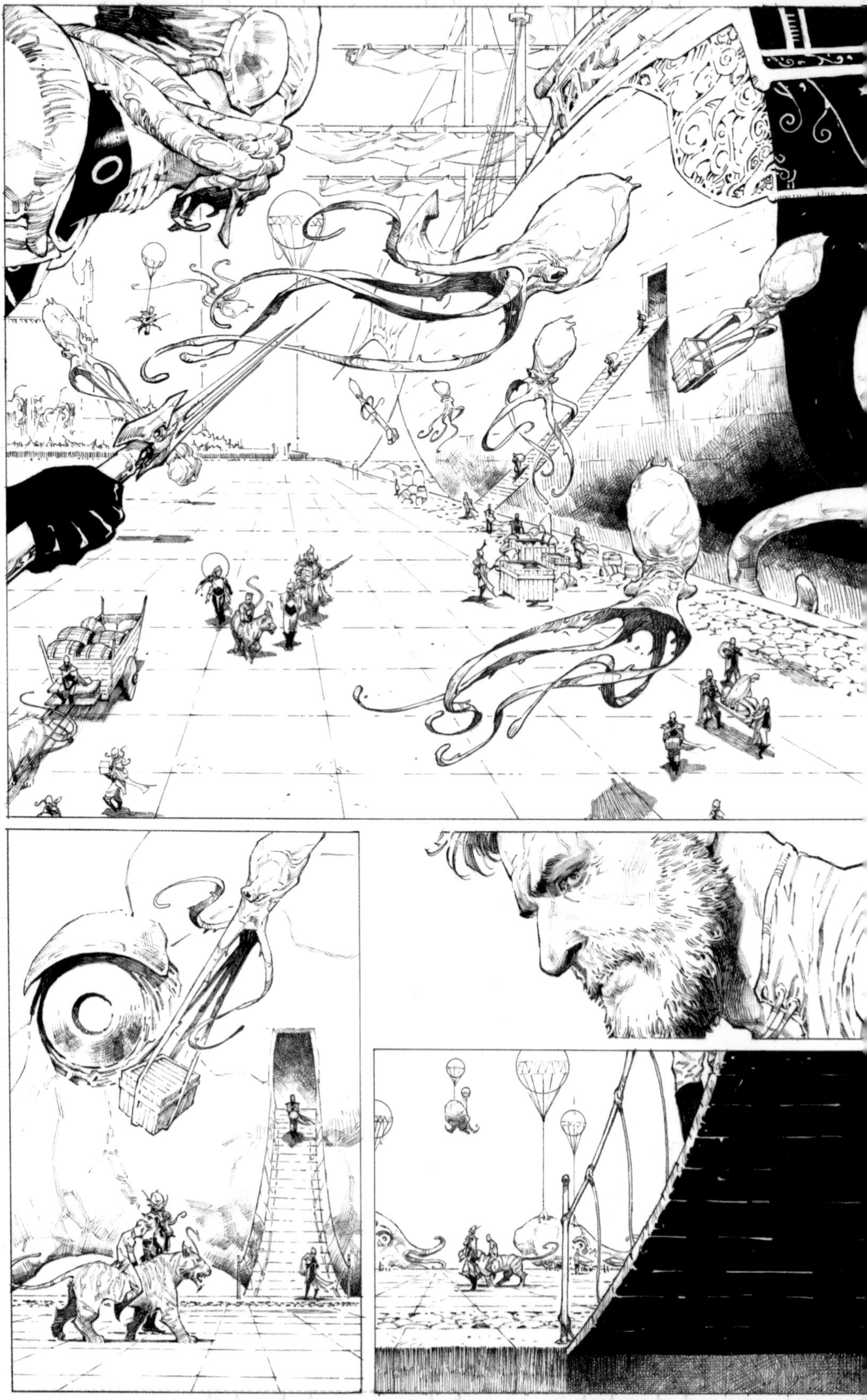

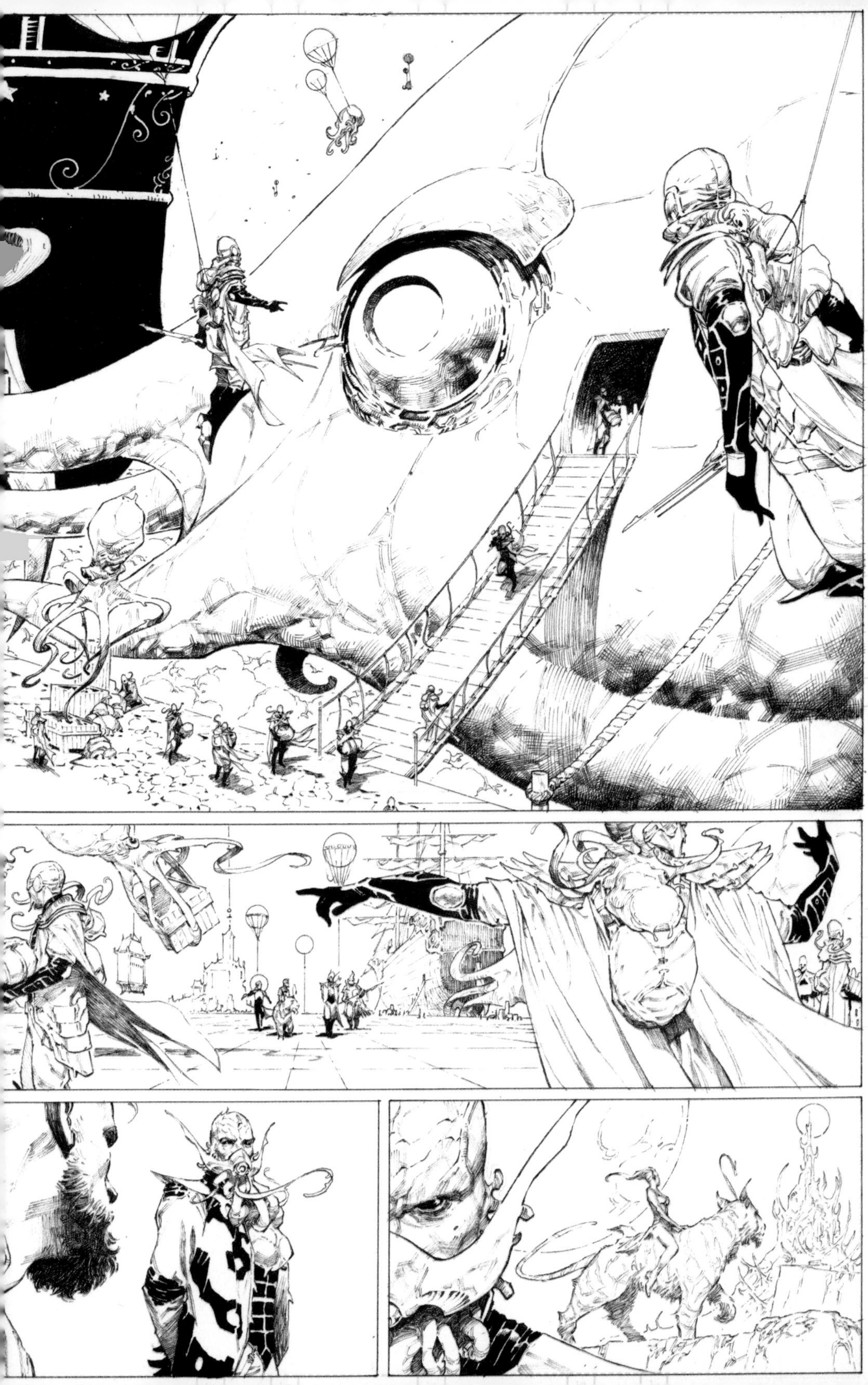

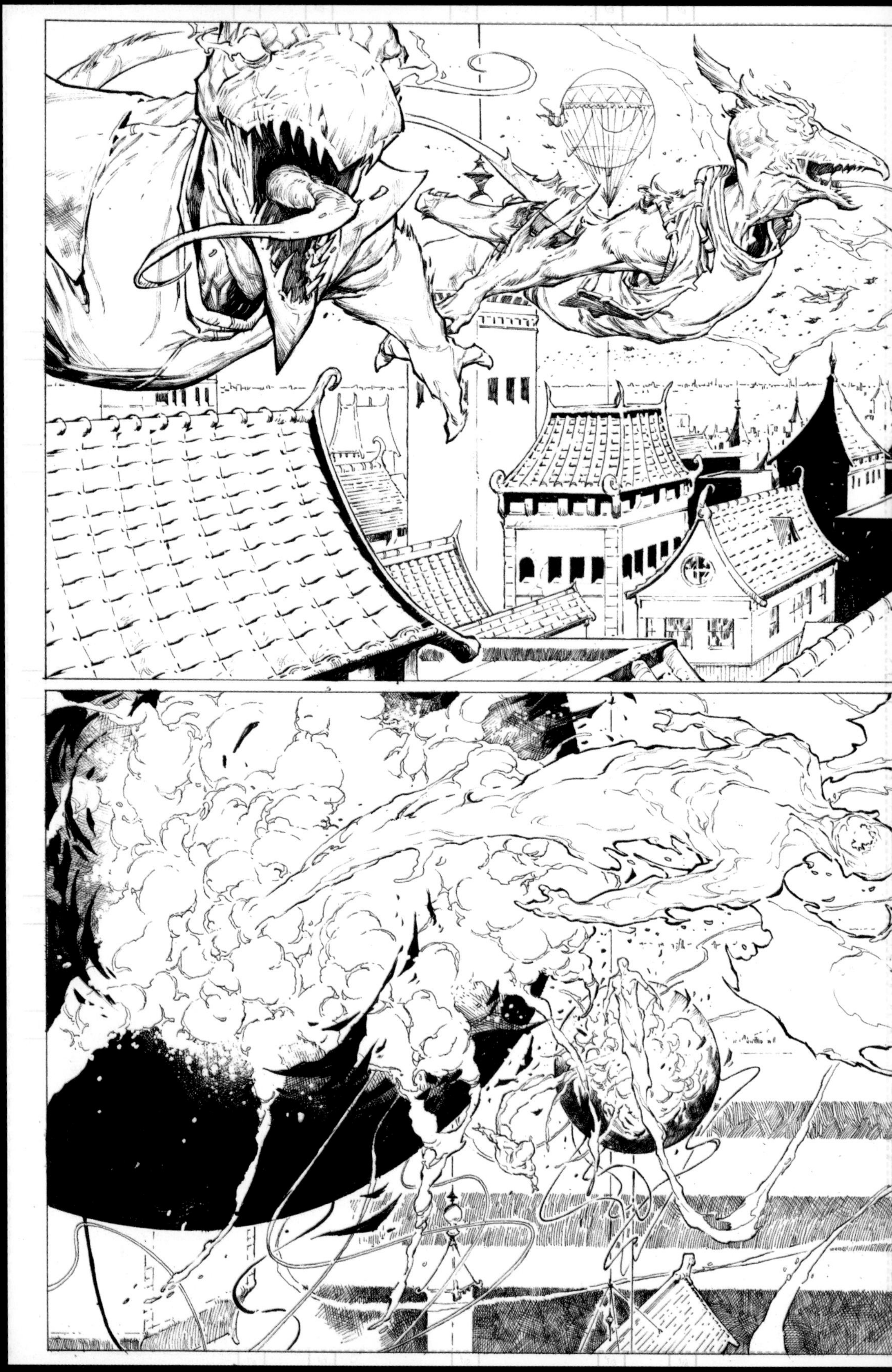

#13 PAGES 16-17 INKS

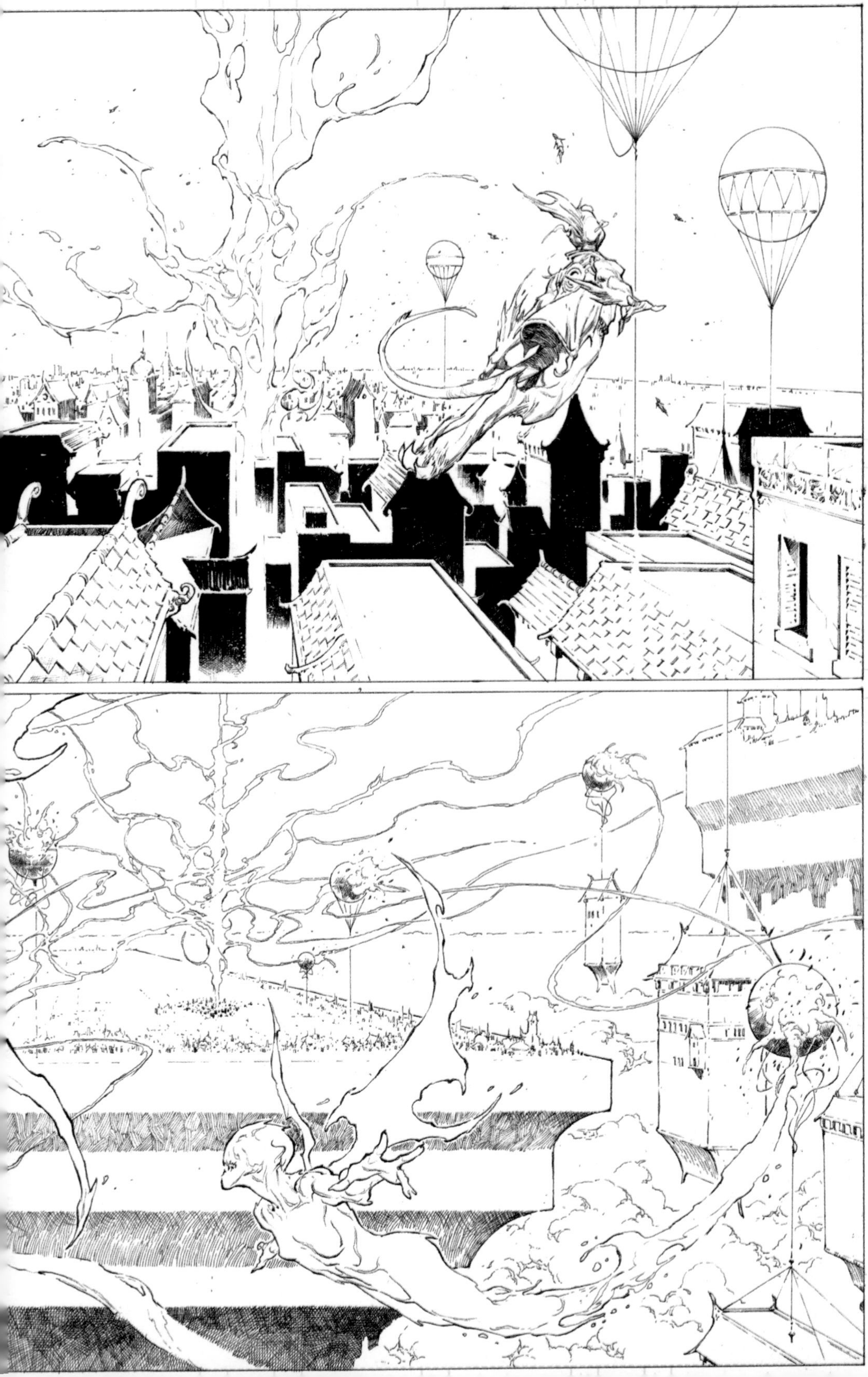

CREATORS

RICK REMENDER is the writer/co-creator of comics such as *Deadly Class*, *Fear Agent*, *Black Science*, *Seven to Eternity*, and *LOW*. During his years at Marvel, he wrote *Captain America, Uncanny X-Force*, and *Venom* and created *The Uncanny Avengers*. Outside of comics, he served as lead writer on EA's *Bulletstorm* game and the hit game *Dead Space*. Prior to this, he ran a satellite of Wild Brain animation, worked on films such as *The Iron Giant* and *Anastasia*, and taught sequential art and animation at San Francisco's Academy of Art University.

He currently curates his own publishing imprint, Giant Generator, at Image Comics while serving as lead writer/co-showrunner on SyFy's adaption of his co-creation *Deadly Class*.

Artist **JEROME OPEÑA** has been working in comics since 2005. He got his start with *Metal Hurlant* for Humanoids Publishing and went on to work on *Fear Agent*, his first collaboration with Rick Remender. The two would work together again at Marvel Comics on such series as *Punisher*, *Avengers,* and a critically acclaimed run on *Uncanny X-Force.*

He currently resides in Brooklyn, New York.

MATT HOLLINGSWORTH has been an avid homebrewer of beer since 1997 and a beer judge since 1999. He's won a total of 18 medals, 13 of them gold medals, in competitions in New Jersey, Texas, Washington, Oregon, and London. He's judged competitions in Oregon, Croatia, Slovenia, Slovakia, and Bulgaria.

In between beers, he's been coloring comics since 1991, including *Preacher, Daredevil, Hawkeye, The Wake, Hellboy, Chrononauts, Wytches,* and *We Stand on Guard*. Born in California, he lives in Croatia with his lovely wife, Branka, and his awesome son, Liam.